P9-EMO-535

"You're in for a fun surprise—just wait and see who walks down the aisle. Don't miss this zany wedding."
—Catherine Coulter

All the stuff she thought she had handled began to come back one at a time. The Samuelsons, Stephanie, Dennis and Dr. Malone, Peaches—and Jake, his timing as bad as ever.

"Charlie!" Jake yelled. "Hold up, will you? I need to ask you something. I need a favor."

"In your dreams," she muttered to herself. If I am afraid of commitment, she thought, Jake Dugan would be a good enough reason.

A flashing red light throbbed over her head and she turned to see that her ex-husband had attached his portable police beacon to the top of his car. He followed her at a safe distance, slowly, so that if a car approached from behind, she wouldn't be mowed down. But then again, she wouldn't need this service if he hadn't shown up in the first place, which was the cause of her walking home in the mud and rain.

She made the right turn into her neighborhood. The flashing red light disappeared and Jake's headlights strafed the houses as he made a U-turn and departed.

She stepped into her house and stepped into sanity. The lights were dimmed, the table set, candles lit, fire in the hearth and two cups of something steaming sat on the coffee table in front of the fireplace. Dennis, having heard her come in, appeared in the kitchen doorway, wiping his hands on a dish towel. The sight of all this peaceful domesticity warmed the heart of the drowned rat, and without stopping to consider the ramifications, Charlene heard herself say, "Dennis, do you still want to get married?"

Also available from MIRA Books and
ROBYN CARR

DEEP IN THE VALLEY
THE HOUSE ON OLIVE STREET

Watch for ROBYN CARR's newest novel
Coming October 2002

The Wedding Party

Robyn Carr

If you purchased this book without a cover you should be aware
that this book is stolen property. It was reported as "unsold and
destroyed" to the publisher, and neither the author nor the
publisher has received any payment for this "stripped book."

ISBN 1-55166-839-4

THE WEDDING PARTY

Copyright © 2001 by Robyn Carr.

All rights reserved. Except for use in any review, the reproduction or
utilization of this work in whole or in part in any form by any electronic,
mechanical or other means, now known or hereafter invented, including
xerography, photocopying and recording, or in any information storage or
retrieval system, is forbidden without the written permission of the publisher,
MIRA Books, 225 Duncan Mill Road, Don Mills, Ontario, Canada M3B 3K9.

All characters in this book have no existence outside the imagination of the
author and have no relation whatsoever to anyone bearing the same name
or names. They are not even distantly inspired by any individual known or
unknown to the author, and all incidents are pure invention.

MIRA and the Star Colophon are trademarks used under license and registered
in Australia, New Zealand, Philippines, United States Patent and Trademark
Office and in other countries.

Visit us at www.mirabooks.com

Printed in U.S.A.

For Sharon Buchholtz Lampert,
for all the years.

Prologue

Charlene Dugan started her day as usual—single. Not just unmarried, but autonomous, independent, free. She was forty-five, in excellent health and shape, attractive, successful in the practice of family law, the single mother of a grown daughter, the single daughter of a widowed mother, the significant other of a handsome, charming man and *devotedly* nonmarried.

Though she had been with Dennis for five years, they did not live together. They each had their own homes and liked things as they were. Well, perhaps Charlene was a tad more committed to remaining uncommitted; Dennis *had* proposed a couple of times. But she had been married once, only long enough to produce one daughter, Stephanie, who was now twenty-five, and she had not been even slightly tempted to marry again in the twenty-four years since. She was content. Satisfied. Fulfilled, even.

On this ordinary unmarried day there were events that, taken singularly—no pun intended—were quite manageable. But when combined, they so rocked Charlene's world that by day's end she was not only ready to consider marriage, she was inclined to do the proposing.

One

Charlene entered the law offices of Phelps, Dugan & Dodge innocent of the trouble the day would bring. She smiled at the young receptionist and nodded as she passed cubicles where clerks and junior associates labored. She stopped in the break room to grab her customary morning cup of coffee and a bagel. Then, as she proceeded toward her office, she heard the muffled roar of her first clients. There was no mistaking the hostile tones of Mr. and Mrs. Samuelson, two of the most objectionable people Charlene had had the displeasure of knowing. She had been selected by family court to arbitrate the Samuelsons' divorce settlement. This was to be their third meeting. The first two had been complete and dismal failures.

Charlene loved her legal specialty. There were very few people who could make the traumas of divorce and custody bearable, and Charlene prided herself in taking families who walked into her office wounded and terrified, and sending them out as people who could cope, people with options.

The arguing achieved fever pitch as she neared her office. Briefcase under her arm, bagel in one hand and coffee in the other, she closed in on the noise. Her

assistant and close friend, Pam London, was standing
behind her desk, arms crossed and toe tapping impatiently as she glared at the conference-room doors. A
disgusted frown twisted her otherwise handsome features.

Charlene was a little confused. "What's going on?"
she asked. The Samuelsons were not supposed to be
in the same room until the arbitrator arrived, for obvious reasons. Plus, they weren't due for another hour.

"They both had an idea they could get to you first,
before the other arrived," Pam explained. "I put Mrs.
Samuelson in the conference room and asked Mr.
Samuelson to have a seat in the foyer waiting room.
But they found each other out and have been in there
fighting ever since. I've tried to separate them, to no
avail." She smiled evilly. "Let's bolt the door from
the outside and let them kill each other."

Charlene handed her briefcase to Pam. "Was he
threatening?"

"Someone would have to take him seriously to be
threatened. He's just a pip-squeak. An obnoxious little
horse's ass. And she's no better."

"Hmm. If anyone was threatening, we could call
the police. Well, call building security to begin with,
but give me three minutes before you send anyone
in."

Charlene and the other senior partner, Brad Phelps,
had the two expansive offices in the back, separated
by their large conference room, while Mike Dodge
was on another floor of the building. Charlene and
Brad had private bathrooms with showers and two

doors apiece; one to outer offices and their respective executive assistants and the other to the conference room. Charlene placed her coffee and bagel on her desk and retrieved something from the top drawer. She stood in the frame of the conference door to watch. And listen.

The Samuelsons faced each other, fists clenched at their sides, their faces red to their scalps. If only they knew how ridiculous they looked. Mr. Samuelson, the shorter of the two, appeared to shout into his wife's heavy, pendulous breasts, and she sputtered obscenities onto the top of her husband's shiny little scalp. How could they not know they sounded so revolting, cursing each other in voices loud enough to carry through these professional offices? Forty years of marriage and five children, come to this.

"I bought that goddamn boat after you walked out!"

"You bought the goddamn boat after I walked out, using the money left in our mutual fund...and you paid for jewelry for your floozies with our IRAs!"

"Since I was the only one who ever put anything in the goddamn IRAs or mutual funds, I figured they were mine to do with as I damn well pleased!"

"And that's why I left! Because you put no value on anything anyone else ever does! I stayed home and raised five kids! I moved fifteen times! I hostessed twenty-five company Christmas parties. I—"

"Played tennis, bridge and golf, got manicures and pedicures and facials, had to build a room onto the house just for your clothes... And you had the god-damn Christmas parties *catered!*''

The loud report, like that of a gun, caused the Sam-uelsons to shut up abruptly and bolt apart, turn and.... And it was only Charlene, in the doorway with a party popper. Confetti drifted lazily to the floor, a curling piece of lavender streamer hanging off Mrs. Samuel-son's large bosom, while Mr. Samuelson's bald head had collected a few glitters.

They both recovered from the sudden fright and looked with some relief toward the arbitrator. This was a couple dissolving after four decades; there were bound to be issues. A certain amount of rage was ex-pected in this field. But as Charlene knew only too well, they must not be allowed to run amok. A little chaos could lead to a lot of tragedy. Domestic discord was the most volatile and dangerous of all.

''You may leave now,'' Charlene said. ''I will ask Pam to get Judge Kemp on the line for me. I'll tell him that arbitration is not possible in your case, and suggest you be bound over for a full divorce trial. You will each have to secure private counsel. I wouldn't consider taking on either of you as a client even if I could. And don't be too surprised if you find the judge considering a hefty fine.'' Mr. Samuelson, ''the only one who put any money in the goddamn mutual funds,'' became especially ashen. ''As an officer of the court,'' she told them, ''I'm obligated to tell him that you were nothing but discourteous and uncoop-erative, wouldn't consider the simplest of requests— like taking a seat in the waiting room—were a continual disruption to the entire office building and have made no progress at all in two meetings. There is very little question, this divorce will cost you more than a boat. Probably more than a boat, a car and a house.''

''Now just you wait a minute—''

''*And,*'' Charlene barked with heat. She was small of stature but should never be mistaken for slight in any other way. ''If you speak to me in a tone that carries even the slightest disrespect...'' she began. The door to the conference room slowly opened and Ray Vogel stepped inside. Charlene had convinced the whole office building to agree to her choice of security service for this very reason. Ray, like his fellow security officers, was big, young, muscled and armed. When he frowned, he looked positively lethal. ''Give me a moment, Ray.'' She turned back to the angry-faced couple. ''The slightest tone of disrespect will be accompanied by a contempt and perhaps assault charge. And naturally another hefty fine.'' This wasn't true, but one look at Mr. and Mrs. Samuelsons' faces said they believed her thoroughly.

''Now wait a minute,'' Mr. Samuelson tried again, but in an entirely different tone. ''There's a lot of emotion here, and I admit we got a little carried away, but we can still work this out—''

''No, you're entirely too late,'' Charlene said. ''We're all done listening to you curse each other, demean each other and make a mockery of a system designed to protect and respect the family.'' Mrs. Samuelson smirked and crossed her fleshy arms over her chest. ''And before you get all smug, Mrs. Samuelson, let me remind you that when push comes to shove, he will probably *still* have the financial advantage in a trial. You might succeed in hurting him, but not without doing substantial economic damage to yourself.''

Her mouth dropped open even as her arms uncrossed and fell to her sides. Charlene lifted one corner of her mouth. ''Perhaps one of the children will take you in.''

Mrs. Samuelson looked stricken.

''Okay, let's go,'' Ray said, holding the door open.

''Wait a minute, wait a minute—''

''Go!'' Charlene commanded. Then she turned around, went back into her office and closed the door. She leaned against it and listened to the murmurings that came from the conference room. She could hear Ray's occasional deep voice urging them to leave. The voices carried a decidedly different timbre than what she had greeted this morning. She looked at her watch—8:07. She went to her desk, took a sip of her coffee and a bite of her bagel. A person shouldn't have to endure this kind of reprehensible behavior first thing in the morning, she thought. She often wished she could just get a glimpse of what these two were like in marriage, because it was difficult not to assume that the divorce was long overdue.

There was a tapping at the door. She checked her watch—8:11. Another fact that never failed to fascinate her—the worse the couple, the quicker they could modify their behavior if money was involved.

Pam stuck her head in the door. ''They'd like to

know if you'd consider giving them another chance,"
she said.

"Ask them if they understand this will be the last
time."

Mr. Samuelson's glittering head and halo of thin,
frizzy yellow hair popped into the door opening. He
came to Pam's shoulder. He grinned triumphantly
while Pam looked down at him with obvious distaste.
"We understand," he said.

"Good," Charlene said. "We'll start with the
boat."

Three hours later, the Samuelsons departed quietly.
Not happily, not even politely, but at least quietly.
They had worked through part of their settlement, and
had kept their rancor under wraps. The pressure for
them to behave had been so intense that Mrs. Samuelson was messaging her temples with her fingertips
as she walked out and Mr. Samuelson was holding his
oversize gut with both hands, lest it explode.

Charlene went into her private bathroom and
splashed cool water on her cheeks. It was a professional coup to be chosen by the court to arbitrate any
kind of settlement. Having made a name for herself in
the practice of family law meant that usually Charlene
was going to be dealing with divorce property or custody—two areas rife with explosive emotions. But this
was hard. It took its toll of a morning.

She heard the intercom on her desk buzz, but she
ignored it, remaining in the bathroom. She sat on the
closed toilet lid, leaned back, kicked off her shoes and

held a cool cloth over her eyes, dampening her short brown bangs in the process.

After twenty years in the business, there were very few surprises. It was always about the boat and the savings account, about who brought home the bacon and who didn't. Even in the new century, when most marriages were made up of dual working partners, it always boiled down to who did the dishes and who earned the highest salary.

She unhooked her bra and let her rib cage expand briefly. She wiggled her toes into the thick carpet beneath her feet. She could not have borne more than three hours with those two. They gave divorce a bad name.

But she had pulled it off, gotten them to sit down and begin dividing things. A few more meetings and it would be done. The judge who had assigned her would be impressed. So what if it took her a while to recover. It was worth it to win the further admiration of the courts. The city was overrun with sleazy divorce lawyers, but there were only a pocketful of respectable unsharky family lawyers, of which Charlene was one. That is not to say her clients wouldn't get what they deserved; she took very good care of them. More important, they would leave the proceedings with their self-respect.

The intercom on her desk buzzed again. "Okay, okay," she said to herself, tossing the washcloth into the sink, slipping her feet back into her shoes and hooking up her bra. She applied some makeup to her cheeks, a little lip gloss to her lips, and squinted critically into the mirror. She looked tired even though she'd slept quite well the night before. She knew what that meant. It was time to seriously consider having her eyes done. A little nip, a little tuck, not a new face, but one that just didn't seem to age at the speed of light.

Charlene didn't give herself much slack; she was a perfectionist from nose to toes, professionally and personally. You don't become successful by relaxing your standards. It was taxing, but nothing worth having came easy.

She flushed the toilet even though she hadn't used it. She just didn't want anyone to think she had locked herself into her bathroom to recover from the Samuelsons. No one should think she *needed* recovery. Not even Pam.

That was Charlene. Always in control. And perfect in every way—without breaking a sweat.

The intercom was buzzing wildly as she headed for her desk. *"What?"*

"Thank goodness, I thought you'd fallen in. It's Stephanie."

"Put her through." Click, click. "Steph, honey, I'm really—"

"Mom, I *hate* him!"

Charlene sank into her chair. Sacramento could be crumbling around them in the throes of a six-point-eight shaker and still Stephanie would assume that the current state of her love life was of paramount concern to everyone. Stephanie didn't even bother to say hello or ask Charlene if she had a few minutes. "Hmm," Charlene hummed, noncommittal.

"I have tickets for *Grease*. Do you know how hard they were to get? How much they cost? And he promised me, *promised* me he'd get the night off. How often do I ask him to do that?"

Probably very, very often, Charlene thought, but she held her tongue.

"Is there absolutely no one in the state of California, in the city of Sacramento, who can stand behind the bar and sling a few drinks so he can go to a musical with me?"

"Stephanie, I doubt it's as simple as that."

"Mom, I've had it with spending every night alone. I don't want to spend the rest of my life like this."

"Honey, I sympathize with you, but you're going to have to work this out with Grant," she said.

"You could hate him too," she whined.

"It's hard to hate Grant. He's such a doll."

"Mom."

"He is. He's good to you. And patient. And smart. And he makes a nice living while putting himself through school. There's a lot to admire about his hard work."

"At the bar. Every night. With drunk women coming on to him all night long. Begging him to take them home."

"My gosh," Charlene mocked. "That must be nearly irresistible for him."

"That's not the point," Stephanie said. "You can

imagine where this leaves me. With two fifty-dollar tickets.''

''Is there no one else who would like to go see *Grease* with you?'' she asked.

''That's not the point either!''

''Then, Stephanie, what *is* the point?'' Charlene asked tiredly.

''The point is, I don't want to be alone all the time. I want my partner, the man of my heart, to spend time with me. To come home to me before I'm asleep!''

Charlene took a deep breath and did not say all the things that came to her mind. Like, *You cannot expect the man of your heart to entertain you all the time.* And, *Didn't you know he was a bartender when you suggested you move in together?* Or even, *Oh my darling, my dearest child, you are so rotten spoiled.*

Stephanie was bright, adorable, funny and sensitive, but she had an overblown sense of entitlement not entirely rare in a twenty-five-year-old. Especially a twenty-five-year-old only child.

''Mom? Are you *there?*''

''Yes, Stephanie. Look, you knew all about Grant's hours and commitments before you—''

''I might want to move back home, Mom,'' she said.

Charlene bolted upright. ''What?''

''I've been giving some thought to moving in with you, Mom.''

''Stephanie, think about what you're saying. You'd be getting a roommate who would nag you to keep things tidy all the time. You would live with someone who is driven almost homicidal by dust bunnies! And you're...how can I put this kindly? Simply not up to the job.''

"You don't have to be mean," she said.

"And you don't have to be sloppy, but you are. We've been over this before, Steph. I love you more than my life, but I won't take you on as a roommate again until I can be sure you can hold up your end of the deal. If you're serious about wanting to live with me, you'd better go home and clean that apartment from top to bottom and prove you can keep it that way." She sighed. "Honey, I suspect you'd be better off trying to work things out with Grant. I know you love him very much."

"I don't want to waste my life waiting around for a man who's...who's..."

"Who's *working?*" Charlene asked sharply. "You'd better think about this, Stephanie. You made a major commitment to him. The two of you have been together a long time. This bartending, this was part of his plan. It's an excellent income for a student. Isn't he almost finished with school?"

"Ha! That'll be the day. He's already talking about getting a master's. And that's only the beginning of my nightmares. He says he's going to test for the police academy."

"Really? Well, I'm not surprised he's taking that direction. He's been real interested in forensics and constitutional law and— Are you so completely surprised?"

"I'm horrified! Straight from spending every night

at the bar to spending every night on the streets getting shot at.''

''Well Jesus, Stephanie,'' Charlene said, out of patience, ''what the hell do you want him to do? Win the lottery?''

''I just don't want to…you know…''

''No I don't know. What?''

''I don't want to end up like you!''

Charlene couldn't get a breath. She didn't want to hear any more.

''Mom, you know what I mean. Don't you? I mean, it figures, with what you do for a living, you'd be pretty suspicious of marriage. Bitter about it.''

Oh boy, this was only getting worse. Bitter? Like a dagger. ''Stephanie, I have a call on another line. Can we talk about this later?''

''Oh, God, now you're mad. Mom, look, I can understand why you'd want your kind of life, and it's right for you and everything, but that doesn't mean that I—''

''Steph, I'm sorry, honey. I *have* to go! I'll talk to you later.''

As she clicked off the line, she felt the rare prickle of tears sting her eyes.

Charlene needed something to shift her emotions back to the stable side, and Dennis came to mind. She decided to surprise him by showing up at his E.R. for lunch, something she made time for only rarely. It was not the nastiness of the Samuelsons that had jolted her—she was used to that sorry business. But Stephanie's remark about her life—or the lack thereof—threatened to ruin her day. What could she have meant? That Charlene didn't need anyone? That was entirely untrue. She needed a lot of people, mostly Stephanie, even when she was the worst brat. And her mother, Lois, who had named herself Peaches for her only grandchild. And of course, Dennis, the most dependable man in the world. In thinking about it, the only thing she *didn't* have in her life was a marriage. And in the presence of all that she *did* have, she didn't need that.

It was true that Charlene was secure as a single woman, had taken to living alone quite easily and felt no desire to have a man's rowing machine stored under her bed. But did that make her bitter about marriage? No! Certainly not!

The best way to drive out any plaguing doubt was to see her man, her Dennis, to feel his arm around her shoulders, to look into his warm, reassuring brown eyes and have him tell her for the millionth time that she was an incredible woman.

It was really *Dennis* who was incredible. Almost too incredible to be believed.

When Charlene had reached forty, after twenty years of backbreaking labor as a studying and then working single mother, she had met Dennis—the perfect man. While hiking along the American River she had twisted her ankle and was rescued by the tall, handsome physician's assistant. His hands on her sprain were gentle, his smile comforting. He helped her to his car and took her to the emergency room in which he worked, where he had her ankle X-rayed. Then he wrapped it himself. Then he took her to dinner. The whole thing had brought about a belief in fate once more, for who could have predicted that she would meet a man so in tune to her every whim. They shared similar tastes in music, in food, in leisure activities. They had both been married once when much younger, though Dennis had no children.

Even though Charlene had declined Dennis's proposals of marriage, she had not done so because of any doubt about their ability to remain perfect partners, but rather out of the common sense of a family law practitioner. "I don't want to screw up a really good thing by overindulgence," she had told him. "Let's not mess with it, especially since it works absolutely perfectly."

And Dennis always said, "You must be right, because I have nothing to complain about. I just thought we could check and see if it could get more perfect."

During their five years together, Charlene and Dennis had set a kind of schedule for their relationship, something that appealed to a woman as strictly organized as Charlene. One night a week they had dinner at her house and Dennis would usually stay over. One night a week they dined at his house, but she rarely stayed the night because she loved her little house in the suburbs. Saturday nights they went out, Sunday mornings they had brunch, and the rest of the time they checked in by phone. They had both togetherness and plenty of time to catch up on work, family, or fulfill other social obligations—he for the hospital, she for the legal community and professional women's groups. Or, they simply spent time alone, something middle-aged professionals who lived demanding, hectic lives needed.

Dennis was, above all, a treasured friend…and when life threw a few curves at Charlene, he was the one for whom she reached.

Charlene was already feeling more secure just thinking about Dennis and their flawless relationship as she pulled into the St. Rose's E.R. parking lot. She was soon distracted by evidence of a recent commotion. A Sacramento Fire Department engine was just departing and a paramedic van was still parked outside. A couple of firefighters in full turnout gear stood talking outside the E.R. doors, and the ambulance was backed up to the dock, doors open, a serious cleaning-up going on.

On a couple of occasions she had gone to the E.R. when Dennis was in the throes of triage, and she had been mesmerized by his commanding nature, his confidence and skill. He was impressive to watch.

But today it appeared the chaos was past. There were a few people in the lobby waiting to be seen, all the curtains were drawn around treatment cubicles and there was a grim hush that lay over the room. It seemed things were under control. She saw Dennis standing outside one of the exam rooms, chart in hand, listening raptly and scribbling quickly as a young doctor spoke to him. A young woman.

She seemed awfully young to be a doctor, Charlene observed, but she had to be if Dennis was writing orders; if she wasn't an M.D., he'd be giving them. She looked about twenty-one and she was very tall. She could look Dennis right in the eye. Charlene, at five foot four, fought down the temptation to feel dumpy. She straightened her spine. She was petite…almost a foot shy of meeting Dennis's gaze. But this one, with her long legs and long auburn hair…

Dennis stopped writing suddenly to make eye contact with the young woman. She looked down as if shaken by something. He put aside the chart and pen and reached out to touch her upper arm. He gave her a gentle squeeze. Charlene saw that Dennis spoke to her softly but intensely. The doctor leaned forward, rested her head on his shoulder. His arm encircled her, stroking her back, and he murmured to her all the while. Charlene could read his lips: "It's okay, okay." The young woman was draped against him, soaking up what Charlene had come for. She wasn't sobbing or crying, but still obviously upset…and Charlene's fiancé held her close and secure. For a long time. Charlene made a U-turn and migrated back to the front of the E.R. before Dennis let the young woman go.

Hmm, she thought. She had never before referred to him as her fiancé. Even mentally.

"Hi, Charlene," Barbara Benn, the E.R. clerk, greeted. "Does Denny know you're here?"

No, she thought, he didn't see me because he was busy caressing a beautiful and obviously brilliant fifteen-year-old doctor. "Ah…I don't think so. You have an exciting morning?"

Barbara leaned over the counter. "Bad accident," she whispered. "We had a couple of fatalities. Very yucko ones.'' Barbara, early twenties with a slight purple tinge to her overly black hair, cracked her gum and rolled her eyes for emphasis. ''Denny worked on one for about forty-five minutes. Awful. Just a kid. I bet he's completely bummed. He'll be glad to see you. Maybe you can get him out of here for a while.''

At that precise moment, Dennis, who she never called Denny, was there, beside her. He dropped his arm casually around her shoulders, but his gaze drifted down the hall toward the departing frame of the young woman he'd just been holding. ''Hi, honey,'' he said absently. ''I can't get away. I'm sorry. It's a zoo.'' His lips fell to the top of her head in a perfunctory kiss before he let her go and followed the young doctor. Charlene was filled with a sense of emptiness that was underscored by her earlier conversation with Stephanie.

There will be an explanation later, she told herself. But as hard as she tried, she could not seem to get past the fact that he hadn't asked her why she had come. Didn't he wonder if something might be wrong? He was probably still very distracted by the fatality...or by the young doctor....

''Whew, it obviously sucks to be Denny right now,'' Barbara said.

''Who's the doctor? The young, beautiful one?''

She turned to look. ''Oh, that's Dr. Malone. She's new. Pediatrician. She's awesome. Everyone loves her. I guess you haven't met her yet.''

''No, not yet,'' Charlene said.

"You'll like her," she said. "She's very cool for a doctor."

No, I hate her, Charlene thought, then retracted the thought with shame. She had *never* had thoughts so jealous and immature where Dennis was concerned! Not even when she had witnessed goo-goo eyes directed at him while they were out together. From young nurses to legal colleagues, women took quick notice of Dennis's classic good looks. Dennis was an absolute *gem.* And, she reminded herself, completely loyal.

Charlene got herself to the parking lot, into the car, and out of the vicinity before she succumbed to the needy impulse to rush to the hospital cafeteria, where she might catch them in the act of holding hands over the tuna surprise, gazing adoringly into each other's eyes.

She drove to her favorite mediterranean café and parked. She sat in the car feeling alone and bereft, feelings that were completely alien to her. Suddenly she knew her life would be awful if she didn't have Dennis in it. And she knew how much *more* awful it would be if some doctor young enough to be her daughter had him. "Okay, it's an age thing," she said aloud in self-analysis. "A little premenopausal panic. Well, I'll be damned if I let myself turn into some wimpy dependent old woman who can't even have lunch because—"

Her cell phone twittered inside her purse. She plucked it out and studied the caller ID—it was her office. She didn't admit to herself that she felt enormous relief.

"Yes, Pam?"

"Char, you've had a disturbing and confusing call from Ron Fulbright, the manager at the Food Star Market in Fair Oaks. Something about your mother. I think you'd better go over there."

"My mother?"

"Yes, something about her not being able to find her way home…"

"What? That's ridiculous."

"Well, that's what I said. To which Mr. Fulbright said this wasn't the first time. They've started having a bag boy keep an eye on her when she leaves the store, watching to see if it looks like she knows where she's going."

"Wait a minute, wait a minute. She drives to the market, right?"

"Apparently she walked."

"But it's drizzling. She wouldn't walk there in the rain."

"Mr. Fulbright has her in his office. You'd better go get her. I could hear Lois in the background. She's…ah…unhappy."

"Well, I imagine so," Charlene said, indignant. "Call him back. Tell him I'm on my way." She clicked off without saying goodbye, put the car in reverse and headed toward her mother's neighborhood.

Lois must have been somehow misunderstood, Charlene thought, and the grocer interpreted this as her being lost and in need of her daughter's rescue. But it was absurd! Lois had only just returned from a rather taxing trip to Bangkok. At seventy-eight, she was anything but lost. She was an independent traveler of the world. Widowed for over twenty years, she was a modern, youthful, brilliant woman who refused to be called Grandma.

Charlene beat down a powerful sense of foreboding, terrified by the prospect of her mother—her rock—falling apart.

Two

Charlene racked her brain for any incident in which her mother had seemed confused or disoriented, but could think of none. She lost her keys, but who didn't? She forgot the occasional name, as did Charlene. Although there was that time, not so long ago, when she put the yogurt and cottage cheese away in the rolltop desk and then couldn't locate the source of the foul odor.... But they had laughed about it later.

When she arrived at the grocery store, she was directed to Mr. Fulbright's office in the back of the store. She heard her mother before she saw her. "May I have a drink of something, please?" Lois asked in a small voice. Charlene was brought up short. She hadn't heard that kind of meekness from her mother since Lois's gallbladder surgery sixteen years ago.

Charlene peeked into the partitioned room. Lois sat hunched on the hard chair beside Mr. Fulbright's desk. Though Lois Pomeroy was petite, she was such a formidable personality, Charlene tended to think of her as larger than she was. And Lois *always* sat or stood straight, her head up. She was prideful and pigheaded. In fact, she was a bossy pain in the ass, who at the moment looked stooped and cowed and...*frightened*. It was very disturbing.

"Anything you like, Mrs. Pomeroy."

"Just water, thank you."

"Be right back," Fulbright said. He nearly ran into Charlene as he exited his cubicle. "Oh, my heavens!" he said, laughing nervously. He grinned at Charlene in a big, perfect Cheshire smile. "Go ahead in," he said.

Lois raised her bowed head and saw Charlene. "Oh. He said he called you. I told him not to."

"Mom, what happened?"

"I just got a little turned around, that's all. It happens to people my age from time to time."

"And has it happened before?"

"Well, no, not really...."

"But Mr. Fulbright said they've been having bag boys keep an eye on you until it appears that you know where you're going. What does *that* mean?"

Mr. Fulbright brought the water. Lois sipped before speaking. "Well, there was one time last year—"

"Last month," Mr. Fulbright corrected.

"It wasn't last month!" Lois shot back. "Sheesh," she added impatiently.

"Yes, it was, Lois. Remember?" he asked too patiently, as though speaking to a child. "You were all turned around in the parking lot. Driving in circles. You went around and around, then back and forth past the store. One of the boys flagged you down and asked if you needed something. Remember?"

"Oh, that was last year!" A little strength was seeping into her voice under the mantle of anger.

Mr. Fulbright rolled his eyes in frustration. He then connected with Charlene's eyes, smirked and shook his head. "Well, if you say so," he relented, but he shook his head. "You have some groceries, Lois. Let me carry them to your daughter's car, okay?"

"Don't bother yourself, I can do it."

"Yes, I know you can, but it's my pleasure. I'm afraid if I don't take good care of you, you'll shop at another store."

"I'm thinking about doing that anyway," she said. "*Been* thinking about it, actually."

Charlene got her mother settled in the front seat of the car, the groceries in the trunk, and stood behind the car with Mr. Fulbright.

"This is an old neighborhood, Ms. Dugan. It's an unfortunate part of the job that we see some of our best customers go through aging crises. Lois got lost about a month ago and couldn't get herself out of the parking lot, much less find her house. She kept coming back to the store, driving around and around the parking lot, until someone helped her. She knows it happened—she started walking instead of driving, and don't let her tell you it was for the exercise." He rolled his eyes skyward, where heavy, dark clouds loomed, just waiting to let go. "Who would take that kind of chance in unpredictable weather like this? A person could drown! It's so she doesn't get too far away from home before she realizes she doesn't know where she is."

Charlene was absolutely horrified. "This is impossible! She just returned from the Far East!" But in thinking about it, Charlene realized that that trip, a tour, had taken place over two years ago.

"Nevertheless..."

"What happened this morning?" Charlene asked. *"Exactly."*

"I had one of the boys watch her walk down Rio Vista to make sure she turned toward her house, but she walked right by. She could have been going to visit someone, so Doug stayed with her just in case. She went another block, doubled back past her street again and finally sat on a retainer wall, in the rain, looking dazed. He asked her if he could help her and she started to cry."

"Cry? My mother doesn't cry! For God's sake, this is crazy!"

Mr. Fulbright touched her arm and Charlene snatched it back as though burned. "She should see her doctor. It might be just a fluke, a medication screwup or—"

"She doesn't take medication!"

"Well, maybe it's something more serious. But Ms. Dugan, it's something."

The passenger door opened. "Are we *going?*" Lois wanted to know, that impatient edge back in her voice. "I could have been home by now!"

Mr. Fulbright crossed his arms. "Or in Seattle," he muttered under his breath.

"Yes, Mom. Coming." Then, feeling protective of Lois, she glared at the grocer for his cheek.

"Goodbye, Lois," Mr. Fulbright said. "See you soon."

"I doubt it," she said, slamming the door.

"Well, thank you," Charlene said. "Though I really think—"

"When you run a neighborhood market in an area with a large retired population," he said, "there are some things you learn to watch for. They're my charges. It won't be that many years before I'll benefit from having people watch after me now and again. Just as the postman keeps track if the mail stacks up, merchants keep an eye out for their regulars."

"Thanks, but—"

"Get your mom to the doctor now. We don't need a senseless tragedy just because it's hard to think about Lois getting older."

As Charlene fastened her seat belt, she muttered, "God, he's annoying."

"Tell me about it," Lois said.

"I guess he knows what's right for everyone, huh?"

"I never could stand that guy. He's a hoverer, you know? Always looking over your shoulder when you pinch the grapes. Probably a pervert. I'm not shopping there anymore."

"I can't say I blame you, Mom. Especially if you're going to find yourself held hostage in the back room." Charlene shuddered, but not for thinking about Mr. Fulbright's back-room office.

"The rhubarb stinks. Smells like fish and tastes like rubber."

"Rhubarb?" Charlene couldn't remember ever having rhubarb at her mother's house.

"Let's get moving. I think I have a hair appointment."

"When did you start caring about rhubarb?"

"My mother always had a rhubarb cobbler on the Fourth of July. I wish I could remember if I made that hair appointment for today or next Tuesday. Damn!"

Charlene drove in silence for a moment. Then, with a sigh, she asked, "Why did you decide to walk to the market today of all days? It's cold, and it's drizzled on and off since morning."

"I needed the exercise."

"Really?"

"Why else would I walk?"

"Well…I don't suppose a checkup would hurt," Charlene suggested.

"I just had a checkup."

"Well, another one won't hurt."

"I'm not going to the doctor and that's the end of it."

"Mom…"

"I said *no*."

"Mom, I'm not going to argue with you—"

"Good! That will be a refreshing change."

"I'm worried, that's all."

"Waste of energy. Worry about something you have some control over. This is out of your hands."

She pulled up in front of Lois's house, parked, killed the engine and turned to regard her mother.

"Why are you acting like this?" she asked in a gentle voice.

"I've had a rough day," Lois said, looking away from her daughter, out the window.

Haven't we all, Charlene thought.

"I have things to do, Aida, so let me get my groceries and get busy."

"Aida? Mom, you called me Aida. I think I'd better get you in the house and—"

Lois groaned as if in outraged frustration and threw open her car door. She pulled herself out with youthful agility and, once extracted, stomped her foot. "You're starting to get on my last nerve! Get me my things and get out of my business!"

That's when she knew. She wasn't sure exactly what she knew, but she knew. The only Aida Charlene had ever known was an old cousin of Lois's who'd been dead over thirty years. And while Lois was admittedly a frisky character, Charlene was unaccustomed to such anger and temper in her mother. Lois was going through some mental/medical crisis.

Trying to remain calm, she went to the trunk, pulled out two bags and handed one to Lois. She followed her mother up the walk to the front door. Lois got the door unlocked easily enough, and they went inside and put the groceries away without speaking. When the bags were folded and stowed on a pantry shelf, they stood and looked at each other across the butcher block.

"I'm very sorry," Lois said. "I'm sorry you were

bothered, sorry I was rude to you and sorry about what's happening.''

"What *is* happening?'' Charlene asked.

"Well, isn't it perfectly clear? I'm losing it.''

Charlene went back to the office in something of a trance. Was it possible that even though she spent a great deal of time with Lois, she'd been too preoccupied to notice these changes?

She threw herself into the accumulated work on her desk, plowing through briefs, returning calls, writing memos and dictating letters. She also spent some time on the Internet, researching dementia in the elderly and Alzheimer's disease.

It was getting late and she should have gone home long ago, but she wanted no spare time between work and evening—she wouldn't know how to handle it. She could research Alzheimer's, but she couldn't think about her mother suffering from it. Tonight was dinner at her place with Dennis. And until she could talk to him, until she could take advantage of his cool-headed appraisal of her problem—not to mention his medical expertise—she couldn't allow herself to focus on it. But when the intercom buzzed and she looked at her watch, she realized she wouldn't even make it to her house ahead of Dennis, much less have time to cook him dinner. "It's Dennis,'' Pam intoned from the outer office.

If he cancels, Charlene thought, I will kill him and hide the body. She picked up. "Dennis, I lost all track of time. I can leave here in just a—''

"Listen, if you have to work late—"

"What? You aren't going to cancel, are you?"

"No," he said calmly. "I was just wondering if you'd like me to pick anything up."

"Oh." The perfect man. The most stable and reliable thing in her life. With Lois falling apart and Stephanie making her crazy, maybe the *only* stable and reliable thing in her life. "Did I just bark at you?" she asked him.

"Pretty much. Bad day?"

"Well, I would reply 'the worst' except that I stopped by the hospital and I know you had a terrible day yourself, one that included fatalities. So..."

"Yes, you were gone by the time I realized you had just made a rare unannounced appearance. I was so distracted at the time. So, what is this? Professional or personal?" he asked.

She thought about dodging the question, but then, after a pause, she slowly let it out. "Personal." It might as well have been a dirty word.

"I should have guessed. I can hear the tension in your voice, and you're working till the last possible minute. I know what that means."

She leaned back in her leather chair. "You do? What does it mean?"

"That you're upset, and you don't want any time on your hands during which you might think too hard, because you're afraid you might become distraught. You never have, but you're still always afraid of that. Of losing control."

Embarrassingly, unbelievably, she began to cry. The

tears had been there all day, just below the surface, but this was the last straw. They suddenly welled up in her eyes, her nose began to tingle and her face reddened and flooded. She pinched the bridge of her nose with her thumb and forefinger, but it did no good. She accidentally let out a wet, jagged breath. She couldn't remember when she had last cried. Probably years ago; certainly pre-Dennis, but he seemed to know what was happening anyway because he said, "Hey, hey, hey. Charlene, honey, what's the matter?"

Of course she couldn't speak. She put the phone down on the desktop, grabbed a fistful of tissues and tried to mop her face quickly and efficiently. She did *not* want Pam to come upon her sobbing. She blew her nose and picked up the phone. "I can't talk about this yet," she whispered into the phone. "Will you…will you pick up something for me?"

"Yes, of course. What shall I pick up?"

"Dinner," she said. And hung up.

Thank God she had her own private bathroom. She flushed her hot, red face with cold water, but it was a while before her tears subsided. The strange thing was that she wasn't sure what brought on the flood. She couldn't tell if it was the picture she had in her mind of Lois sitting hunched and frightened in the warehouse-like office, or if it was Dennis giving voice to her fear of losing control. Or could it be a mental image that she couldn't let come into clear focus of Stephanie fetching *her* from the grocer's back-room office?

When she was finally leaving, Pam was standing

behind her desk, putting some things away and other things in the tote she carried to and from work.

"See you tomorrow," Charlene said, ducking.

"Char?" Pam queried, leaning over her desk to get a closer look at Charlene. "Have you been crying?"

She stopped short but didn't turn. "What makes you think I've been crying?"

"Your eyes are red, your nose is red, your eye makeup is making tracks down your cheeks, I heard a tugboat horn come from your office and—"

"Don't be ridiculous," she said. And she left quickly.

Charlene lived in a new home in a small, gated neighborhood just east of the city. It was under thirty minutes to her office or the courthouse if traffic was reasonable, and only a half mile from the freeway. This gave her quick access for convenience and no traffic noise for peaceful living. The length of drive was perfect for making cell-phone calls, thinking through a work problem or giving herself a stern talking-to.

Tonight's self-talk was about keeping perspective. About staying cool. She was accustomed to giving herself pep talks—she was a hardworking single mother, after all. She took her issues one at a time, sorting them out calmly, logically.

First of all, the Samuelsons were a perfect example of the bad-divorcing couple. She decided to write them off as the cruel, ignorant people they were and place them in the chilled mental compartment in her mind that she had labeled *icebox*. She'd freeze out their influence over her mood.

Second, Stephanie was a wonderful girl, a jewel of a daughter, but she was a tad spoiled. It wasn't her fault, exactly. Between Charlene, who always worried about doing a good enough job as a mom, her exhusband, Jake, who was a very doting father, and Peaches, who was destined to have only the one granddaughter, Stephie was doomed to play the royal chick. So, she was spoiled. She liked having her way and having people cater to her. She wanted to graduate from princess to queen, and in order to do that she had to find a prince, marry him and turn him into her king. It looked as if she was going to succeed, too. Unless she drove the prince away with all her imperial demands.

Grant Chamberlain was a remarkably good choice for her daughter; Charlene wished she'd been that lucky twenty-five years ago. He was twenty-seven, a disciplined ex-army noncommissioned officer from the Special Forces, getting his degree on the GI Bill and supporting himself by tending bar. He was handsome and genuinely kind. Charlene admired him and approved of the way he treated her daughter, which was with respect and more patience than she usually deserved. Charlene was not totally unsympathetic. She could understand some of Stephanie's problem, what with their conflicting work schedules. Stephanie got up early to teach English to surly eighth-graders while Grant slept in. When she got home, he had already gone to work, where he stayed until the wee hours.

Grant took his days off during the week, which he filled with classes and study groups while Stephanie worked. When Stephanie was off on the weekends, Grant worked his longest hours…and made his best tip money. So this was hard. Work in the adult world was hard. There you have it. Who among us, she thought, isn't working hard? Long hours?

She let go a huff of laughter. *She doesn't want to end up like me, huh? I'll bet she doesn't. I work like a farm hand!* But she not only loved her work, she loved her life. She'd much rather be tired at the end of the day than whining that she wasn't having enough fun or getting enough attention. And that was *that*.

Next, she thought about Dennis and Dr. Malone, but by now she was in command of her senses again. It had clearly not been passion with which Dennis had touched the young woman. It was comfort. Paternal. There had been a fatality. A child. Barbara Benn had said Dr. Malone was a pediatrician. That explained everything. She settled her mind on that matter as well, and let it go.

But on the matter of Lois, she was at sea. She could feel the sting of tears come to her eyes at the smallest thought of her mother stooped and confused and lost. It was more than she could bear. Had she taken her completely for granted? She was in her late seventies, after all. Charlene knew she was lucky to have had her for so long, and in such excellent health of body and spirit. This time of life, she reminded herself, eventually comes to everyone. As some wise old sage had said, old age is not for wimps.

She pulled off the interstate onto the access road that led to her neighborhood. Within a quarter mile of her house, her car seemed to lurch oddly to the left and drag as if being tugged from behind. It was an ominous sensation. She slowed and pulled onto the soft, muddy shoulder. As she did so, she could feel the left rear tire go flat.

What little sun there was behind heavy clouds was almost gone, so she grabbed the flashlight from the glove box, got out of the car and shone it on the flattened rubber. "I can't believe this," she said aloud. At that very moment, she felt the first drop quickly followed by the second. Then the heavens opened up in earnest and a deluge poured down on her, drenching her to the bone. As she stood beside the disabled car, practically drowning, she saw the glare of approaching headlights. The car slowed, pulled to a stop behind her. There was not so much as a single house on this half-mile stretch of road that led from the interstate to her subdivision, so the odds were excellent that this was one of her neighbors, on his way home. Then she considered how her day had been going and thought her chances of being murdered were better.

A man got out of his car. She shone the flashlight on his face—and groaned. She was only slightly happier to see her ex-husband and not a serial killer.

"Charlie?" he said. "What the hell you doin' out here?"

She almost laughed, but it was more a sputter, given the heavy rain. "Oh, gee. Thinking," she replied.

"Well, Jesus, think in my car!" he said, grabbing for her arm.

"I can't," she resisted. "I'm soaked."

"Yeah, I can see that. Come on."

"I'll ruin your upholstery."

"Oh, that's funny. My *upholstery?* I'm way ahead of you. Come on!"

For lack of a better option, she went to the passenger side of his car and got in. She had to kick aside what appeared to be dirty clothes and a pair of running shoes, while he lifted a stack of file folders spewing loose papers off the seat so she could sit down. He pitched some fast-food bags into the back seat, pulled a blanket from same and drew it around her shoulders. The car was only a couple of years old at worst, but the interior was a wreck. Like his little house. His life.

"Why would you have a blanket in the back seat? Dates?"

"You're a riot, you know that?" he replied irritably. "This is a stakeout car—I practically live in it. There's also a first-aid kit, water, pick and shovel, fire extinguisher and other emergency items. You never know what's going to develop. Or what you might have to dig up." He pulled the blanket tighter around her. "So, what were you thinking about, Charlie? That flat tire?" he asked. "Wishing you could say 'April Fools'?"

God, she thought, it *was.* April first! How sad that none of her stuff could be joked away.

He was the only person who called her Charlie. Well, he and his cop friends. "What are *you* doing out here?" it finally occurred to her to ask, but she knew the answer. He had to be coming to see her. The question she couldn't answer yet was whether he was going to make her laugh or piss her off. There was a fifty-fifty possibility.

"I stopped by your office, but you were already gone...."

"I *know* I gave you my cell-phone number," she said.

"I had to see you in person for this," he said.

"Is it about Stephanie?" she asked.

"No, it's a favor. I need your help on something. But what about Stephanie?"

"You didn't hear from her today?"

"Not a peep. Why?"

"Well, wait a minute. I don't want to breach a trust. Does she usually talk to you about her relationship with Grant?"

"No, I wouldn't say that. She complains about Grant. She whines about Grant. She snivels, gripes, moans and groans, but no, I can't say she has ever *talked* to me about Grant."

A chuckle escaped Charlene. Jake also had a way with the unvarnished truth.

"There are times, Charlie, when I think I almost like the boyfriend better than my own daughter."

She shrugged and chuckled again. Guiltily. "She's been a little high-maintenance lately," Charlene commiserated.

"Y'know, I forbade her to move in with him. I absolutely forbade her," he went on. "She totally blew me off, called me old-fashioned, overprotective, the whole bit. Told me she knew what she was doing. And now what? All she does is bitch. Things just aren't going too well for the little couple. I guess Mr. Grant isn't courting her enough, huh?''

"Well, what do you say to her when she lays all the whining on you?'' Charlene seriously wanted to know.

"I tell her to grow the fuck up.''

God, he was a clod. "Oh, that's sensitive. You don't really say that, do you?''

"No, I *think* that, but I don't say it. If I *said* it she would cry. And you know what happens to me when she cries. It takes the bones out of my legs and I crumble. But I'd like to say it. I gotta tell you...I've been *thinking* it a lot lately.''

"I've even thought that about you,'' Charlene taunted.

"You look good, Charlie,'' he said. "You put on a little weight?''

She ground her teeth. She wanted to kill him for that. "About Stephanie—''

"You're right, I shouldn't be too hard on the kid. She going to learn about successful relationships with us as role models?''

She let out a huff of indignant laughter. "You weren't so hot, maybe. I think I was a fine role model.''

"Hey, hey, hey, I didn't mean to say you were a bad parent. Jesus, Charlie, you were the best parent in the world. There *is* no better mother than you. Hell, I wish you were *my* mother! I just mean about relationships. We weren't, either one of us, able to make one stick.''

"Yeah, well, I only tried once, remember. You tried, what? Five times?" She shivered. She was cold, miserable, wet and a quarter mile from a warm fire, a glass of wine and stable, consistent Dennis. For some reason it didn't occur to her to ask Jake to just drive her home.

"Four. I don't think you can say five since I married the same woman twice. You remember Godzilla? What a disaster that was. But I was married to Stella for seven years, you know. That would almost be considered a success.''

"I still can't imagine why you left Stella. You must be crazy.''

"Me, crazy? Gimme a break. It's Stella who doesn't have too many arrows in the old quiver, if you get my drift.''

"Stella? She's mother earth!''

"Yeah, she's a good kid at heart. It's just all the yoga, natural food, crystals, wood-nymph music, beads, bangles and fucking affirmations. People can be too positive, you know. It's wearing. But never mind, she was always great with Stephie.''

"Maybe Stephanie can move in with Stella," Charlene said.

"What's'a matter, Mom?" he said, jostling her with an elbow. "The little chick threatening to move home?''

"She suggested she might...."

"And if I know you, you talked to her about her commitment to Grant because there's no way you want Stephie, who is an even bigger slob than me, back in your tidy little nest." He slapped his knee and giggled. His laugh was contagious but his giggle was positively repellent.

"No," she lied. "I told her she should consider moving in with you."

"Yeah, sure," he said. "Y'know, I admit I regret the way I played it."

"Played what?" she wanted to know.

"I wish I'd done what you did. Stayed out of the game altogether. Refused to hook up at all, with anyone. Just flat-ass refused to get together with anyone who wasn't absolutely perfect. Period."

"That isn't what I did! There *wasn't* anyone...starting with you!"

"We don't have to sing the 'Jake was a lousy husband' song again. We're all getting a little tired of that one. I was young, you were young, we were stupid."

"*You* were stupid," she said.

"Yeah, yeah. So what we have here is me, getting married all the time and never able to make it stick, and you, with an obvious fear of marriage—"

"I'm not afraid of marriage!"

"Oh, really?" he asked, eyebrows arched sharply.

"Not at all!"

"Afraid of commitment, then?"

"Don't be ridiculous! Dennis and I are totally committed."

"Just afraid to take the next step and make it legal?

I mean, I can understand, it's only been, what, five years or so...."

"For your information, we're planning to get married, we just haven't—"

She stopped suddenly. She had no idea she was going to say that. Or what she was going to say next.

"Just haven't what, Charlie? Picked the century yet?"

She stared at him blankly for a moment. Her life flashed before her eyes. Well, maybe not her life, but certainly her day, and the way it had seemed to happen to her through a series of random disasters. April Fools'? Maybe she was the only fool.

"And that's why Stephie is all fucked up about marriage," he said. "Because between the two of us we can't come up with one decent relationship. Know what I mean, Charlie? Admit it, you're as reluctant as I am impetuous. Huh?"

"You know what?" she said to him. "I had to co-parent with you, but the baby has grown up. She's an adult, whether she likes it or not, and while she might need her parents, she has had plenty of time to adjust to the divorce. And I'll be damned if I'm going to talk about this whole thing with you for another quarter century! Leave me alone for a while, will you?"

She opened the door and got out of his car, the blanket still wrapped around her shoulders and dragging through muddy puddles behind her. His ability to insult and enrage her had not lessened in twenty-five years. She went to her car and retrieved her purse and briefcase, locked the door and started walking. Stomping.

"Charlie, what the hell are you doing?" he called out of his opened window. She stomped on, muttering incoherently to herself. He could still, with such ease, provoke her into irrational behavior. Here she was, walking down the soft, muddy shoulder of an isolated two-lane road in the dark, in the rain. It was worse than irrational, it was suicidal. But right that moment it made more sense than sitting in the car with him.

"Charlie, this is stupid!" he yelled.

God, he was following her. In the car.

A car going in the opposite direction whizzed by. The splash off the tires provided a fine spray of mud to add to the rain, which had lessened to a heavy drizzle, but was not quite enough to wash the streaks of mud off her face and coat.

All the stuff she thought she had handled began to come back one at a time. The Samuelsons, Stephanie, Dennis and Dr. Malone, Peaches—and Jake, his timing as bad as ever.

"Charlie!" he yelled. "Hold up, will you? I need to ask you something. I need a favor."

"In your dreams," she muttered to herself. If I *am* afraid of commitment, she thought, Jake Dugan would be a good enough reason.

A flashing red light throbbed over her head and she turned to see that her ex-husband had attached his portable police beacon to the top of his car. He followed her at a safe distance, slowly, so that if a car approached from behind, she wouldn't be mowed down.

But then again, she wouldn't need this service if he hadn't shown up in the first place, which was the cause of her walking home in the mud and rain when she had a perfectly good cell phone in her purse.

She made the right turn into her neighborhood in ten minutes. She could have been faster if the weather had been decent. The flashing red light disappeared and Jake's headlights strafed the houses as he made a U-turn and departed. It was then that she realized she wore his blanket around her shoulders. She shrugged it off on the front walk and hung it over the wrought-iron entry gate.

She stepped into her house and stepped into sanity. The lights were dimmed, the table set, candles lit, fire in the hearth and two cups of something steaming sat on the coffee table in front of the fireplace. Dennis, having heard her come in, appeared in the kitchen doorway, wiping his hands on a dish towel. The sight of all this peaceful domesticity warmed the heart of the drowned rat and without stopping to consider the ramifications Charlene heard herself say, "Dennis, do you still want to get married?"

Stephanie moved a cherry around in her Coke with the straw, staring into the mix, daydreaming. She sat at the far end of the bar near the cash register, and when Grant was between customers, he spent a few minutes leaning across the bar talking to her.

This was how they'd met. She'd been at the bar with a couple of girlfriends and had flirted with the cute bartender. That was two and a half, almost three years ago. It was a lot more romantic then than it was now.

A guy, carrying his drink, sauntered over and sat down beside her. "Tell me you're not waiting for someone," he said to her.

"Okay. I'm not waiting for someone."

He smiled. He wasn't bad-looking, with a nice shape to his face, curly hair and friendly brown eyes. A sharp dresser. He rolled his eyes heavenward. "Thank you, God." He refocused on her face. "So, tell me your heart's desire and I'll bring it to your feet."

I must be getting old, Stephanie thought. Bar talk used to be fun...and now it only sounds stupid.

"Hey, Freddy," Grant said, slapping a cocktail napkin down in front of him. "You meet my girl?"

"Your girl? *Shit.*"

"Freddy, meet Stephanie. Stephanie, meet Fast Freddy."

"Fred," he corrected with a casual sneer directed at Grant. "Darlin', if you're mixed up with this guy, you're making a huge mistake. Let me take care of you."

"What can I get for you, Freddy?" Grant asked. Grant had that look—narrowed eyes, forced smile, sunken cheeks. He was working on being polite. This was not a good sign for Stephanie. If Grant had appeared to actually like Fred, Stephanie might have shunned the man. But Grant's dislike provoked her into overt friendliness. It was all about the way things had been going lately. The squabbling. The complete failure of compromise. The need to do something to perk things up, to get Grant's attention.

"I'm good," Fred said, lifting his half-full glass. "Fix up the lady, here. My treat."

"You think she buys drinks at my bar?" Grant asked with a mean laugh.

"You mean she's *really* your girl?" he asked, incredulous.

"Really. As in, we live together. Another Diet Coke, Steph?"

"No, thanks. So," she said, turning her full attention and sweetest smile on Freddy. "How long have you two known each other?"

"From the Stone Age, man." He sipped. "Like, high school."

"Jeez, I thought I'd met all Grant's high-school pals," she said.

"That should tell you something," Grant said, turning away to serve other patrons.

"He's always been the jealous type. I get all the girls. But until this moment it meant nothing."

She laughed at his absurdity. "These come-ons, Freddy. Stale. Old. Completely transparent."

"I know. I'm thinking of getting a writer."

"Ah, the Cyrano de Bergerac syndrome."

"Spoken like a movie buff...."

"English teacher."

"No kidding?" He seemed to relax into himself. "I'm a history major. I taught for two years. I really liked the kids, but the pay sucked."

"So I've noticed." She glanced at Grant and saw

him glowering. Her eyes went back to Fred. "What do you do now?"

"I'm a day trader. Stocks. Commodities."

Her eyes actually lit up at the word *day,* but Freddy might have thought she was responding to *trader.* "Really? Sounds interesting. Tell me all about it."

On the night Charlene and Dennis decided to get married, they changed a flat tire in the rain, traded their wet clothes for warm terry robes and then spent a quiet evening talking about the day's events over a light dinner of hot soup and cold salad. "You go first," she said to him. He, somewhat reluctantly, told her about an auto accident that had taken two lives— a grandfather who might've had a coronary at the wheel and a nine-year-old boy who wasn't buckled in and upon whom the emergency team had exercised every gift modern medicine had to offer before they let him go. It was Dr. Malone's first fatality as a pediatric resident.

"Now you," he said, and she skipped the Samuelsons and Stephanie's remarks and went straight to her mother's crisis. Tears threatened again. Charlene honestly didn't know if she was going to get through this without endless crying.

When she was finished, Dennis said, "You know, it could be a number of things—from the predictable old-age dementia to Alzheimer's. It could even be small strokes...or maybe she was just very tired or had other worries on her mind. Then again, maybe it only appeared she was confused and lost when she was daydreaming.''

''Do you think it's possible?'' she asked hopefully.

''I think she'd better see a doctor, a specialist. There's a good geriatrics doctor at St. Rose's. People like him. If you can get Lois to go, I can get her a quick appointment. He owes me.''

Dennis always made everything all right. No matter what the crisis, he could be counted on. ''I would be so lost without you,'' she said.

''So that was what had you crying? Worrying about your mother?''

''Yes. Silly, isn't it? I usually check things out before I overreact.''

''And were you so overwrought that you walked home from your car in the rain?''

She grimaced. Ah yes, there was something else she hadn't mentioned. ''Jake was on his way here to ask me a favor,'' she said. ''He pulled up right behind me, moments after the tire went flat. It started to pour so I got in his car to sit it out. Then he asked me if I'd put on a little weight.''

Dennis couldn't help himself. He started to laugh.

''I wasn't amused,'' she said.

''I don't imagine you were.'' He had no trouble envisioning her as she jumped out of his car and, furious, walked the rest of the way in the rain. ''Just tell me one thing. You didn't suggest we get married because Jake made you feel fat, did you?''

''No,'' she said. ''But by the time I got here, soaked and mad, I realized that the one thing in my life that

I have always been able to count on is you. And I'm stupid not to tie you down and get you off the market."

"Charlene, I've been off the market for five years."

"And I've been crazy to let you run around loose. Dennis? Do you think it's a bad idea? Because—"

He covered her hand with his. "I think it's probably about time."

She sighed in relief. For some reason, all she wanted was to have this one part of her life settled. Mapped out, covered, secured. Done.

"Why don't you take a soak while I clean the dishes," he said. "Then I'll start the bedroom fireplace and meet you in there."

She had a moment's hesitation. "Dennis—"

"It's all right, Charlene," he said, reading her mind. "We've both had rough days. I'm thinking along the lines of a little CNN before sleeping."

By the time she got out of the bath, he had already nodded off on top of the comforter. At 5:00 a.m. she felt his lips touch her forehead as he prepared to leave for his early start in the emergency room. She could smell the coffee he'd made, and although he was clean shaven, there would be no evidence that he'd used the bathroom sink; Dennis was as immaculate as she. She couldn't have asked for a better night's sleep, all her worries and anxieties put to rest by the best companion of her life.

Yes, it was probably about time.

Three

When Charlene entered her office, Pam London was taken aback. "Wow," she said, her mouth dropping open in surprise. "Look at you."

"What?" Charlene asked, but she smiled because she knew what Pam saw. She'd seen it herself in the mirror that very morning.

"You look ravishing. You haven't looked this good since you got back from Mazatlan."

"Ravishing?"

"My, my, yes." Pam squinted a bit, studying Charlene's face. "What is it? New makeup?"

"Not exactly. Come into my office, will you?" Pam followed, notepad in hand, and shut the door behind her. "Dennis and I have decided to get married," Charlene said, skipping any preamble.

Pam didn't make it very far into the spacious office before she sank into a deep and comfy leather chair. Speechless.

"This can't possibly be a surprise," Charlene said. "Can't it be...?"

Charlene, businesslike, began taking papers out of her briefcase and placing them in separate stacks on the desktop. "To the contrary. Some would even say this is way overdue, that we should have done it years ago. After five years, it seems almost like a mere formality.'' Indeed, on the very night they had made the decision, nothing special set it apart from any other night they spent together. Except maybe the changing of a tire in the rain, which Dennis accomplished while Charlene held the flashlight.

''I guess I thought—'' Pam didn't finish.

''You thought we didn't need marriage?''

''Well…that's what you always said.''

''And it's still true. We don't *need* marriage, but wanting it is a different story. To make our commitment complete.''

''That's lovely.''

''You are the absolute first to know. I haven't even told Stephanie yet, or my mother. Lois thinks I'm completely hopeless, so she's going to flip, and Stephanie… Well, I haven't talked to her since yesterday.'' And in thinking about that conversation some of the glow threatened to fade from Charlene's features. She would have to call Stephanie and tell her about her grandmother; they were very close. But as for the marriage plans, she could wait. In fact, Charlene was still smarting a little from Stephanie's words and didn't look forward to calling her at all. ''But I wanted to tell you immediately,'' Charlene said to Pam. ''Because I'd like you to stand up for me, if you will.''

''If? Of course I will! But what about Stephanie and Lois? Won't they get their noses out of joint if I—''

''No, no, no,'' Charlene insisted. ''This is all going to work out fine. And I want you with me on this.

Like you've been with me on everything. I couldn't have built this practice without you, Pam.''

"I don't know what to say."

"Say you will."

"Of course," she said, flattered. "When is this going to happen?"

"I don't know. In a few weeks. I have about four major crises to work out before I can think about the actual event, but once I get things under control, I'll make some arrangements. Something very small, very quiet, very quick."

Pam smiled lazily. "Quick? Are you pregnant?"

"Ha-ha."

"And you are doing this quickly because...?"

Charlene stopped shuffling papers, put her briefcase under her desk and took a seat. "Now that we've decided, we're anxious to have the formalities out of the way. But there is another matter that concerns me. My mother is experiencing some memory problems. Some confusion. I'd hate to call it dementia, but until she sees a doctor, I have no other terminology."

"So the call from the grocer was the real McCoy," Pam observed.

"I didn't want to admit it. I was hoping he was just overreacting, but she *was* confused. It's possible she really couldn't find her way home from the store and had to be rescued by a bag boy. I have no better explanation because she can't remember much about the incident."

"My goodness, how scary," Pam replied, as surprised now as Charlene had been yesterday.

She nodded. "I owe Mr. Fulbright an apology. And a debt of gratitude. I hope these aren't the early symptoms of Alzheimer's."

"And that's why you're going to hurry and—"

"That's a factor, not a reason. My mom has a problem, and I don't know how serious it is, but before things get any worse, if they're destined to get worse, and while everyone in my family and in Dennis's family are all relatively healthy and alert, we're going to have a small, pleasant ceremony."

"Well, this must be the right decision, it sure has worked wonders on you. You look positively radiant. How do you feel?"

Charlene folded her hands together on top of her desk. "I can't explain it, but if I'd known I was going to feel this great, I'd have accepted Dennis's proposal years ago. I've never felt so comfortable…so *serene*. I have total peace of mind."

Pam leaned back into the folds of the chair, stretched her long legs out in front of her and admired Charlene's shimmer. "You're glowing. It's amazing."

"I can feel it."

"You and Dennis must have had some romantic night last night—the sparkles are still floating all around your aura." Pam's eyes became moist. "I'm so happy for you, Char. No one deserves this more than you. I'd be honored to witness for you."

Pam stood, dropped her notebook on the ottoman and moved toward Charlene. She opened her arms to embrace her, tears glittering in her eyes.

But Charlene didn't cry. She was a little embarrassed by what Pam had said…and its contrast with the truth. There were no sparkles of romance glittering around her, but rather the warm glow of complete contentment. There had been no sex, no breathless passion in the wake of a profession of the truest love, but rather the intimate dialogue of close friends as they comforted each other after their terrible day.

But wasn't that what true love really was? Friendship and trust? Knowing the person you counted on was there? And being there for him?

So, Charlene asked herself, what exactly was she glowing about? She frowned over Pam's shoulder as she admitted to herself that it felt vaguely like relief.

Charlene patted Pam's back and said, "There, there." Then she handed Pam a tissue and said, "High on my list of priorities, after a nice little wedding, is a week off. Not a honeymoon, but rather a vacation. Sometime later this spring possibly, after we've tied the knot, had Peaches to the doctor, cleared some time from our schedules and have things under control. We're talking about a cruise. Dennis and I have both been under so much pressure lately, I'm surprised we even have the energy to get married. To that end, I'd like to make a dent in the 'pending' list and clear some time."

"When are you going to tell Stephanie and your mom?"

"Well…"

"That's not much of an answer," Pam said. "What's going on?"

"To tell the truth, I'm a little miffed at them both.

Peaches knows she has a problem that could be serious, and she told me to butt out. Said she was sorry to be losing it. Her exact words were, 'I'm sorry that obviously I'm losing it.' Jesus. As for Stephanie, she doesn't stop talking about herself long enough to check and see if anyone else has a life. She's so self-absorbed...."

"She's twenty-five."

"And spoiled and selfish. But I will have to speak to her about Peaches. You know how close those two are. And hopefully we will tell them both this weekend."

"How do you suppose they'll react?" Pam said, a devilish flicker sparkling her eyes.

"Hmm. Peaches will probably be astonished and Stephanie will... Stephanie will probably be relieved that I'm not going to die an old-maid divorce lawyer." She shook her head while Pam laughed. "So," she went on, "I have a full calendar today, culminating with a meeting this evening here with Bradley himself of Bradley & Howe regarding the Omagi custody. I doubt I'll get home before ten. I'm due in court in an hour. Child Protective Services continue to harangue Leslie and Tom Batten, and I've filed an injunction to hold them off until we can have a hearing. Then I have a lunch and a meeting with Carl Dena regarding the transfer of one of his companies into his son's name, since his son's been managing it for about ten years anyway. Can you see to these items, please?" She passed a neatly printed list to Pam. "And will you please add one item?"

"Sure."

"I ran into Jake last night. He wanted a favor, but we got sidetracked talking about Stephanie and he forgot to ask me. Will you give him a call? Ask him what he needs?"

"Sure."

"And if it sounds like too much trouble, tell him you can't fit it on my calendar. I've already done plenty for him and I don't—"

"He probably just wants some simple legal thing for free, like a paper filed for a friend," Pam said as she scribbled, not even looking up from her notebook. "If so, I can probably get it done without even bothering you."

"Your discretion," Charlene said dismissively. "I've got less than an hour to go over my notes for court, so let's get to work."

"Gotcha. Coffee?"

"Hey, that would be great. I forgot to grab some as I passed the pot."

"You have a lot on your mind. By the way, will you be living in your house or Dennis's?"

Charlene responded with a blank stare, her mouth slightly open. How could that have not even come up in the conversation that followed "Do you still want to get married?" "Um, my house, of course," she said to Pam unconvincingly.

"You didn't even talk about it, did you?"

"You know, we talked about so many things...."

"Oh brother," Pam said, heading for the coffeepot.

One of the things Pam London appreciated about working for Charlene Dugan was the quality of the work environment and the high measure of independence and responsibility Pam was afforded. She was an experienced paralegal, an executive assistant, and passed off secretarial work to office clericals and legal research to law clerks. Pam had helped build Phelps, Dugan & Dodge; she'd been with Charlene for sixteen years, beginning in the early, lean years.

Pam remembered with nostalgic fondness the old brick walk-up they started in, when they both were young and energetic, when Stephanie was just a bitty little thing with freckles. They couldn't afford a secretary so Lois, who was about to retire, helped out with typing and filing in the evenings and on the weekends.

They'd been through a lot since then, both professionally and personally. Pam had lost her mother to cancer and eventually moved back in with her father. She told herself she did it for him, but it was as much for herself. Meanwhile, Charlene finally moved out of her mother's house. Together they built a strong reputation in the legal community. The work was challenging, the pay excellent, the people were of the highest caliber and her days flew by.

Pam and Charlene were too busy to worry that they didn't have dates. And now, against all odds, Charlene was actually getting married.

It was 7:00 p.m. when the door to Charlene's office opened and she came marching out, briefcase in one hand, sheaf of papers to drop on Pam's desk in the other, coat over her shoulders. And a scowl on her face. "Last-minute change of venue," she said. "I'm going to Bradley & Howe."

"When did this happen?" Pam asked.

"About ten minutes ago, when I called to confirm our meeting here. It's a sleazy trick. This guy is creating diversions, pretending the meeting was always scheduled for his office. What bullshit. I left a message for Sherry Omagi on her voice mail, but if she shows up here, tell her she can drive over to Bradley & Howe if she wants to, but it doesn't matter. I'll meet with the attorney whether she's there or not, and I'm not backing down."

"Go get 'em, tiger."

"You ever get through to Jake?"

"Oh, yeah. There's some woman he met…I think he said he met her in a bar…?"

"No," Charlene said facetiously. "Jake? In a bar?"

"She's divorced, has a couple of kids by two exes, neither of whom share custody or pay child support. Now ex number one wants custody of child number one. And of course she's broke."

"Does the ex have money?"

"Don't know that yet."

"Well, I can't see a judge handing over a child with a lot of back support owed. Abuse?"

Pam shrugged. She didn't know the answer to that either. "He abandoned them…as did ex number two. I put her on your calendar for next week."

"Why'd you do that?" Charlene asked.

"Because you just can't say no to Jake," Pam returned, smiling gently.

"That's what you're for! You *can!*"

"Char, it's easier this way. Believe me. It'll take hours of pestering off the clock." She glanced down at the papers Charlene had given her. "Where are you with CPS versus Batten?"

"We'll revisit this issue in one month with a hearing in family court. We've got a TRO. The CPS has been temporarily restrained. They've been told to leave the Battens alone unless they have a police matter to investigate."

"In the hot file it goes. You'd better hurry."

"Don't work too late," Charlene said.

"Since there's no meeting here, I'll close up in ten minutes."

"Have a nice evening," Charlene said, pulling the door closed.

"You bet," Pam said to the closing door. "You bet," she said more quietly to the empty room.

She cleaned off her desk at a leisurely pace, giving that last client who might show up at the wrong place for the right meeting a few more minutes to appear. She cleared her computer screen, locked her desk drawer and placed her calendar open on top of her desk, scanning tomorrow's schedule. Yes, yes, I love working here, she said to herself. I'd be lost without this place.

Lost.

Pam pulled her gym bag from the cupboard behind her desk and went into Charlene's executive bathroom; she only used this private facility when Charlene was out of the office. There she affected a transformation—from sophisticated career woman in light wool suit, silk blouse and pumps, to weight trainer in spandex, sports bra and cross-trainers.

She pulled her shoulder-length auburn hair into a clip and couldn't resist the urge to preen a little in front of Charlene's mirror. She was *cut;* nicely muscled, her percentage of body fat low. Looking fine. Weight lifting was more than just a hobby, more than a means of staying in shape. It was something she did to keep her spirits from sinking.

It wasn't as though she had a bad life. In fact, by almost anyone's standards she had a *great* life. She loved her job, was in outstanding health and had a terrific home life with her Great Dane, Beau, and an elderly but extremely fit father who traveled quite a bit, leaving her to enjoy the luxury of free rent in three thousand square feet with hot tub. And she had friends, from work, from the neighborhood and from the club where she exercised.

But there was no man in her life and there hadn't been in years. *Years!* And she was no longer too busy to notice.

She also remembered the ones that hadn't worked out, the ones who did come around but were completely wrong for her and the ones who caught her eye and already had the stamp of another woman on them. She was luckless in this department. What was worse, she had absolutely no idea why. If her father asked her one more time, "Any new prospects, honey?" she might strangle him. As objectively as she could judge, she thought herself to be of at least average attractiveness. Oh hell, *above* average! She was intelligent, industrious and clean. She had a sense of humor, she read good books and, unless she was missing some vital signal, she was actually popular. She got along with everyone, on both personal and professional levels. In fact, she was one of those women who, after writing of her dilemma to Ann Landers, was likely to get the response, "If what you say about yourself is true, you'd have been snapped up years ago. There must be some little thing you're overlooking."

It wasn't like Pam to sulk. In fact, it was rare for her to give in to this sense of disappointment, this feeling that she had somehow failed. She'd stopped trying to figure out what terrible flaw she had long ago. Was this because Charlene was getting married? But that was silly. Charlene and Dennis had been together for years and, as she'd said, this was really only a formality.

Pam had accepted that not everyone gets a partner and she knew a lot of single people who were not looking, were not trying to find a mate. She was thirty-nine and had stopped allowing herself to be set up at about thirty-five. She wasn't interested in making man-hunting a life's work.

The paperwork she would take home was already packed into her briefcase. As she pulled her raincoat out of the closet, there were two short taps at the outer office door before it swung open. "Locking up, Ms. London?" Ray Vogel asked her.

"As we speak," she said, taking her coat off its hanger.

"Whoa, Ms. London," he said, grinning. "Look at you! I always figured you for a gym rat."

"A what?" she said, laughing in spite of herself.

"Wow, look at that six-pack," he said, referring to her muscled abs. "Where do you work out?"

"Just a neighborhood tennis and fitness club."

"You compete?" he asked.

"Me? Get serious!" But she had an unmistakable urge to flex.

She slipped into her coat, pulled the strap of her tote over one shoulder, gym bag over the other, followed that with her handbag strap, then grabbed up her briefcase and suit-on-a-hanger. Keys in hand, she joined him at the office door. He took the keys from her hand, eased her out the door, flicked off the lights and locked up for her. "You could compete," he said, handing her back the keys. Then he took some of her burdens. "Come on, I'll make sure you get to your car."

"You don't have to do that, Ray. I get myself there every night."

"Tonight's my treat," he said. "You know, I could tell. That you work out. I thought about just asking, but I didn't want to, you know, be…um…" He was clearly searching for a word.

"Nosy?" she supplied, humor in her voice.

"That's not what I mean. I was working on a way to ask you if you were, you know, married. Or involved."

She almost dropped her suit. She stopped walking and turned toward him with a look that verged on alarm. "What?"

He shrugged. "Married? Involved?"

"Why?" she said, confused—and very shocked.

"I thought we could grab a drink some night. Maybe something to eat." He took her elbow in hand and led her the rest of the way to the elevator. He pressed the down button. "You know, a date."

It was almost scary, the way he proposed this only minutes after she'd been flexing her thirty-nine-year-old muscles in front of the bathroom mirror, bemoaning her absolutely solitary life. She was going to be a long time in recovering from the sheer blow. "Are you serious? You have a thing for older women?"

"Why wouldn't I be serious? How much older can you be?" he countered.

The elevator arrived and they stepped inside.

"I could be a lot older, Ray. I could be your mother!"

"Come on," he said, brushing her off.

"How old are *you?*" she demanded, feeling a blush rise up her neck.

"Now, if I'd asked you that question, I bet you'd get all piss— All bent out of shape," he said, correcting himself. "I'm almost twenty-eight."

"I could be your much older sister," she said. "I'm almost forty."

"Oh yeah?" he said, looking pleased with himself. "How *almost?*"

"Thirty-nine and three quarters."

"No shit. I mean, no kidding!"

"How 'almost twenty-eight' are you?"

"Twenty-five," he said. He grinned devilishly. Handsomely. "I took you for about thirty."

"Ray." She laughed at him. "You're a terrible liar."

"Okay, thirty-one. No more than thirty-three, tops. So, about that drink—"

The elevator deposited them on the main floor and they stepped out onto the marble floor of the foyer. "You really have made my day," she said with laughter in her voice. She couldn't wait for her father to next ask about prospects. "But I'm afraid I couldn't possibly have a drink with you."

"You're involved," he said. It was not a question, and it reeked of disappointment.

"Ray, I'm pretty sure we wouldn't be right for each other." She stopped at the glass revolving door.

"I'm mature for my age."

"Me too," she said.

"I get done here at about ten. You should be finished working out by then."

"Good night, Ray," she said. She took her bag and briefcase from him and went through the revolving doors.

He followed her. "I'm going to change clothes, drive over to the Plum Tree—they have good Chinese and a nice, quiet little bar. Very cozy neighborhood place. Not too loud."

"I'm going to work out, then I'm going home,"

she said, heading for the parking lot. "To tuck in my dog and walk my father."

"Oh man, you're making it very tough, Ms. London," he said from the glass doors. "I don't know how to compete with a dog and a father. Play fair."

She threw her head back and laughed again. "You are very flattering. Have a nice evening."

"You're breaking my heart!"

She shook her head. Nice joke, she thought. The kid doesn't know from broken hearts. She unlocked her car, threw all her stuff in ahead of her and got in. She turned on the engine and the lights, then looked one more time toward the office building. He stood there, watching her go. Tall, handsome, young. *Young.* As she pulled out of the lot, the face in the rearview mirror grinned stupidly back at her. "Oh, for God's sake!" she snapped at herself. "Don't even think about it!"

Dennis could hear the commotion of happy family life as he stood at the front door of his sister Gwen's house. He didn't hurry to ring the bell, just listened for a moment. Gwen was forty now and had had her children in her thirties—Richie, when she was thirty-one and Jessica, when she was thirty-three. They were at a great age right now—lots of fun and not much work. They didn't have to be bathed anymore, and they were too young to drive. But this was not a quiet or calm age. He could hear the choppy piano practice in which Jessica was engaged and a steady thumping coming from somewhere inside the house.

"Richie! That basketball is for outside!"

The steady thumping would be his nephew, bouncing the ball against a wall.

"I'm keeping time for Jessica," he yelled.

A *living-room* wall.

He rang the bell. The door was opened by the kids, who immediately shrieked in happy surprise and threw themselves on him. He lifted them both, looping an arm around each skinny waist and balancing their wiry bodies against his hips, then carried them through the foyer, past the living room, to find his sister in the kitchen.

"Well, look at this. Your uncle Dennis is psychic. He knew I needed a break from you ungrateful monsters."

"I eat monstrous children for breakfast," he said in his growling voice and gave them a powerful shake that sent their limbs flailing.

"Take them away for a while and I'll make it worth your efforts," she said.

He growled again and carried them upstairs, knowing he wouldn't get a single peaceful word of conversation with Gwen until he'd given them some quality time. An hour later, the kids clean and tucked in their beds, Dennis migrated back to Gwen's kitchen, lured by the aroma of freshly brewed coffee. She brushed a strand of hair out of her tired eyes and slapped a box of Girl Scout cookies onto the kitchen table between two cups.

"Where's Dick?" Dennis asked.

"In New York, on business," she said. "The dick," she whispered, making her brother laugh.

"Had enough mommying for one day?" he asked, sitting down behind one of the cups while she poured.

"You're the guardian for those two, right? Because I might not live to see the end of this job. God, they should bottle that energy." She filled the second cup. "Charlene working?"

He sipped. "Mmm, good. Yeah, she has a meeting." Gwen yawned. "Am I keeping you up?" he asked.

"God, I'm sorry, Denny. I had to work at the school today, plus I took Dick's turn at Jessica's soccer practice, and then there was this Brownie meeting about the cookies. You know, THE cookies," she said, smacking the box till it fell over. "The effing cookies," she added, again whispering.

"Won't you be glad when they get a little older and you can swear again?"

"Jesus, you don't know the half. How's your life?"

"I'm getting married."

Her mouth fell open and she was momentarily speechless. "You're getting *what?*" she asked when she recovered from the shock.

"Married," he said again.

He sipped again from his cup while she studied his passive face.

She had wondered if this day would ever come again for her brother. She didn't want him to be alone. Even though he had her, Dick and the kids, it was not the same as a spouse, a partner. When he'd started dating Charlene, she'd grown excited. Hopeful. But five years had passed in relative sameness, and while they were obviously very close, nothing like marriage—or even living together—ever materialized.

Gwen put her elbow on the table and held up her head with her hand, staring at him while he sipped his coffee. Is this what happened when you were almost fifty and getting married? Matter-of-fact? Is it just another chore? Like deciding to update the will or go see the tax attorney?

She lifted one skeptical eyebrow. "You look ecstatic," she said doubtfully.

"It seems like the thing to do, don't you think?" he asked.

"It's not a colonoscopy, Denny. You're getting *married!*"

"I really am happy about it. It's just that...there's something I hadn't accounted for."

"Lay it on me," she said, slowly testing her own cup of hot coffee.

"I was completely unprepared for how this would bring back memories of Sarah." Gwen stopped sipping and gave Dennis her full and, for once, unsarcastic attention. She slowly lowered her cup to the saucer. "Even though I asked Charlene if she wanted to get married two, probably three years ago, it never occurred to me that in saying yes she would unleash so many memories for me."

"Good ones?" Gwen asked. "Bad ones?"

"All of them, from the time I met Sarah and first

held her close, to the time three years later that I held her cancer-ravaged body as we said goodbye.''

''Oh, Denny...''

''I have no idea why this is happening now. Really.''

''Maybe it's the idea of remarrying,'' she offered.

''Sarah died eighteen years ago. And we were only together for three years. It doesn't feel like *re*marrying. It feels like *that* was another life.''

''Well, then, what could it be? Are we close to any anniversaries? Of your engagement to Sarah? Your wedding, her illness, her death?''

''No, thank God.''

She reached across the table and squeezed his hand. ''Maybe it's just time for you to revisit this thing. You know, like post-traumatic stress. Maybe this is how you complete the cycle, bring closure. I mean, is it even possible to marry Charlene without your last marriage crossing your mind?''

''I never thought I'd love like that again,'' he said, looking anywhere but at his sister.

A moment of silence passed between them...and stretched out. In a way, Denny and Charlene had been acting like an old married couple since the week they met, but was that a good thing? ''And have you?'' she asked very quietly, drawing his eyes back to her face.

''Of course!'' he insisted. ''My God, Charlene is extraordinary. I know *you* agree.''

''I do,'' she said. In truth, Gwen was one of Charlene's biggest fans, but that wasn't really the issue here. The issue was her brother, who was morose on the day he announced his formal engagement. Despite his insistence to the contrary, the bold and passionate way he had loved when he loved Sarah had been buried with her. While Gwen was mostly concerned with her brother right now, it did cross her mind that Charlene might be getting shortchanged.

Gwen had been eighteen when her twenty-eight-year-old brother met and fell helplessly in love with Sarah Brown, a slender beauty with dark hair and vivid eyes. Dennis had described his first true love to his sister as kind, patient, good-natured and possessing a dry humor.

They met while Dennis was teaching high-school chemistry. Sarah was the photography and audiovisual teacher at the school and there was such chemistry between them—an intended pun they overused—that the principal asked them to stop looking at each other during school hours. They got married the second school was out—a sweet little ceremony in the park—and spent the summer in Europe.

What they had together was so obvious, so intense, so devoted and delicious, it became the benchmark for what Gwen wanted for herself. Perfect love.

And then Sarah died, a slow and miserable death from ovarian cancer.

"I don't know if I ever told you this, Denny, but one of the things that I have always most admired about you was…is…your ability to take the pain and disappointment in life and turn it into something positive and beautiful. Like letting the experience of Sarah's illness and death turn the chemistry teacher into a physician's assistant who can help people daily. I love that about you.''

He looked wistful, his eyes cloudy. ''She was so amazing,'' he said.

''Dennis, look at me,'' she said.

He obliged. ''You've told me that a number of times, Gwen. I appreciate it.''

''Denny, is this some kind of red flag? Maybe you and Charlene shouldn't be getting married....''

''I was so lonely by the time I met Charlene,'' he said. ''Dating never did do it for me, you know? I was so grateful to finally find someone who liked the same things. Someone I could talk to. I suggested we get married or at least move in together six months after we met.''

''I didn't know that,'' she said.

''She told me she'd never been happier, more in tune with a person...and she didn't want to screw it up by changing everything so soon after we'd fallen into such a lovely little routine.''

Routine, Gwen thought. Yes, that would describe it.

''The day I met Charlene was one of the best days of my life. The past five years have been some of my most contented.''

Gwen couldn't bear the flat expression on his face, the murky look in his eyes. Sarah's death had been a painful loss for Gwen, too, and for everyone even remotely related to them. They had been a beautiful, joyful young couple, without so much as an argument between them, and were now scarred by the utter tragedy of a life cut short. And almost overnight Dennis became a young widower locked in a powerful grief that lasted years. It was almost too much to bear remembering. She was afraid she might cry just thinking about it.

Now he was getting married....and he sounded perfectly miserable.

In utter frustration she tore open the box of cookies and stuffed one into her mouth. She went for a second, then a third, chewing slowly and with much difficulty. Her cheeks puffed out and her teeth were smeared with chocolate. It took a long time to make room for two more, which she had to break into chunks to push into her mouth. Dennis watched this display in frowning confusion, but she didn't see him. She had closed her eyes as she struggled with the clump of chocolate. When she was finally done, she wiped her mouth with the back of her hand, looked at her brother and said, "Just don't bubble over with happiness, okay?"

"That was disgusting," he observed.

"Thank you."

When Charlene arrived at the law offices of Bradley & Howe, Sherry Omagi was waiting in the foyer, looking as nervous as a cat. Charlene pasted that smile of confidence on her face. She hadn't spent as much time as she should have preparing for tonight, for she'd had only one meeting with Sherry, but it should be cut-and-dried. Sherry was willing to discuss visitation, as long as she maintained custody, and would not ask for support payments. She was a self-supporting accountant who worked mostly at home and the child was young, circumstances that all heavily favored the mother.

"He's already here," Sherry said, wringing her hands. "I saw him go in."

"Sherry, I want you to calm down and let me do the talking."

"I'm so afraid," she said. "Frankie means everything to me."

Charlene pulled her client along with her to the elevators. She pushed the button for the third floor. "Now, we've talked about this, Sherry. Your ex-husband is entitled to some quality time with Frankie, and the same is good for Frankie, but that's no reason you can't retain primary custodial care. You should rethink the issue of compensatory support as well."

"I don't need support," she said. "Kim isn't as attached to Frankie as I am. He only wants him because I want him. He's even said that having him is *stupid*."

"People say things in the heat of the moment."

"He said he's sick of Frankie shitting all over the place. Really, Charlene, I worry about Frankie in Kim's care. I don't know that he'd be…safe."

"Well, there are definite messes involved when you have little ones running around. This is the first time you've indicated Kim could be abusive. Are you serious about this?"

"I just don't know. I suppose that's just my temper talking, but still. Charlene, I just want custody. That's all."

"Compromise will get you a lot further, Sherry. Especially since it's the best thing for the entire family."

"But it hardly costs anything to keep Frankie. Really."

"But it will, believe me. Wait till he wants to drive. Wait till college. We have to settle these things now, make it part of the divorce settlement."

The elevator arrived on the third floor and Charlene got off. When she realized that Sherry wasn't beside her, she turned around. Her client stood in the elevator, paralyzed. "You're kidding, right?" Sherry asked.

"About what?"

"About driving. About college."

Charlene laughed. "I have a twenty-five-year-old daughter—it's nothing to kid about."

"Charlene, Frankie is a goose."

Charlene's expression was frozen, her mouth hanging open slightly. She did a memory check of all the times Sherry had said things like, "Frankie is such a precious goose," and "I don't know what I'd do without my little goose." She couldn't remember one time she'd actually been informed that this was not a minor child.

"A goose...with tail feathers?"

"Beautiful tail feathers."

"The kind of animal down comforters are made of?"

Sherry gasped. "God forbid!"

"Oh my Lord," Charlene prayed.

That night Jake entered Coppers. The bar, once named Toppers, had been rechristened when the owner realized a large percentage of the clientele was from the police department. Jake stopped first at the bar, procured a beer, said hello to a couple of guys he knew, and finally migrated to a booth near the back. A woman waited there, nursing a cola.

"Hiya, Merrie, honey." He slid in across from her. "You're all set. You have an appointment with Charlene next Tuesday—10:00 a.m. Can you do that?"

"I reckon so.... But does she know I ain't got no money?"

"She understands about that. Charlene is good, Merrie. You're going to need someone good to get ahead of this guy."

"Jake, I just don't get it," she said, shaking her head. "He didn't want nothing to do with us. Only saw Josie one time, that's all. Never gave me any money, let the apartment lease run out with me sitting there with no place to go. And now? He wants his daughter so she can have a good life? What does he think she's been having the last eleven years up till now?"

Meredith was a thin, washed-out blonde, all of twenty-seven years old. She was just a little bitty thing, about five foot two, a hundred and ten pounds maybe, soaking wet. If it hadn't been for her little tiny breasts, she'd look like a kid. A tired and worn-out kid. She had hardly any fat on her, and her eyes were big and blue and innocent...but she was not. She'd had a hard life. Even before this. She'd been only fifteen when she'd gotten pregnant with the child in the custody dispute. Her ex, Rick, had been thirty, and quite possibly agreed to marriage as a means of escaping any charge of statutory rape.

Meredith was broke, not terribly bright and didn't live the most wholesome of lifestyles. She also had a daughter at home, aged eight, fathered by another man who was not her husband. Rick, on the other hand, was forty-one, stable and married with a second child. He made a good living, lived in a decent house and went to church on Sunday.

Jake saw a dark shadow on her cheek. "Merrie?" he asked, leaning across the booth and squinting. "Merrie, you got a bruise?"

Self-conscious, she touched the exact place. Then she reached into her purse to retrieve her compact and studied her reflection. She powdered the spot. "It ain't no big deal. Not really."

Jake took a long pull at his beer, pursed his lips and looked away, trying to mentally gather restraint. "He's really starting to piss me off, Merrie."

"*You?*" She laughed.

"When did this happen?"

"He came over this morning when I was getting ready for work. He found out where'd I moved to and that you were helping me out, helping me get a better job. He wanted to talk to Josie and I wouldn't let him past the door. He found out about the whatchamacallit…order of protection." She laughed hollowly. "It made him mad."

"Jesus Christ. You call the police?"

She looked into her cola, defeated. "I just took the kids over to the neighbor's, told her to be sure he didn't bother them and then came on t'work." She looked up. "I know I should've called the police like you said, but I'm just so tired of him. Of everything. And I didn't want to be late for work again."

"You gotta do this by the book, Merrie. Follow through. Or you're gonna be *real* late for work, you know what I mean?"

"Oh, I don't think he'd actually kill me," she said quietly. "So, how'd you talk your ex-wife into helping me out? You don't have to pay her for this, do you?"

"No, nothing like that. She likes having me owe her. It makes her feel powerful." He grinned.

"You must have a pretty good relationship with her, even after the divorce."

"We were married one twenty-sixth of the total time we've known each other, and we've gotten along better in the last twenty-five years than we got along in that one. Most of the time I irritate the shit outta her." He grinned, as if it was an achievement. "But, like I said, she relishes opportunities to remind me that I am a lowly cop and she is a big fucking attorney." Merrie lit a cigarette. "Hey, I thought you quit."

She exhaled away from him, trying to spare him the secondhand smoke. She touched her purplish cheekbone. "I'm under a lot of stress."

"Soon as this is over, you gotta try to quit again. That stuff isn't good for the kids. Y'know?"

She shook her head. "How'd you end up single?

Good-looking guy like you, with such a big heart? Seems like some woman'd have you locked up tight.''

"They do that regular, Merrie, honey. Regular."

"Well, listen, I gotta git," she said, stubbing out the barely smoked cigarette. "Get the kids home and in their own beds before my neighbor has a fit. Jake, I don't know what I'd do if you weren't such a good guy."

"Hey, no problem. C'mon, let's go."

"You think I'm going to get through this, keep my Josie?"

"I'm telling you, Charlene is the absolute best lawyer in family law in this city. Judges pick her to arbitrate all the time. She's so good she even took a case to the Supreme Court. And she's a nice person. You'll like her. She's got a lot of… What's the word I'm looking for? She's got a lot of spunk, that's for sure, but that's not it. She's got class, but that's not it either…. Dignity. She's got dignity. You spend a little time with her, you feel all cleaned up."

They exited the bar and stood outside in the wet, early-spring night. "You never should'a divorced her," Merrie said.

"Ha. That was not one of my options."

Four

The sun came out on Saturday morning and Charlene took it as an omen. She was preparing the brunch for her mother and daughter over which she would give them the good news.

"Let's not overcook that quiche," Dennis said.

They were making brunch. *They* would convey the news. She mentally lectured herself to start thinking and acting as a couple. This should not be a challenge; they'd been together for years.

Dennis put a sprig of mint in the festive-looking bowl of multicolored melon balls and poured four mimosas. He snapped open and refolded the linen napkins, peeked in the chafing dish at the ham and bacon and turned on the coffeepot. Charlene brought the warm croissants to the table, unfolded the napkins and put them in decorative rings, checked the meat in the chafing dish and turned down the temperature, then drank one mimosa. Rather quickly.

Dennis noticed. "There isn't any reason to be tense," he said. "I'm sure they approve of me."

"It's silly, isn't it? But I am tense. Why is that?"

"Are you afraid to get married?"

"No. In fact, since we made the decision, I've never felt more relaxed. Secure. Pam says I glow."

"You didn't like the way I folded the napkins?" he asked. And if she wasn't mistaken, asked rather testily.

"I wanted to use the napkin rings—I just bought them. If you don't like them, take them off." She took a breath. "Dennis, there are a couple of things we haven't talked about yet."

"Like?" He left the napkin rings alone.

"Insurance? Joint accounts? Prenup?"

"Those things don't matter to me," he said. He'd already told her that he had set aside some money for his niece and nephew, for college, and he naturally assumed Stephanie would remain her beneficiary. "Anything you want is fine with me."

"Well, here's something we haven't discussed. Where are we going to live? I assumed we'd be living here."

He stared at her for a moment as she fussed with the napkins, then he picked up a mimosa and drained the glass. "You did?"

"It seems like we spend more time here," she said.

"That's because of your schedule. You don't exactly keep regular hours."

"I don't punch a clock, no."

"Exactly! And when we have plans and you can't get away until the last possible minute, I come for you here. Then I bring you back here."

"I thought you *liked* it here," she said.

"I like being with you," he countered. "And coming here rather than asking you to drive back into the city is the gentlemanly thing to do.''

"Oh. You're being a gentleman? You don't like it here?''

"I like if *fine,*" he said snappishly. "But it's for your convenience that we spend more time here. My house is actually closer to your office and the courthouse. If your clothes were in my closet, it would work out even better for us to meet there.''

"Your place would make a nice rental," she said.

"You don't like *my* house?''

"I love your house, but this house has a larger master bedroom and bath. Plus, I just bought it.''

"It would make a nice rental," he said, a little edge in his voice.

"I don't want it to be a rental!''

"Really?" he asked. "Why not?''

"It's my house! I don't want to rent it out!''

"And you think I'd like to rent mine out because...?''

"It's older, larger and there are more rentals in your neighborhood.''

"It's an historic district!''

"You don't seem as attached to your house as I am to mine.''

"It's a restored home! I restored it!''

The doorbell rang. They stared each other down.

"We're going to have to put this discussion on the back burner," she said.

"Where it will stay good and hot," he added testily.

They went to the door together, plastered smiles on

their faces and swung the portal open to greet Stephanie and Lois. They welcomed with hugs and cheek presses, pulling the guests inside. Dennis quickly replenished the mimosas that had been guzzled while the brunch guests shed their wraps. He presented full, fresh glasses to Lois, Stephanie and Charlene, then he put an arm around his fiancée's shoulders and said, completely sweet-natured, "Let's not make them wait. Let's have a toast."

Dennis and Charlene were both professionally trained in the ability to act contrary to emotions when necessary. Dennis couldn't let his stress or fear or even anger show in the emergency room, especially around the patients and their families. As for Charlene, she was a gifted litigator; no one knew by her expression what she was thinking…and at that moment she was thinking she had just met a side of Dennis she had never before known.

"What are we toasting? New car? Vacation? Raise? Bonus?" Stephanie asked, taking a preliminary sip.

"At long last, Dennis and I have decided to make it official. We're getting married."

Stephanie stopped in mid gulp. She and Lois exchanged shocked looks and then said in unison, "Why?"

As toasts go, it wasn't all Charlene had dreamed of. She much preferred the reaction she had gotten from Pam. Happy tears seemed more apropos.

"We felt it was time," she said somewhat wearily.

They relented. "Oh. Well then, congratulations!"

"Yes, of course. How wonderful."

Dennis raised a glass. "To new family ties," he proposed.

"Hear, hear," they intoned.

"Now, what have you made for brunch?" Lois wanted to know.

"Well, don't fall over in excitement," Charlene said.

Stephanie whispered to her grandmother, "I think she's in need of a little more bride-to-be attention, Peaches."

"But they always serve such lovely meals," Lois protested.

"Come ahead, then," Dennis said. "Come and sit—you'll love this."

It was true—Dennis and Charlene had gotten quite good at this sort of thing. It was not entirely insensitive of Lois to concern herself first with brunch and second with the upcoming nuptials. In their five years together, Charlene and Dennis had established a reputation for giving the best parties, with the most exquisite ambience and the most delectable food. They had a keen eye for putting the right guest list together, and whether the affair was large or small, elegant or casual, it was always polished. Perfect.

They sat Lois and Stephanie down and served them a wonderful brunch. Once their appetites were sated, they turned their attention to the prospect of a wedding. Charlene gave them the standard line, that it would be small, simple and soon, possibly in a few weeks.

"What do you mean, small wedding? What do you mean by small?" Stephanie wanted to know.

"Well, we've talked about a quick trip to Lake Tahoe," Charlene said.

"Or, we could throw caution to the wind and go all the way to Las Vegas," Dennis threw out.

Charlene looked askance at him. She thought his tone was a little edgy and suspected he was still miffed about the house issue.

"Most likely, we'll go down to the courthouse, get it done and spend our time and money on a vacation later," Charlene clarified.

"And deprive yourselves of guests?" Lois asked. "How completely unlike either one of you."

"I have to admit, I'm pretty surprised," Stephanie agreed. "I would have expected a rather lavish affair."

"As in big, white wedding?" Charlene asked, frankly shocked.

"Oh, not as in big, white, virginal wedding," she clarified. "Something that would fit your personal style more—which is almost never simple, small and soon. I've seen you plan a Christmas party for months, a Fourth of July barbecue for weeks. It's so unlike you to just throw something together."

"Well, that's just the point!" Charlene said in frustration. "We want to get married and don't have time for a big deal. It's a little more complicated than a dinner party, you know."

"Hardly. You can take as much or as little control as you like," Lois declared.

"Peaches is right, Mom. These days you get a wedding planner."

Charlene was a little slow to respond because she was watching her mother. It didn't escape her notice that Lois seemed positively sharp as a tack today...and this pleased Charlene greatly. This was the mother she knew and, as it happened, took for granted.

"I can't believe a planner eliminates all the work. Surely there's still copious shopping, ordering, listing, planning..."

"As much as you want." Stephanie shrugged. "Remember Jennifer Johnson, my sorority sister? She's in med school and said all the time she could spare was a two-hour meeting every couple of weeks. Her mom and dad live in another state, so they couldn't help. The solution? She had a meeting with the planner to talk about what she liked, made final selections that were brought to her and showed up to say 'I do.'" Stephanie popped a melon ball into her mouth.

"That couldn't be done in a month."

"Maybe not, but if all you want is a nice party, something you wouldn't have to have a hall reserved for months in advance, you could have a very nice wedding with good food, music, flowers and lots of fun planned in two or three months. You could be a June bride." She leaned over the small round table. "You're not, you know, in the family way?" she whispered. Then giggled.

"She's afraid I won't make it," Lois said.

"Mother! What an awful thing to say!"

"Aren't you?"

"Peaches, that's a little melodramatic, isn't it?" Stephanie wanted to know.

"It's true. She's completely freaked out because I got a little turned around at the grocery store."

Annoying though the direction of conversation was to Charlene, it was also endearing. That was her mom; she rarely spoke as you'd expect an eighty-year-old woman would. Freaked out, indeed!

"I heard it was very turned around," Stephanie said, giving her grandmother a sidelong glance.

"It could have been *very*. Whatever. She's afraid if she doesn't get married quickly, I won't even know I went to the wedding."

"You are so irritating," Charlene said to them both, but she managed a smile. At least Peaches had a sense of humor.

"I wouldn't mind having guests," Dennis said.

The women turned as one to stare at Dennis, as if they'd forgotten he had a role in this event.

"Well...I wouldn't," he said.

"But you said it should be simple and small and quick," Charlene said.

"No, you asked if it *could* be simple, small and quick, and I said that would be fine, if you wanted it that way. I always say that. Anything you want is fine with me. But if you're tempted to have a larger party, a reception with guests, I would enjoy that. My first time around, we didn't have a big wedding, just a few friends in the park."

"Why didn't you say so?"

"You didn't ask. You seldom ask me what I'd prefer.'' He let his gaze drop as he sipped his coffee—to miss her glower.

"Was that a jab?" Peaches whispered to Stephanie.

"Very definitely," Stephanie whispered back. "The wedding tension has begun."

"No, it hasn't," Charlene said. "This could work out fine. I went to the justice of the peace with Jake."

"Maybe we should do things differently," Dennis suggested. "For luck."

"Well," Charlene began patiently, "Stephanie's right. We've entertained on any excuse in the past few years. It seems kind of strange to conceal the wedding."

"It *is* a celebration, after all," Lois said. "I wouldn't mind having something to dress up for. You *are* my only child, you know. And you eloped the last time."

"I just said that, Mom," Charlene reminded her.

"I know. I heard you."

"You two have always been such party animals," Stephanie said. "In your own very special, uptight way," she added softly.

"I think I can remain mentally competent for a few more months," Lois said.

"Mother, for heaven's sake—"

"I don't know why you don't check it out," Stephanie said. "I mean, before you decide to elope to Tahoe, you might as well see what you're dealing with. That's what I plan to do."

"Seek out the help of a wedding planner?" Lois wanted to know.

"Oh, yeah. I figure I'm going to need one."

"Big event, huh?"

"I'm thinking ice sculptures."

"How is it that doesn't surprise me?" Charlene asked.

"I'll get the name of Jennifer's wedding planner," Stephanie offered. "By the way, where will you guys be living?"

"My house," they said in unison, and the subject was immediately dropped. Again.

Meredith Jersynski arrived at Phelps, Dugan & Dodge ten minutes early. All she knew about law was what she had learned from late-night *Law & Order* reruns on television; her divorce had been accomplished without her ever stepping into a courtroom. She did know enough to try to look as if she could win a case if she went to court, so she wore her very best dress and jacket. She pulled her flouncy blond hair back and clipped it conservatively, but she was a little short of cash, so her dark roots remained too evident. She went light on the makeup, put the run in her hose on the inside of her leg, wiped the dust and scuffs off her old pumps and prayed she didn't look like an eleven-year-old dressed up in Mommy's clothes.

The law offices occupied the entire fifth floor and Merrie couldn't help gaping in awe as she took in her surroundings of dark polished wood, plush leather, immaculate granite and tile, classy prints and fresh flowers in rich vases. A job emptying trash cans in a place like this was more than she aspired to. To reach this pinnacle, to be a lawyer in a place like this, it must make a person so proud.

In Charlene's office there was a little sitting area made up of a sofa, two comfortable chairs, a coffee table and end tables. Meredith sat in one of the chairs, perched self-consciously on the edge. Pam sat in the other chair with her notebook and Charlene sat in the corner of the sofa across from Merrie. Coffee was served; Meredith's cup rattled on the saucer. There was a tape recorder under the coffee table, which Charlene could operate with the toe of her shoe.

"Pam will take some notes even though we're taping this. It's all for the sake of accuracy. I don't trust my memory with anything."

"It's all right," Meredith said.

"Tell me about it," Charlene said. "Take your time."

"Which part?" Meredith wanted to know. "Rick showing up and wanting Josie?"

"Maybe you'd better start at the beginning. When you met him, dated him, married him?"

A rueful laugh escaped Meredith. "Well, that all happened real fast. And it was over with real fast, too."

"Go ahead," Charlene urged.

"Well, let's see. It was in Odessa. I was living with my aunt and uncle at the time. My folks was... well...my daddy was gone, my mama was remarried to a guy I didn't get along with too good, my uncle had a place I could work in and—" Realizing she'd strayed quite a bit from the point, she stopped and cleared her throat.

"Rick was this older guy who came into my uncle's place. He offered to drive me home after work and I accepted. He got fresh with me right then and there. There weren't no date, of course. I pushed him away and said no, and figured I'd never see him again, but he came back, brought me a nice present and took me home again. This time he at least bothered with a little sweet talk. I must've had a crush on him because I gave in. Too fast." She grimaced in embarrassment. "I'm a sucker for presents."

"That was when?" Charlene asked.

"About twelve years ago."

"You got pregnant right away?"

"He came around for a week or two. Probably less than two. And yes, I got knocked up. And my uncle, he came unglued. Knocked me near into the middle of next week. By this time I hadn't seen Rick in at least a couple of months. All I really knew about him was his last name and he'd said he was from Sacramento. But he had a real unusual last name. So my uncle tracked him down, found out where he worked and who his people were, and called him up."

"To tell him you were pregnant?"

"Well, I reckon. And to scare him into marrying me. I wasn't yet sixteen. And he was near thirty."

Charlene and Pam looked at each other; Meredith looked so young now, this man must have had a shine for real young girls. In Charlene's experience, those kinds of shines didn't often disappear over time. She tried to push the assumption from her mind and let the young woman finish her story.

The thing she was having trouble rectifying in her mind was Jake's interest in Meredith. Either his tastes in women had made yet another metamorphosis or he had taken a paternal interest in this one.

"So, did he come back for you then?"

"No. He said it probably wasn't his. That he wasn't the first. My uncle went crazy again...said he wasn't going to keep a whore around his place. But the baby was Rick's and I knew it was and I swore it was, and so me and my aunt and uncle came here, to Sacramento, tracked him down, said we'd get a blood test, and he said okay." Compound sentence finished, she took a breath and sat back in the chair.

"He then married you?"

"Yes. We got this little apartment where I practically never saw him. He'd come around about once a week, maybe twice. Spend the night, leave some money, take off again. Until I got big with Josie and then he stopped spending the night. About three weeks after she was born, he said we were getting divorced and I'd better find myself a baby-sitter and a job."

"And...?" Charlene prompted.

"I found a baby-sitter and a job," she replied, confused.

"You didn't get in touch with your uncle? Couldn't he have helped you?"

"Oh, Ms. Dugan, my uncle might've helped me eventually, but only after he'd beat the tar out of me. Then if he could help me, I'd end up with Rick, who wasn't nice to me and didn't like me. And he didn't want Josie, that was for sure. And she's the prettiest little thing. And smart? Girl's as smart as a whip! Her teachers are always making a fuss over her.''

"Okay, you got a baby-sitter and a job."

"I'd gotten on with the neighbors by then, and I may not be the smartest person in town, but I put by a little cash when I could. I knew Rick wasn't good for much, and he wasn't good for long. I got a job like the one I'd had in Odessa. In a club.''

"Country club?'' Charlene asked hopefully.

"Dance club.''

"Dance?''

"Strip. My uncle had a little strip club.''

Charlene took a breath. "When did you next hear from Rick?''

"About three months ago. I ain't heard a peep from him in all these years. Josie's eleven…and she's scared to death she's gonna have to leave me and Angie.''

"Angie?''

"I had another baby three years after Josie… another pretty little girl. She's eight. I didn't marry her daddy, but her daddy sees her sometimes and even gives me a little money now and again.''

"Her daddy is—?''

"A bouncer at one of the clubs I danced in.''

Charlene took a breath. "Meredith…I have to ask you this question. Are you, or have you ever been involved in prostitution?''

"No, ma'am! I mean, I ain't gonna sit here and

pretend I didn't ever find one of the gentlemen attractive…and I been known to accept a gift if the giver is a nice sort…but I didn't ever sell anything to anybody!''

Pam and Charlene exchanged looks.

"If there's a custody dispute, your ex-husband will very probably say you were a prostitute."

"He can't prove nothing like that."

"No arrest record?"

"I didn't say I wasn't ever arrested…but I ain't never been a prostitute."

"What were you arrested for?"

"I was holding for someone one time. He must have seen an undercover cop in the bar and passed off to me." She shook her head. "I ain't the smartest girl in town, Ms. Dugan, but I ain't ever done wrong on purpose."

"Did you do time?"

"No, I got probation…and I don't do drugs, either."

"Okay, let's fast-forward. Did your ex-husband tell you why he wants custody of Josie?"

She shrugged. "He's married now, has a daughter of his own, and he says he wants to give Josie a nice home."

The room was silent for a moment. Two of the three people present were seriously wondering if this might not be a good idea.

"And…did you talk about visitation? Joint custody? Any compromise?"

"No, we did not," she said emphatically. "Because

right after I said no he got me with a left hook to the jaw and liked to have knocked me out. So I took my girls to a shelter and got me one of them…you know…protection things.''

''Temporary restraining order?''

''Yes. Told him to stay away. Then I moved where I thought he wouldn't find me. Ms. Dugan, he *gave* me custody and divorced us and never sent us no money or visited Josie…. He *can't* have her now!''

''Well, Meredith, I'm not going to mislead you. This is not going to be a slam dunk.''

''I reckon Jake must've known that much because he wanted me to see you. He says you're the best lawyer there is.''

''Isn't that nice of Jake,'' Charlene said, and though she smiled, she had strong homicidal urges toward her thoughtful ex-husband.

Speaking of the devil himself, Jake was sitting outside Charlene's office, waiting, when the door opened. Meredith flew right into his arms, hugging him. ''Jake, you're right about Ms. Dugan. She's just about the nicest person I ever met.''

''I told you so, didn't I?''

''I have to visit the ladies','' she said. ''Then we can go.''

''This way, Meredith,'' Pam said, leading her down the hall toward the community ladies' room. Charlene and Jake were left alone.

Jake stood. ''She's something, isn't she?'' he asked, wiping at a stubborn spot on his pant leg. ''I appreciate this, Charlie. It looks kind of bad for her and the kid, doesn't it?''

Charlene shook her head. "You really tossed me a winner this time, Jake. The girl doesn't stand a chance."

"If anyone can help her, you can."

"Every time you bring in one of these 'favors,' she's worse off than the one before."

"Charlie, you might be the first break this kid's had in her life."

"Well, remind her to call me to set up another appointment."

"Will do. Give it your best shot, will you, Charlie? She's a good kid. She's had a lot of bad luck, you know?"

"I always give it my best shot, Jake."

When he was gone and Pam returned, Charlene was waiting for her, leaning a hip casually against Pam's desk. She was wearing a rare look—desperation. "Got any ideas?" she asked Pam.

Charlene shook her head. "You?" she asked.

Pam shook her head as well. "I wouldn't want to be her."

"How about them? The kids? I don't even know where they'd be better off."

"That's a good place to start. We should find out if the ex-husband's got anything to offer," Pam said.

"If he does, it shouldn't be hard to get support in exchange for shared custody. After all, he's been delinquent for eleven years."

"Jake could get us—"

Charlene was shaking her head. She employed the services of a number of investigators and each had certain specialties. Maxie Preston was not above using her sex appeal to put a gentleman suspected of the occasional indiscretion at a disadvantage. In lay terms, she wasn't above setting traps. And she was a tiny blonde, something she had in common with Meredith. She did not, however, look like a mere child.

"I don't want to use Jake on this," Charlene said. "I think I'd rather use Maxie."

"Maxie?" Pam asked. "She's pretty high dollar for a pro bono. Why not let Jake help with this?"

"Because Jake's not objective, and if there's one thing we really can't afford on this case it's getting a loose cannon like Jake involved."

"But Maxie…? You know I have this problem with the way she works," Pam complained. She'd never been comfortable with that whole scenario.

"She doesn't have the same constraints as we do, but she gets the job done."

Pam made a face.

"Tell you what—you set her up on this investigation. You call her, meet with her, tell her what you want. Agree?"

"Agree." Pam sighed. "That Meredith. Jake sure can pick 'em."

"Haven't we always said so."

Pam left a message with Maxie's voice mail, and the call was returned an hour later. By the background noise, Pam assumed Maxie was in her car. "My schedule is really tight, but if this is something urgent, I'll make room."

"You decide," Pam replied. "We have a client, a very tiny twenty-six-year-old divorcée with an eleven-year-old daughter. The ex was forced to marry her as a minor, when she may have loosely resembled an eleven-year-old child. He abandoned her and the child almost immediately, never paid support and has returned to her life to sue for custody. It's our concern that—"

Maxie cut her off. "You don't have to explain. I did the math."

"There's also a chance he's a good guy who wants to do the right thing. He's forty-one, married, has a child from the second marriage…. The only hiccup in that theory is that, according to our client, he slugged her."

"Yeah," Maxie said. "I'll bet he's a peach."

"You know what Charlene wants? Pay records, work history, et cetera."

"Et cetera meaning kinky habits. Fine. I'll need the usual retainer, a workable timetable—say, at least a week, preferably three—and I'll have to interview the woman. I can go see her at work. Tell her I'm coming."

"The usual retainer?" Pam asked.

"Four hundred. Cashier's check. I'm going to be working not far from your office tonight. I should be wrapping up at around eight. That too late for you?"

"No, I'll be here," Pam said, fully expecting Maxie to offer to stop by and pick up her check.

"Good. Swing by Romeo's. I'll meet you in the ladies' room."

"The ladies' room?"

"I'm working the bar. Nice gentleman whose wife keeps finding lipstick on his collar. But hey, a girl's gotta pee, huh?"

"Oh, Jesus."

Maxie laughed loudly, then honked the horn and yelled, "Nice signal, dipshit! So, Pam, shall we say eightish, in the ladies'? I'll be the one wearing the provocative décolletage."

"See you then," Pam sighed, hanging up quickly. What was it Charlene always said of this private investigator—*she got the job done.*

Charlene left the office at six for a dinner meeting, leaving Pam to clear away the remnants of the day and lock up. Pam didn't mind the task. In fact, she quite liked it. It gave her a sense of completion to be the last one in the office at night, and often the first one to arrive in the morning. And tonight she had time to kill before meeting Maxie. There were still people about in the building, in the law offices—associates, paralegals, clerks, until late at night, sometimes midnight. They were tucked away in offices, cubicles, conference rooms and the centrally located law library.

After filing some case books back in the office's central law library, Pam returned to her desk—and found a long-stemmed red rose. She touched it suspiciously and lifted it gingerly. Then she lay it back down on her desk and began to gather her things together. A few days before, she had found a note on her calendar, wishing her a good day. Then there was a scribbled invitation to meet him in the evening for a beer at a quiet little neighborhood sports bar. She had put both in her purse, unwilling to have them found in the trash by even the janitor. He should not be doing things like this, she thought. He had absolutely no guarantee she wouldn't go to his supervisor and complain, insist he be sent looking for work elsewhere.

Unless he had seen some kind of sparkle in her eyes that suggested he was on safe ground. She'd have to check that, make sure she offered him no encouragement.

She went into Charlene's bathroom, dug around under the sink and found a bud vase. She'd make sure she offered him no encouragement tomorrow, but for now she'd enjoy the rose. Then she thought better of it, returned the vase to its storage place and went back to her desk where she pitched the rose into the trash can.

But there was something she couldn't hide even from herself. It felt very nice to be pursued, even if there was no possibility of an eventual relationship. And she knew, even if no one else noticed, that she was dressing differently. She chose the silkier dresses over the wool, opted for the shorter skirts, sheerer blouses, and took pains with her hair and makeup.

Pam packed her tote and briefcase, slung her raincoat over her arm and headed out the door, snapping off the lights. The dead bolt turned, the office lay still. Ninety seconds later the dead bolt turned back, the lights flashed on and Pam plucked the rose out of the trash can and slipped it delicately into her tote.

Romeo's was an upscale steak house attached to a large downtown hotel. It was frequented by businessmen and women who traveled to Sacramento and those who worked in the downtown area. The bar and restaurant were furnished in dark woods and leathers, a motif that lent itself to wealth, secrecy and warmth.

Pam didn't see Maxie so she settled into a chair at the bar not very far from the hallway to the rest rooms. She decided a glass of wine while she waited wouldn't kill her. A glance at her watch told her she had at least twenty minutes, and the place was not crowded. There were a couple of women across the room engaged in deep conversation, a group of young men on the other side of the bar standing around a high table and a couple snuggling in a booth in the corner.

"What can I get you?" the bartender asked.

"Just a glass of Merlot, thanks."

He brought it back in moments and she had a five-dollar bill on the bar. "You're taken care of. The gentleman." He inclined his head, and Pam followed the direction to a gentleman of about forty-five on the other side of the bar. He lifted his glass and gave her a smile.

"Oh," she said. "Listen. Thank him, but please, tell him I'm…that is, I…I'm meeting my fiancé."

"I'm sure he'll understand perfectly," the bartender said. But he left her five on the bar.

Fiancé? Hah!

She sipped her wine and tried not to look at the snuggling couple in the booth across from her. The raven-haired beauty was all over her date. Pam wasn't sure where the woman's hands were, but it gave her a shiver just to consider. She looked instead at the group of young men. But when she noticed that one of them resembled Ray just slightly, that shiver was back—personalized.

Ever since Charlene had announced that she was getting married, Pam's perspective on her own romantic life had gone berserk. She found herself thinking obsessively about a certain young security guard, even thinking she saw him when he was nowhere near. The temptation grew daily, even though she hadn't seen him in a while. There were times her fantasy life was so rich and deep that if he should come upon her suddenly, she might faint into his arms and beg him to— She was clearly out of control.

She risked her tender, neglected libido and stole a look at the passionate couple only to find the woman looking at her. It was just a glance, but the woman gave her head a little, almost imperceptible toss in the direction of the rest rooms. Then she gave her gentleman friend a little nuzzle. The woman slid out of the booth, gave her short leather skirt a little tug and walked to the rest rooms. There was something about that walk and the low-cut sweater that struck Pam. She glanced at her watch. Eightish. She lifted her glass and carried it with her.

"Right on time," Maxie said as she pulled the lush

black wig off her head and gave her blond hair a healthy ruffle to bring it back to life.

Pam availed herself of one of the lounge chairs in the rest room to watch the show and enjoy the rest of her wine. The ladies' room was deserted except for the private detective and the paralegal, but something told Pam that the presence of other women wouldn't have much effect on Maxie. "Amazing," she said. "So, this means...?"

"It means I'm done for the night." She pulled the pink sweater over her head and revealed a tiny microphone in her push-up bra with a threadlike cord that snaked around her torso and into her skirt. "He wanted to get a room. He said he's separated, which will come as a surprise to his wife." She picked up her purse, turned it inside out—which made it a completely different article and much larger—and put her wig and sweater inside. Off came the leather skirt, inside of which was a neatly folded brown silk blouse. Tucked into her panty hose was a slim, flat recording device. "We were barely past the introductions before he was trying to slide his hand up my leg. Imagine his surprise if he'd run into this?" She laughed, tapping the recorder.

Maxie turned her black leather skirt inside out so that it became brown leather, shrugged into her blouse, freshened her lipstick and was ready to go.

"Miraculous," Pam said.

"Check please?"

"Check?" Pam asked.

"Your reason for meeting me here. The retainer!"

"Oh!" Pam put down her wine and retrieved an envelope with the check and some vital information about the people involved. "You know, what you were doing with that man…"

"Look, my job isn't seducing perfectly innocent men, getting them into trouble. My job is responding. If they're not screwing around, they're perfectly safe."

"You were responding a lot," Pam said.

"I was sealing the deal. My client needs to get out of that relationship before he gives her something bad. But you know what? Ninety percent of them don't."

"Come on!"

"Seriously."

"Then why hire you for this? If they don't intend to—"

"They want the goods, but they don't want to be alone." Pam's mouth hung open slightly. Was being alone so bad that you had to put up with something like that? "I don't think we should leave together," Maxie said. "It might draw attention to me. Enjoy your wine for about three more minutes."

"Sure."

"Thanks for stopping by," she said, then winked and slipped out the door.

It took Pam a little more than three minutes to recover. She just wasn't sure about Maxie's methods, and had voiced her concerns to Charlene many times. She found Maxie deceptive and treading a fine legal line, but Charlene insisted that Maxie only brought subtle troubles into specific relief.

Back in the bar Pam noticed that the man who had bought her the wine had moved on and was sitting at a table with two young women; he didn't even notice her as she passed. Maxie's mark was waiting impatiently, fidgeting in the booth. Shortly he would know he'd been shafted, but he might not know the degree for a while. Then she discovered that the young man she thought vaguely resembled Ray actually *was* Ray.

"I didn't think I could be this lucky," he said. "I was about to leave and I thought I saw your car, so I came back in to see if you were in the bar or restaurant."

She was unable to not smile. "What if I'd been on a date?" she asked.

"Well, I'd have had to beat him up and abduct you," he said, then continued more seriously. "Really, Ms. London. Don't you think I have any manners? I'd have nodded and left quietly and you would have explained that you knew me from work."

He seemed to have lovely manners, actually.

"What do you think? Can I buy you a drink? A cup of coffee?"

She slipped the strap of her purse over her shoulder. "I'm sorry, Ray. Not tonight. I really have to get home. I was here meeting a client. I've had my limit and it's been a very long day."

"I'm a little on the used-up side myself, so I won't argue. But I will take you to your car."

"You really don't have to," she said, but she walked alongside him just the same.

"You say that whenever I offer, and I think you'd be secretly disappointed if I didn't."

More like secretly devastated, she thought. "I remember this about you young guys. You're cocky."

"Is that right?" He laughed. "Know what I remember about you older women?"

They arrived at her car. "What?"

He leaned so close to her that she could feel his warm breath on her face when he talked. And his breath was sweet with the fragrance of something vanilla. "Nothing. You'll have to teach me."

That she could teach him anything scared her. Pam had not been without men in her adult life, but she didn't consider herself either experienced or especially talented. There was hardly a waiting list.

"Ms. London, I peeked in your car," he said, close enough so that if she leaned ever so slightly, she would be touching him. "To make sure it was yours, you know?" She nodded, but weakly. "Is that my rose you're taking home?" he asked. Again she nodded, the bones in her legs turning to rubber. "That makes me happy," he whispered, and his lips brushed against her cheek so gently she wondered if she had imagined it. Then, with a knuckle, he stroked the place lightly.

"Here," he said, taking her keys from her and opening the car door. "You're tired, remember?"

It was a good thing he did that, she thought. Because she couldn't speak or move and she was that close to suggesting something she remembered from high school, something that had to do with the back seat of a car.

She slid behind the wheel. "Good night, Ray," she whispered. "Another time?"

"Absolutely," he said, closing her into her vehicle.

As Pam walked into the house from the garage, she came upon her father, just returning himself. He wore his shorts and had his gym bag slung over one shoulder, his tennis racket sticking out. He was a man in excellent physical and mental condition, and it was not at all unusual for him to have an evening game. "Hi there," he said. "I left you a note. I had a couple of sets with Hank, then we had something to drink. I've already walked Beau. Are you just getting home?"

"I had to meet a client to deliver a check."

"I saved you some stir-fry, if you're interested."

"Thanks, but I don't think I'm hungry."

"Pam? You feel all right?"

"Sure. Why?"

"You look a little flushed...a little feverish."

"Oh really?" She touched her cheek and could feel the heat. In fact, she hadn't stopped feeling it since she'd left Ray. It was amazing; all that steam and all he'd done was touch her cheek. "I had to turn the car heater on. Maybe I overheated myself."

"Spring is on us. Going to be getting real hot around here pretty soon," her father observed.

You don't know the half of it, she thought.

Five

Agatha Farnsworth checked her reflection in the dressing-room mirror. Pastel suit with knee-length skirt, check. Beige shoes with a low heel, check. Cream-colored, high-collared blouse, check. Spectacles, check. She didn't need them, mind, but the spectacles lent the touch she needed. The whole ensemble was accompanied by her soft brown hair, cut to the smooth pageboy style and kept an unthreatening color rather than her natural hair, which was fiery red and fiercely curly. Having it straightened was quite a chore, but smooth hair lent itself better to the image she wanted to create. The first rule of bridal consultants—no one draws attention away from the bride. Agatha, costumed so, could be swallowed up by the wallpaper.

She was so completely suited for this. Her distinctly refined British style brought customers to her in droves. They were confident this was a woman who could deliver the exact sort of class and panache they were looking for, whether their pleasure was barefoot in the park or the top of the Ritz. She was good at her job, certainly, but it was the accent that added that little extra expectation of a perfect wedding.

Even though every wedding oozed stress, it also blossomed in joy. Agatha was good at defusing angst in its earliest stages and even better at showering the brides, the mothers and the maids with the perfect amount of fuss. They ate it up. She made their experience peak.

And it kept her from thinking too much about herself.

She looked at her watch at the exact moment she heard the tinkling of the doorbell. She smiled. Promptness would be a plus. She walked into the showroom, but found only an older gentleman there, casually browsing through the invitation book.

"May I help you with something, sir?"

"Oh, hello," he said pleasantly. "I'm here to see Agatha Farnsworth."

She immediately extended her hand. Father of the bride, perhaps? It was unusual, but not unheard of. "How do you do? I'm Agatha."

"Dennis Gardner," he said, shaking her hand.

"Oh, of course, the groom. It's a pleasure."

"Are you surprised?"

"Well, you've caught me. It's actually quite unusual to have the groom's participation in the wedding plans. Especially at this stage, this first meeting with the consultant."

"Admit it," he said, grinning. "You thought I was the bride's father."

"I thought no such thing!" she lied, laughing. He could *not* have detected that very thing from her expression. She was a pro!

"Who usually shows up for the initial meeting?" he asked.

"Most often? That would be the bride and her mother."

"In this particular case, you got lucky."

"Now, Mr. Gardner, if you think I'm going to exchange mother-in-law jests with you, you're mistaken. I'd be laughing myself out of a perfectly good job."

"So, when does the groom usually show up?"

"When the bride brings him, kicking and screaming, to view the invitations, flower arrangements, dining choices, et cetera. It will be a pleasure to have you involved from the beginning, Mr. Gardner."

"Please call me Dennis. I keep expecting my father to walk in."

"Very well, Dennis. Do we expect your fiancée? Ms. Dugan?"

He looked at his watch. "She's running a little late. Something urgent came up, but she hopes to be along as soon as possible."

"Wonderful. Why don't we retire to my office. I'll get you settled with a cup of tea or coffee and you can look through some of the wedding books. You'll have the advantage over her, I fear, viewing my wares first, but I assume you've discussed what sort of affair best reflects your personal taste."

He thought about this for a moment, a slight frown crossing his features, and said, "Tea would be wonderful."

She wasn't fooled in the least. They obviously

hadn't discussed it at all. They'd decided to get married, to have a wedding, and hadn't the first idea what would suit them. She smiled and nodded. "Come along, Mr....ah...Dennis. This will be far less painful than you think."

Agatha's office was small and perfectly designed for intimate conferences. She used a table instead of a desk, which made looking through albums easier, and kept most of her paperwork at home, carrying only the essentials with her in her briefcase. There was a phone, a fax and a bookshelf filled with design albums that held everything from sample invitations to fabric swatches. Two chairs faced each side of the French provincial table—chairs usually inhabited by ladies. Dennis Gardner, tall and strongly built, looked too large for his.

She excused herself and brought back a tray bearing cups too delicate for this large man's fist, but they were all she had available. "You did say tea?"

"Yes, thank you," he said, accepting the dainty china cup.

She took her place on the opposite side of the table. "So, Dennis, what was it that prompted you and your fiancée to consider the benefits of a wedding consultant?"

He took a sip of his tea and placed the cup on the table. She noticed it was nearly empty after one sip and made a mental note to stock mugs for future use since it appeared that more men were getting involved in the wedding plans.

"Charlene and I have been seeing each other for

years, but our decision to get married was sudden, so we haven't given the matter much thought. We've both been married before, both have busy careers and it just seemed like too much of an undertaking. But then her daughter came up with the suggestion that we talk to a consultant before abandoning the idea. Do you remember Jennifer Johnson?''

Agatha beamed. "Of course! A young doctor marrying another young doctor."

"Jennifer was a sorority sister of Charlene's daughter, Stephanie."

"Ah, I see. Jennifer's wedding was a huge success, if I do say so myself."

"So I hear. Stephanie couldn't believe we weren't having a party at least, especially given the fact that Charlene and I love having guests."

She folded her hands on the tabletop. "Perhaps you'll decide I can be of assistance."

"You'd probably rather wait for Charlene, but I'm curious about what something like this costs. Do you mind…"

"Not at all." She reached into her briefcase, which stood open on the empty chair beside her, and withdrew a brochure. "You'll see that my fee is hourly, but do remember, Dennis, that I am very experienced. I don't waste time on fiddle-faddle. Also, I have established relationships with various vendors and merchants. Sometimes I'm able to book events on short notice, whereas you might be told that reservations are made many months or even years in advance. And finally, do note, while you're under absolutely no obligation to use the Bridal Boutique for any of your apparel or notions, there is a substantial discount if you do. Of course, they count on me to bring business their way. That's why they provide this little office for my use.''

"You work here? For the boutique?''

"I work as an independent consultant, but in addition to my hourly fee, which is competitive, I receive a commission on sales.''

He rested an ankle on his knee and looked over the top of the pamphlet, making eye contact. "Your rates may be competitive, but you're expensive.''

She smiled confidently, again folding her hands demurely. "When the florist loses your order, the limo has a flat tire and the maid of honor gains twenty-five pounds between the fitting and the wedding, I'm worth every penny.''

He admired both her confidence and her poise. "I'll just bet you are. And if a gentleman wanders in here in mid-April looking for a June wedding that's memorable…?''

"I would venture to say you couldn't do it alone. A wedding consultant with contacts and favors to call in would be indispensable.''

"But it could be done?''

"Dennis…*anything* can be done.'' She fairly beamed.

His cell phone rang and he plucked it out of his pant pocket with some difficulty, squirming about in the chair. "Who do you suppose this could be?'' he asked facetiously. "Hello, Charlene.'' He listened…

and listened some more. "Let's do this," he finally said. "I'll just treat this as a fact-finding mission. I'll gather information from Ms. Farnsworth about what she can do to help us, and if you finish up within the next thirty or so minutes, call. I don't want to keep the lady longer than that."

Agatha made a dismissing motion with her hand. She was patient.

But he said goodbye, clicked his phone closed and put it in his shirt pocket.

"It's perfectly all right, Mr. Gardner—"

"Dennis. Please."

"Dennis, I'm sorry. What I mean to say is, I'm very much accustomed to working with busy people who have tight schedules. I know I'm the one who must be flexible. I'm paid quite well for that."

"Yes." He laughed. "I see that."

"I can stay as late as you need me. I have no other appointments this evening. Or, if it's more convenient to reschedule, that's easily done as well."

"Agatha, you are far too accommodating. I could get used to it."

"It's my pleasure. Your fiancée is obviously a busy woman."

"She's an attorney. I know what she's working on right now, and I understand the urgency only too well. She's doing a pro bono case on a custody dispute, and it's possible there's abuse involved."

"How dreadful!"

"It's actually a favor for her ex-husband. Someone he asked her to help."

"Truly? Her ex-husband?"

"That's a fact. He's a police officer."

It was rare for Agatha to be taken aback, but this had the effect. "Well, may I say, you're a sporting man, Mr. Gardner."

This brought a burst of laughter from him. "I guess it must seem so, Agatha," he said, not begging that first name out of her another time. "There are a couple of incidental facts that would probably make the scenario more understandable. One, Charlene has been divorced from her ex-husband for twenty-five years. And two, I work in an emergency room. I'm a physician's assistant. Unfortunately, I've seen some terrible situations resulting from domestic crises, so I'm only too happy for Charlene to do whatever she can before someone, especially a child, gets hurt. It takes precedence over planning parties…even wedding parties."

She found herself simply staring as he spoke. "How very noble, Dennis," she said from her heart, momentarily spellbound. What a wonderful man! What a wonderful couple they must be, championing the underdogs of the world.

"Ahem." She cleared her throat to break the spell. "Well, would you like to glance through some wedding albums while we wait for Ms. Dugan? We have invitations, flowers, cakes, reception halls, outdoor facilities, everything you can imagine in connection to a wedding party. We even have the makings for a skydiving wedding."

"Sure, I'll have a look through."

She heaped a couple of heavy albums onto the table before him. "Perhaps by the time your fiancée is free, you'll have a suggestion or two for her. And allow me to get us more tea."

The next thirty minutes turned into forty before Dennis's cell phone rang again. All he said was, "Perfectly understandable. Don't worry a bit, we'll talk later."

"I expect that was disappointing news for you," Agatha observed.

"More disappointing for you. Charlene isn't going to make it. I'm afraid I've wasted your time."

"Not at all! I believe we've at least had a start. You now have an idea, however vague, of what can be done for you. We'll simply reschedule, at your convenience. Would you like to ring me when—"

He looked at his watch. "What I'd like to do is buy you dinner. It's the least I can do."

"That's really not necessary, Mr. Gardner."

"I don't know about that. It's necessary that I eat, and it's getting late. And you said you had no other appointments."

"Thank you, that's very kind. But I fear your fiancée might find it inappropriate."

"My fiancée who is presently doing free legal work for her ex-husband's new girlfriend?" He laughed. "Come, Agatha. I'll buy us a nice casual dinner, you can tell me your favorite wedding stories, and if Charlene finishes up, she'll join us."

"Are you certain?" she asked.

"Completely. Otherwise, I might be offended."

* * *

Before even beginning to decorate, Lois put on a Christmas CD and to the orchestral strains of "We Three Kings," she pulled the heavy boxes of decorations out of the guest bedroom closet. It was smart of her, she now commended herself, not to store these in the attic after putting them away last Christmas. At her age, getting them down had begun to require assistance from Charlene or Stephanie or Dennis—or all of them. It made her feel so much better to be able to do this herself; the worst part about getting older was becoming dependent.

It was unseasonably warm and sunny, a perfect day to get a jump on the outdoor work. She separated the twinkling lights from the other decorations and opened up the garage door. She turned the stereo high, left the door to the house open and let the music drift all the way to the front yard. The first thing she did was put the plastic wreath on the mailbox.

Jasper Conklin was tinkering in his garage when the music drew him to the front yard, where he observed his next-door neighbor positioning her ladder beneath the eaves of her house. He simply watched, mystified. Could she be putting up Christmas lights in April? Could that be "We Three Kings?" He watched her for a while. She was remarkably spry for her age, but then, as long as he'd lived next door she had lived alone and always did her own yard work—mowing, pruning, digging, planting, hauling. He hadn't been surprised to see that, while she'd hired a painter for the outside of the house, she did the trim herself. Even the eaves.

Now there she was, standing atop the ladder, stapling lights to the house.

Jasper had never had much of a relationship with Lois or her family and it was entirely his fault. He was unfriendly and solitary, a manner brought on by the long infirmity of his deceased wife. And though she had been gone for four years now, he was just barely coming out of his shell. This—his elderly neighbor putting up Christmas decorations in April—was urging him out of his garage and across the lawn.

"Well now, Lois, what are you up to?" he asked.

She jumped a little in surprise and looked over her shoulder at the gentleman standing there. She frowned. Though he looked familiar, she couldn't remember his name. It was maddening; it happened to her all the time lately. "I thought I'd get a jump on it this year," she said, turning back to her work, the heavy stapler weighty in her hand.

"I'll say," he replied. "Nice day for it, isn't it?"

She not only couldn't remember his name, she couldn't seem to remember if they were friends. But they must be for he spoke with such cheerful familiarity. He looked like Albert Finney, and she wondered if that was his name. Albert? She turned back to him, looked him right in the eye and said, "Well, Albert, *you* must think it's a nice day, the way you're dressed."

Jasper smiled at her kindly. He had had absolutely no idea Lois was suffering from delusions. In the end his wife had had quite a terrible time with dementia.

She had been considerably younger than Lois, the dementia was worsened by drug psychosis resulting from years of taking pain medications and sleeping pills. But although that had been perhaps the most difficult part of her illness, it had also been sweet in its vulnerability, precious in its unexpectedness. He smiled again, remembering with fondness some of the things she'd come up with.

"Lois, why don't you get down from there and let me put up the lights," he said.

"Oh, Albert, you don't have to do that. Anyway, it makes me feel so accomplished to do it myself."

"There must be something you can do that doesn't involve a ladder," he suggested.

"Well, I could get the Christmas dishes out and make us a cup of tea or hot chocolate." She grinned mischievously. "Or maybe a nice spiked eggnog."

"Hmm. We better stick with the nonalcoholic libation. How about coffee?" He ran a finger around the collar of his shirt. It was getting warmer by the day. He wondered when she was going to come out of it and discover that it was April. But more important than that, he wondered if the realization was going to prove painful for her. "Are the Christmas dishes handy? You won't have to go to a lot of trouble, will you?"

"Why, not at all. I've already got all the boxes out. I have decorations all over the living room, waiting to be hung, strung and put about."

"You haven't, by any chance, gone looking for a tree, have you?"

"Not as of yet," she said, getting carefully down

from the ladder. He put out a hand to help her descend. "I'll do the house decorating first, then go."

"Now, if memory serves," he said, "last year your daughter helped with the decorating."

"Yes, but I thought this time I'd surprise her," Lois said proudly.

"Oh, something tells me she's going to be surprised. Incredibly so. I was just thinking to myself, that neighbor of mine, she's never passed on the work of the yard and garden to hired hands or offspring. You've always been such a workhorse, Lois. I think it's kept you in shape."

"Thank you, Albert. You've always been so kind. So thoughtful."

Beyond casual greetings across the yards, they'd had very little contact in thirty years. Certainly they had never been social or relied on each other. He sheltered his poor sick wife and their piteous lives behind drawn blinds and sullenness. Was it odd that he'd come out now, friendly and helpful? Probably not, he considered. A vulnerable woman in need of help, in need of caretaking—this was a situation he understood. In fact, this was as good, as familiar as he'd felt in a long time.

"Run inside then, Lois, and find those dishes and get the coffee brewing. This shouldn't take me but a minute, then I'll come in. By the way, do you have today's paper?"

"I've already tossed it," she said. "Why?"

"I didn't get mine," he said cagily. "If you didn't toss it far, may I have it?"

"Certainly!" she said, and went into the house through the garage.

Jasper stood there a moment and then, for better or worse, got on the ladder and completed the job of attaching the twinkling lights to the eaves.

Lois stared into her poinsettia-decorated teacup, her hands beneath the table and folded in her lap. She was completely morose.

"Come, Lois," Jasper said. "Decorating out of season is a completely harmless thing. Don't let it ruin your day. The sun is shining and you don't have chest pains."

She looked up slowly and regarded him thoughtfully. "We've never before shared a cup of coffee and we've been neighbors for thirty years."

"The shame of it," he said. "It's my fault. My wife was ill, you know. For some twenty-five years I tended her."

"One would think you could have done with some friends, particularly neighbors," Lois said.

"One would, wouldn't one," he said, and laughed with embarrassment. "I didn't start out stupid, Lois. I evolved. I was thirty when I found and married Jean, thirty-one when a car accident left her with a spinal cord injury and limited range of motion. A quadriplegic for all practical purposes, and all this before our first anniversary. I cared for her with the help of nurses and aides."

"So you were too busy for friendships," she said.

"No, Lois, I was too *angry*. Enraged! I'd been completely cheated of a wife, of a family. Never mind the cheat Jean suffered, in terrible pain most of the time. So I had all this rage and couldn't show it. Then there was shame. There was never a time I let a person into our world of disease and dis-ease that I didn't see pity. And, of course, we were lonely. The strange thing about loneliness is that instead of reaching out, the lonely withdraw.'' He shrugged. ''It makes absolutely no sense.''

''What brought you out today?'' she asked.

He grinned at her and patted her hand. ''I couldn't resist, Lois. If it had been just the lights, I might have thought it was a party. But 'We Three Kings' gave you away.''

She brought up a hand from her lap and, with her fist, gave the table a heartfelt pound. ''It's the most maddening goddamn thing!''

''Christmas lights in April is not so bad,'' he said.

''If you know that's what you're doing it's not,'' she barked. ''But, if you're dead sure it's December, it's a giant pain in the you-know-what!''

The garage door squeaked open. ''Mom?'' Charlene's voice called.

''Shit,'' Lois said.

''Shh,'' Jasper comforted, patting her hand. ''Just act natural,'' he said.

Lois blinked in confusion of a new sort. *Act natural?*

''Mom, what are you— Oh! Mr. Conklin. How are you?''

"Very well, Charlene," he said, standing. "And you?"

"Fine," she said slowly, perplexed by the scene before her. She took in the table, the Christmas dishes. "Mom?"

"*You* stopped by, Charlene," Lois said patiently. "Did you want something?"

"I...ah... Mom, what's the Christmas stuff out for?"

"Oh, that," Lois said.

"My doing," Jasper said. "We got talking in the yard, your mom and me, about putting up lights for a party. I offered to help her—"

"Just a hen party, Charlene, nothing that will interfere with your wedding plans. I won't even invite you, how's that?"

"Of course the lights were in the last box we opened," Jasper said.

"I used to be more organized."

"Then we got to looking through all the decorations and talking about swapping some. Just for variety. Get something new and different, you know, without spending a nickel."

"What a splendid idea!" Lois chirped, forgetting for the moment that she shouldn't act as if she was hearing this for the first time. "Every time I think about it, I like the idea more."

Charlene had that look on her face. She wasn't buying it.

"Wonder if any other neighbors want to get in on this?" Lois asked Jasper.

"Not too many, Lois. At our ages, we'll forget who we loaned what to."

She burst into laughter. "Isn't that God's truth!" Then she sobered slightly. "But Jasper, you're just a kid."

"Fifty-nine this November. I just took early retirement from the post office and I'm bored to tears already. I'm thinking about getting a job."

"Fifty-nine, hmph. I could be your— Well, Charlene. What can I do for you? It's not like you to drop by in the middle of the day like this."

"I had a deposition in Fair Oaks and he canceled, which put me in your neighborhood in actual daylight. I wondered if you'd like some company for grocery shopping."

Lois leaned toward Jasper. "She's afraid I'll get lost in the parking lot."

"I was trying to be helpful!"

"Thanks, Charlene, but I've just been to the grocery. You go ahead."

"You're sure?"

"Yes, I'm sure. Besides, I have to go over to Jasper's now and check out his Christmas stash."

"Lois is fond of poinsettias and I'm pretty much a Santa man," he said, plunging his hands into the pockets of his shorts and rocking back on the heels of his sandals.

"Well…" Charlene said doubtfully, helping herself to a sugar cookie from the Christmas plate on the table. She chewed for a moment. "I guess I'll get back to the office then."

"Have a nice day, dear," Lois said.

"You, too. See you again, I hope, Mr. Conklin."

"I look forward to it, Charlene."

As she was leaving she could be heard to mutter, "Retirement. Shew." And the door closed.

"That went well," Jasper said.

"Except for one little thing," Lois replied. "I can't for the life of me remember when I last went to the store."

"Not to worry. We'll take care of that."

Grant had midterm exams coming up. He had packed his class schedule because he was so close to finishing, to getting his degree. That meant two classes three days a week and four classes two days a week—on his days off. Usually he worked until 2:00 a.m., then got up and went to school. He had a three-hour break around noon, in which he would go back to the apartment he shared with Stephanie to make himself a sandwich and pack a gym bag. He often could have used a nap, but would end up spending the time cleaning up the apartment. It was a perpetual mess. Housecleaning was not one of Stephanie's gifts. She never contributed to the household chores and it had become a huge bone of contention in their relationship.

He would then head back to the university from two till four, then to the campus weight room. He was diligent about his exercise routine because he was determined not only to pass the police exam and physical, but to breeze through the academy—which many claimed was as difficult as marine boot camp—when he was hired as a police officer.

That pretty much put a cap on his energy level. Most nights he just looked forward to going home to a nice tidy apartment where he might have a beer—something he couldn't indulge in on nights he tended bar—put his feet up and maybe nod off in front of the news. After a rest, there would be more studying.

What greeted him as he entered the apartment put the skids on his plans.

"Hi, sweetie," Stephanie said. "I thought you might be working out. I was thinking about going down to the exercise room myself." She laughed at herself. "I guess you can see how far I got."

Her books, purse, sweater and a stack of student papers from the eighth grade sat on the dining table that he had earlier cleared off. She wore her sweats and fuzzy slippers, had pinned up her long, curling hair, and the clothes she had worn to work were lying in a heap in the middle of the bedroom floor, except for the panty hose and shoes, which she had shed in the living room. The *middle* of the living room.

She had obviously had a snack. A glass, plate and bag of chips littered the coffee table along with the mail; chip crumbs speckled the freshly vacuumed carpet. She had the newspaper spread open on the sofa while she read it.

They lived in a small apartment and it didn't take much out of place to make it look a mess. How Stephanie managed to scatter so much stuff through a tiny space in such a short amount of time was amazing. And annoying.

"I thought we'd get dinner out and maybe see a movie," she said.

Grant ground his teeth. Don't, he told himself. Don't get mad. She just doesn't get it.

"How about that, sweetie?"

"I can't, Stephanie. I have to study. I have exams coming up."

"You're running a 4.0. Aren't you?"

"And I'd like to keep it."

"But it's your night off!"

"I've had a really long day. I'm tired, and I still have studying left to do."

"I worked all day, too, you know. I'd like to have an evening out. I'm alone every night of the week."

"Be my guest," he said. "Maybe while you're out, I'll fix myself some dinner and clean the apartment...*again!*"

"That was totally sarcastic!"

"Look at this place! Stephanie, I used my break today to clean the apartment!"

"I worked all day. I'll clean up later."

"But you won't. You didn't work all summer and you never cleaned up!"

"Grant, are you going to harangue me about that again? Because if I want to be lectured about tidiness, I can go spend the evening with my mother."

He gritted his teeth against telling her that that would be a good idea. Instead, he said, "I'm going to take a shower."

Grant returned to the room a little while later. He felt better after the shower, but there would be no relaxing with a cold beer tonight. "I'm sorry if I was sarcastic, Stephanie."

"It's okay. Now, how about the Olive Garden? We can have a little pasta, salad, wine…and then to put us in a better state of mind, let's see a movie that makes us laugh."

"Tell you what, I'll go to the restaurant with you and then I'll go over to the library to study. I'll have to skip the movie, but I won't be late."

"Is that the best deal I'm going to get tonight?" she asked teasingly.

"'Fraid so," he said. "Get cleaned up and let's go."

"Now?"

"It's almost six. I'm hungry. And, for the hundredth time, I have studying to do."

"But I just ate," she said, indicating her dirty dishes on the coffee table. "I didn't know you were going to want the early-bird special."

"What did you have in mind?" he wanted to know.

"How about in an hour…hour and a half?"

Maybe it was being tired, or the pressure of work and school, or the irritation that was becoming commonplace in their home. Whatever it was, he had had it. He grabbed his jacket from the hall closet and swung his book bag over his shoulder. "It doesn't look like this is going to work out, Stephanie. So I'll grab a bite on my way to the library and you do whatever floats your boat. Okay?"

"Grant! Where are you going?"

"I just told you! I've told you twenty times already!"

"If you walk out on me like that, don't expect me to be here when you get home!"

"Stephanie, if you're not here, maybe the apartment won't get any messier!"

By the time he reached the bottom of the apartment-building stairs, he completely regretted his short fuse. It looked as if they were on the rocks and he had no idea how to mend their ailing relationship. It made him feel inadequate, like a failure. He loved Stephanie, but at some point she had stopped being the kind, happy girl who he wanted to marry.

Stephanie sat on the floor of the apartment and flipped the TV channels with the remote. She had stacked sixty essays from eighth-grade English on the coffee table, but she doubted she'd start on them tonight. Her tiff with Grant was bothering her; her concentration was off. She was distracted. Bored.

What did he want from her? To be waiting at his beck and call, ready to jump in the car and go to dinner when *he* was hungry? Where did this tidy-apartment stuff come from? When she met him he had lived with a couple of guys and they were slobs, all of them. So how was she to know he'd turn into a neat freak when they moved in together? Neatness wasn't in her nature, that's all. But she put her dishes in the sink, kicked her clothes into the bedroom closet and punched up the couch cushions.

The phone rang. She lifted the cordless and could see by the caller ID that the caller was at the security gate. "Hello?" she queried.

"Steph? It's Fred. Want some company?"

There were dirty dishes, clothes on the floor, a week's worth of mail opened and scattered on the table, papers to grade on the coffee table, and Stephanie was dressed in sweats and a T-shirt. No bra. Company? Grant had made the bed, vacuumed the carpet and dusted the furniture, but he hadn't done anything with the bathroom. And Lord knew, Stephanie hadn't cleaned it in ages. She was in absolutely no state for company. But Grant was gone—and Fred was calling.

"Fred, what a surprise!"

"I thought I'd drop by, pay you a visit. You gotta be bored, home alone every night."

"You got that right. I'm starving. Want to go get a pizza?"

"I could go get one and bring it back to the apartment," he offered.

But she didn't want to entertain him in the apartment. "Fred, I haven't been out in ages. How about Carbones? It's right down the street."

"Anything you want, baby," he said, and Stephanie remembered back to a time Grant used to say that to her.

"Oh hey, the gate just opened. What's your apartment number?"

"Just park in front of building eight, Fred, and I'll be out in a couple of minutes. I'm fixing my hair."

"Sure, but hurry up. Now that you mention it, I'm starving."

Maybe a little jealousy would get Grant's attention. She remembered when he had more time, was more devoted to her and never complained about her shortcomings. So she was a little messy. *He* worked long horrible hours. There had to be a compromise in there somewhere. Maybe, if she could just get her devoted man back, she could learn to be tidier.

But for now, she was going to get pizza with Fred. He was a little strange, but he was fun.

When she opened the apartment door she gasped; there he stood.

"I recognized your car," he said, shrugging.

"Didn't I ask you to just wait for me?"

"Oh, sorry. I wanted to do the gentlemanly thing."

"The gentlemanly thing is always to do as the woman asks."

"Gee, I'm a screwup." He shrugged. "Come on, I'll treat."

Stephanie didn't enjoy Fred's company much; he was a self-absorbed braggart who seemed intent on telling her about every one of the women in his past. But, he did pay for the pizza and beer, and he did distract her from her annoyance with Grant. When he drove her back to her apartment at eleven, Grant's truck was still not home and she got fired up all over again.

Without realizing she was going to do it, she said, "Freddy, I have two tickets for *Grease*. How would you like to go?"

* * *

Dennis and Charlene rescheduled their appointment with Agatha Farnsworth for one week later. Dennis was sitting in the parking lot in front of the Bridal Boutique when Charlene called him. "You're not going to believe this," she said. "I have a client in jail and he needs bail. I can't reach a relative and Pam must be at her gym because I'm only getting her voice mail."

"Do you like this client?" Dennis wanted to know.

"Yes, I do. Why?"

"Because if you didn't like him you could let him sit there until we've seen the wedding consultant and had dinner."

She laughed at this idea. "He's going through a very nasty divorce. His wife, a real barracuda, had him picked up on bogus kidnapping charges during his legitimate visitation. He's been through enough. I'm going to get him out of jail and then I'm going after her."

Dennis could see Agatha moving around inside the boutique. She wore a peach-colored suit and dark silk blouse. She moved gracefully around the store, tidying up.

"I wouldn't want to sit in jail if it were me," he told Charlene. "I think I'll see if I can buy Ms. Farnsworth dinner. If you get done downtown before too late, meet us at The American Grill."

"There's a hex on this wedding-planner thing," Charlene groused.

But Dennis, who was actually not very disappointed, said, "It'll all work out."

He went into the store and Agatha greeted him with a smile that soon faded. "Oh, Dennis, where is your fiancée?"

"Bailing a client out of jail," he said. And he smiled.

"Are you amused by that?" she asked, confused.

"In a way. Let's go have dinner. If it's not too late when Charlene finishes, we can come back here and look through some of your wedding books, talk about some ideas."

She frowned. "Are you sure this is a good idea?"

He smiled more broadly. "Absolutely sure."

Six

The kiss of death was saying you wanted to clear your schedule to get married and take a short vacation. Suddenly all of Charlene's clients ran for the phone to call her with one legal problem after another. While one client was falsely accused of kidnapping, another actually had her pet goose, Frankie, abducted by her ex-husband. In the first case, the courts could assist, in the second case there wasn't a lot of law on the books to help out with the custody of a goose. And that was just the tip of the iceberg. Everyone wanted to sue right now...and no one wanted to reconcile their bad marriages. Every will was being contested, every argument reached its peak and every adoption seemed to be falling apart.

New clients could be shuffled off on partners and associates, but many of these new legal issues were arising out of old client files, and Charlene couldn't abandon them. Her clients relied on her.

Three weeks had passed since she and Dennis decided to get married, and their time together had been more scarce than usual. She had missed the first two meetings with the wedding consultant and was determined to make the third. She was on her way to meet

Dennis at Flamingo Bay, a trendy restaurant near the river. They would have a bite to eat, talk a little about their personal expectations of a wedding and then keep the appointment with Ms. Farnsworth, who Charlene hadn't even met yet.

But all that changed in an instant when her cell phone rang and Jake gave her some most unwelcome news. She made a U-turn with one hand on the wheel, punching up Dennis's number with the other.

"I'm sorry," she said to her fiancé, though her voice was not in the least apologetic. "I can't make it. I just got a call that one of my clients has been hospitalized. I don't know her condition, but I have to go."

"You're on your way there?" Dennis asked.

"Yes. Absolutely."

"What hospital?" he asked.

"County."

"Can I help? Should I meet you there?"

"No, I'll be fine."

"Okay. Then do you want me to go ahead to the wedding store at seven-thirty?"

Charlene was stumped for an answer. She finally heard her own drawn-out silence and shook herself mentally. "Ah...um...anything you want, Dennis. I don't know how long I'll be. This could be complicated...there are minor children involved in a custody dispute. Let me call you after I've assessed this situation," she said. She didn't realize what she was saying, what she was feeling. It didn't occur to her, and wouldn't until much, much later, that she was having an episode of déjà vu mixed with present urgency. Half of her was in the here and now, the other half had traveled a long way back in time.

Charlene had been in situations like this with Jake before, the first and most ancient of which occurred shortly after they met, over twenty-six years ago. They had been in a criminal justice class together at Berkeley and had just barely started dating. She wasn't sure she even liked him. In fact, she was pretty sure it wouldn't work out. He was too immature, too squirrelly. Indecisive, easily distracted and whimsical. She was serious, had serious plans.

But that night, as she was waiting for him to pick her up for their third date, an incident occurred that changed the course of both their lives. It started with Jake being late. She was not surprised; she had already judged him to be irresponsible. Even then, she was controlling and not about to let him get away with it. So she called his apartment. He answered, but was nearly incoherent.

What she understood from patched-together pieces of their conversation was that a crime had just taken place. One of his neighbors in his less-than-swank apartment complex had physically hurt a child. A *baby*. Jake was incensed. At first she didn't even recognize his voice and then she could hear his red-hot rage. She could hear him trembling in anger. He had called for an ambulance and the police. He had thought it might be the 911 operator calling back, because she had asked him to stay on the line and he'd hung up on her. He was too busy to stay on the line. He was holding the suspect.

Charlene had gone to the apartment at once, partly to be sure Jake was all right and partly because of her own insatiable urge to be near the action. By the time she arrived, the place was a swirl of carnival-like emergency lights—ambulance, fire truck, police cars. The ambulance doors stood open and a woman peered inside, wringing her hands nervously. To the left was a man talking calmly to police, holding something like a rag or ice pack to his face. And to the right was Jake, speaking less calmly to police, flailing his arms in description, his face red to his scalp.

What Charlene didn't know as she pulled up to that scene was that Jake had noted immediate evidence of sexual abuse as well as battery on this sweet little nine-month-old baby boy. Unmistakably, rape.

As she parked behind the police and got out of her car, all hell broke loose. A paramedic jumped out of the back of the ambulance, took hold of the young woman by her upper arms and shook his head sadly. The woman collapsed in agony. A cry of rage exploded from Jake. He blew through the police officers like a bull, crashed into the suspect and began to pummel him. He was completely out of control.

It took four officers to pull him away and hold him while they cuffed and removed the suspect, who later was convicted and put away for a nice long time. While the police held Jake, he lunged with such force his feet left the ground. They might as well have been holding a bird by the wings. He screamed obscenities with such wrath his voice was hoarse and almost soundless. "You cowardly, slimy, stinking son of a bitch! You want to beat up on someone? You want some action? You try *me* sometime, you fucking *animal!*"

What Charlene was *not* thinking as she missed yet another date with Dennis and drove toward County Hospital was how Jake's fury and outrage had sewn the seeds of their relationship. His complete and unadulterated indignation that something this wrong could happen to an innocent had caused him to go berserk. When he was done screaming, he had cried. And when he'd shed enough painful tears, he had put his fist through the wall. It had taken her hours to calm him down and convince him that the police would do their job, that the perpetrator would come to justice.

And it also had excited her; she loved being close to that kind of energy.

Oh yes, she'd loved his slim grasp on control, his passionate desire to destroy that pervert. She didn't dare leave him alone. Jake had had a shower, washed the blood off his knuckles, then let her comfort him while he became contrite and worried that his temper might hurt his chances with the police department. This was what really drove him, he confessed—helping people before it came to this tragedy and then, failing that, getting the scum that would sink to such depths of depravity off the streets.

She, for her part, was prelaw, and that night she knew she would be a family lawyer, an advocate for children. Women who found themselves trapped in nightmares like the one she had seen would come to her and she would liberate them. Family law would be her life. She saw it as clearly that night as she could see it now.

Between the two of them, that night so long ago, they were practically Robin and Marion. Of course, they never did go out on their date. They spent the entire night in bed, where the passion of outrage turned into the passion of healing, which quickly turned into the passion of passion.

But Charlene wasn't thinking of any of that, even though she was possessed of a familiar emotion and strongly suspected she'd done all this before. She was consumed with thoughts of Meredith Jersynski in the hospital and what she would find when she got there.

She had expected to find Jake waiting for her in the E.R., but he was not. Instead, seated in the chairs outside the exam rooms was another police officer Charlene happened to know, Jake's friend and co-worker, Sam Jordan. She was brought up short by the surprise. "Sam?"

He looked up. "Oh, hi, Charlene. Jake said he called you."

"Did he ask you to wait for me?" she asked.

"No, I'm waiting for Merrie. She's one of our special projects. Did Jake tell you what happened?"

"No. Is she going to be all right?"

"Someone took a shot at her, Charlie. She was about a block from Coppers where she serves, and someone took a shot at her. Right through the windshield."

"My God!"

"Missed her, but she ran her car right into a pole, hit her head and lost consciousness for a little while. Looks like she's going to be just fine, though."

"Except that someone shot at her."

"Yeah, except that. Someone tried to kill her, and for what?"

Charlene just shook her head. For what, indeed? It looked, for all practical purposes, like Meredith was going to have a hard time keeping her daughter away from the father, so all he had to do was exercise a little patience. Why screw it all up by getting in trouble with the law?

"You called Meredith your what? Your project?"

"You know," he said, glancing down the hall toward the exam rooms to see if she was coming yet. "One of our girls."

"What do you mean, one of your girls?" she asked.

"Jake didn't explain?"

"No! Go on."

"We have a few girls—sorry, I'm such a dope—*women* we're helping out. Women who are trying to get on their feet after a bad deal. Like getting out of a bad marriage. Abuse or whatever."

Charlene slowly sank onto one of the chairs. "Whatever?" she pushed.

"Well, let's see. We have a couple of women coming out of the bad end of addiction, trying to stay clean, earn money and get their kids back. One we're helping keep safe from a pimp—but she's gotta stay out of the business, you know. Merrie here, she came out of a shelter. We got her a job waitressing at Coppers. Old cop bar. And we found her an apartment in the same building as one of our guys. We have a fund that subsidizes her income until she can get on her feet.'' He took a breath, looked down at his hands. ''Jake said you were doing a pro bono on this here. Gee, Charlie, we can't thank you enough for that. Legal help, decent legal help that is, gets real expensive, puts a drain on our resources.''

''I didn't know.''

''Didn't know you were doing a pro bono?'' he asked, confused.

''No,'' she said. ''No, I didn't know there was a group of you doing things like this.''

''Yeah. We keep it kind of quiet. There's no waiting list to get in the program or anything. I mean, we're official and everything. We even got set up with a lawyer and accountant, both volunteers because we're tax free....''

''Exempt,'' she corrected. And then she thought back over all the favors Jake had asked of her over the past several years. Had they all been for these ''projects?''

''How many of you are there? Doing this?'' she asked.

''I think we're up to thirty now...something like that. We keep an eye open for anyone who has a good chance of getting out of the system, with a little help. 'Course, we got people in the shelters and recovery programs who also keep an eye open, and they know we're real picky. It has to be special circumstances, like this one."

"What makes Meredith special?" she wanted to know.

"She's sincere, determined. She put the kids first, and went to the shelter on her own steam. Her story stays the same so we're sure she's telling the truth. This kid hasn't had a break in a long, long time. And she's clean, not using anything or selling anything. She just needs a second chance." He grinned. "Her kids are real sharp. Little Einsteins.

"Now, I figure the thing to do is get her to a safe house. No one knows whether that bullet went into her head or the upholstery in the car, so we have an edge here. They were careful with the accident report and the emergency room docs are going to cooperate with us. So, we know more than he knows, right?"

"Did you have someone pick up the kids?" she asked.

He nodded. "Right away. They're at the substation now, waiting for their mom. Then I'll take them all to a safe house. And we have someone sitting at Merrie's apartment to see if anyone shows up there looking for the kids."

"And where's Jake?"

"He decided he wanted to have a little conversation with the ex."

"Uh-oh," she said.

"He won't blow it, Charlie. He's one of the best interrogators I know."

"But he's a hothead. And this girl's important to him."

"They're all important to him."

"She isn't...? Are you sure she's not...a girl-friend?"

Sam laughed. "Absolutely sure. Why? You think she's his type?"

"He's had many types, Sam," she said. "Where does the ex live? I'd better get over there before he screws up my custody case."

Just as she wrote down the address, Meredith came toward them wearing a white bandage on her forehead. She was clearly flustered, but thanked Charlene for coming to the hospital and begged Sam to hurry up and get her to her daughters.

"Do everything the police tell you, Meredith," Charlene said. "When you get to a safe place, call my cell-phone number. If I don't answer, leave your new number on the voice mail. And don't worry. You're going to be all right now."

Dennis decided against Flamingo Bay and went instead to a dilapidated steak house at the bottom of the city, near the river. The down on its luck end, not the renovated, chic river walk full of pricey restaurants, clubs and shops. This place was a little on the edgy side. The owner was an old guy who had been there over thirty years; improvements were made every twenty or so. Charlene wouldn't eat there. She said it made her skin crawl. So Dennis went in protest. He ordered a New York strip, bloody. French-fried onion rings, greasy. Beer, tall and icy.

It wasn't Charlene who was going to pay.

Dennis was not a guy who thought of himself as remarkably intuitive. His instincts were good in the E.R., but everywhere else they were so-so. But there was something about Charlene's phone call that set off alarms. First of all, he knew, without her saying, that it was Jake's friend in the hospital. Second, it would have been Jake who called. Third, Charlene couldn't give him a straight answer as to when she would be finished with this mission because she was making herself available to someone else. Not Dennis. Not the wedding planner.

She was the *lawyer*. She didn't have to sit vigil at anyone's bedside. There was no lawyering work to do at the hospital. As long as she had her phone she could check the client's condition, leave her number and get on with her day. Or evening, as the case may be. There were dozens of clients—hundreds—all in various stages of domestic crisis. Sadly, this was not the first one who had been hospitalized in the midst of a court case. Sometimes a client made the initial call to the lawyer from the hospital! Charlene was *very busy*, often late and frequently interrupted. But she maintained a personal life, however thin her time was stretched.

She should have said, "Go ahead to the shop. I'll grab a sandwich and meet you there." But she hadn't.

And when Dennis had asked, "Should I meet you there?" she could have said, "Oh darling, would you?" But she hadn't.

Charlene was in another world—Jake's world.

In point of fact, Dennis had seen less of Charlene in the three weeks since they'd decided to get married than ever before. She blamed a combination of unusual circumstances ranging from her mother's confusion and forgetfulness to getting her taxes filed to having an extraordinary number of complicated cases rise up without warning. But the bottom line was, they hadn't spent a night together in weeks and their frequent phone conversations were businesslike and brisk.

Dennis, annoyed, didn't think about the fact that he'd worked several double shifts in the past three weeks, voluntarily, making himself less available to his fiancée. That was not the point. *She* was too busy for *him*.

He arrived at the Bridal Boutique a little early; Agatha was just nibbling on the last of a homemade sandwich. She patted her lips with a linen napkin and said, "I should put you to the task of teaching my clients punctuality, Dennis. You are ever prompt."

"I'm early. I didn't mean to interrupt your dinner."

"Think nothing of it. I was finished anyway." She folded the napkin and placed it inside a plastic container.

"Charlene isn't going to make it," he said.

"Oh dear. You could have just phoned, Dennis. I do understand. People don't hire wedding consultants if they have time on their hands, but only if they're incredibly busy."

"I don't know how you make a living. It's very un-American, you know. To be so polite."

"You saw my price list," she said with a sly smile. "And I'm not American. Did Charlene have another emergency?"

"Unfortunately. And I did a stupid thing."

"What's that?"

"We were supposed to meet for dinner at one of Charlene's favorite restaurants. One of those grassy places with lean meals and natural foods. Something to keep us from getting fat and going into cardiac arrest." He shrugged. "But since she couldn't make it, I...I..."

"You opted for the meaty, greasy, cardiac-arrest diet," she finished for him.

"How did you guess?"

"You have a terribly guilty look about you. Don't worry, I won't tell."

"Thank you. You're not only accommodating, you have the discretion of a priest. You should be rewarded."

"Never mind, Dennis. It's my pleasure."

He looked around and noted that they were alone in the shop. "Are you finished here?"

"Nearly. Why?"

"I'm going to need ice cream. Or medication."

"I shouldn't leave the shop, Dennis. The store manager, Mrs. Simms, has gone out for something. And there is the matter of my continually going out for meals with you. I'm concerned that it wouldn't be thought suitable."

"Let me ask you something. Do you have a miserable time with me?"

"I think you already know the answer. Last week we laughed so hard I feared the restaurant manager might ask us to leave."

"Then don't worry so much about impropriety. You know, Americans don't have nearly the manners and discretion of you Brits. No one will notice."

"I've noticed. Three dinners in three weeks. That might be excessive."

"But tonight is only dessert. And coffee. Or maybe drinks. And Charlene may yet join us. In fact, grab some of your sample books and bring them along. You said you were flexible, Ms. Farnsworth. I think we'll have to take this meeting at a restaurant."

"Well...I suppose. And we'd best study the sample books. As it goes, making even a late-June wedding date is going to prove a challenge. Are you absolutely sure about this, Dennis?"

He rubbed his stomach. "Acid indigestion. I'll never learn."

"And you think Charlene will be along later?" she asked.

"Very likely," he lied. "I have my phone with me."

At seven-forty-five Agatha had a vanilla ice with raspberries and Dennis had a lemon ice and wafers. At eight-thirty Agatha had a glass of pinot noir and Dennis had an Irish coffee. At nine-thirty Agatha had a brandy and Dennis had a scotch. But in all that time they only talked about the business of weddings for roughly ten minutes. And the sample books never came out of the car.

Dennis asked a couple of simple, uncomplicated though personal questions. *What was it like growing up in England? What does a young English girl aspire to? And what brought you to the United States?*

He learned quite a bit more than he had expected, but not more than he desired. Agatha, it seemed, came from a simple, healthy, almost idyllic childhood in the English countryside. She was educated in public school, and spoiled a bit as the only child of an older couple. She had great fun in school and university, and married before finishing her program. Again, idyll. Her husband, Martin, a young barrister, adored her. They traveled a bit before settling into a flat just outside London. He went to work in a small but promising firm and she took a job at Harrod's. First Jason, then Sylvia were born. It seemed she lived a charmed life.

Then the unimaginable happened. While Agatha was away on a week-long buying mission for the store, a faulty furnace killed her husband and children in their sleep with carbon monoxide gas. All of them were gone in the blink of an eye. Agatha was only twenty-eight, just a girl.

In the two years that followed she watched her parents age and deteriorate. They didn't have the energy to assist Agatha through her grief; the tragedy sapped their strength and they opted for a retirement home in the south of France, where they could be cared for and enjoy less hostile weather. Even though there was still plenty of family in England—aunts, uncles, cousins by the score—Agatha just couldn't stay in the familiar English countryside. She couldn't enjoy the sights in London. Life for her would never be the same and she had to reach hard, very, very hard, to find something that would change the darkness that wanted to swallow her up. She desperately needed a change so complete it would lift her out of her old life.

And so, with her family's reluctant blessing, she decided she'd try California.

She wiped a tear from her eye. "I can't believe what I've done," she said. "Dennis, I'm thoroughly embarrassed. And dreadfully, dreadfully sorry. I don't know what came over me."

He reached for her hand. "Please don't apologize, Agatha. You can't know how perfectly I understand."

"I didn't mean to take advantage of you because you work in the healing profession. I suppose people tell you their troubles all day long."

"I've been known to have those kind of days, but—"

"But I've never divulged so much personal information to a client. Good Lord, you're not even a client, but a prospective client. I've deuced this job for certain!"

"Agatha, take it easy. You've only—"

"I've never bared my soul, dished out my heartache like that. How awful! When people ask me if I'm married, I say no. When they ask why I came to the States, I say, 'For a change of scenery.' But this!"

He actually laughed softly.

"Forgive me, please. I promise you, I will never—"

"Agatha, stop!"

"I don't know what came over me."

"Maybe you found yourself a friend?" he suggested.

"More than likely I found myself a glass of strong wine and drank it too fast."

"No." He laughed. "It's only a sympathetic ear, that's all. You must have sensed that I wouldn't mind if you talked about your husband and children. When I was a much younger man, I was widowed. It's been many years, eighteen to be exact. I would say I've recovered as much as can be expected, but I'm no stranger to the pain of loss. And loneliness."

"Oh, Dennis," she said, now gripping the hand that had reached for hers in comfort.

"So you see? Somehow I just asked the right questions. You knew you could talk about your personal life with me because I would understand. And you know what's happened?"

"I'm a little afraid to ask," she said, sniffing.

"You have a new friend. You don't have to feel so lonely here anymore."

Patrick Jersynski lived in an upscale town house in the cul de sac of a moderately rich neighborhood. In front of his town house Jake's Chrysler was parked, blocking the driveway, and in the cul de sac Jake paced. He looked as if he'd slept in his clothes. His shoes were scuffed, his pants wrinkled and the collar of his white knit shirt stuck crookedly out of a striped crew-neck sweater. The stripes were gold, brown, beige and black—circa 1990. His hands were plunged deeply into his pant pockets, his head was down, and he didn't even look up as Charlene drove around the corner.

"Oh, Jesus," she said to herself. "He's over the top."

She parked behind his car and killed the lights. She opened the door and stood, calling to him over the top of her car. "Jake?"

He stopped walking and looked up. He recognized her and jogged over. "Charlie, he hasn't fired a gun. Two uniforms came with me. We told him there'd been a shooting and we were waiting for a warrant to search his premises for a weapon. He invited us in and let us search. He asked us to be careful not to break anything because he hasn't done anything wrong. He has an alibi. He has a sick kid and, except for a stop off at the pharmacy for a prescription, he's been at work or at home. And his hand hasn't fired a gun."

"This could all be an ugly coincidence, Jake," she said. "Meredith's car might've gotten in the way of some random shot. Or, maybe this guy hired a shooter, but I honestly can't imagine why he'd need to. If he can make himself right with Meredith and the courts, he's going to at least get visitation…there's just the matter of back support and amends. All he has to do is be a little patient. Why would he need to shoot her?"

Jake rubbed a hand along the back of his neck. "He

asked about Merrie. Asked if the kids were all right and was there anything he could do."

"Jake, is it possible the person we should take a closer look at is Meredith?"

Jake pointed at the town house. "Look at his place, Charlie. He's got a little money. He could fix Merrie up with back support and she'd live better than she ever has. Her kid could have a father, to boot. Why would she run away from that with a lie? There's something rotten here and I can't figure it out."

"We're not going to figure it out here in the street. I'll call his lawyer tomorrow. I've been avoiding that, hoping for more information on this guy first, but nothing is forthcoming."

"Let's go get a drink," Jake said. "It's been a long damn day."

Stephanie had made a terrible mistake. She should never have led Freddy on. He was calling her several times a day, at the junior high where she taught and at home. She'd received a bouquet of flowers in seventh period from "your new best friend" and there were ten hang-ups on the answering machine when she got home.

Now Grant was at work and Freddy was calling and calling and calling. Finally, in frustration, she picked up the phone. "Stop! You have to stop calling me!"

"Hey, what's the trouble?" Freddy said.

"Listen, you have to hear me—I am not available! I can't date anyone! I live with my fiancé! If you don't go away and leave me alone I'll have to tell Grant!"

"Why would you do that? You wouldn't want to be responsible for me getting pounded, now, would you? Because the boyfriend...he works every night and you get so lonely."

"Freddy, you are twisted," she accused.

"But you invited me to see *Grease* next weekend...right?"

"I'm uninviting you! Leave me alone!" And she slammed down the phone.

It rang but she didn't pick up. This time, because he knew she was there, he left a message. "Stephanie," he called in a singsongy voice. "Stephanie? Guess who made a killing in the market today? You're making a big mistake brushing me off. You really don't know what you're giving up.... We could have some fun. Maybe you should take some time to think about this. I'll give you—" The answering machine cut him off. Before he could call back and talk into the machine all night, she disconnected it and unplugged the phone. She ran into the bedroom and unplugged the extension.

The apartment was finally quiet.

Seven

Dennis insisted on following Agatha home. She didn't live far from work and wasn't a bit concerned about driving alone late in the evening, but after three hours of talking, a couple of drinks and a good cry, Dennis said he'd feel better seeing her home. If she didn't mind.

Mind? She thought it very chivalrous indeed. She had quite forgotten how nice it was to be in the company of a gentleman.

It was just after eleven when they both pulled up in front of Agatha's little house. It was in old Sacramento, in a section only a couple of miles from Dennis's own house. Young moderns had revisited the neighborhoods, rebuilding and improving. She'd been renting the place for that past year and it looked something like a gingerbread house. It was sweet, tiny, and surrounded by shrubs, trees, vines and flower beds. There was a winding walk up to the porch; a light shone warmly from inside.

Dennis got out of his car. "Agatha, this is priceless. Did I tell you that I live in an older home not far from here?" he asked her, staring appreciatively at the house. "I renovated it myself."

"You think of this as an older home?" she asked, laughing. "I would consider it a newer model. I find it quite hard to live in anything under four hundred years old," she said. "I suppose the polite thing to do would be to offer you coffee or tea to make the remainder of your drive less taxing. After all you've put up with tonight."

"And I think I'll accept," he said, and walked up on the porch.

Once inside, there was even more for Dennis to appreciate, particularly the homey touches she had provided—old English mixed in with American. It immediately struck him how much more comfortable he was in a house like this than in a new, starkly white, modern construction. Charlene liked the bright, clean look of newer styles; he thought of them as cold. "This reminds me so much of my mother's house," he said. "I'm drawn to these classic neighborhoods. They have so much more character."

"The neighborhood might be old but my neighbors are mostly young. Career couples, small children and singles. My parents' cottage was similar to this house. It too had a porch, fenced garden, outbuilding and attic with dormer. Well, I'll set the kettle to boil. Do look around as much as you like."

The furniture was old but sturdy, decorated with hand-tatted doilies and antique antimacassars. The Oriental carpet was threadbare around the edges, but that didn't detract from its rich color and texture; in its day it must have been beautiful. The wood was dark, stressed and highly polished, and a faint smell of lemon oil hung in the air. There was a dry sink in the small dining room upon which she had placed a crystal decanter set and glasses. Dennis lifted one of the decanters, uncorked it and whiffed a very fine brandy. Agatha had such excellent taste.

"I rented the house, furnished, from a gentleman whose elderly mother had to be moved into an assisted-living facility," she called to him from the kitchen. He could hear the water running behind her voice. "The decanters are mine, the crystal from Ireland, the linen and lace also. I didn't bring much, but there were some things I couldn't leave behind."

"Will you buy the house eventually?" he asked her.

The water stopped. She stood in the kitchen doorway, drying her hands on a towel. "I'll go home to England...eventually."

This hit him with sudden, unmistakable sadness. When he looked at her, he knew he couldn't hide that emotion from showing in his eyes. She was lit from behind by the kitchen light and seemed almost ethereal. Mystical. There was a glow behind her hair, almost like a halo. He couldn't take his eyes off her. He was in a trance.

She cleared her throat and broke his spell. "There have been so many times I've wondered if I'd ever find someone special again, after all I've been through. It was hard for me to believe people get two chances." She smiled wistfully. "Just knowing your story, Dennis, knowing about you and Charlene gives me so much hope. Thank you for sharing it with me."

He nodded toward a picture on the buffet of a family of four. He suspected a relative or close friend. "Who is that?" he asked.

"My family. Me. Martin and the children. It was taken five years ago, not long before they died."

He frowned. "It doesn't look anything like you," he said.

She took off her glasses and placed them on the dark cherry table. "I try to project a much quieter image for the work I do. It's very important I cater to the brides, you see. They're my bread and butter."

He stared at her with his mouth slightly open. "Damn shame," he said. There was nothing homely about Agatha in her present incarnation; she was lovely. But the woman in the family portrait was much more provocative, with her fiery-red hair, all ablaze in long curls, a mischievous twinkle in her eye and a come-hither tilt to her smile. She was a vixen. "If you don't mind, I think I'll have a brandy rather than tea or coffee."

"It's entirely as you wish, but I'm concerned about your driving. I understand the laws in this country are very strict."

He smiled, poured himself a small draft in the snifter. "I'm not driving anytime soon," he said softly. He extended the glass toward her. "Will you join me, Agatha?"

He could see a very slight movement, as though she started to accept, then withdrew. "I've had my doubts about dinner and ice cream…and of course, I've had second thoughts about you following me home to be sure I'm safely tucked away. There's no question about it, having you in at this late hour is inviting gossip. But joining you in a brandy…? Dennis, I know that eventually Ms. Dugan is going to disapprove. Strongly.''

"Has it escaped your notice, Agatha, that Charlene hasn't called? Her ex-husband has called her out on an emergency and I haven't heard a word from her all evening."

"She can't help but notice the empty bed."

"We don't live together."

"Really? In these modern times? Astonishing!" Then it crossed her mind that the fact did put a slightly different stamp on it.

"Charlene likes her independence," he said, and even he noticed there was an edge to his voice. "I didn't mean to sound annoyed. I'm not. Oh, I was annoyed earlier this evening, before I stopped by the shop to cancel our appointment. Since then, I'm afraid my fiancée hasn't even crossed my mind. I should probably be ashamed of that."

"I should say so," she said. But it was then that she accepted the glass.

"It must have occurred to you by now that this has nothing to do with the bridal business."

"Oh?"

"Or with Charlene."

"She *is* your fiancée."

"But this—me being here, having a brandy with you—is only about you and me."

Well, at least he was the first to say it. Over the past three weeks her affection for him had grown proportionally. She found herself hoping against hope that he would come, and Charlene would fail him, stand him up yet another time. Agatha's meager protests against dinner, dessert, the lateness of the hour they dallied together at her house were halfhearted. She wanted nothing more than for him to stay.

As for Dennis, he was growing more and more attracted to her by the day, by the moment. He found himself driving by the Bridal Boutique on his way home from work, hoping to catch a glimpse of her. While he'd been more than a little put out with Charlene's many schedule conflicts, at this point he was not a bit unhappy that she was elsewhere.

Still, neither of them knew what they were going to do with the situation.

Agatha walked into her small living room and chose to sit in a chair with an ottoman. She didn't trust herself otherwise. This was becoming very tense. She knew the remainder of the night could answer some questions—and she welcomed his attention. Yet this could not possibly be more wrong. He belonged to someone else! She was the wedding planner!

Dennis took the corner of the sofa nearest her. He sat forward, his elbows resting comfortably on his knees. "Agatha—"

"Dennis, I must be frank," she said, interrupting him. "You have me at a disadvantage. I'm completely unprepared for this…this…situation. Since losing my husband five years ago, I don't know that I've been alone with a man, unless it was on an elevator."

"I apologize if I make you nervous, Agatha."

"But, you see, I'm not in the least nervous. In fact, I haven't enjoyed myself this much since my husband was alive. I'm rather embarrassed to admit, I don't want you to leave."

"And I didn't follow you home to be sure you were safe. I just couldn't stand to see the evening end."

"But if you stay any longer, someone might do something he or she will live to regret."

He seemed to think about this for a moment, then put his brandy on the coffee table. He half rose, leaned across the short distance that separated them and gently touched his lips to hers. She met his kiss, though hesitantly. Her eyes slowly closed and he moved over her mouth softly but purposefully. Her lips parted slightly, and with a tenderness that promised future tempest, he probed the inside of her mouth with his tongue. He gave her lips a delicate nibble, then withdrew and returned to his seat.

"Well now," she murmured, shaken to her core.

He smiled handsomely. "I'm not going to do anything tonight that could prove regrettable," he said. "I wouldn't put you in a position like that. But I'm not leaving either. Not until you ask me to. Because, Agatha, I haven't enjoyed myself this much in a long time either."

"But you're to be married, Dennis!"

"Oh, I doubt that."

"Well, blimey," she said. "Looks like I've lost myself a perfectly good client!"

* * *

Long before Agatha finished weeping through the story of the loss of her family, long before Dennis insisted on following her home and long before Stephanie disconnected her phone and answering machine, Charlene was left to follow Jake away from the Jersynski house. She found herself parked behind him in the driveway of his small house. She wasn't entirely surprised. Jake wasn't in a mood conducive to a public gathering.

He didn't bother to wait for her, to escort her up the walk and to his door. He got out of his car, slammed the door, let himself in the house, flicked on the porch light, and was out of sight before she'd even gathered up her purse and coat. By the time she entered his house she could hear him talking on the phone in the kitchen. "What time was that? And they said what? Oh, that's beautiful! Fucking beautiful!" He paced in the small kitchen. "Okay, I've got a pen, give me the number. Got it. How are the kids holding up? Okay, I'll be in touch. And Sam...is her story still— Never mind, never mind. I'm going to talk to her myself, tomorrow." He turned off the phone and slammed it onto the counter just as Charlene entered the kitchen.

"You can catch more flies with honey," she said, throwing her coat over the back of a kitchen chair and her purse on the table.

"Imbeciles. Doesn't anyone care about keeping this woman safe?"

"Jake, stop it, please. I'm exhausted and I'm starving," she said, and sank into a chair.

"I am way too old for this shit," he said, running a hand through his errant, curly hair. He leaned wearily against the kitchen cabinet. "The medical secretary in the E.R. went on break and someone from a ward upstairs relieved her. Someone called and asked if Meredith Jersynski had been brought to the emergency room and was she all right. The stand-in receptionist said she'd been discharged."

"He was one up on you."

"Fools. This wasn't supposed to happen," he said. "We were on top of it. We had her covered."

"I know," she said, sympathetic. And now they didn't know anything again.

"She's a good kid, Charlie, I'm sure of it. Just a simpleminded little girl from Odessa. I mean, she might not be the sharpest knife in the drawer, but there's not a mean bone in her body. And she loves those kids. She'd do anything for those kids...and she was only a kid herself when she had 'em."

"Jake, this isn't your fault. This can still work out for her."

He hung his head for a minute. "I should've never gone over there. Now he's on to us and knows we're on to him."

"Well, you could have waited a little while...."

"I'm a screwup."

"You're not a screwup," she protested. "I said you were a hothead. There's a difference."

"Yeah, not much."

"Yes, much. You're one of the best cops I know, with one of the worst tempers. You'd think in twenty-five years you'd have mellowed out."

"I *am* mellowed out! Can't you tell?"

She actually thought about this for a moment, frowning. It was possible. She looked around the kitchen. "Your house is in really good shape, Jake. I'm not sticking to the floor or anything. And there's fresh fruit in the fruit bowl. Since when do you eat things that are good for you?"

"Since I got a cleaning lady," he said. Charlene picked up an apple. "I have beer and Jack Daniel's."

"No Château Ste. Michelle Chardonnay?"

"Not hardly."

She rubbed the apple on her skirt, shining it up, and bit into it. He poured himself two fingers of Jack, neat.

"I'll have one of those," she said. He gave her a look, his eyebrow raised. "Long day," she said. "Long month."

"Your funeral," he obliged doubtfully.

"So, when did you decide to have a clean house?"

"Don't start pushing my buttons, Charlene. I've had a long day, too."

"I'm not trying to push your buttons," she said, chewing the apple. He handed her a drink. She handed it back. "Could I have a little ice and water?"

"Sure. Wimp."

"I'm genuinely curious. What happened?"

"Nothing *happened*. There's a list of people about four miles long who need a second chance, a little work, a break. So, I have this girl who cleans the house and washes the clothes once a week, and I have this kid who does the yard. What's the big deal?''

''Oh, no big deal. It's just that I never knew you to notice anything was messy. The Jake I know would be glad to help someone with work, if he had any work to be done, but he'd never imagine that he—''

''See, now *that* was a button,'' he said, interrupting her.

''Jake, I thought the girl…Meredith…I thought she was someone you were dating.''

He laughed at that, threw down his Jack and poured himself another. ''Get serious.'' He pulled out a kitchen chair and sat in it wearily. He was looking a little worn. Tired. He gave her a lopsided smile and shook his head. ''Does she look like my type? She's about Stephanie's age.''

''Men never seem to be bothered by those silly age things. They date and marry girls younger than their daughters all the time.'' She sipped. ''And you've had many types.''

He scrunched his eyes up and peered at her through slits. ''Button?''

She took another big bite of apple, put it on the table, stood up and shrugged off her suit jacket. She sat back down and sipped her drink. ''Tell me how you got started in this little rehabilitation program of yours?''

''I don't know,'' he said, stretching. ''Accidentally.''

''Come on,'' she said. ''Hardly anything is an accident with you.''

''Well, I didn't start it up, if that's what you mean. It was a fluke. Remember that old joke? Guy is sitting in a bar and a hooker walks up to him and says, 'I'll do anything you want me to do for a hundred bucks, but you have to tell me what you want in three words or less.' And he says, 'Paint my house.'" She laughed at him. No surprise. He had always made her laugh. "That's about how I got started in this program. There was this hooker, just a young thing. Jesus, she was a kid. Anyway, she wanted to get away from her pimp, but she couldn't support herself. And even if she'd tried, he'd have found her and knocked her around again, put her back on the street. So, I rounded up six guys who needed their houses cleaned."

"Young? How old is young?" she asked.

"Oh, Charlie, you don't want to know. We were taking a big chance here. This kid was not legal. The 'right' thing would have been Social Services, but y'know…" He rubbed a hand through his hair again. The long day was showing on him—five o'clock shadow, rumpled clothes. But once he started talking about this project of his, a spark lit behind his eyes. A fire. "I just didn't think the system could keep her safe."

"You thought you could keep her safe *better* than the system."

"Okay, so don't hold that against me. We did, when it was said and done. We had work for her, cleaning, then we had to find a place for her to stay. One of the married guys offered to take her in, give her a bed in the basement rec room. His wife taught school and it was summer break and she was a toughie. If she could manage the thugs she had in the classroom, we figured she could manage Nicole if she gave them any trouble.

But Nicole didn't give them any trouble. Man, she wanted *out*."

"What about the girl's parents?"

He gave a huff of laughter. "You know *that* story." He rubbed the rim of his now-empty glass with a fingertip. "I'm a father, Charlie. You think I'd take on this little pro if I thought there was any chance she had decent parents who would protect her? It was pretty obvious her situation at home put her on the streets. And I put my job on the line. So did the other guys."

"So...it started with her?"

"Sort of. The thing is, word leaked out, like it always does. And we found out that there was a bunch of people getting themselves way too involved with these second-chancers. There were a couple of women cops who were giving shelter to battered women, moving them in and out of their houses like they were running bed-and-breakfasts. We had the homeless living in garages, doing odd jobs. We even had a kid washing dishes and busing tables, living in the back of Coppers." He gave his head a sharp nod and smiled crookedly. "It's been working out real well."

"Sam says you're organized."

"In a way. We got an accountant, just to keep us out of trouble. Every once in a blue moon we'll throw a picnic or dance, and put the money in the pot."

She watched his face while he described what was completely selfless charity work, but with no ego. If he was proud, it was of the program; he wasn't boastful.

"Jake," she said, smiling, shaking her head.

"What?"

She laughed at him. "I so frequently think about why I divorced you that I hardly ever remember why I married you in the first place."

"Yeah?" He puffed up. "I thought you said it was the length of my—"

She hit his hand, shutting him up, but she laughed. "Believe me, it wasn't that." She grew more serious, wistful. "I sometimes forget how inherently *good* you are."

"Yeah, baby," he joked.

She touched his hand. "You shouldn't listen to me when I say you're a bad role model. I'm glad you're Stephie's dad."

"Don't get goopy, Charlie. I'm just an average guy doing a below-average job."

"No. You're way above average, going the extra mile." She drained her glass and put it on the table. "I have to go. I'm absolutely exhausted."

"You sure? I could order a pizza."

"No thanks," she said, standing. She picked up her suit jacket to put it on and she wobbled a little.

"Whoa there," he said, standing. "That drink go straight to your head?"

"It wasn't the drink. I think I stood up too fast."

He held her jacket for her to put on. "I don't know, Charlie. I don't know if I want you driving just yet. Maybe I should take you home."

"Ha! You've had twice as much to drink." She put an arm through a sleeve.

"Yeah, but I'm better at it." He turned for her to put in the other arm.

"So you'd like to think. You—"

Both arms in, she found herself facing him, standing almost unbearably close. He was grasping the front of her jacket. Neither of them moved. In her heels, she was almost his height, and she could feel his breath on her face. Slowly, so slowly she was barely aware of it, his hand let go of one of her lapels and rose, a bit awkwardly, to her face. He lay his palm against her cheek; his hand was rough and calloused. His fingers, fanned, reached into her hair. She closed her eyes and turned her face into his hand, kissing the palm.

"Aw, Charlie," he said, his voice raspy. "You're gonna hate yourself…"

She lifted her lips from his palm and looked deeply into his eyes; his, moist and green and steamy as jungle grass, and hers, hot as fire.

His arm circled her waist and he devoured her mouth. She met him with her own and opened her lips under his, a taste coming to her that she recognized, that she knew well, that she remembered and on occasion longed for.

Jake's hands immediately moved from her waist to her rib cage and up, moving over her underarms to the front of her shoulders and over the top, slipping her jacket off, down her arms. She let it drop to the floor. Her hands came together behind his head and she pulled him harder against her lips while she kicked off her pumps. With one arm around her waist, Jake moved the other under her legs and lifted her into his arms just as her second shoe fell. And he carried her to bed, where they tore at each other's clothing, throwing it every which way.

It was perfectly choreographed, smooth as a ballet, from touch to kiss to lift to the gentle tumble onto the bed.

This had happened before. And not just twenty-five years ago.

It was complicated, but then, when was it not? Charlene had great passion for Jake. She always had—at least since their third date. There were issues and emotions upon which they were as melded as soul mates. When it came to police work, law, right versus wrong, the underdog, Charlene and Jake could stand side by side and provide a united front against injustice. Also in the area of sex. Their bodies fit together as if they were made for that purpose alone. Since their very first coupling, each had known instinctively how to please the other—what to touch, how much pressure to bear, whether to hold back or forge ahead.

They also knew when to speak and when to shut up. In bed, at least.

The moment they were naked, skin against hot skin, they came together like long-starved lovers. He was inside of her in seconds and she was ready for him in less time. He held himself above her and she pulled him into her. With her legs wrapped around him, they rocked together, erupting into a mutual orgasm that left them shuddering and panting. It was as though neither of them had been sexually satisfied in so long they were like overripe plums that fell from the same tree at the same time and exploded on impact with the ground.

Then they collapsed into grateful relief. Jake rolled over, next to her, and drew her close with one arm while he reached down to the foot of the bed with the other, and pulled the quilt over them.

"We didn't even make it under the bedspread," she whispered.

"That happens sometimes," he said. And, beneath the quilt, he gently caressed her. Patiently and softly. Because he knew, when they recovered a little, they would do it again, but this time slowly. Carefully. Taking their leisure of each other.

But, most of all, not talking about it.

"It" was the difficult and complicated relationship they had shared for over twenty-five years. Though Charlie had passion for Jake, undeniable passion, she couldn't stand being married to him. Couldn't live with his mess, his childishness and high energy, his short fuse. He didn't ever turn his short fuse on her, but it detonated all around her. Something on the job would work him up and he would slam around for hours, maybe days. It was impossible. He called himself "flexible," but the truth was, he couldn't stick to a plan. He was almost never on time, was easily distracted and forgot important things, like meeting her at the hospital when she was about to give birth. And he took too many risks, personally and professionally. He was just a big, dumb kid in a man's body. He spit, went to boxing matches and never read books. Of any kind.

As for Jake, he was in love with Charlie and always had been. Desperately, passionately, hopelessly. But he couldn't please her, except when he hunted down criminals or made love to her. In those two things she could find no fault. But she was rigid and had been set in her ways since she was twenty. She had this thing with being perfect—if she said dinner at six, she didn't mean 6:03. From the day he met her she had had her life mapped out, exactly the way everything was going to happen for her, from college to law school to interning to her practice. She even had the date she was going to pass the bar written in her diary. Jake knew he wanted to be a cop, but beyond that he wasn't sure of anything.

Stephanie. Now, there was something she hadn't planned on. But then, neither had he. Despite the fact that Charlene and Jake couldn't get along for five minutes, they'd done all right with Stephanie. It seemed there was one thing that gave them the impetus to compromise...and they both loved her more than life.

He touched her breast and kissed her neck. "I'm getting too old for this, Charlie."

"Oh? You could've fooled me."

He raised himself up on an elbow and looked down at her. "Y'know, this has happened to us from time to time, and we kind of go along with it because—"

"Shh," she implored.

"No, this time I have to say something here. This is the first time either one of us let this happen when we were in a...you know...committed relationship."

"Please, Jake, can we talk about this later?"

He kissed her below the ear. "If you promise. I have to talk about it this time."

"I promise," she said, and there was such a sound of sadness in her voice, such a dark liquid swell in her eyes, that he let it go and instead kissed her neck. Then her shoulder. Then her breast. He feasted gently on a nipple until he heard her sigh. Jake might not be a Rhodes scholar, but he knew how to take Charlie's mind off her troubles. Obviously, something was wrong in Dennyland.

She couldn't see him smile because it was dark and he was using his mouth to rouse incredible, breathtaking sensations in her.

By the time he came into her for the second time that night, they were once again starving for each other. It was spectacular. It always was. It never failed, even when there was anger between them. That was the hardest part about failing at everything else. Charlie had opted to go it alone. She rarely had a man in her life and Jake strongly suspected she hadn't been in bed with one until Dennis, while Jake had kept trying to find a woman with whom he had this kind of incredible chemistry.

Charlie curled up next to him like a kitten, all soft and small and innocent. She sighed deeply, sleepily. She wasn't going to be talking tonight. So, what else was new.

Jake knew better than anyone that there was no getting Charlie to do anything she didn't want to do. So he decided to just enjoy the moment, holding her silky skin against him, her even breathing telling him that for once she wasn't tense or sleepless, for once she was completely relaxed and he had done that for her. There was plenty of time for talk later. He'd get up early—it was unlikely he'd sleep much—and put on a pot of coffee and they would talk about it. "It." The way they never did, in a quarter of a century, quite finish with each other. Their marriage, such as it was, was like a car wreck. They got behind the wheel of their union, neither of them experienced enough, patient enough, nor willing enough to keep it on the road. They ran it into a ditch and abandoned it.

At least they hadn't abandoned Stephanie. He smiled at that thought. Pain-in-the-ass spoiled though she was, she was also bright, beautiful, compassionate and definitely good down to her last polished little toenail.

He pulled Charlene closer. Maybe now, mellowed, they could try this again. He'd do anything. Anything. Take Prozac and calm down; stay tidy and timely. He could do it. God, he loved her, had always loved her so much....

It was the phone that woke him, and his very first urgent thought was, *Please don't let anything have happened to Merrie, please.* He swung his legs over the side of the bed; he thought better sitting up. The clock said midnight. He picked up.

"Hello? Yeah, honey, what's the matter? Oh, really? Explain it to me. Slowly. Take a breath." Charlene sat up behind him. He looked over his shoulder and gave her the shush sign. "Well, you're in luck.

We've been working together on a domestic thing. Your mom is doing the custody part for the woman and I'm trying to get evidence on the ex-husband, so, we put on the coffeepot and mapped out our joint investigation. Your mom was just getting ready to go…she's in the bathroom. No, no, let me be the one to tell her…and explain. Okay? We'll come right away. You got your phone? Good. She'll call you from the car.''

"Jesus," Charlene said. "What is it?"

"It's Peaches, honey. She's in the hospital."

Eight

It was safe to say that Charlene wasn't in control of her actions when she heard that Peaches was in the hospital, a respirator breathing for her. It was Jake who made sure she was tidied up enough to go to her mother's—and daughter's—side. When Charlene started frantically searching the floor for clothes to throw on, Jake slowed her down and said, "Whoa, now, just a little spit and polish. You don't want to look like you just tumbled out of your ex-husband's bed...."

Babbling incoherently, she let him help. A quick shower, a little talc and a touch of mousse, probably years old and left behind by some old wife or girlfriend. A dab of lipstick, then back into a lawerly suit after a whisk of the lint brush.

And then, of course, Jake had to drive while Charlene spent the fifteen-minute ride on the phone, getting the details, placing calls, leaving messages.

Messages for Dennis. Messages of desperate apology, completely unlike Charlie in the first place, and in the second place, she was sorry she had missed their appointment with the *wedding consultant!* Would he ever forgive her? As Jake overheard, it had been their *third* attempt to get together with this person who would help them plan their wedding. Their wedding? Jake almost took the car up a pole when he heard that. What was up with Charlie?

He had never seen this before. Yeah, she'd been in and out of his bed over the years, reluctantly admitting she liked sleeping with him despite the fact she did not get much pleasure from having him as a husband. It was regular, it was cyclical, and he looked forward to it. She never interfered with his marriages, she never came around if she was dating someone. She called the shots, but she always knew what she wanted. This remorseful Charlie was someone he'd never met.

On her third call to Dennis's voice mail, ''Dennis, you must have your phone turned off for a reason. Maybe you have an early morning, whatever.... But I'm so sorry I missed our appointment for to-night...and as soon as I know the details about Mother, I'll leave you a message and...and I hope you're all right, darling....''

Jake hit the steering wheel with the heel of his hand. Charlene didn't notice.

As it turned out, Peaches had been caught in a fire. She wasn't burned, but she suffered some smoke in-halation. Apparently she'd left the stove on and either fallen asleep or suffered a small stroke. In either case, it was her neighbor, Mr. Conklin, who had noticed the smell of smoke through his open window and rushed to save her. She was not seriously hurt; the night nurse hastened to tell Charlene that Peaches's condition was stable. But she had been so distraught and combative they'd had to give her a powerful tranquilizer. She was sleeping deeply and comfortably now and a full examination and diagnosis was to follow.

Just as bad as the sight of Peaches lying prone in a hospital bed, being helped to breathe by a respirator, was Stephanie's face—ashen and afraid. The poor girl looked stricken.

"Oh *Mom!*" she cried when Charlene walked into the room. She flew out of the chair and into Charlene's arms. Stephanie was taller than her mother by four inches, and with her chunky, thick-soled shoes giving her even more height, towered over her. But Charlene held her, stroked her back and murmured that it was all right. Of course Charlene wasn't sure it was, but that was what she promised just the same.

"I was so scared," Stephanie whispered, her voice jagged. "I couldn't *find* you!"

"Goddamn phone," Charlene cursed in a profound lie. But what was she supposed to do? Explain? She couldn't even explain the events of this evening to herself. In fact, she couldn't stand to even think about it.

"But imagine, finding you at Daddy's at midnight!"

"Believe me, no one is more surprised than me. It was work."

Jake, who stood behind Charlene, looked at the floor. He had gotten her to the hospital in record time, looking fresh as a daisy, and as a reward for his goodness he had been privy to her desperate messages left on Dennis's voice mail. Nothing made a guy feel better than getting out of bed with a woman and having the first person she thinks to call be another guy.

"I can explain all that later, Stephanie. Tell us what happened to Peaches."

"The fire was in her kitchen, probably a pan left on the stove. She was asleep or passed out or stroked out on the couch in the den. The TV was on, so she might've just forgotten about it, but they're going to check her head...her brain...anyway. Fortunately, she forgot to close the kitchen window, and Mr. Conklin, you know, next door? He smelled smoke." Stephanie slanted her eyes to the figure sitting on the other side of her mother's hospital bed.

For the first time Charlene noticed that Jasper Conklin sat vigil. He looked devastatingly concerned, and this made her frown. What was this man's sudden interest, after all these years? "Hello, Mr. Conklin," she said warily. He gave a nod. She then gave Stephanie her attention again.

"So, it's not as bad as it looks. She's been sedated and the respirator is only *helping* her breathe. She might even get to go home tomorrow. Oh, but now that's going to be a problem, because Mr. Conklin says her kitchen's a wreck."

"Smoke damage," he said quietly. "And...water damage."

"Mom, Peaches was really acting up when the paramedics brought her here. I've never seen her so upset and...and uncooperative. She was coughing and gasping for breath and she still wouldn't let them put oxygen on her. They were talking about restraining her. She was like a bad two-year-old. They were asking if Peaches had been showing symptoms of confusion and disorientation and Mr. Conklin told them she had. Just lately."

Again Charlene looked past her daughter at her mother's neighbor. He shrugged his shoulders lamely.

"Mr. Conklin, will you come into the hall and tell me about it?" Charlene whispered.

"Sure," he said, slowly getting to his feet. He was looking a little older tonight; being tired and frazzled had taken its toll. As he moved slowly around the hospital bed, he gave one of Peaches's hands a pat.

"Honey, stay here with your dad while I talk with Mr. Conklin."

"Okay," Stephanie said. The moment they had stepped into the hall, Stephanie turned her distressed whisper on her father. "Oh, Daddy, I was a wreck. Do you have any idea how weird tonight was?"

He had some ideas, but held his tongue.

"First of all, I had unplugged my phone because...because I had all these papers to grade. I plugged it in to call Grant at work and it rang before I could dial. And then I couldn't find Mom! Do you know how strange *that* is? I mean, that phone is her lifeline. And if she doesn't answer her cell phone, Dennis answers his."

"Well, modern technology isn't always what it seems...."

"What was she *doing* at your house?"

"Like I said, we're working on this case.... I talked

her into a pro bono custody case for a friend, and we… She ran into some trouble. The friend. It's pretty complicated, but it's just police business.''

"Okay, okay…but, you're not in a fight, are you?"

"Who?" he asked, perplexed.

"You and Mom?"

"Huh? Oh, no. No, not at all. We're actually working together on this." He rubbed his chin as if in thought. "Very amicably, as it happens."

"Well, that's a relief. I don't need Peaches on the machine, Grant at the bar and you and Mom bickering." And Freddy the Stalker, who she was not entirely sure was only a pest.

"We don't bicker," he said, a half smile on his lips.

"Only most of the time. Probably where I get it from."

He threaded his hand through her pretty hair, grasping the back of her neck under the heavy honey-colored mane. "We all do pretty well for as goofy as we are."

"Oh, Daddy." Her eyes welled up with tears. "I can't stand that this is happening to Peaches. What are we going to do?"

"Our best. That's all we can do. We'll get her the help she needs."

"Did Mom call Dennis? Because he didn't answer his phone either and this is his hospital…you know, where he works. He knows everyone here. I was stuck making decisions for Peaches, which I hated to do without talking to Dennis first."

"She called him. Left him messages. I think I counted four."

"I wish he was here...."

"Steph? I didn't know they were getting married. Your mom and Dennis."

"Gee, I'm sorry, Dad. It never occurred to me to tell you. You just found out tonight?"

"Yeah," he said. "More or less." She said she was dreadfully sorry so many times that he wondered if Dennis would catch on. It was odd for Charlie to gush and grovel that way. More typical of her was a quick explanation, followed by a brief and not terribly sincere expression of regret. Then it was over.

From what Jake heard, Charlie was writhing with deep internal guilt. Guilt that she probably wouldn't feel so profoundly if she hadn't been roused out of her little love nest by her mother's accident. Jake knew from experience there was nothing like an accident to make you feel as if everything you did was wrong.

"You're not upset about it, are you, Daddy?" she asked.

"Upset? Why would I be upset?"

"I don't know. You seem a little...you know... sad."

"Stephie, it's been a long day. I've been to two too many hospitals tonight. I'm shot." And a little sad that Charlie would use him like that when she had a sure thing planned with Dennis. Even though he didn't like Dennis all that much, he wasn't going to cuckold him.

"Maybe you should go home, get some sleep."

"Probably. First I'm going to see if your mom needs anything."

She smiled at him. "I bet there are a lot of women who wish their ex-husbands were as nice as you."

He thought about where he'd been an hour ago, about that brief fantasy that maybe they could try again. He smiled back at her. "You don't know the half, punkin."

Charlene spoke quietly to Jasper Conklin. "Naturally, I have a lot of questions—"

"And I probably know every one of them," he said. "You want to ask me a few things, or should I just start shooting answers at you?"

"Have I missed something, Mr. Conklin? When did you and my mother become such good friends?"

"Will you at least call me Jasper? Or, if you prefer, you can call me Albert. That's what your mother calls me, though I have no idea why."

"Albert?"

"I suppose this looks strange to you, Charlene. We've been neighbors for so many years without— Well, you knew my wife was an invalid."

"I knew that, yes."

"She was very dependent. Most of the time I needed nursing help. She died four years ago."

"Yes, I know. I'm so sorry."

"A blessing." He shrugged. "I regret that I didn't get to know my neighbors better years ago, but the time for regrets is past, isn't it? Regret seems to have been a constant companion of mine for a long time. I spent twenty-five years regretting that I had to care for a sick wife and then four years regretting that she was gone. I took retirement a year ago and I've been bored to tears. And lonely.''

''With all respect, Mr.... Jasper...''

''I know, I know. My sudden interest in your mother has to do with finding her putting up Christmas decorations in April, Charlene. And realizing how much I miss having someone to take care of. Someone who really depends on me.''

''Ah. I didn't think it was a decoration-trading scheme.''

He grinned. ''Good alibi, wasn't it?''

''Fair.'' She shrugged.

''Well, I recognized the confusion. In fact, I recognized need, and it was familiar to me. So I decided that, even though it was overdue, it wasn't a bad time to become a good neighbor.''

''You've been looking out for her.'' It wasn't a question.

''In a manner of speaking.''

''You don't have to, you know. You could have simply called me and—''

''Please, don't insist that I stop, as though this is some burden thrust on me. It turns out I'm comfortable in this role. I've had tons of practice. I haven't felt useful in years, and for pity's sake, Lois likes me and the rest of you are busy.''

She sighed deeply. ''But she's my mother, Jasper. I can't step aside and give you the responsibility. You can't imagine how much I owe her.''

"Oh, but I can. I've been your neighbor, remember. I might not have been outgoing, but I wasn't blind. I saw her go off to work every day till she was sixty-five, and then she worked part-time and volunteered. She did all the work that house required and helped take care of her granddaughter in the bargain. She's a helluva woman, that Lois. I'm glad to hear you say it, that you owe her. Damn fine gesture for a daughter, if you ask me." He leaned close and whispered, "A busy daughter who could probably use a little help now and then."

She felt deeply grateful. "You're very sweet."

"All the women say so," he said with a laugh. He rarely ever talked to women.

"Go home and get some rest, Jasper. You must be exhausted."

"Actually, I feel pretty good. Probably that hospital coffee your Stephanie forced on me. But, I'm going to go home now and let you see to your family." He took one of her hands in both of his. "Promise you'll call on me?"

She nodded and tears came to her eyes. How strange life was. All through high school she'd thought of him as the grouch next door. Mr. Crabapple. Even though he was only twelve years older than she, it had seemed like a huge age span then. She and her friends would come roaring up to the house in their noisy cars, squealing and honking, and this grumpy old coot would come outside in his flannels and yell at them to *shut up!* Self-absorbed teenagers that they were, they never worried about his poor sick wife, about his perhaps desperate need for rest. He must have celebrated the day Charlene left for college, and mourned the day she came back, child in tow.

Now he was offering to help her.

She gave him a kiss on the cheek. "Thank you. I think you saved her life."

"Heavens. And she may save mine if she lets me be of service again."

Life was strange indeed, Charlene thought as Jasper's words burned into her memory, taking her back to her youth. *I saw her go off to work every day till she was sixty-five....* There were things she hadn't allowed herself to think about for years and years.

She sent Stephanie and Jake away and plopped herself down at her mother's bedside. She took Peaches's hand in hers and settled in for a long and reckless bout of remembering.

Lois moved them into that little house in Fair Oaks when Charlene was ten. She could vaguely remember Mr. Conklin moving in at about the same time. Charlene's father was not with them during the move, but not too long after, he made one of his appearances.

That was what Nate Pomeroy did—appeared. And disappeared. Then he'd appear and disappear again. He was a piano player, a lounge singer, a band manager, a music man, a fly-by-night. Because Charlene and Lois didn't talk about him too much, Charlene wasn't clear on how her parents had gotten together in the first place. There was a picture Lois kept in the bottom of her underwear drawer—Nate and Lois, dressed up, she holding flowers and wearing a hat with a veil. It had been a very small, very intimate little wedding in Charlene's grandparents' living room. By the time they moved into the little house in Fair Oaks, Charlene didn't have grandparents anymore.

When she was little, she knew her father as the handsome, funny, playful, happy man who just kept showing up and darting into her life like a beautiful exotic bird, filled with stories, laughter and small gifts.

Lois was a librarian with firm hours, a steady paycheck and a quiet lifestyle—except for Nate. Before buying the house, they had lived in a tiny two-room apartment. If Nate was around, Charlene slept on the sofa, and if he was not, she slept with Lois. From the time Charlene was five, whether or not Nate was in residence, she would go to school in the neighborhood of her mother's public library building, walk to the library after school, and they would take the bus home together. Charlene learned to sit quietly and do homework or read for several hours at a time when she was very young. She was extremely disciplined.

When Lois managed to purchase the little house in Fair Oaks, Charlene still went to the school near the library, until she was in junior high and old enough to be left on her own until dinnertime, when Lois was off work.

And every so often—Charlene couldn't remember exactly how often—Nate Pomeroy would saunter up the walk to the front door with flowers, candy, some kind of toy, trinkets, cheap costume jewelry or silk scarves—anything colorful, feminine and irresistible.

Charlene would scream in delight and throw herself on him, overtaken with sheer joy, but Lois would cross her arms over her chest and glower at him. It would sometimes take him days to win her over, but only seconds for Charlene to fall under his spell.

Nate was wonderful for a little girl, a fantasy father. He would take her to movies, to the zoo, to the park, to the river, to San Francisco. Sometimes, as she got a little older, they would conspire that she would skip school so they could do something special, like drive to the coast or up to the mountains. He always knew actors and musicians playing Tahoe clubs or San Francisco theaters. She idolized him.

Lois remained cool and distant for a while, but eventually she warmed up. And just about the time she'd start to relax and enjoy a sort of family routine, Nate would get restless again and be gone. Poof. Sometimes he didn't even leave a note. Weeks or months would pass before he returned. As Charlene got older, the stretches of his absences grew longer…and her resentment deeper.

Now that she was an adult, she understood the scenario better. Lois had fallen under his spell, married him, had a child with him, and either would not follow him around in his nomad-like existence, or had not been invited. Lois had already been thirty-two when she married Nate; in the fifties she would have been considered an old-maid librarian.

In high school Charlene was less impressed with her father's irresponsible behavior, and met his visits in much the same stiff manner that Lois did…and again, much like Lois, she warmed up eventually. By then Nate appeared about once a year and stayed for as long as a few weeks. She also noticed that he began each visit by talking about what a fool he'd been to let this precious family life slip away from him. Who needed the boys in the band? He needed his two beautiful girls! His home, his security, his sanity! There must be something he could do that would keep him close to Fair Oaks, even if he had to work in San Francisco or Lake Tahoe and drove home every week for a couple of days. Maybe he could be a lounge singer in Sacramento, or give piano lessons right in Fair Oaks. Charlene would grow excited by the prospect of having a full-time father.

Then he would go and Charlene would be shattered.

Charlene misled her friends and later Jake, making it sound as though her father was a presence in her life and simply traveled for his job. She made it sound as though he wrote, called, came home regularly, supported the family financially with his work. In reality, she doubted Nate ever gave Lois a dime, and she was a little afraid to ask Lois if she gave Nate money. Afraid Lois had.

Lois was a great mother as mothers go, but she wasn't exactly a tremendous communicator. Charlene remembered back to an incident in her junior year of high school. Nate had come, won them over in a few days and settled in like a father who'd doted on his wife and daughter for years without interruption. He went to church with them, attended the high-school football games, chaperoned the dance, did card tricks for her friends, helped them decorate the homecoming floats…and then left a note saying a gig had come up in L.A. and he didn't know how long he'd be gone. Charlene had thrown herself on her bed and wept hard, burning tears. Lois came into her room, sat down beside her, touched her back with gentle affection and said, "Shall we talk about it, Charlene? Your father?"

She had said, "No! I don't want to talk about him! Not ever!"

And Lois had said, "All right, but tell me if you change your mind. And remember, I'm always here."

And that was it.

From the time she was a little girl, Charlene had learned to keep her feelings to herself, the way her mother did. She was ambivalent toward her father, adoring him and detesting him. As she got older, it took him longer to melt the ice that encased her heart, but she never asked her mother the burning question, "How did we get mixed up with a guy like this?"

Small wonder, then, that she ended up being helplessly attracted to Jake, a fun-loving boy who might never grow up. Jake, who could make her laugh till she wanted to fall down, and who could bring her such forbidden sexual joy she wanted to never get back up. Jake, who had such passion, for justice, for adventure and for her. From the first time she kissed him, there was something so familiar. Even though there was no physical resemblance at all, the first time Lois met him she said, "Oh boy."

Charlene got pregnant before she got married, which didn't give her a lot of time to plan things. And she couldn't find her father for the wedding. When Stephanie was close to arriving, a telegram found Lois. Nate was dead. Shot by a jealous husband in southern California.

Charlene demanded that her mother go with her to L.A. to retrieve the body and have a look at where he'd been and with whom. She wanted to lay the whole thing to rest once and for all. Jake offered to take her, help her get through it, but she didn't want Jake right then. She wanted only her mother. Lois went because she was worried about the pregnancy; Charlene was overwrought.

Lois tried to talk to Charlene about Nate, about their disjointed family life, about how she was never sure if letting Nate in and out of their lives did more harm than good, but Charlene wasn't interested in going over it. She wouldn't listen. She wanted to be finished with all that. Through her tears she said, "He'll never let us down again."

What Charlene didn't realize, didn't prepare for, was the legacy he left like a splotch on her future. For years to come she would make decisions and choices based on the disappointments of her youth because she hadn't ever confronted and untangled them.

She came out of the experience—twenty years of abandonments by a father she craved—a determined young mother. She was done screwing around with confusion and focused her attention on doing *everything* right. But she went over the edge. Already very disciplined, Charlene became controlling. She became the kind of college student who mourned over an A−, the kind of mother who never let her daughter near a smudge.

There just wasn't room for a guy like Jake in a deal like that. He didn't have the constitution for it. Besides, at his young age, he couldn't concentrate long enough to keep Charlene happy.

Fortunately for everyone, the situation made Jake angry enough that he demanded to be a huge part of Stephanie's life. And to soothe his weary manhood, he found himself a woman right away, whom he dated, married and divorced in about eighteen months. This, in Charlene's way of thinking, established him as very much like her philandering father...and therefore hopeless.

But every so often she would find herself helplessly drawn to Jake. It was a damnable thing! She knew he wasn't good for her, knew he'd only disappoint her again and again, but she found herself needing him. Though they never actually reconciled, they would fall into an amicable pattern that usually included sleeping together, but never living together. And sure enough, just like with her father, this perfectly wonderful spell with Jake would end because he would let her down. Take her for granted. She would back off, put distance between them until, once more, some force brought them together again. Then he would do something to screw it up. Again and again.

In her total desperation not to get mixed up with a man like her father, she *became* like her father. She moved in and out of Jake's life, hurting him and causing him pain for twenty-five years, while he was helpless to reject her because he loved her so. But she didn't see that.

Charlene didn't find Dennis for twenty years, twenty long, confusing, difficult, often lonely years, which culminated with perfect Dennis, a man tidy and dependable and classy and reliable. Maybe they didn't have some of the things Charlene had with Jake, but they did have trust, mutual respect, companionship. He was a man who would stay and stay the same. No one knew better than Charlene how vitally important that could be.

Stephanie insisted on a final cup of coffee with her dad, even though he was clearly tired to the bone. Good sport that he was, he gave her another half hour, because he knew she wasn't ready to go home and face the rest of the night wondering what was going to become of Peaches. They sat in the deserted hospital coffee shop, sipping on vending-machine coffee that had a distinctly cardboard taste.

"It's just that she's had such a tough life," Stephanie said. "I hate to see her wrap it up like this—confused and disoriented and constantly getting lost or hurting herself. I wished for her a rockin' old age."

"Yeah, well, it's pretty much rocked up to now, wouldn't you say?" Jake wanted to know.

Stephanie shrugged. "I think there have been some perks these past few years, now that Mom's doing better financially and I'm out of school. There were a couple of trips, a couple of retreats. But up until then it was work, work, work."

"The way of the world, my princess," Jake said. He had that look on his face; it was so like Charlene's look. That *When do you suppose she's going to get it?* look.

"Come on, you know what I mean—the whole single-mother thing. She not only raised Mom by herself, she then mostly raised me. If she wasn't actually doing the baby-sitting, she was helping to pay for the baby-sitter. And all this on a librarian's wage."

Jake looked a little perplexed. "I understand your grandfather traveled a lot while your mom was growing up—"

"That's what Mom likes people to think. That's what she even told me—'Your grandpa was in a traveling band and we learned to get along without a man around all the time.' But if you ask Peaches, my grandpa was a real flimflam man. He probably only spent a year in total with Mom and Peaches her whole life."

Jake gave Stephanie his full attention, and he looked more than a little bit surprised.

"Peaches took the bus to work until I was in junior high. Mom had a car before Peaches did."

He sat up a little straighter. "Your mom's father wasn't around at all when she was growing up?"

"Hardly at all. Peaches said Mom adored him. She used to sit on the front step and wait for him, used to haunt the mailbox for letters that never came. It broke Peaches's heart, but there wasn't much she could do. She didn't think it would be better to refuse to let Charlene see her father at all."

"No, I don't suppose. It's so funny I never knew any of this."

"Well, since you and Mom didn't stay married for even a year…"

"I remember when your granddaddy died. You were about to be born. I wanted to go with your mom to where he was buried, but she didn't want me with her. I was worried about her, what with her being so pregnant with you. But Peaches said she'd be all right, that I should let her have her way. I think you were born about a month later, if that."

"I *know*, Dad. He died in Los Angeles, where he'd been living for a few years. Turns out he was actually shot by a jealous husband. Peaches said shooting was too good for him."

His mouth hung open. He was sure Lois and Charlene had said it was a heart attack. "Wow!"

"She didn't tell you anything about him, did she?"

He laughed in embarrassment. "Okay, we haven't always been real honest with each other, but at the time he died we were *married!*"

"It's definitely not your fault, Daddy. She didn't tell me, either. Peaches said she refused to talk about her father. He must've hurt her too much when she was growing up by being so absent all the time. That's what Peaches said."

"But Peaches told *you*," he said.

"Well, I asked a lot of questions about my grandpa. And remember, when I was little and curious and full of questions, Mom was in college and law school. That left me and Peaches together all the time. She showed me some old pictures, told me he had been a musician. He was pretty unreliable and didn't live with them much when Mom was growing up, but when he did come around he was great fun. But then he'd up and leave with no warning. It would make Peaches furious, but in those days you didn't get divorced unless there was some horrendous reason.'' She laughed ruefully. ''I guess it wasn't horrendous enough that he was a no-good, cheating bum who never made a single rent payment in his life.''

Jake whistled low and checked out the coffee-shop ceiling for insight. ''You ever ask your mom about this stuff?'' he asked.

''I asked her a few times. She wasn't very forthcoming, just answered my questions yes and no. 'Yes, he died before you were born. No, he wasn't around much when I was growing up. Yes, I suppose I missed him, but you can't really miss what you don't have. No, I wasn't that sad when he died because he hadn't been a big part of my life.' We might as well have been talking about the postman.''

''Shew.'' He rubbed his head.

''Surprised?'' she asked.

''Why didn't anyone tell me about this before?'' he wanted to know.

''Who knew you didn't know? Who knew you wanted to know? What difference could it make to you? We still have Grandma and Grandpa Dugan up north. It's not like I was traumatized…or even deprived. Three grandparents is actually pretty good.''

He just nodded, then he reached across the little

table and held her hands. "Growing up with Peaches was a good life for you, wasn't it, honey?" He saw her eyes mist over again. "I suspect you went into education because of your grandma, didn't you, punkin?"

"Sort of. Literature was probably because of her. And education was a way to get paid for studying great books. Mom and I both grew up at the library."

"Yeah, I'll bet." He drained his paper coffee cup. "Don't worry about Peaches, honey. Everyone will pitch in, make sure she's okay. I don't think you have to start counting her last days just yet."

"I guess."

"And honey? Maybe you shouldn't mention to His Denniship that your mom was slightly out of touch at my place. Hmm?"

She got a sly smile. "Oh?"

"I know they're all way liberated, but if it was me I'd be bothered. So, if she wants him to know, she'll tell him."

"Yeah, okay."

"You like him, right?"

"Sure. He's a great guy. I think he's what you would call steady." She shrugged. "Whatever makes her happy, y'know?"

"I know," he said. "Want me to follow you home? Make sure you get in all right?"

"Dad!" She laughed. "When I first moved out on my own I could get home at 2:00 a.m. without anyone sitting up, tapping a foot, waiting. So, lighten up."

"Lighten up, lighten up," he mimicked. "Would

you like company to your car in the hospital parking lot?''

''Now, *that* I'll take!''

However, when she got home, she deeply regretted her cavalier attitude. On the welcome mat in front of her apartment door was a bud vase and single red rose. There was a note attached, but it was unsigned:

Should a nice girl like you be out so late?

The hair on the back of her neck prickled and a chill ran through her. She knew it had to be him. He'd grown tired of just calling and calling and had come to her door.

She had not yet mentioned any of this to Grant, or to anyone else. It was her misjudgment and she was embarrassed. She wanted it to go away before she owned up to doing the very thing she criticized other, stupid young women of doing.

She let herself into her apartment warily. She bolted the door behind her, checked every nook and cranny and made sure the windows were locked. Sometimes you just know what you know, and she knew he was out there, nearby.

She heard the key in the lock and her heart hammered. She pushed her hand against her chest as if to slow it. When Grant walked into the apartment, she let out a huge sigh.

''Oh, Grant! I'm so glad you're home! I've done the dumbest thing. I should've told you before, but I felt too stupid.''

"What?" he asked, tossing his keys on the counter.

"The rose? Did you leave it outside?"

"What rose?"

She went to the door, opened it and looked out. It was gone.

"What rose?" he asked again.

"This is all your fault!" she accused Grant. And then she started to cry.

By the time Charlene was done remembering her childhood it was nearly dawn. She probably should have come to some huge conclusions about where she was coming from, where she was going. Instead, she stumbled upon a partial answer and finally admitted to herself how much losing her father had hurt.

The sound of a metal chart being flipped open brought her out of her hypnotic state and she turned to see a young doctor enter the room. She stood and faced him.

"I'm Dr. Moore," he said, extending his hand.

"Charlene Dugan, Mrs. Pomeroy's daughter."

"Good to meet you. Well, we're going to take out the tube, turn off the respirator. I'm going to schedule a brain scan and MRI, some routine blood work. It could be anything from a series of what we call silent strokes that, over time, cause memory problems and confusion, or late-onset dementia, maybe even Alzheimer's, that contributed to her mishap last night."

"Could a stroke have made her lose consciousness?"

"We know what made her lose consciousness, Mrs.

Dugan. She fell asleep. She had a blood-alcohol level of .06 percent.''

''What? She doesn't drink much. A little wine, a little toddy…''

''She most probably forgot she'd had a drink and had another, and maybe one more,'' he said, scribbling in the chart all the while. ''It happens. Sometimes with medication, patients forget they've taken their pills, and take more. Same with meals,'' he added, looking up. ''I had a patient whose spouse was wasting away because his wife kept insisting they'd eaten already…when they hadn't.''

''I'm sorry,'' Charlene said, getting back to the original point. ''Are you really saying that my mother was drunk?''

''Well, not drunk as a sailor, but certainly relaxed enough to fall asleep.'' He flipped the chart closed. ''I'm going to complete her tests by noon, discharge her into your care and have you schedule out-patient visits to do some testing for Alzheimer's. I know this is going to take some enormous adjustments on your part, but given the circumstances of last night, you're going to want to check into some companion care. We have some informational brochures for you….''

''Dear God,'' she said in a breath.

She heard him before she saw him. Someone was running down the hall and suddenly there he was, skidding to a stop by grabbing the door frame, his silver hair mussed, unshaven, but wearing the scrubs he would be working in. ''Char!'' he said.

''Oh, Dennis,'' she returned with relief.

"God, I'm so sorry!" He walked into the room and took her immediately into his embrace. "I turned my phone off because I had an early start. Jesus, I'll never do that again."

"It's all right, Dennis. My phone wasn't working last night and they had to call Stephanie to the hospital. Everything that could have gone wrong…"

He turned directly to Dr. Moore. "Pete? Everything under control?"

He extended his hand, and the sight of them shaking, knowing each other, made Charlene feel safe and secure for the first time. This was how she had felt when she met Dennis, that he could keep her safe. With him, she would be taken care of. He wouldn't let her down, disappear, drift away or forget he'd made promises. This business of his phone being turned off was more than rare—it was almost nonexistent.

"I think we've got everything covered," the doctor told Dennis. "Not too serious this time. I'll let Mrs.…um, Charlene can fill you in, and if you want to call me later, I'd be glad to talk to you about nursing care, support groups, extended-care homes."

"We'll take care of her for now," Dennis said. "Can I go ahead and turn off that respirator?"

"Sure, that would be great. Be sure and stop at the station and make a chart notation. Let the IV run out. We sedated her on top of the alcohol, so she's sleeping very soundly, but pretty soon—"

"She'll be up and growling. Let's get that tube out before her eyes even open."

"Good idea."

Yes, Charlene thought. This is what I need most. Someone stable, mature, calm. Willing. I don't need to be chasing some hothead off to a perp's house and holding him off a bad guy. I've got bigger things on my plate. I need someone stable and consistent and predictable.

God, she thought, did I almost lose my mind?

Never again.

Nine

Charlene took a cab to Jake's house to fetch her car. She did this on the sly, without Dennis knowing, although she expected the whole scenario might eventually come up for discussion. Maybe Stephanie would make some innocent remark about where Charlene was found, or perhaps Charlene herself would bring up the subject, just to make it appear less forbidden. For the moment, she was opting for discretion, though the word that should probably have come to her lawyer's mind was *indiscretion*.

The cabdriver was singing along with Smokey Robinson. "I did you wrong, my heart went out to play...."

"Would you mind turning that off, please?" she asked.

"Whatsa matter, lady? You don't like Smokey?"

"It's getting on my nerves."

"Hey, you're the fare," he obliged, clicking off the music.

Heart went out to play, indeed.

It wasn't Dennis she was worried about. He was as solid as a rock, without a jealous bone in his body. She did this for herself, knowing she could only confront one issue at a time. So, when Dennis went to work in the E.R., she walked out the hospital door, through the parking lot and down to the convenience store on the corner. From there, she phoned for a cab...and waited forty minutes.

It was almost 8:00 a.m. by the time she got to Jake's, and it was immediately obvious he wasn't letting her get away with anything. He had his garage door open and he was sitting on a lawn chair on the driveway. He wore his sweats—old ones—and held a steaming cup of coffee. Beside him was an empty lawn chair, he was that sure she'd come alone.

She approached him with caution. He watched her walk toward him and didn't move. Nothing moved. His eyebrows didn't lift, his lashes didn't flutter, his lips didn't twitch. She stood before him, contrite. "Sometimes I don't think," she said.

Silence hung between them. He watched her face, but couldn't look into her eyes because they were downcast. He let the silence stretch out; he had a lot of experience with this sort of thing from interrogations. It was especially tantalizing when you knew more about the situation than the suspect, but the suspect didn't know how much you knew. His favorite opener had always been, *Why not go ahead and try the truth first, because you don't know how much I know.* "Coffee?" he finally asked the suspect.

She raised her eyes. "Jake, I came to say I was sorry."

"You came to get your car," he said, standing up. "And you promised you'd talk to me about our...what should we call it, Charlie? Our relationship?" He walked into the garage, toward the door. She didn't want to notice the way his sweats fit so keenly over his muscled butt. He stayed in shape, that was for sure. He had chopped off the sleeves of his sweatshirt and she *hated* noticing his biceps.

"That was before Peaches got hurt," she said to his back.

He made a half turn. "Cream and sugar?"

She sighed. "Black," she said. She had no intention of drinking another cup of coffee.

She tapped her foot nervously while she waited for him. She wanted to get home, shower, clean up, make a few calls, go over to Peaches's house to see how bad it was. There were clients who were not going to be pleased to have their cases delayed or pushed off on an associate, but there wasn't much she could do about that right now. She had a million things on her mind, making it difficult to sort out priorities. But that was what she was best at—prioritizing. Right now her number-one priority was getting the hell out of here. Where *was* he? How long was he going to drag this out?

He finally reappeared, carrying two mugs. "Here," he said. "You can't drink it black."

She looked into the mug; it was milky. Cream and sugar.

"Sit down, Charlie. Tell me about Peaches."

For that she could sit. She told him what the doctor had said, that Peaches would be discharged by noon, that she was awake, alert and stable before Charlene left her, and that the days, months and perhaps years ahead were probably going to be very challenging. "Do you want to hear something astonishing? The doctor said that people who read a lot are less likely to get Alzheimer's. And he hopes that means that if Peaches does indeed have Alzheimer's, it will be less severe. And also, that the later the onset, the slower the progression. Surprising. So, there will be several doctor's appointments in the coming days and weeks, I suppose. More tests, et cetera."

"Are you scared?" he asked her.

"Scared? No. I'm concerned."

"Ah. And sorry."

"Of course I'm sorry! I wouldn't wish this on anyone, least of all my own—" She stopped. That wasn't what he meant.

Jake watched her face, her eyes, her grip on the mug. By now he had pieced together her childhood from a combination of his own remembering and what Stephanie had told him last night…or rather, early this morning. How had he gone twenty-five years without knowing the accurate details of Charlie's childhood? And why had she kept these details from him? Was she ashamed of her father? Her childhood?

Charlene had been raised in a household of confusion, with a father who was in and out like their house was a train station. And not even the fact that her mother was always there, a constant source of love and support, was enough to eliminate Charlie's abandonment and control issues.

In the few short hours since Stephanie had filled him

in, he'd realized a few critical things. One, when he married Charlie twenty-six years ago, though he loved her madly, he'd been twenty-four and stupid and hadn't paid attention to what was going on around him. Some of that couldn't have been helped; twenty-four-year-old men tend to think with their peckers and have the maturity of rock stars. He hadn't realized that, when he acted like an undependable jerk, Charlene was naturally afraid that she'd married a man like her father. Second, when her father actually died, and she conveniently never told him the truth about the man or his death, she went into a serious tailspin...and incredible denial. *She* wasn't going to have the kind of life her mother had; *she* wasn't going to put up with that irresponsible crap from anybody, especially not a man.

Third, she hadn't fallen out of love with Jake when she divorced him twenty-five years ago. She'd merely run out of courage. And faith. She wasn't brave enough to chance that theirs could be a marriage more successful than her parents', and she had utterly no faith in Jake. Or herself.

Jake had thought through the whole thing—including the many times he and Charlene ended up in bed together over the years, and then she tried to pretend it hadn't happened when he tried to discuss it. Probably the most important conclusion was this: Charlene was headed for a meltdown. Mega.

"So. Tell me what you think we should do now, Charlie."

"Nothing. We do nothing at all. I'm sorry, I know better. *I knew* better. I think it was stress."

Stress? his lips silently questioned. He didn't laugh, but his mouth might have quivered with the desire.

"Don't laugh at me, you bonehead."

He leaned his elbows on his knees and held the coffee cup with both hands. He allowed himself a chuckle. "Look, there's a lot more going on here than we can untangle right now, or even over breakfast. But there's one thing you should look at, Charlie. This is a bad time to be getting married. Give yourself a break."

"How would *you* know?" she asked angrily.

"Oh, man, I am an expert on that, okay?"

"If I don't know after five years that I love Dennis, when am I going to know? Huh?"

"Maybe when you stop crawling into your ex-husband's bed."

She shot to her feet, indignant. Her coffee slopped onto her suit. "You jerk. Now look what you did!" She brushed impatiently at the stain.

Jake didn't stand. In fact, he leaned back and stretched his legs out lazily. "Somehow I knew that was going to be my fault."

"It was an *accident!* And I'm not talking about the coffee. It was an emotional night. I was tired, stressed out, very grateful to you for the way you…you…. I don't know. I admire your compassion…I told you that. We're not meant to be together, we've proven that. But not everything about our relationship was terrible. It's a *curse* that we always had it good in bed! A goddamn curse!''

"That kinda depends on your perspective," he said.

"I made a mistake, and I'm embarrassed. Leave me alone about it."

"You've made that mistake a lot over the years. Have you been embarrassed every time?" he asked, knowing the answer already.

"This was the first time I was planning a wedding."

"That's what I'm saying, Charlie. Red flag."

"But he's good for me," she said, and her voice had grown whiny. Wheedling. "He's very stable—"

"Steady."

"Yes. Steady. Like a rock. He doesn't have a whole trunkful of character flaws, he delivers on all his promises and he doesn't mind that having things tidy and well organized is important to me. We don't fight. We don't even argue. I don't ever have to wonder where he is, when he'll return, whether he's faithful."

"No," Jake said, slowly coming to his feet. "You have to wonder those things about you."

"Jake, I'm warning you. You're really making me mad."

Making you, period, he thought. Got you figured. Know your number. Have you in my sights. But he said nothing.

She, on the other hand, put her almost empty mug on the driveway and started digging in her purse for her keys.

"You have a song?" he asked her.

"What?" she asked, totally confused.

"You and His Denniship, you have a special song?"

"For God's—"

"We had a song."

"We were children!"

"I still hum it. 'I may not always love you. As long as there are stars above you.'"

"Listen, *drop* it. I should have my head examined for even letting you bait me for this long." She resumed digging. Keys were even harder to find when you were pissed off. "Now that I think about it, every time we've had this little…indiscretion…you won't let it go. You always want to talk about it—"

"'God only knows what I'd do without you,'" he sang, off tune. "You gonna tell him? Cleanse yourself?"

Her head snapped up and tears came to her eyes. "God…"

"What if I tell him?" he asked.

She stared at him for a long moment, her eyes filling. "You hate me that much?" she asked him.

He stepped toward her and he lifted her chin with a finger. "Hate you? Charlie, I've been in love with you since the minute I saw you, all those years ago. You left me with our baby and I was devastated. Hate you?" His finger dropped. He slid his hand into the pocket of his sweats and pulled out her keys. "You left them on the counter last night." She snatched them out of his hand. "You okay to drive?"

"Damn you!" she snapped, and stomped to her car.

"Postpone the wedding, Charlie," he said to her back. "Do yourself a favor."

She reached the end of the driveway and whirled back to face him. "This is none of your business!"

He waited till she got into her car and couldn't hear him when he said, "I wish that were true."

Agatha moved with ease through a morning of challenges. She began with an emergency fashion alteration as a pregnant maid of honor blossomed out of control with triplets. Next, a photographer had absconded with his deposit and the film from a wedding, so she was working with the videographer to create stills out of movie film to give the bride and groom captured memories of their special day. A florist had made a critical mistake on an order and all the flowers were the wrong color, clashing with the dresses. Agatha had driven to a flower warehouse north of town and filled her trunk with peach roses, carnations and miniature daisies, then delivered them to the church and hired two young women from a competing florist to re-create all the arrangements on the spot. Plus, she managed a substantial refund. But her coup was achieved when she convinced a hotel that had mistakenly double-booked their reception facilities to keep her party in the room they were scheduled to have and move the other wedding party to a smaller and less convenient site. People liked to please Agatha, and promises of future business didn't hurt.

All this was done with her usual poise and grace, despite the fact that she hadn't gotten much rest the night before. She and Dennis had sat up and talked in her tiny living room until almost 4:00 a.m. She knew almost everything about him now, from the details of his first marriage and Sarah's death, through the years that led up to when he met Charlene. She had told almost everything about herself, for there was so much more to her than just the sad tragedy that had robbed her of her children and made her a widow. It had been such a long time since she'd felt such intimacy, such trust. It was as though they'd known each other for years, when it hadn't yet been a month.

She had always assumed that she'd be too afraid to let down her guard, given her losses. But Dennis had driven caution from her heart, and instead she was filled with longing. She was embraced by his charm. All through her hectic morning she smiled whenever he crossed her mind. Oh, she had fallen for him. Thoroughly.

Before he left her at that wee hour, he as much as said the same. Not in so many words, perhaps. "I don't know exactly how I'm going to accomplish this," he had said. "Charlene has trusted me completely for five years, and in all that time, I've never even looked at another woman. But we can't possibly get married now. In fact, I don't see that we have any future together."

She told him she hoped it wasn't anything she had done. He said that in the short period of time he'd known her, he had come to realize that his relationship with Charlene was almost platonic. They were fond of each other, had much in common. The feelings they shared were so comfortable, they could easily be mistaken for love. But now he knew he wanted something more.

Then he had taken her hands very gently into his and said, ''It was everything you've done—the way you smile, the light in your eyes, the ripple of genuine pleasure in your laugh, the curve of your neck, the small crease of concern between your pale eyebrows when you're unsure.'' And this had made her heart hammer in her chest. Oh, she had fallen badly.

She couldn't deny it or stop it. Once she felt his affectionate gaze touch her face, she was lost. It had been so very long since there'd been love or passion in her life. Truthfully, she hadn't thought there would be again. What she'd been trying to do was live her lonely life as gracefully as possible.

He had kissed her goodbye, and in that kiss was all the promise of wonderful nights and weeks and years to come. She was as foolish as any thirteen-year-old girl.

She was thirty-three and he was fifty. Ordinarily she would take the age difference quite seriously, but after what she'd been through, she couldn't imagine giving it a second thought. If Agatha had learned anything, it was that life was not to be taken for granted, and to be twice loved was rare. This was so much more than she dared hope for. It was unimaginable that she's quibble about something so inconsequential as their ages.

They hadn't made any plans to see each other again. She had no idea what to expect, for that matter. However, when he walked into the shop at noon, it was as though they'd planned it. Her schedule miraculously cleared. She was usually booked solid through the day but she saw that there were no more commitments until 2:00 p.m.

She beamed, inside and out. "What perfect timing!" she said. "It happens I have a break. I hope you're free for lunch."

The look was still there in his eyes, that look of deep affection, but there was a slant to his mouth and wrinkle on his brow that hinted at sadness. She had a glimmer of intuition—*Oh no, he regrets this!*—but she beat it down.

"I have deli sandwiches in the car," he said. "Can we go to your house, so we can talk undisturbed?"

"Of course," she said, ever accommodating. But she felt a surge of panic.

"I don't have much time. I have to get back to the hospital. Do you mind if we take two cars?"

"That's fine," she said, forcing a smile. "I'll meet you there."

Once she was driving, she decided it was a good thing she had a little time alone in her car. Even though it wasn't far to her house, she needed that time to compose herself. Be gracious, she told herself. You were attracted, but he didn't make any promises. You fell for him, but it was your own doing. He didn't seduce you unawares. Be adult—people move in and out of relationships all the time. It was just a few evenings spent together, a few hours of chat, and no mat-

ter how intimate it might have felt, it was certainly
not a betrothal.

And, she reminded herself, the complication is that
the betrothal lay elsewhere. She comforted herself that
if this experience happened only to show her that it is
still quite possible to find love and happiness in this
world, that would be enough.

She unlocked the door for him and walked ahead
of him into the house. She tossed her purse and keys
onto the coffee table. "Shall I get us sodas?" she
asked.

"Please," he said, and proceeded to set out place
mats on her table, placing the sandwiches and napkins
on top of them.

It took her only seconds to bring back the drinks
and sit down. "Tell me at once, Dennis. I can see it
in your eyes…something has gone wrong. Don't make
me wait."

"That's exactly what I have to do, Agatha—is ask
you to wait. To be patient with me. I'm afraid something has come up."

"Oh…?"

"It turns out that Charlene had a very good excuse
for not making our appointment last night. Her mother
was involved in a house fire and was taken to the
hospital."

"Oh, no!"

He nodded. "While I so cavalierly turned off my
phone, in a huff because she was doing work for her
ex-husband, she was sitting vigil at her mother's bedside. When I turned on my phone and collected my

messages, she had left several. She was frantic, verging on hysteria. And I wasn't there for her.''

"And is her mother going to be all right?"

"Yes, thank goodness. She forgot she was cooking, fell asleep, and was rescued by a neighbor. She's going to be discharged today. She's had symptoms of confusion and forgetfulness lately. She's seventy-eight.''

"The poor darling," Agatha said, not thinking of her own disappointment at all, but rather of her own mother's aging, fraught with hardship and loss. She found herself thinking she must plan a trip to see her parents soon. "At least she'll recover. Charlene must be so relieved.''

"As you can imagine, I feel like a complete cad.''

"Oh, Dennis, don't be too hard on yourself. We all make misjudgments from time to time. But at least…''

He waited expectantly. She seemed to struggle with the words.

She took a bolstering breath. "At least you found out before it was too late.''

"Too late for what?"

"You must know I wouldn't hold you to anything muttered at four in the morning. Especially given that you were under completely misguided impressions.''

"Agatha, wait. You don't understand. This doesn't change the way I feel. It only changes my circumstances for the moment. I had fully intended to tell Charlene today that we have to call this whole thing off. We're not meant to be married. But after listening to her desperate messages, I didn't have the heart. I rushed to the hospital and found her more vulnerable than I've ever seen her. Because this is a medical crisis, she relies on me completely.''

She couldn't believe her ears. He meant it? That he was changing all his plans because of her?

"I'm going to have to help her through this. I owe her that much. Please understand.''

"But Dennis—'' she began. "Do you mean to say—'' She stopped again. She didn't want to get ahead of him, didn't want to make assumptions.

He covered her hand with his and gave it a squeeze. "I told her that her mother's health is the priority issue right now, that we can worry about our plans later. One thing at a time. And of course she agreed. But then the very next thing she said was, 'I would be so completely lost without you.' I've never seen Charlene like this. It's very unusual. She's extremely independent, incredibly unsentimental. Sometimes she's a little too tough, if you know what I mean.''

Agatha nodded, but she wasn't really listening. His voice started to fade from her ears after he said he was going to have to help Charlene get through her crisis. There was such a vagueness to that, an indefinite quality that indicated he might linger in this limbo for a while. Tell him you can't do it, her common sense was urging her. Just tell him that you understand, but that you can't see him until he finishes his business with Charlene. Nothing personal, no hard feelings, but it would be wrong to have these little dinners, ice creams, intimate discussions that reach deep into the morning hours and end with kisses so promising, they made her ache for hours afterward. He'll understand. He's a perfect gentleman. He wouldn't want you to compromise any values.

It would simply be safer, she was telling herself. Why get so thoroughly involved? Agatha was not so far past reality that she had forgotten that once one makes an emotional commitment of the heart, no matter how far the body had gone, turning back without great pain was impossible.

Tell him, Agatha! Just tell him you can't see him again until he's past this crisis with his fiancée!

"Charlene is usually very practical. Very sensible. And certainly not dependent. In fact, I would say she's always taken our relationship for granted, a thing that I was forced to admire while at the same time it irritated me. She's frightened, that's all. I don't think it will take much more than a medical report, a plan of action and a good support system for the care of her mother before she's on her feet again, solid as a rock, and forgetting we even had a dinner date. A couple of weeks, perhaps. Or, it's possible I'll find her back to her old self in just days."

Tell him, Agatha! If not for the sake of your poor, battered heart, then for the sake of propriety.

"I hate to ask this of you, Agatha. I think you know...I've...well, even though it's crazy and unexplainable, I don't want to be with anyone but you from this moment on. I don't know how or why this happened, but there it is. I think I'm in love with you."

Be that as it may, her sane mind was saying, we have a slight complication, and that is that you have a fiancée who depends on you and I won't allow you to lie to her, so we must not be together again until you've resolved this—

"A few days, a couple of weeks. I swear to you, I won't let this drag on. I only want to do the right thing. I'm going to end my engagement with Charlene as soon as possible. It's never been my style to lead anyone on. Two women is one too many."

Oh, Agatha, are you crazy? Speak up! This script was last heard on a *Dynasty* rerun! He's about to have his cake and eat it, too.

"I'm sorry for the complications," he said, touching her cheek tenderly with one knuckle. "I am so grateful for your patience."

She opened her mouth to tell him that, while she understood completely, she thought it imperative that they stay apart until he had finished his sad business. "Will I see you tonight?" came out instead.

From where Grant sat on the sofa in his living room, he could see the mound of linens in the bedroom move slightly. Stephanie was beginning to wake. He could also see the pile of dirty clothes on the floor at the foot of the bed, the school papers and books stacked high on the dining table and the dishes and pans in the sink and on the counter. The kitchen had been clean when he'd left for work, dirty when he got home—as usual. The kitchen and bathroom were perpetual messes that he'd long since given up hope he'd ever get control over, or that Stephanie would ever pitch in. Sometimes the simple task of putting soap in the dishwasher and turning it on took more domestic talent than Stephanie could muster.

Grant hadn't slept at all last night. He'd been doing a lot of thinking, trying to figure out what to do. Stephanie might have unknowingly brought the conflict to a head when she introduced Fast Freddy into the scenario, his sudden and discomfiting presence a direct result of Stephanie's constant dissatisfaction with Grant. When Stephanie had shrieked, "This would never have happened if you worked a normal job with normal hours like a normal guy!" Grant knew they were doomed. From this point on it could only get worse.

Stephanie moaned and rolled over, twisted in the sheets and quilt. She was slowly coming around and it was almost noon. It had been a late night. Or rather, an early morning. She had left a message on the school district's voice mail that a substitute would be needed for her class due to a family emergency. What she didn't know yet was there was about to be yet another emergency—their separation.

Grant loved her, there was no question about that. In fact, it had pretty much been love at first sight. Here was a young woman so full of love and life and laughter, she was irresistible. Added to that her natural compassion, the patience she used to teach surly teenagers and the devotion she had for her family.

But she was also spoiled, selfish and shortsighted.

To see Stephanie out in the world, the perfectly put-together beauty that she was, it was impossible to imagine what an unbelievable slob she was. He hadn't seen the bathroom counter since she moved in. Grant was a long way from fussy, but this amount of disorder put him on the defensive, had him fighting for his life in the squalor that was supposed to be their happy home.

But that was only one issue, and there were many. The constant bickering was killing him—about his schedule, his plans for the future, her loneliness, and, not the least, *marriage*. How anyone, especially a young woman whose parents were divorced before her first birthday and whose grandparents allegedly lived together about a month a year, could introduce the idea of marriage as a cure into a relationship as troubled as this one was beyond Grant.

She moved again, moaned, and Grant knew that the time had come. He had to get this over with. He went into the kitchen, poured coffee into the two cups he had searched for and washed that morning, and took them into the bedroom, where he sat on the edge of the bed. "Steph?" he urged. "It's almost noon. Time to wake up."

"Hmm? Can't I sleep a while longer?"

"I have to talk to you before I leave."

"Leave? For work?"

"Sort of. Here, I brought coffee."

She smiled sleepily, but the sight of her swollen eyes from last night's crying was almost enough to make him lose his nerve. She took the coffee cup, hummed appreciatively and said, "You are too good to me, Grant Chamberlain."

"I love you," he said.

"Aw," she returned, placing the palm of her hand against his cheek. "That's so sweet. See, I think we'd do a lot better if we just had more time together. You're usually asleep when I get up and I'm asleep when you get home, and it just can't—"

"Stephanie, I have to tell you something and you have to be quiet and listen. It's real important that you listen and not fight with me. Just this once."

Her swollen eyes opened fearfully. "What is it?"

"I love you. I always have loved you and I'm a little afraid that maybe I always will. But I can't marry you. You know why?"

"Why?" she asked weakly.

"Because we're not happy. You're not happy with me."

"But *Grant*—"

"No! You have to listen. I know all couples have their problems. I know everyone argues sometimes, and even have some real huge battles. But there isn't hardly anything about me that you like. You don't like my job, my goals, my dreams. When I'm not home you complain, and when I am home we fight. We're opposites to the core. I like it tidy, you wouldn't know tidy if it bit you in the butt. To tell you the truth, Steph, I don't know if you're going to find a guy who will be able to hang around, spend a lot of time with you, have plenty of money on hand so he doesn't have to work long hours, and will be happy about all the housework he'll have to do just to keep from attracting the health department."

She sniffed loudly and lifted her chin. "It's the new

millennium, Grant. The woman doesn't have to do all the—"

He tipped his head and grimaced at her ridiculousness. "I'm not going to argue about that again," he said. "I work full-time, go to school full-time, and if anything gets done around here, it's because I—" He caught himself. There he was, doing just what he said he wouldn't do. "Stephanie, you want a baby, right? If you had a baby, you think you could even find it in this mess?"

"That was just *mean.*"

"Steph, last night put the cap on it, so to speak. When I came home to find you hysterical because that asshole, Freddy, had been pestering you, scaring you, I realized our problems are out of control. Bigger than we are. You're not happy. You're worse than not happy, you're miserable. You think if I change my work schedule, you'll be happy. Or if I decide not to be a cop, like your dad, you'll be happy. Or maybe if I don't complain that I have to dig around in a mound of dirty dishes to find a cup to wash every morning, you'll be happy. All problems considered, you still think we should go ahead and—"

He stopped talking as her eyes welled up and one large pitiful tear spilled over and rolled down her cheek. He wiped it with the knuckle of his index finger.

"I work hard, Steph, and I plan to keep working hard. I don't just want to be a cop, I want to be the chief of police. Maybe the commissioner. I've wanted that since I was about four. Nothing's going to change that.

"I'm going to leave, Steph, and give you your life back. Give you a chance to find out what it takes to make you happy. Because, baby, happy people just don't live like this. And when I do get married and have a family, it's gotta be with someone who is on my team, who is proud of what I'm doing, and who I can't wait to get home to. And to someone whose team I can get on. I just can't get on this team. It's a goddamn wreck. You'd expect this from a teenager," he said, throwing his arm wide to indicate the unkempt bedroom. "Not a grown woman."

"Leave?" she choked. "You'd do that to me?"

"Yeah, I'm afraid I'm going to do that to you. Oh, I'll pay the rent and leave the furnishings that are mine. At least for a while. But my advice? I think you should go move in with your dad. Charlene would never put up with this mess, and your dad will make you feel safe."

"With Freddy stalking me and Peaches in the hospital, you'd—"

"I'm going now, before this gets any worse. Every week I stay we fight more and this place makes me angrier. It's gone too far. I don't want a life like this. Not with every day being miserable. Not with complications like other guys."

"But I would *never*—"

"Steph, I don't have any more compromises in me. Maybe with me gone, you'll figure out what you *really* want."

"So you're going to walk out on me, leave me to handle this lunatic who's putting roses on my—"

"Not to worry, baby. Fast Freddy isn't going to bother you again. I guarantee it. Meantime, think about moving in with Jake. He'll spoil you, make you feel like a little girl. You'd like that." He walked to the bedroom door. "Or you could live on your own, get your life under control. And maybe grow up."

"Grant, please don't do this to me," she said, her voice trembling. "Please don't go."

He left the room. At the apartment's front door sat two stuffed duffel bags. He was leaving behind his TV, furniture, dishes and linens. He didn't think he'd ever get that stuff back, but it didn't matter. If she needed it to get by, she could have it. He looked over his shoulder and saw her standing in the bedroom door frame, comforter wrapped around her, tears streaking her face.

"If you need me, I'll be at my folks'."

"I hate you," she said in a mean whisper.

It made him stiffen in hurt, even though he knew she didn't mean it. She loved him, but she only loved him best when she got her way. Just the same, he said, "I know. That's why I'm going."

Ten

Lois was fatigued and her throat hurt from the respirator. This caused her to stoop just slightly when she left the hospital. She also shuffled a bit rather than marched. The woman who had spent years saying "Stand up straight" and "Pick up your feet" was painfully aware that she could do neither. "A little bit of tranquilizer goes a long damn way," she muttered on her way to Charlene's car.

"What, Mother?"

"Nothing," she said. "Let's get out of here. I want to get home and call my lawyer. I'm going to sue the bastards."

"Mother, I'm a lawyer. And just who are you going to sue?"

She stopped midstride and glared at her daughter. "I'm going to sue whoever put these marks on my biceps when they were trying to tie me down to a gurney, and I'm completely aware of your profession. I doubt you'll be objective enough to help me."

She resumed shuffling toward the car and Charlene muttered, "I'm thinking of a lawsuit myself. I'd like to go after whoever gave you the nasty pill."

"When was the last time you found yourself losing

your marbles in public, Charlene Louise? Just see if it doesn't make you the slightest bit cranky.''

Charlene's purse started ringing and she actually welcomed the interruption, especially considering that her middle name was *not* Louise. Pam was calling; she had been checking in almost hourly with regular updates on how she was rerouting Charlene's most critical cases. ''Have we heard anything from Maxie Preston?''

''Nothing yet,'' Pam said.

''Hmm…well, do me a favor. Call her and tell her my client was shot at early last evening.''

''Dear God.''

''She's okay, but understandably, we have her under wraps. And no, they didn't pick up Jersynski. He had an alibi and no apparent weapon. This whole thing has me pretty baffled.''

''I'll call her,'' Pam said. ''Then there are the Samuelsons,'' she went on. ''They don't want to wait for the judge to assign another arbitrator. They want you and only you.''

''Ugh! Just when I thought I had a way out.''

''They're at your complete disposal. If you find you have a few free hours, you have only to let them know.''

''I thought it would feel better to be so loved,'' she groused. ''Tell them I'm embroiled in a family emergency, and if they want me they'll have to be very patient. And tell them if they're *not* patient— Oh hell, you know what to tell them. Just be sure they know they're still on very thin ice with me.''

"Will do."

"Scare them."

"My pleasure. Give my love to Peaches."

"That might be harder than you think. It's a little prickly around here."

Pam laughed. "Where there's a will," she said.

"There's usually a thorn or two...."

She was putting the phone back into her shoulder bag as they arrived at the car. She reached for the passenger-door handle and her mother slapped her hand. "I'm losing my mind, not my ability to open a goddamn door!"

"Mother, if you don't stop swearing at me, I'm going to start shopping for a home."

"Go ahead, do what you want. I don't care. If it makes me feel goddamn better to swear, I'll swear! I heard you say I was prickly. Let me prickle!"

"Well, you may be losing your marbles, but certainly not your hearing." With a sigh of resignation, Charlene walked to her side of the car and got in. "I'm going to take you to my house, Mother, where we'll have a bite to eat and—"

"Take me to *my* house!"

"Mother, your house is badly—"

"Take me to *my* house or I'll take a cab while I can still remember the goddamn address!"

Charlene, gripping the steering wheel, glared at her mother. Her mother glared back, pursed lips and all, like a video portrait of her childhood. Charlene finally said, "You're not going to make anything about this easy, are you?"

"Let's just remember which one of us is impaired, shall we? Then I suppose we'll remember which one of us has it *easy*."

Charlene bit her tongue and drove—to her mother's house.

This is what it can be like for some people in old age, she reminded herself. That was one of the things she'd been thinking all morning, while she tangled with Jake, gave instructions to Pam on how to manage the office in her absence, even as she drove to her mother's house to assess the damage. She thought about how precarious life can be for someone like Lois…or for someone like herself at the age of seventy-eight. But the numbers didn't matter; it wasn't really important when it happened, whether at sixty or ninety or a hundred and ten, the reality was that at some point she was going to be old and probably impaired physically or mentally—or both. Not very many people were lucky enough to live full, conscious, robust lives and then one day nod off and not resurface. Oh, that's what everyone hoped for, that they'd just buy the big one at about the same time life became more of a struggle than a joy, but before it got too painful or difficult. But it didn't usually happen that way.

Yet another reason she needed to marry Dennis. She didn't trust Jake to get home to dinner on time, much less be a conscientious partner in old age.

When they pulled up to Lois's house, the garage door was open. "Who could be in there?" Charlene asked aloud.

"Probably that neighbor...what's his name."

Curiosity got the best of her and she went ahead into the house, leaving her mother to follow. She heard whistling and found him scooping up charred debris in the kitchen. He wore rubber boots and wielded a wide-based janitorial broom. A big trash can stood in the middle of the room and several filled and tied-off garbage bags stood around. "Hello!" he said cheerfully.

"Mr. Conklin?" Charlene questioned.

"Dear God!" Lois gasped, looking at damage that was breathtakingly bad.

"You just keep turning up everywhere," Charlene said, pleasantly surprised to see him again so soon. "How'd you get in?"

"The door was left unlocked, Charlene," he replied. "Lois, it looks a lot worse than it really is. There's serious redecorating to be done, and you'll need new appliances, but there isn't any structural damage at all, and I think the wiring is mostly fine. I know a man who's a cheap but good electrician just in case."

"My God, what a disaster!" she said. She let her purse drop to the floor, pushed back the sleeves of her sweater and took a giant step into the blackened kitchen.

"Watch your tracks," he said. "Even though the firemen tracked soot all over the house, I think the carpet is going to make it after a good shampoo."

"It better make it. I just put it in a couple of years ago."

It was a dozen years, Charlene thought. At least.

"There's just me in this house. I hardly put my foot on the floor," she added.

Which was true enough. Just Lois, semiretired thirteen years ago, completely retired the last eight. About a hundred and twenty pounds on a little five-foot-two-inch frame. Not real hard on the carpet, but hell on wheels in the library.

"I've got my work cut out for me," she said.

"Mom, we're going to get some help with this," Charlene said.

"We?"

"Yes, *we*. This isn't a simple clean-up. It's going to take some reconstruction, and your insurance company will pay for most of it."

"I'm used to doing most of my own repairs," she said, but a little less snappishly than before.

"Charlene's right, Lois. I said it wasn't as bad as it looks, but it's not as though we can mop up here and call it a day."

"We?" they both asked him.

He smiled. They were like two peas in a pod. Tough, independent, bossy women who liked calling the shots.

"I thought maybe you'd like to be nearby while all the work is being done, so you can supervise, oversee, boss around the subcontractors, so I tidied up the guest room at my house. It would put you close to the work. I'm sure whoever you hire will need to consult with you on a daily, if not hourly, basis." Then he smiled.

"Good idea, Albert," Lois said, while Charlene

smirked and crossed her arms over her chest. Sneaky
devil, she thought. Appealing to her mother's stubborn
and controlling nature.

"Mother, I'd much rather you stay at my house. I'll
bring you over here however often you—"

"Nonsense, I wouldn't be comfortable in your
house. I've heard too many stories about the ruined
relationships when old women move in with their
daughters and there's a power struggle for who's in
charge."

Charlene smiled patiently. "Oh, Mother, but you're
not like that—"

"I know I'm not. *You* are!" Charlene's mouth
dropped open as her arms fell to her sides. "Now,
Albert, let's see this guest room of yours...."

"Certainly, Lois. Come along."

He grasped her elbow and was careful to lead her
out of the kitchen by way of all the plastic garbage
bags he'd spread across the carpet to the door. And if
Charlene wasn't mistaken, he threw a slightly amused
yet superior look over his shoulder.

Charlene stood in Jasper's hall while her mother
inspected the guest room and bath, as discriminating
as any tourist visiting a five-star hotel. The accom-
modations were adequate, not unlike the room Charlene had grown up in. These little suburban homes
were clones of each other. Most were pleasant three-
bedroom houses with eat-in kitchens and two-car garages sitting on good-size lots with large California
trees. They weren't new, but sturdily built forty-year-

old houses wearing many coats of paint, havens on quiet streets, with neighbors who had known each other for years.

It was probably best, she relented, to leave her mother in the neighborhood. As forgetful as she was becoming, moving her to Charlene's house might only aggravate the situation.

"Well, what do you think?" Lois asked Charlene.

"I think it's very generous of Mr. Conklin."

"Mr. Who? Oh, you mean him? Yes, I suppose it is."

"Lois, even though the fire was in the kitchen, your clothes are going to reek of smoke. I would have started some laundry for you, but I didn't want to meddle."

"Bull feathers, you meddle at will," she said.

"Well…" He laughed. "True enough. I held myself back. Why don't you go next door, gather a laundry basket of clothes to wash over here, and I'll put on some coffee. How does that sound?"

"Very practical. I'll get right to it."

As she toddled off, Charlene was struck again by how much she had aged in the last few days. "Do you think it's a good idea to send her on a mission like that? Alone?"

"If she doesn't come right back, I'll go over. But let's get that coffee going, Charlene, and talk. Let me give you some peace of mind, if I can."

"I won't turn down that offer," she said, following him into the kitchen. "I could use more of the latter than the former."

"It's not that complicated, Charlene. In fact, I'm surprised by how simple this is."

It turned out that, even though Jasper had lived next door with his handicapped wife for twenty-five years, Charlene had been too busy building her career and raising her daughter to notice the details of the Conklins' lives. In fact, Jasper not only worked full-time but did almost everything for his wife. She wasn't able to wash herself after the accident, and feeding herself was an enormous challenge that ended in a feeding tube.

"In all the time I spent resenting the labors of my marriage, it never occurred to me until she was gone that I had a real talent for caring for her. I had felt useful and needed. Much of the work I actually enjoyed. While it was hard, it was also helpful. When she was gone, my life became so desolate and empty." He laughed in embarrassment. "I spent so many years thinking my life was desolate and empty because of her and her many needs, when in fact it was just the opposite. Now, of course, I am the guilty party."

"Guilty?" Charlene asked.

"I hid us from the neighborhood, from my co-workers. I should have brought her out and the world in. The visiting nurses tried for years to encourage us to be more social, but I refused. My poor wife. She must have been so lonely."

"Poor Jasper," Charlene said. "*You* were lonely."

His eyes showed his gratitude for that understanding. "Ah! So, here I am, alone and retired. And if there's one thing I have a sure talent for, it's taking care of someone with medical problems. You think your mother's quite a challenge right now, with this new wrinkle in her health. Well, let me assure you, this is barely anything at all. And she seems quite comfortable with me."

"You're proposing to take this on? As some way of repenting for being resentful of your wife's ill health?"

"Don't be silly, there's no possible way to make amends for that now. Don't you understand? It turns out this is what I *do*."

The front door squeaked open and Lois came into the kitchen with a laundry basket in which she had a little more than laundry. In addition to clothes that smelled of soot and ash, she had a houseplant, a calendar, a bottle of perfume, a shoe, a winter coat and a collection of plastic hangers. Also, she seemed to be wearing at least four sweaters, one over the other. Charlene squinted in confusion. Pink, red, blue, white.

"You have quite a collection there," Jasper said, as if this were completely normal. "A plant for your room, some essentials, some laundry. Let's see if we can throw these sweaters in the wash or if they have to be sent to the dry cleaners."

He took her by the elbow and escorted her down the hall toward her room and the washer and dryer. Momentarily he was back.

"I don't want to mislead you, Charlene. I'm not licensed as a caretaker, but I'm thinking of looking into that. I'm not a rich man by any means—I have only the post office pension, and my social security hasn't even kicked in. So, I'll be happy to look after Lois for a while, to see how it goes, but I'm afraid she'll have to pay me rent. Something to cover the food and utilities. Maybe a couple hundred a month. And bear in mind, if this experiment goes in the direction I hope, I might consider taking in a couple of elders. It just depends.''

"It just depends," she repeated.

He sighed and sought the answer from the ceiling, then looked back at her. "I'm sorry for your misfortune, but when I discovered I could be of some use to your mother, I began to feel needed again. And I won't lie. Happy.

"Let's be clear about this, Charlene. I'm not doing you a kindness. It may seem so, but it's not. Care workers are in business, and while I haven't worked this end of the business before, don't think I don't know it well enough. I had to use every agency in town, hire every kind of helper from nurses to aides, been through it all right up till the hospice people came. I do know what I propose.''

"Yes, I suppose you do," she relented. He had lived next door for thirty years; it was almost certain he wasn't dangerous or larcenous. Besides, what did Lois have to steal but a few old books?

A crash from the back of the house brought Charlene bolting to her feet, while Jasper calmly rose, moved to the pantry for a dustpan and broom and said, "There will be a few adjustments to make, but everything is going to work out just fine. You'll see.''

"Alllllllbbbbberrrrrrt," Lois called from her bedroom.

"I imagine that was the flowerpot. She wanted it on the bed of all places."

"Are you going to tell her your name?" Charlene asked.

"What's the point? The only important thing is that I answer. Coming, Lois," he called. "Go home. Change into some comfortable clothes. Call your daughter and Lois's insurance company. Maybe even consider a little nap—I know you didn't get much rest last night. I'll make us a nice casserole for dinner. I have nearly mastered the art of casserole."

"On the one hand, I feel like I'm only just getting to know you after having you next door for so many years. On the other, you seem like an old friend. Honestly, Jasper, I don't know how I'd manage without you. You're a godsend."

"Well, Charlene, it's going to be nice to have some company for a change."

Stephanie cried for almost two hours. She was just winding it up when her mother called and explained about Peaches moving in with Mr. Conklin. "Stephie, are you all right? Your voice sounds…thick."

Ordinarily Stephanie would have explained that she was crying her heart out because that asshole, Grant, had walked out on her. Then would come the laundry list of everything he'd done wrong. But instead, inexplicably keeping her problems to herself, she said,

"Maybe I'm coming down with a cold or something. Or maybe I'm just exhausted."

"Did you get some sleep?" Charlene asked.

Here was another chance to unload on her mother. "Not very much, no. Did you?"

"I'm afraid not. You didn't go to work today either?" Charlene asked.

"No. I wasn't up to it. I'll take something for a headache and lie down for a nap."

"Well, do. We can't let ourselves fall apart now when Peaches needs us most. And if you're completely sure you're not coming down with something, you can come over to Mr. Conklin's for dinner. But only if you're completely sure. I don't want Peaches getting sick on top of everything else."

"I understand, Mom," she said, her voice grave. "But she is all right?"

"She's a pistol, but all right. I think she had one of her little spells this afternoon. She was wearing four sweaters and one shoe. But she snapped right back to her old self. She's in a lousy mood, but then I guess I would be, too."

"Are you going to get her in to the doctor soon?"

"I made an appointment before leaving the hospital. Day after tomorrow I'm taking her for a consultation and probably some neurological testing. Dennis gave me the name of someone he thinks is good."

"Can I go? Hear what he has to say?"

"Of course. Can they spare you at school?"

"They'll have to spare me...if Peaches needs me.

Tell her I love her, and if I don't think I have a cold or flu, I'll see you guys.''

"Good. If I don't see you later, I'll call.''

After that, Stephanie stopped crying and stood under a steaming hot shower for a long time, till the water started to run cold. When she dried off and stepped out of the shower, she decided she wasn't going to cry anymore. She wasn't going to be a big stupid baby. Everybody but Peaches called her spoiled and immature. Well, not everybody, but three of the most important people in her life.

She stepped out of the steamy bathroom into the master bedroom and critically eyeballed the wreckage. Oh, she knew it was disastrously messy. She wasn't an idiot. It's just that she had no talent for housekeeping, and no aptitude for keeping it so. Then there was the interest factor—zero.

But she began to clean, filling bag after bag with refuse from the bathroom, bedroom, kitchen and living room. In between gathering up clutter, she turned on the dishwasher and began doing laundry. She had done three loads of clothes before she realized that all of Grant's clothes were gone…and that none of the mess on the floors belonged to him. Even with his schedule he was able to keep his laundry in check. She cried a little more. What was the matter with her? Why hadn't she figured out even the most rudimentary of household chores?

In two hours time she had put a substantial dent in the squalor. At first it was all about Grant, about proving she could change and get him back. While she worked, she fantasized about how impressed he'd be, then how sorry and remorseful he'd be that he'd walked out on her and hurt her so. And they would turn over a new leaf…and he would make a few compromises, too.

She stopped cleaning just long enough to call the school district and leave the message that she'd be out the rest of the week, due to a family emergency. Then it was right back to work, hauling the trash out, emptying and reloading the dishwasher, folding and putting away clothes. She ran the vacuum, dusted the furniture, polished the glass and scrubbed the little kitchen floor. The sticky, grimy, brown-tinged kitchen floor. And slowly, remarkably, she became sympathetic toward Grant. *She* became sorry and remorseful. In fact, as she broke her fifth nail digging the crusty buildup out of the corner, she muttered, "I think I'd have left me, too."

And she wasn't done yet. The stove and refrigerator weren't cleaned, the laundry wasn't finished, there was ironing to last through three movie rentals and the bathroom was tidied but she needed special chemicals to handle the scum on the tiles and tub. But the improvement was obvious enough to make her actually feel proud. She was starting to feel that this was not about bringing Grant home, but about proving that she was an adult, capable of adult responsibilities.

She looked at her watch and saw that it was nine o'clock. She had missed dinner with Peaches at Mr. Conklin's house, but that was okay. There was time enough to check out that situation tomorrow. But it wasn't too late to clean the refrigerator and go to the grocery store.

Hours later she was carrying two armfuls of grocery bags up the stairs, bags filled with bread, soup, fresh fruits and vegetables, and a couple of rented movies. Also included was a notebook, she intended to start keeping a journal. Halfway up the stairs to the second-floor apartment she paused, feeling that familiar prickle on the back of her neck. Danger. She felt watched. Stalked.

She slowly turned and scanned the parking lot but saw no one. Ahead of her, just a few steps away, were the apartment doors—hers and the next-door neighbor's. There was no hallway to contend with, no dark entry. And most importantly, no one there. But she stayed on her guard as she balanced the sacks of groceries and opened the door. Once inside, she locked it and put a dining-room chair against it, just for insurance. That done, the nervous prickles went away. She wasn't going to let him scare her.

The message light on the phone was blinking—two new messages. She pressed play.

Charlene: "Well, honey, I guess you didn't feel well. I hope this means the ringer on the phone is turned way down and you're sleeping. Give me a call tomorrow and let me know how you're feeling."

Freddy: "Hey, Buttercup. Just wondered what you were doing, if you were bored or hungry for pizza or lonely, because I'm available for anything. Made a lot of money on the exchange today and just looking for someone to share my good luck with, you know? So,

call me and I can be there in no time. The number
is—''

She hit the delete button and called her mother. He
hadn't said anything scary and she wasn't going to let
him get to her. Instead, she was going to try out
Grant's suggestion, that she think about what kind of
life she wanted. And what it would really take to make
her happy.

Stephanie ate a small salad and microwave burrito
at nearly midnight and fought the urge to call Grant
at work. He'd be getting off at 1:00 a.m. There was a
huge temptation to tell him she'd cleaned the apartment from stem to stern and was turning over a new
leaf—no more slovenly habits, no more whining and
complaining, no more trying to change him. She was
going to change.

Instead she got out her journal and made her first
entry. *Today Grant left me.*

Outside her apartment, in the after-midnight shadows, a figure crept along the windowless side of the
apartment building. He wore dark clothing and stepped
lightly. The front of the sixteen-unit building was lit
by parking-lot and building lights, so he sprang out
onto the sidewalk. With hands in his pockets, he
walked quickly and purposefully down the concrete
toward Stephanie's unit. He took the stairs two at a
time. He pressed himself up against the door as if to
listen, and stayed that way for a long time. Then he
carefully and quietly began to descend the stairs while
pulling his cell phone out of his jacket.

Before his foot could touch that last step he was grabbed by the arm, whirled around and slammed against the building, in the dark, under the staircase. The noise was loud enough to have disturbed the occupants of the ground-floor apartment opposite Stephanie's had they been at home. The cell phone flew from Freddy's hands and he looked up into the enraged eyes of Grant Chamberlain.

Just in size alone, Freddy was doomed. He had been exercising his fingers on the computer keyboard while Grant had been training for the police academy fitness test.

"About to make a call, Freddy?" Grant asked, keeping his voice low so Stephanie wouldn't hear.

"I...gee...I was just in the neighborhood and thought maybe Stephanie was, you know, waiting up for you. Or maybe wanted some company till you got home."

Good, Grant thought. He doesn't know I moved out.

"You get off early?"

"No, Freddy, I've been waiting for you. You've been giving my girl some trouble and she wants you to stop calling her, to stop leaving little notes at the door. You with me, pal?"

With that last, Grant gave him a nice hard slam against the stucco wall.

"Don't know what you're talking about, man!"

"Yes, you do, you little shit. You're a weirdo who slinks around after dark to sneak up on women who've told you to stay away."

"Bull—"

Grant gave him another meaningful shove. "I'm only going to tell you this once, Freddy. Don't mess around with my girl. You hear me? Because you will pay so big if you ever pester her again."

"Look, man, I—"

"There are a few things you don't know about Stephanie, Freddy."

"Let me go, Chamberlain. We both know you outsize me. We both know you can fight and I can't."

"That's a real good place to start, Freddy. I don't necessarily like to fight, but I won't hesitate. In fact, I don't necessarily like to kill, but hey." He shrugged.

"Aw, come on, man," Freddy whined. "I could call the police, you know."

"Yeah, if you could just get your hands on that phone, you could, couldn't you. Why don't I help you a little. Police," he called. "Oh, pol-eeeece."

"Jesus, you're—" Freddy stopped as he heard a car door open. A man stepped out. He wore a long, dark trench coat and he sauntered toward them. There was just no other word for it. He *sauntered*, full of confidence and meanness. Grant continued to press Freddy against the wall until the man came close, then turned him toward the man.

The man flipped open an ID wallet with one hand and a big, dangerous-looking flashlight with the other. He shone the light on the ID badge that, along with his picture and preposterously large badge, said, Jonathan "Jake" Dugan. Freddy stared at it openmouthed.

"Jake Dugan, pleased to meet you."

"Jake Dugan as in Stephanie Dugan," Grant clarified, lest there be any doubt.

"You don't want to be hanging around here anymore, now, do you, son?" Jake asked. And he smiled. It was an evil and terrifying smile that Jake had perfected over the years, one he used to frighten young wannabe felons and teenage brats. He opened his coat to put away his wallet and expose his very big gun.

"Hey, I don't want any trouble. I was just—"

"Save it," Jake said. "She's my little girl and I'm a little protective. You understand? So, just get the hell out of here and don't come around this neighborhood again. As in *ever*. If you meet someone who lives in this complex here, meet someone else. Do we understand each other?"

Grant gave him a shove in the direction of his cell phone. When he bent over to pick it up, Grant put a boot in his backside and sent him on a sprawl. Freddy rolled and sat up, glaring at the two of them with barely concealed rage, but he wasn't about to do anything physical. To keep some dignity he picked up his phone and stood slowly. He turned and walked, but did not hurry away. He walked across the parking lot and down past several buildings before getting into his car, which was parked a very obvious distance from Stephanie's building. The gate opened in response to the car's weight and out he went.

"You still think that was the right thing to do?" Jake asked Grant.

"I guess so. What would you have done?"

He shrugged. "Something like that, I guess." He

tilted his head toward the stairs. "You going up there?"

"I can't, Jake. It doesn't work for us anymore."

"That a fact?"

"But I'll be damned if I'll let some slimy little weasel like Freddy give her any trouble."

"You probably nipped it in the bud, but I'd keep an eye on him."

"I told her I thought she should go to your house. Stay with you a while."

"Yeah, well, there's something going on up there," Jake said, rubbing the back of his neck. "She hasn't even told me you left. And ordinarily she'd be on the phone wailing and complaining and cursing the day you were born."

"You think I should check on her?"

The light from Stephanie's living room clicked off and the apartment darkened. It was 1:00 a.m. Grant looked up the stairs longingly.

"There isn't anything wrong with her. I talked to her around six or so. Asked her how her grandma was and she said she was thinking of going over for dinner with her mom. She was okay. Not cheerful, exactly. Distracted maybe. But okay. Come on. It's late."

Jake walked toward his car, but Grant stood where he was, looking up the stairs.

"You still think it was the right thing? To leave?" Jake asked.

"Yeah," he said. "I had to."

"Well, come on then. Leave."

Grant sighed, kicked at a pebble and went to the car.

Jake looked at him a long time before turning the key. Grant wore a look of misery and desire. It drew his features down long and sullen. "Candy-ass," Jake muttered, and started the car.

While Lois was undergoing some cognitive and memory testing, Charlene and Stephanie were sitting in the doctor's office where they were learning about a world they had never, until now, had to think about.

"The symptoms Lois is experiencing could be traced to any number of causes, including Alzheimer's disease. 'Silent' strokes, patterns of tiny dead cells inside the brain that can cause memory loss, mood swings, confusion, even trouble walking occur in as many as one out of three elderly individuals, people over seventy. Their effects are cumulative over the years and put people at risk for full-blown strokes. Alzheimer's, as you probably already know, is escalating dementia, and, as I explained last night, progresses more slowly the later the onset. Hardening of the arteries causes dementia, as do a number of other conditions and diseases. The preliminary testing we did before Lois left the hospital points us in the direction of silent strokes or Alzheimer's or both."

"And does that explain the mood swings? The swearing and general grouchiness?" asked Charlene.

The doctor, who was quite young, smiled. "Both the condition and the frustration of experiencing these maddening symptoms explains the mood swings and anger. I'm going to prescribe both a blood thinner to prevent further strokes and an antidepressant that doesn't have a strong side effect of lethargy and sleepiness. Plus, there's a new drug that has proven beneficial in slowing the onset of Alzheimer's.''

''But if you're not sure she has—''

''It's a process of elimination. She is, at the very least, a strong candidate. I'd call it pre-Alzheimer's.

''I strongly encourage you to attend a support group for the families and caregivers of Alzheimer's patients where you'll learn not only a great deal about the disease, but how to manage Lois's care. There are some things you should look into right away. Her medications, for example. It's very common for patients with dementia to forget they've taken their drugs and overdose. I recommend a locked medicine drawer or cabinet and someone to give her the pills as prescribed. Companion care would be a serious need, I would think. She doesn't need to be fed and bathed, but she has already had a mishap. Mental stimulation and physical activity both play very big roles in slowing the progression, in giving our patients more quality time. Senior day care and support groups for the patient can be a good way not only to manage time so you can both work and spend quality time with Lois, but also serves as a good diversion for her.'' He took a breath. ''Above all, don't panic. I think Lois still has years at home, with her family.''

''Before a nursing home, you mean?'' Stephanie asked. ''Peaches would die in a nursing home!''

''We advocate keeping our patients at home with

home care for as long as possible. In the best cases, with good nursing help, they never go to nursing homes. But even in the most dedicated families, there is usually a point at which the patient requires more care than the family can manage...and that's what nursing homes are for. Before you let the very idea upset you, let me assure you that we have some very nice facilities...and they're getting better all the time.''

Peaches had always taken care of *them*. Neither Charlene nor Stephanie had ever imagined the day that they would be called upon to take care of her.

Stephanie had not been to school all week, and she still hadn't told anyone that Grant had left their apartment. After three days of scullery work, she was now too ashamed to tell anyone that she had used her days off to try to put her life in order.

Her self-project didn't end with housework, though admittedly she could now see the drastic need. She also went to a bookstore and did a little self-help shopping. She avoided all the ''how to get a man'' books and gravitated instead toward the ''improving the mind and spirit'' category. She needed to feel in control of her destiny, instead of like a passenger on a runaway train. It was time to explore gratitude and positive thinking. She could no longer take everyone's love and devotion for granted without giving anything back.

Her journal entries were growing long and filled with self-examination.

He was right. It took me five hours of backbreaking labor to scrape the first layer of mess out of this apartment, and that was only the beginning. How have I lived like this and not seen it? Is it like the woman who suddenly realizes she's gained a hundred pounds and can't imagine when or how it happened? And to top it off, when he did come home, I did nothing but nag and complain. So he left. What would I have done? So now the new Stephanie Dugan is going to shape up and get a life. Every day I'll keep a chronicle of what I'm doing to become a better person. First, I'm going to tidy up my surroundings, then my attitude, then my personal goals. I'm going to find out what my life is for.

Once she caught up on the chores, she decided to make helping someone a priority. That was a lesson her grandmother had taught her early in life—if you volunteer, you'll feel better. Peaches had put in years of reading to the elderly and infirm and blind. She had taught adults to read even when she had a full-time job and a family to take care of. Well, now Stephanie needed to help someone—and Peaches needed her help. She would dedicate herself to her grandmother and stop focusing so much time and energy on *herself.*

Stephanie was reinventing herself, and she wasn't going to tell a soul. Because it wasn't about getting attention…but about giving it.

Eleven

Pam entered the conference room at 7:00 p.m. to spread out and organize her work on the large conference table. Her arms were laden with current files, calendar, day planner, legal pad, pens, highlighting markers and her bottled water. The office phone was now turned to voice mail, a welcome relief from Charlene's clients. Where to start with this mess? Charlene had twenty-two pending cases and Mike Dodge didn't do divorce or custody. He was in San Francisco at the moment, and he specialized in trusts, wills, probate and taxes associated with inheritance. Since it was routine for Charlene to refer those clients to Mike anyway, there were none in her caseload now.

Twenty-two. That didn't even touch the number of cases that were considered open without pending court dates. It was Pam's job to figure out the routing of the caseload. Charlene was spending lots of time away from the office, taking care of her mother's appointments with doctors. In addition, there was the reconstruction of a charbroiled house and all that went along with it, from refurbishing to redecorating. Charlene needed breathing room.

Pam's days, on the other hand, were getting longer

and she was suffering under a different kind of strain, that of trying to appear rested, well organized and stress free so that Charlene could handle her many personal issues with as little worry as possible.

Pam hadn't heard a word about the wedding. She supposed it had been pushed back till a more manageable time, but she didn't dare ask.

She shook her head in bemusement when she picked up a file. The one case Charlene was passionate about keeping up with was the pro bono for Meredith Jersynski...and this one was a dog. A loser. Not only that, but she paid Maxie out of personal funds, and Maxie was a high-priced investigator. The relationship Charlene had with Jake was some strange inseparable bond that exceeded their common parenthood to Stephanie. The only one who seemed not to know this was Charlene. Pam wondered how Dennis coped with that.

She reviewed folder after folder, making notes and lists and changes, stacking up the finished work as she went, checking off files as she completed each review.

Schedule court date for Patricia Lombardi custody hearing
Reschedule Samuelson arbitration
Separation agreement for Larsens—Assoc.
Adoption final—Cardens
Intake for divorce—Janice Timmons

Timmons? The name took her breath away for the moment. She flipped through the file and read the suspicious single page. It was only Janice Timmons's intake information—address, phone, date of birth, date of marriage. Pam had not been aware of this. The appointment had obviously been set up by the appointment secretary before Charlene's mother had been hospitalized. Janice was a twenty-something-year-old court reporter in the Superior Court. She had married her college sweetheart just three years ago in a storybook wedding they had all attended. When they toasted the bride and groom, there wasn't a guest present who didn't think this love affair would stretch into old age. They seemed made for each other; they were positively enraptured.

And here she was, divorcing. It was all so fragile.

Such was the life of family law. There were blissful moments, like successful adoptions, the reuniting of families, the lawful return of property. There were times that justice, however bittersweet, was finally reached, like winning a wrongful-death civil suit or getting a handicapped child into the right kind of educational facility. But there were terrible disappointments here as well, like Janice and Bill Timmons, so in love, and parting company after only three years. How did things like this happen? Pam had asked herself many times. And why, knowing how tenuous even the most solid relationships are, do we long for a mate?

Ray knocked at the conference door and stuck his head in. "Late night?"

She put down her pen and wished, for the millionth time, that her heart wouldn't pick up speed when she saw him. But wish it or not, it hammered in her breast. "There's a lot going on," she said.

"It's almost nine, Ms. London. Have you eaten?"

She looked at her watch in shock. A few lists, a couple of schedule changes, and almost two hours had gone by. "Ah…um…haven't even thought about food."

"Well," he said, entering the room despite the fact that she hadn't invited him. He had a take-out bag. "I brought you something anyway. Vegetables and rice. A little chicken. Tea. You have to keep your strength up."

"I don't have time to eat, Ray," she said, tearing her eyes away from his face and picking up the pen again. She looked down and pointed the pen at the legal pad, but he lifted her hand off the paper.

"Don't be so pigheaded. Have something to eat," he said. "I'm on my break."

She dropped the pen and leaned back in her chair, sighing in resignation. She was starving, and for more than mere food. "I'm never going to get done," she complained.

He began to empty the bag of small cartons, cups and plates. "What's up with Ms. Dugan? Jake said something about a fire?"

"You know Jake?"

"Just sort of. I know the boyfriend, Grant Chamberlain."

"You do?" she asked, stunned. Sometimes the world was shockingly small.

"Yup. I took a couple of classes with him at Sac

State. I met Jake at JT's—the bar where Grant works. And then, of course, Jake was just here…when was that? A week or so ago? With a woman?''

''Wow. It's always amazing how many connections there are in a town this size.'' She would have to run for her life. Now it was settled. Even if she had momentarily toyed with the idea of toying with— She couldn't let her mind wander in that direction. Whatever she'd been thinking, she'd stop it at once.

He pushed a plastic plate and fork at her and she moved aside her tablet, calendar and files. Despite all her good sense, things started to happen to her vision. When he lifted his fork to his lips and slowly drew the chicken and vegetables into his mouth, she saw the top button of his uniform shirt unbutton itself. Then two more buttons opened, then another. The ripples in his tanned, hairless chest sent a rush through her that made her catch her breath.

''You okay, Ms. London?'' he asked.

No, I'm delusional from overwork. She looked down at her plate and muttered, ''Uh-huh. Yeah.'' She took a few bites with her eyes closed. In her mind she was seeing his handwritten notes, left at different times during the day when she might be away from her desk. It was odd that she never saw him hanging around, but she found plenty of messages just the same. *You look beautiful today* and *Just tell me when.* Boyish, silly messages.

She looked up as she realized he had left two such notes on her desk that very day, one before lunch and one after. And it was now 9:00 p.m. She also noticed his shirt was completely buttoned, and blinked in surprise. "Ray, what are you doing here this late? Didn't you work a day shift today?"

"Yep."

"Shouldn't you be off now?"

"Yep. But you're still here, just like you've been here late every night this week. No breaks for supper, and far as I can tell, you aren't having anything brought in to eat."

"So?"

"So? So I thought maybe you'd appreciate this."

She laid down her fork. "It's very nice of you, but...I'm concerned by all this attention, Ray. I think you're making too much of—"

"Too much? Not enough, I think." He smiled. "Some women like that sort of thing," he said. "And so do you, though for some reason you try to hide it."

"I'm too old for you!"

"Fine, then just eat and I'll go."

She became silent. Was that what she wanted? For him to go? And not come back? It was an awful thought, but she also had to think about what the partners would say if they found a middle-aged executive assistant fiddling around with a twenty-five-year-old security guard. It could cost her her job.

For now she would just eat the dinner, thank him and send him on his way with a calmly delivered explanation of the facts of life. She lifted her fork. "This is delicious. Thank you."

"You're welcome. The Plum Tree. Best Chinese in town. Right down the street."

"Listen, Ray, I'm a little tense," she said.

"Seems like maybe you've been under a lot of pressure."

"A lot, yes. And let me be honest, I don't really know how to handle your...your...pursuit."

"That so?" he asked. "I would've thought you've had a lot of practice."

"At—?"

"Handling pursuits. Men must pester you all the time."

"Me?" Pam asked. "No! I'm hardly ever asked out on a date."

"Impossible," he said. "As smart and pretty and healthy and positive as you are?"

"Wouldn't you have a lot more in common with a younger woman?" she asked him.

"Well, Ms. London, I'll let you know if our relationship ever gets beyond me leaving you notes and flowers, and walking you to your car. Okay?"

It's never going to get beyond that, she thought, but for some reason she couldn't say it. She watched him eat, his fork carrying small bites back and forth from his paper plate to his mouth, sensually chewing, slowly swallowing. She was growing hypnotized by the slow, sexy movement. He locked onto her eyes, held her, and delivered a mouthful to her on his fork. She opened her mouth for him and closed her lips around his fork.

It began to happen to her again; the delusion returned. His shirt unbuttoned itself, his chest was revealed, his slow breathing expanded his pecs and strained his shirt—and she was lost.

She didn't know what was happening to her. She was tired, that was one thing. And although she had accepted her state of singleness, just having this sexy young man around was underscoring her aloneness, leaving her feeling hungry for attention, craving affection. And now, as they sat across from each other at the conference-room table, eating Chinese, she was hallucinating.

"I just want to get to know you," she heard him say, but his voice was distant and faint. "We could just see what happens."

His hand reached across the table, touched hers, and she thought she heard, "You know it would be good. We'd be so good."

She was doomed. Her eyes drifted closed and she could feel his presence coming closer. His breath was hot on her neck and she felt his lips sear her flesh. "Let yourself, Pam. Let yourself go. You know we'd be so, so good...."

Pam had the feeling she was floating into his arms, that he pulled her to her feet, embraced her around the waist and gently lowered her to the boardroom table. He pulled apart her silk blouse so that her bare chest pressed against his. Never before had she known such longing. She sighed as she strained toward him and—

"Ms. London?"

Her eyes popped open and the fully clothed, politely patient and deadly handsome Ray tilted his head inquisitively as he studied her.

"I'm not the hottest ticket in town, but I've never had a girl nod off on me before."

Her cheeks flamed a scarlet so hot she thought she might pass out, as embarrassed as if he had actually seen the fantasy that had overtaken her. She was no longer sure what he might have said, what she had dreamt. Had she moaned? Writhed? Said his name?

She put down her fork. "Ray, this little flirtation has been fun, but there's something you'd better get straight. I'm not going to lose my job over you. Got that? I've...really...got to...get going." She pushed her plate toward him, gathered up and stacked the client folders. She virtually flew into her office, tossed the folders into the file drawer without putting each one in its place and locked it up. Forgoing all the closing-up rituals she typically engaged in, she simply grabbed her purse and ran. *Ran.* With no time to wait for the elevator, she took the stairs. She raced past the ground-floor security desk and was out the door and behind the wheel of her car in a flash.

She looked back at the office building in time to see Ray appear in the doorway, looking toward her, unmistakable disappointment drawing down his features. Well, there, she thought. He got the message. She started the ignition and drove too fast out of the parking lot.

And she thought, I am so screwed up.

Charlene rarely took personal days. An admitted workaholic, she usually had to get out of town to keep herself from going into the office on her rare vacations. She was a little worse than driven—she was compulsive. She moved at a brisk and efficient pace and was capable of doing several things at once. The hardest part about being needed to help while Lois kept appointments with doctors and reconstruction companies was the time spent *waiting*. It was tempting to use that time working in one fashion or another—on the cell phone or laptop—but that made Lois feel like a burden. "I know you're too busy for this, Charlene. Go to your office and I'll get Mr. Conklin to take me on all these errands. Or I can always get a cab."

"Don't be silly," she said. "Besides, I want to hear what the doctors have to say. Having a cell phone and laptop computer just makes the whole process of being away from the office that much easier." But she resisted as much as she could, forcing herself to leaf through a magazine or read a few pages from a book.

There had been lots of tests to determine the cause of Lois's symptoms, everything from blood work to imaging to neurological and psychological tests. She did everything from laying still in a long, skinny, clanking MRI tube to repeating words from memory and getting scores. It was tedious and often discouraging. Lois knew she wasn't scoring as well as she might have even two years ago. "I feel like I'm working with half a brain," she complained. "It's maddening."

Wedged into the tight schedule of medical professionals was the matter of the burned house. Reconstruction companies sent out representatives, one after the other, to bid on the job of repairing the kitchen.

Not only was it far more expensive than she had guessed it would be, it was going to take much longer. And, of course, the insurance company had a million excuses why they wouldn't be responsible for the full amount. "I'm a lawyer," she had said to the adjuster. "Are you sure you want to screw around with me?" To which he had answered, "It will be our absolute honor, ma'am."

There was no possible way Lois could have done this alone. In fact, Charlene couldn't do it alone. She called Dennis for every medical question, and Jake or Jasper for every building and reconstruction question.

Having Lois staying at Jasper's house was perfect. As one doctor told Charlene, "Jasper might be more than willing to look after your mother and give her lodging, but he can't take the place of a close family member. It's very important to Lois that you're nearby and involved. She needs to be close to the familiar." Charlene agreed, but at the end of every day filled with appointments, phone calls and as much time at her office as she could squeeze in, there was still dinner at Jasper's with her mother and often Stephanie, with Dennis or even Jake dropping by. After Lois was settled for the night, Charlene made the long ride home exhausted. Five a.m. with her usual exercises and low-fat breakfast came mighty early. She was so busy making sure everyone was getting what they needed, she hadn't taken her own emotional temperature in weeks.

Together she and Lois chose the company that seemed best suited for the job, and by the questions Lois asked the young representative, one would never know she was showing the early symptoms of dementia. That's what made this all so hard. She not only had lucid moments, she had lucid hours and even the occasional day without doing or saying anything entirely off the wall.

Then came the day Lois had to go to the library where she read books onto tape as a volunteer. "You could go to work for a few hours if you want to," she invited Charlene. "You could just drop me off and come back later."

It was very tempting, Charlene thought. Every day the work that accumulated on her desk grew taller. But she didn't want Lois to be "left." "Are you sure *you* want to do this?" she asked her mother.

"I'm not going to give up my volunteer work until I absolutely have to."

"Or you could ask Jasper. I'm sure he'd be delighted."

"I could, but I've never liked asking."

That was Lois in a nutshell, and one of the things that was going to make taking care of her so difficult. She didn't like to ask for help. And, if the help was going to act put out about it, she would feel terrible. "Let me go with you, Mom," Charlene said. And in thinking about it, she grew happier about the idea. The work would always be there. "It will be like revisiting my youth. It's been years and years since I've gone to the library just to poke around, play with books, find something to read that's completely entertaining."

"I'm surprised you can stomach the idea, after being held hostage in a library all your childhood, then spending so many years in law libraries.''

''The library has always been a comfort, like a second home.''

In jeans, tennis shoes and a T-shirt, as opposed to her usual lawyerly suit, Charlene looked like a young girl. And like a girl, she sat on the floor in the adult fiction section, the D-F aisle strictly by happenstance, and paged through novel after novel, just visiting the books. The construction of the ''to be read'' stack had always been her favorite part about reading when she was a preteen. She liked to play with her books in much the same way a cat plays with a lizard before she bites off its head. The covers were the first to catch her eye, then the title. She'd then read the jacket blurb, but the most important factor was the first page or two.

While she consciously looked through books and Peaches sat in an enclosed room behind the periodicals reading into a tape recorder, Charlene's subconscious was remembering her childhood by the sounds and smells of the library. *We didn't do too badly, Peaches and me,* she thought. In the first apartment building they had lived in, Lois had been the only woman with a child whose husband was seldom around. But the neighbors were friendly and supportive. In fact, there were lots of them who would have kept Charlene after school, but that wasn't what Lois had wanted to do. ''She'll get her homework done at the library, plus read a little extra. It'll be good for her.'' And now that Charlene remembered it, the neighbors also weren't judgmental about this man who wandered through their lives every now and then.

Then there was the purchase of that new little house in Fair Oaks, surrounded by trees and rolling hills, in the shadow of the mountains. What an achievement that was. Now, having worked as she had, raising a daughter of her own, Charlene finally realized what it must have taken for her librarian mom to save enough money to get into that house.

When they'd moved, they'd only had enough furniture for one and a half rooms—the bedroom set they shared and a couch, small chair, coffee table, lamp and two TV trays. Again Lois saved, pinching those pennies. The very first purchase of furniture she indulged for the new house was white Provençal-style bedroom furniture for Charlene, so that she could have her own space, her own grown-up bed.

She had three books in a stack and was staring at the first page of the first, not really absorbing the words. Instead she was thinking, *So, my father was a real screwup, but a fun guy. So he wasn't real reliable, but then it turns out we never relied on him anyway. So, just how messed up am I because of my father? Probably about as much as I want to be.*

"Mrs. Dugan?"

She looked up into the frowning face of Elizabeth Nelson, the children's librarian. "We need you. Could you please come and do something about your mother."

"Oh God," she said, jumping to her feet. She ran, streaking through the library at breakneck speed, back through periodicals, where she'd left Lois. The door was ajar and a young man was looking inside. Charlene pushed him aside, maybe roughly, but then she was stopped by what she saw. Her mother stood in the corner of the small study cubicle, slowly and rhythmically banging her head into the wall. Charlene was momentarily paralyzed. Then she recovered, took three long steps into the room and grasped her mother's shoulders. "Mom?" she said, stopping her and turning her around.

Long streaks of tears coursed down Lois's cheeks. She bit her lip and shook her head, a deep and horrible sadness so penetrating Charlene felt it in the pit of her stomach. "Mom, what is it?"

"Oh, Charlene," she said shakily, her voice a hoarse whisper. "I don't know the *words*."

"Oh, Mom," she said, pulling her close and holding her. "Mom, it's okay. You'll know them later today. You'll see."

Lois sobbed into Charlene's shoulder. "Do you know what it means if I can't read? Do you know what that means?"

"Mom, you're okay. It's a hiccup. The words will come back later today. Or tonight. They're not gone forever."

"How do you know?" she asked.

Charlene brushed the tears from her mother's cheeks, first the right side, then the left. "Because when they're gone forever," she whispered, "you won't even know they're missing."

For a moment Lois just looked at her in confusion,

and slowly she began to recover. First the terrible grief left her eyes, then her lips relaxed. Then, remarkably, a half smile played on her lips and she let go a little huff of laughter. "Oh, what a comfort *you* are."

Charlene smiled back. "Let's go home, okay?"

"Might as well. I'm done reading for the moment."

"I'll bring the book," Charlene said. "I'll mark the page and you can look at it later."

"Eternal optimist."

Lois walked out of the room ahead of Charlene. People had gathered outside, waiting to see who the kook was who had been banging her head. Lois lifted her chin and met their eyes with challenge, until one by one they turned away. It made Charlene feel, for the moment, so very proud of her mother's courage.

Charlene doubled back a couple of steps, popped the tape out of the still-running recorder and slipped it into her pocket.

It was the situation at the library that cautioned Charlene enough to suggest to her mother that they have some legal documentation in place before some unfortunate incident made it necessary. "Leave it to a lawyer," Lois said.

"A power of attorney isn't really quite enough," she explained. "That allows you and someone you appoint to take care of certain legal matters, like the sale of a house or the purchase of a vehicle. But if you appoint a conservator, you don't have to worry about legal and financial responsibilities. And if, in a forgetful moment, you make some sort of mistake—

like give your life savings to a charity—you'd be protected. Your conservator, your legal guardian, could get it back."

"I'm not going downhill that fast, you know," Lois pointed out.

"Of course not, and I can understand why a woman as independent as you wouldn't want to give up control. But what if a workman needs to be paid and you're a little...how should I put it—"

"In another mental zone?" Lois supplied.

"Okay," Charlene agreed slowly.

"I'm not ready," she said. "No legal papers yet. Workmen can wait. God knows they've kept me waiting often enough in my life."

"Okay, there are two ways to do this. We can go to some family court judge together, fully understanding what's happening and making legal preparations before it's necessary. Or, I can go to court later and declare you incompetent. The latter is usually very uncomfortable for everyone."

"Lois, as difficult as it is to think about, I think it's very prudent. Caution is the watchword here," Jasper said.

"Then I'll make you my guardian," she said to Jasper.

"Mother! Now that hurts!"

"Well, you and I don't agree on anything, especially how and where I should spend my time or money!"

"I'm not going to be anyone's guardian," Jasper

said. "How about another family member? What about Stephanie?"

"Well now," they both said. Both women erroneously thought Stephanie would be easy to control. Neither of them had been acquainted with the new, improved Stephanie.

She called Stephanie to ask if she could sneak away from school to meet them at the courthouse.

"I know this is short notice, but we need to see a judge in family court about a legal guardian for Peaches, in case she becomes incompetent. You know, for medical and financial decisions. A judge I'm close to, Judge Kemp, is going to squeeze a little time out of his schedule to meet with us. Peaches won't let me be the responsible party...."

Stephanie giggled. "Bet that really pissed you off," she said.

"She's willing to let it be you. And I trust that you'll absolutely listen to my advice on any of these matters, especially with your grandmother's health and income at stake."

"Whoa," she said almost reverently. "Me?"

"Yes, you. Did you hear what I said? About listening to me?"

"Listen? Of course. I always *listen.*"

"And pay attention," Charlene stressed.

"This must be sheer hell for a control freak like you," Stephanie suggested.

"You are the serpent's tooth, for sure."

So they were to meet outside of Judge Kemp's office, where Stephanie would, with a bit too much glee, agree to be Peaches's working brain. Charlene decided it was rather fitting as they'd always sided against her anyway, made her their common enemy on issues like bedtime, curfews, dating and chores. Grandmothers and granddaughters, bonded for life by the simple tension between mothers and daughters. *I can't wait until she has a child,* Charlene found herself thinking. *I'm going to quit work, take over its life, spoil it rotten and overturn all her decisions.*

This was a big moment, and despite the attempt at levity surrounding Peaches's choice of conservator, they all knew there was no going back from this. Not only would this remain in effect till the last breath Peaches took, but she was not going to get better. The best they could hope for was that she wouldn't get worse quickly.

Here they were, the three women of this family, charging out of denial on bulls and into the truth. Together.

Twelve

Charlene was very grateful to Stephanie for offering to take Lois out to lunch and then home. She knew that Pam was holding the flood of legal work at bay, trying to make it seem manageable, with all the tenacity of the Little Dutch Boy. She could see the stress building behind her assistant's eyes. But now that Lois had been thoroughly examined and was on medication, and the reconstruction in her house was well under way, Charlene could spend a little more time in the office and a little less time running errands.

There was no mistaking the relief that flooded Pam's features when she walked in. "Hello!" she beamed. "How are we doing today?"

"Pretty good, thanks," Charlene said, and accepted a frighteningly thick stack of messages.

"It's not as bad as it looks," Pam said. "Five of them are from Dennis."

"Dennis? Well, why didn't—" She stopped mid-sentence and reached into her purse for her phone. She took it out, looked at it and turned it on, feeling ridiculous. "I think I'm the one getting Alzheimer's. I was in a meeting, turned off the phone and forgot to turn it back on." On the small face it said, "5 missed calls." "I wonder what's so urgent. Will you see if you can get him on the line for me?"

"You bet."

The minute Charlene was inside her office, she was shaken by a feeling of being *home*. This week of so many family chores was not done begrudgingly. She was devoted to Lois, but it was here that she thrived and did the life's work that made her soar, that mattered most to her. It was here that she prepared to win battles for people who could not win them for themselves. For women and children who had no other champion; for families who couldn't resolve painful issues for themselves. For couples who couldn't keep it together anymore, and the kids, who, without some dignified conclusion to their parents' crisis, would flounder into confused adults who would only repeat the cycle.

This was the work that defined her.

Her intercom buzzed. Pam said, "I have Dennis on the line, and Maxie just called to say she's on her way in." She felt her pulse pick up speed as she wondered what Maxie had learned. It had been weeks of getting nowhere on the Jersynski custody matter. Then her eyes caught the stack of folders in her in box—all open cases. With that distraction, she took Dennis's call. "Hi, Dennis. I'm sorry, I was in a meeting and forgot to turn my phone back on. I'm forgetting a lot of things lately."

"You have a lot on your mind. Can you get away for lunch?"

"I can't. I just walked into the office, and if you

could see the relief on Pam's face, you wouldn't leave her either.''

"I haven't seen you in days...."

"I've been so busy...."

"The only time I saw you last week was at Jasper's house, with Peaches and Stephanie. We haven't had a private conversation in... Jesus, Charlene, I don't even know how long."

"What can I say? It's not deliberate. And things should lighten up soon, now that we have Peaches stabilized and the work on her house has begun." Charlene heard Maxie's voice in the outer office, but she couldn't hear what she was saying. Then her voice was joined by another familiar one, that of Jake. And Dennis was saying, "...really need to talk, Charlene. It's important."

"I know, Dennis, I know. The wedding. And we will, I promise. But right now there are people waiting to see me, a pile of work that could sink a battleship on my desk, and I'm simply exhausted. Can I call you back?"

"This is very important."

"I agree. And the very second I get a minute to call my own, it's yours. All right?"

Her intercom was buzzing and she said, "Send them in." Suddenly Dennis was no longer on the line and she wasn't sure whether or not she'd even said good-bye. But the thought went away quickly as she went back into action, ready to champion a young woman trying to hang on to her kids.

The personal importance of this case to Charlene

was evident purely in her acceptance of this impromptu meeting. Ordinarily she was too busy to condone this sort of interruption, and too well organized to suffer the consequences of a schedule breach. But all of her organizational skills were becoming lax along with her memory, right at the time she needed both the most.

"I trust this means you have some earthshaking information," she said to Maxie, giving Jake an informal nod of hello. "Have the two of you met?"

"We run into each other from time to time," Maxie said.

"We tried to arrest Maxie here for solicitation once, as a matter of fact. Turns out she was working all right…but not as a hooker. I'll have to tell you about it sometime."

"It was one of my highlights," Maxie said without humor. She took a seat and addressed Charlene. "What I have is a lot of very interesting innuendo and no conclusion."

"Shoot."

"Okay, first of all, there's nothing on the ex-husband. He's clean. You know I have no respect for a man who abandons a child and its mother. However, it appears that's the only truly bad thing he's done. He's not a perv, a felon or an abuser. And here's another thing you don't hear from me very often. If he slugged Meredith in the face, I bet she provoked the hell out of him."

Jake whistled. Both women glared at him and he looked over his shoulder as though he couldn't possibly be the guilty party. He decided it was time to take a seat and try to be quiet.

"I'm not saying I'd blame her. She'd have to be mad as hell at the guy, knocking her up at sixteen, abandoning her to the streets of Sacramento with a baby, then coming back around a dozen years later to pick up the kid. I'd have a few choice words for him if I were her. He'd wanna belt me after a few minutes, too.

"Now, here's what I know about the custody thing. The kid he has with the second wife is nine, and she didn't just have a sick day from school—she has cancer. Childhood leukemia. She's been very, very sick and spends a lot of time in Texas at a big cancer hospital called M.D. Anderson. Rick Jersynski said he just wanted his daughters to meet. He said he would have waited, but the sick child said it was her wish to have a sister. And guess what? Rick came up with one.

"It was the mother, the second wife, who hired an investigator to get the goods on Meredith and convince her husband that they would be a better family for the girl. Whether or not that's the case, it's the mother I worry about and I'll tell you why. I found out from a source in the hospital that they've failed to find a match for a bone marrow transplant in the family. I think the mother has ulterior motives."

"And not the father?"

Maxie shrugged. "This illness has really broken him down. He seems oblivious. The mother, however, seems angry. Motivated. She's the one who hired the detective, called the lawyer."

"I talked to the lawyer," Charlene said. "He's sticking to the case on its merits. Which is exactly what I would do. Did you get any information about the shooting?"

"Nothing," Maxie said. "Jake?"

"We're not pursuing it. I want to, but unless we have something substantial to take to the prosecutor, there isn't even a felony here."

"Someone tried to kill her, right?"

He shrugged. "Someone fired a gun inside city limits, but there doesn't seem to be a witness who saw a gun pointed at Merrie's car. In short, we can't say for sure that any attempt was made on her life."

"Well, for Chr—"

"I have a question," Maxie said. "Has anyone talked to the daughter of Meredith and Rick?"

"About…?"

"About whether she'd like to meet her dying sister?"

Charlene didn't answer right away. Finally she said, "Given the fact that he wants to take her away from her mother, there seems to be substantial risk in putting her in that household, even for a visit."

"What if all he wants is a bone marrow transplant?" Again Maxie was answered with silence. "I'd be real careful about giving up vital organs, but I hear a bone marrow transplant isn't that big of a deal. You have sore hips for a few days…up to a week. But more to the point, if that's all they want from the girl, this could all be over with a simple blood test. Apparently they've had zero luck with matches."

"You know," Charlene said, "there are ways to do that without even exposing Meredith's daughter. We could get a blood sample from the cancer patient and take it to the potential donor, instead of the reverse. Meredith could learn whether her daughter is a match. We wouldn't even have to tell Rick Jersynski. If they sued in civil action for the results, they'd be exposing their motivation." Charlene smiled impishly. "Wanting to give your daughter a good home is one thing. Wanting to give your daughter a good home in exchange for her cells is quite another."

"Well, that's all I got," Maxie said, standing. "Finding cheating husbands and laundered money is a whole lot easier than this stuff."

"Thanks, Maxie. You're brilliant."

She winked and dazzled them both with her smile. "Yeah, I know."

When Maxie was well out of earshot, Jake whistled. "She expensive?"

"Does she look expensive?" Charlene asked.

"I'll split it with you," Jake offered.

"My treat," Charlene said. "If it turns out Jersynski just wanted his oldest daughter's bone marrow, he's going to pay for the whole case. And I probably won't even have to ask twice."

Stephanie drove Peaches back to Fair Oaks. It was not difficult to see that the older woman was sulky and depleted. "You know what I learned today?" Peaches asked. "There's nothing quite so exhausting as signing a paper that says you're okay about not making any more of your own decisions.''

"It's not really like that, Peaches. I mean, I certainly don't intend to step in and make decisions for you. I can hardly make decisions for myself."

Peaches patted her granddaughter's thigh as they drove. "I think you do a fine job. I'm very proud of you. And this—taking on this responsibility. It's very grown-up of you."

That's my grandma, she thought. Never plays the pity card. "It's just a formality, Peaches. It's there if we need it, and we don't need it right now."

"Still…"

"Where would you like to have lunch? What would taste good?"

"I'm not very hungry…."

"Let's stop for some caffeine. Some perk-up. Maybe a muffin. How about it? My treat?"

"Only if we can put sugar and chocolate in with the caffeine."

"Hey, I didn't know it came any other way."

The weather was perfect; a lush and velvety springtime in northern California. It would soon be May. Summer was nearly upon them. They sat at a small table under a tree; Stephanie cleaned the bird droppings off their chairs first. "Looks like this could be a little war zone."

"I'd rather deal with a little bird-shit than be stuck inside," Peaches said, drawing a sharp laugh out of her granddaughter. There was no mistaking it; Peaches's language was getting a little more daring.

"You know, it's not that I don't trust your mother," she continued.

"I know."

"She's very smart. About these things especially."

"I know, Peaches."

"You should listen to her, you know. When it's time for decisions about things, ask your mother. Listen to what she says."

"Why didn't you just let her be the guardian?" Stephanie asked.

"Because she would try to be perfect and she would drive me crazy. She needs less to control, not more. I did her a favor."

"Peaches, do you like it at Mr. Conklin's house?"

"It's okay. It's fine for now."

"You wouldn't consider staying there for a long period of time, would you?"

She sighed deeply, her knuckled hands wrapped around her coffee mug. "If I have to stay somewhere and have a round-the-clock keeper, I'd rather it be one of those assisted-living places. I'm doing this more for him than me. I recognize I need the guest room, but..."

"He's talking about going professional," Stephanie said. "Taking in a few people who need companion care. He has two more bedrooms in that little house."

"I know. Sheesh. What some people do."

"Kind of bizarre."

"Some people are needy. Some people like to be needed."

"Peaches…Grant and me…we're not together anymore."

Peaches snapped to attention, and stopped her reaction short of a gasp. She was speechless.

"It happened a couple of weeks ago, right after the fire. We'd been doing a lot of fighting. About everything. It wasn't working out. So, he left." She shrugged and her eyes got a little glassy, but she didn't break down. "It's been very hard."

Peaches squeezed her granddaughter's hand. "Is that why you haven't been yourself lately? Why you've been upset?"

"Partly."

"You've been so quiet, so introspective. I thought it was all this business with me, with my illness."

"I've had a lot of thinking to do. I've been thinking about you, too, but I honestly haven't been too worried, because I know we're going to work things out. I know you're going to be okay."

"Oh, Stephie, you didn't have to go through this alone. You could have come to your mom and me. We have such a lot of experience with men leaving."

"Well, that's just it. Two generations of being shafted by guys. Somehow I don't think any advice you could give me would…would…"

"Don't say any more, Stephie. Bad track record, I know. And you don't want to be the third in a series."

"Peaches, he didn't leave me because he's a bum. He left me because I'm *impossible*."

"That's not true, honey. That's just not—"

"It *is*. Peaches, I can't believe what he had to put up with! I have so much growing up to do."

"We all do, honey. We all do."

"Peaches, have you thought about moving back into your house after the work is finished?"

"I'd like to do that, but I don't kid myself. It may not be possible. I did almost burn the place down."

"Because I've been thinking, that maybe we should be roommates. We could stay together in your house until…well, just until."

It was all Peaches could do to keep from climbing over the little patio table and embracing her granddaughter. "Oh, honey. I don't know if you really want to take that on."

"Take *that* on. Do you mean you?" Stephanie said, adding a laugh. "But I love you!"

"It's more than me, it's me and a disease. A progressive disease. And not only that," she said, giving that hand another squeeze. "This thing with Grant may yet be worked out."

"Well, I'm not going to worry about that right now," Stephanie said. "Instead, I'm going to worry about getting my life together. Prioritizing. Working on the things that matter to me most, and doing the things that are going to have meaning for the rest of my life. Believe me, a Saturday night with Grant at home instead of working isn't going to be the most important thing in the end. In the end, I don't want to have wasted a minute with you."

Peaches stared at her granddaughter in wonder.

"My dear child, you're more grown-up than you give yourself credit for."

"Peaches? Let's not tell Mom any of this yet, okay? About Grant, about you and I possibly becoming roommates…"

"Lucky for you I most likely won't remember you ever mentioned it."

"You make bad jokes."

"You'll appreciate that someday, believe me. Oh, Stephanie. Before I forget—" She stopped right there, rolled her eyes and smiled. "I love you. You are the greatest thing my daughter ever did for me."

Charlene stood at her office window and watched the shadows of the setting sun play on the hillsides of the Sierra Nevadas. The afternoon had flown by and she had only put the smallest dent in her work. But she couldn't deny it felt good to concentrate on something other than her mother being sick or whether workmen would show up on time.

In her years as a lawyer she had drawn up hundreds of powers of attorney, settled just as many wills and written quite a few living trusts. Usually the families she served were much more desperate than hers. It was typical for people to realize they needed this kind of help when the central character was already well beyond self-care. She had always said—and Lois had always agreed—there was no reason on earth for them to be less than prepared. After all, they were a very small family, a family of only three women. And they knew how to take care of each other.

But nothing had taken it out of her like drawing up a conservatorship for her own energetic, independent mother, even though it was for her safety.

There were other associated feelings that confused her and made her feel guilty. For example, Lois needed her and she *really* wanted to be there for her mother, but *there* wasn't where she wanted to be. She wanted to be *here!* This was where she felt she could perform at the peak of her abilities, and she was hooked on that performance high.

There were two sharp taps at her office door just before it opened. Jake stood in the frame. "Charlie, I have some news." He stepped closer. "Hey, hey, hey, what's this I see?" For a second she didn't realize what he was talking about until he reached toward her face with the back of his hand. She turned quickly away and brushed at her cheeks, then retreated behind her desk. She was getting very uncomfortable with the frequency that this was happening.

She turned back to Jake. "Stephanie, Peaches and I were at Judge Kemp's office to get his signature and seal on some important papers today. Stephanie is now my mother's legal guardian. Just to be ready, you know? Because she's going to need us to…you know…think and remember for her."

"So soon? Charlie, didn't she just start showing symptoms of—"

"She almost burned her house down!"

"Hey," he said, palms toward her, holding her off. "I just asked. If you all agree to the arrangement, who am I to question it?"

She took a breath. "Sorry. It was harder than I thought. There have been so many confusing issues lately. Leaves me wondering, you know?"

"Wondering what?" he asked hopefully.

"Oh, never mind.... Suffice it to say, there seem to be a lot of issues right now."

He was quiet, looking down at the tops of his shoes. She wasn't the only one with issues. He hadn't spent so much time thinking about a woman since Charlie left him over twenty-five years ago. It was like falling in love with her all over again, even though he'd loved her all along. Had she at least decided it would be a disaster to marry Dennis?

He took strange hope in her tears. She was so good at compartmentalizing, something men usually managed better than women. In their relationship it was Charlie who could box things up in neatly tied little packages, out of sight and mind, while Jake stewed. He looked up at her, his eyes soft. "Yeah. A lot of issues, huh?"

"I admit to being a little emotionally unstable right now, okay?"

He laughed. "Really?"

"Try not to be a pain in the ass, Jake. My life is a wreck."

"Well, maybe this will make it easier. I talked to Merrie this afternoon. The kid has such a soft heart. She's going to get in touch with her ex and ask him about his kid's leukemia."

"I wonder about this guy, Jake. Do you think if the situation were reversed, he'd help Meredith?"

"I don't know, Charlie. But I do know this. It isn't the stuff you get that makes you the better person, it's the stuff you give."

"Oh, Jake," she said, her eyes welling up with tears anew.

"Hey, Charlie, you're nothing but mush today." He pulled her into his embrace, giving her a comforting hug, patting her back.

The sound of a man clearing his throat drew her misting eyes to the doorway, where she saw Dennis, standing there in his work scrubs. She knew this didn't look good. All she'd done lately was make excuses as to why she couldn't see him, and now he had made a surprise appearance at the worst possible moment. She extracted herself from Jake's arms and glared at him as she felt him hang on a moment longer than he should have.

"Am I...interrupting anything?" Dennis asked, a sour note to the question.

"Oh, Dennis, of course not! Come in, sweetheart."

Sweetheart? both men thought.

Dennis entered the room just as Charlene began to walk across to welcome him with the appropriate kiss. "We finally cleared that custody case off the books—and it all happened to revolve around a little girl who's dying." She pecked his cheek and sniffed. "I don't know what's the matter with me. I'm a basket case. I'll cry over every little thing these days."

She looked at Jake, but held Dennis's hand. "Tell Meredith to call me if she has any problems. Mean-

while, I'll call the lawyer and tell him he'd better warn his clients to behave, for the sake of the little girls.''

"Thanks, Charlie. Do your stuff," Jake said. He made to leave, but as he was to pass Dennis he felt short of stature. And like a simple laborer in his wrinkled shirt, worn leather jacket, while Dennis wore scrubs. Dennis, who had *two* degrees. And he acted smart about everything, while Jake knew one thing: police work. That he was good at it didn't really cut any grass right now because even though he'd had the good woman in his bed just recently, Dennis of the two degrees seemed to have her *concern.* "How you doin', Denny?" he asked. He loved the way Dennis blinked in irritation when Jake called him that.

"Good, Jake. Yourself?"

"Never been better, pal."

And out the door he went, feeling like a loser, but acting like a cocky guy who couldn't care less. It was not an easy act.

When Jake was gone, Charlene fell against Dennis's chest, and his arms automatically held her, gave comfort. She mumbled against him, "Can you forgive me?"

"There's nothing to forgive, Charlene...."

"Oh, but there is. I've completely neglected you. Jake's gotten more of my time than you have, and that's just unforgivable." She pulled back and looked up at him. "It was just business, but that's over now. I hope."

"It's been a very stressful few weeks."

"And this morning I took Peaches and Stephanie

downtown where we had papers drawn up for conservatorship based on incompetency. Peaches turned her life over. Dennis, she was so brave about it, but..."

"It was the right thing to do," he said, stroking her back gently. "We really have to talk, Charlene. It's important."

There is a tone that a man or woman uses that imparts the news better than the news itself, and Dennis had that tone. That *deadly* tone. Oh no, she thought, panic settling over her. "Dennis, I know I haven't taken enough responsibility for the wedding, but if you'll just give me another chance, I promise you—" She held on to him tightly, pressing her head against his chest.

"Listen to you," he said. "I want you to stop worrying about that. I'm not upset about that."

"You sound upset. There's something in your tone of voice..."

"Let's slow down. You need less to worry about. Take some time."

She pulled away just enough to look into his eyes. It was unmistakable. She was losing him. "You must think I don't want to get married, when I was the one who asked you."

"Now seems not really the time. Wouldn't you agree?"

"Agree to what?"

"We should probably postpone our plans."

She could read it on his face—if she'd give him just the slightest chance, he'd tell her he'd reconsidered. He didn't want to get married. Her common sense was saying walk away. Every instinct was telling her that marrying Dennis now was the worst possible idea, and maybe she shouldn't marry him ever. But instead of paying attention to these signals, she was overcome with guilt. She'd done him wrong. And fear. If she didn't have Dennis, would she ever have stability in her life? "I'm sorry. I know life has been complicated. Confusing. But I want us to get married, especially because of that. It's the only thing I'm sure of."

"I've never heard you talk like this," he said.

"Dennis, let's have dinner together tonight. Someplace quiet and dark. Where we can talk. Please?"

"I can't," he said, shaking his head. "I have to pull a double shift. Things are pretty backed up in the E.R."

"Tonight? Can't you—"

"Can't help it, Charlene. But I wanted to see you to tell you. Seems like there have been a lot of phoned-in excuses lately, and—"

"Tomorrow?" she asked.

"That might work. I'll call you," he said.

"Should I cook? Would that be better?"

"Sure," he said. He kissed her on the cheek, and out the door he went.

It's all wrong, she thought. He wants out. It's over and he's having trouble with the words. And I can't let him go.

Pam was packing up her briefcase at 9:00 p.m. The days were getting harder, longer and lonelier. There had been no more little notes or gifts or surprise dinners. She had gone and done it—driven him away. He had finally gotten the message that she didn't want to be courted by him. And now she was miserable.

Maybe he just had some time off, she thought, so she asked the guard at the security desk on the ground floor. "Hi, Ed. I haven't seen Ray Vogel around lately. Is he on vacation or something?"

"He quit," Ed said. "Went to work somewhere else."

"Oh." Hmm. He didn't even come by to say good-bye.

Well, what did you expect? she asked herself. You were distant, you avoided him, then you had a huge fantasy in his presence that he interpreted as you falling asleep. And you capped it off by bolting.

When she got home the house was empty. She dropped her purse and tote on the kitchen chair, kicked off her shoes and peeled off her panty hose right there, poured a glass of wine and went outside to the patio. There she relaxed on the chaise and asked herself, for the thousandth time, if she'd been wise, or if she'd made an error in judgment. In the first flush of red wine she considered that she'd used the best possible judgment for the situation, but she wanted him. Wanted him.

It was almost time for the ten o'clock news, when her dad came into the house with the dog. Beau found her at once. He bounded through the house in search, then nosed open the back door and leaped onto the patio, jumping expectantly around the lounge where she reclined.

"Well, young man, did you have a run?" she asked, petting his head and rubbing his ears. He instantly calmed to soak up the attention; the Great Dane sat politely, all one hundred and twenty pounds of him. And her dad was then behind him, winding the leash up as he came outside.

"Yes, the lad has had a good run. Have you been out, Pam?"

"No. As a matter of fact, I'm only getting home from work."

"You've been putting in some very long days lately. You know what they say about all work and no play."

"Dad? When was the last time I asked your romantic advice?"

He moved over to the chaise, and she slid her legs to the right so he could sit. "It's been a very long time. You almost never ask, and when I intrude, you usually tell me to butt out."

"Rudely?" she asked.

"Absolutely," he returned.

"All right, I have a question for you. What do you think about dating when there's an age difference? A considerable age difference. Say, fifteen years."

"Well, I say that the age difference matters when you're young and when you're old. Right now, it won't matter at all. But later, when you're older, imagine how old he'll be."

She smiled at him. Of course he would assume she was considering an older man.

"You remember Charlie Broadman? He's seventy-five and his wife is fifty-five. He's a damn happy man, but I don't know his wife well enough to ask her if she's still happy. Look at them sometime, see if the picture they make together is something you could live with.''

''I remember when he married her. She was young. Thirty-five? Didn't he have children nearly her age?''

''Something like that,'' her dad said. ''So, there's some serious space between them that I'm sure didn't matter so much when they were thirty-five and fifty-five. And I expect she keeps him young. But Pam, the bigger question is, how much time does anyone have? You might avoid a relationship because of the age difference, and he may never get to the age when it will really make a difference. Or, perhaps you'll be the one to go. We don't know these things, after all.''

Pam's mother had died when Pam was twenty-five. Her mother had only been fifty. And her dad, now seventy, was the picture of health and vitality.

She touched his hand. ''Dad. He's twenty-five.''

The look that came over her father's face was priceless, worth a fortune if captured on film. His white eyebrows shot upward, his mouth made a perfect O and his cheeks became rosy as his eyes glittered. He recovered quickly, patted his daughter's hand and said, ''Pam, dear girl. Some people don't recognize a gift when it sneaks up on them and bites them in the butt.''

Charlene went alone to the small, dark, quiet Italian restaurant at about seven. She ordered lasagna, antipasto and garlic bread to go. Then she went to St.

Rose's emergency room. She hoped Dennis hadn't eaten yet, because she had to make amends for things she had no intention of telling him about. Things like sleeping with Jake, not thinking about Dennis much, not missing him, not wanting to get into bed with him even now, and mostly for not wanting to marry him and fully intending to do so anyway. She knew she was a little unstable, but she was dangerously practical. She knew what she needed, what she had to do. She wasn't going to continue stumbling stupidly through life making bad romantic decisions and go into old age without connections she could depend upon.

But Dennis wasn't at St. Rose's.

"Could he be working in another part of the hospital?" she asked the receptionist in the E.R.

"I doubt it," she said. "Dennis doesn't float. He's assigned to the E.R. permanently. But, just to be sure, I'll page him for you."

Charlene tapped her finger impatiently on the desk, waiting for the phone to ring after the page. But it didn't. The receptionist paged again, and again there was no response.

Charlene went to Dennis's house and let herself in. It was, as usual, neat as a pin and tastefully decorated, as if it were a model home on display. But there was no one at home. She sat at his kitchen table and ate her half of the dinner, complemented by a glass of red wine from his wine rack. When she was done eating, she called Dennis's sister, Gwen, and to the sounds of kids and ruckus in the background, asked her when she might be free for lunch. Gwen said anytime, and Charlene asked her for Friday. Then Gwen asked, "Are you and Dennis doing okay?"

"We've been under a lot of stress lately, with my mom's newly found condition," Charlene said.

"He told me all about that. I'm so sorry. Peaches is doing all right, though?"

"Remarkable, under the circumstances."

"I've been worried, Charlene. I thought maybe something was wrong. Dennis has been acting… well…sulky. Quiet. Unlike himself."

She had noticed; this was her fault. She wasn't sure she could still undo the damage, but she said, "I'll pay closer attention and see if there's something bothering him."

"I didn't mean to put it on you," Gwen said. "As if you don't have enough."

"Oh, you didn't, Gwen. Caring about Dennis is my greatest pleasure."

Gwen sighed. "You two are so amazingly sweet. I'll look forward to lunch."

Amazingly sweet, Charlene thought. Lunch would be fine. Gwen was top-notch. But the real reason Charlene called was so Gwen could say, "Would you like to speak to Dennis? He's right here."

She watched a little television as she worked on the note she was going to leave him. She tore up several versions that ranged from *Where are you, you bastard?* to *I'm sure there's a reason we've had this miscommunication.* She thought a lot about Dr. Malone, the young, tall, beautiful, seventeen-year-old doctor. It would be hard to lose to her, she secretly admitted to herself.

At ten-thirty, about a half hour before the evening shift wrapped up, she called Dennis's cell phone. His voice mail came on and she left the message. "Hi, it's me, and I'm still up if you want to come over after work. I'm just missing you. Call me back on my cell. I'm on my way home from Mother's."

Fifteen minutes slowly dragged by before her phone rang. "Hi, Charlene. Thanks for the offer, but I'm exhausted."

"Oh, poor you. Long day in the E.R.?"

"You can't imagine. I'm going to need to get right in bed."

"Want some company? I could drive over to your place…"

"Oh, not tonight. Forgive me? I'm done in."

"Don't give it a thought. Let's talk tomorrow. Maybe we'll finally get to have that slow, quiet, wonderful Italian dinner…hmm?"

"That would be nice. Have a nice sleep."

"Love you," she said.

"You too," he replied.

It took a few minutes for the truth to settle in. She slowly packed up every trace that she'd ever been in his house, including the bottle of wine minus one glass. She turned off the lights, locked the door behind her and drove away.

The curse of the Pomeroy women had struck again.

Thirteen

Spending the night with Agatha had been the farthest thing from Dennis's plans. Indeed, he had considered it a stroke of good fortune to learn that Charlene was in her office and not at some doctor's appointment with her mother, or at Jasper's, where there was no privacy. If he didn't catch her at the office, he wouldn't find her alone until she finally went home, late at night.

At last, a private moment? He went there after work with the purpose of having a serious talk with her about their future, or the lack thereof. Talking to her there, where she would be at her professional best, was the perfect setting for this difficult discussion.

Catch her, he did, but in the arms of her ex-husband. And she'd been crying. Again. Dennis was unable to go on. Not only was she crying...she was crying with *him*.

Dennis had never been bothered by jealousy and he wasn't jealous now. But he was angry. Regardless of all the stressful events in the past few weeks, Charlene should be moving closer to him, basking in the warmth of intimacy. Instead, she was becoming more emotionally unavailable by the day, all the while screaming about how much she wanted to get married. Indeed, all evidence pointed to Charlene not being in love with him, yet desperately insisting they marry. And soon. And every time he turned around, he was running into Jake! He hadn't seen so much of Jake in five years as he had in the past few weeks. This was getting too ridiculous. All he wanted was for this fiasco to end.

So he made up a lie. There was, of course, no double shift.

In a snit, he drove to Agatha's house, parked in the driveway and went into her backyard garden where she kept a small patio table and two chairs. He felt instantly serene, at peace again. All the tension of unfinished business with Charlene was gone. All the anger at finding her with Jake disappeared. He forgot there was anything to be upset about.

He paged Agatha, left his number and held his small phone as he waited only moments before it rang.

She gave herself away at once by the breathless, hopeful tone in her voice. "Yes, Dennis?"

It made him smile. "Guess where I'm calling you from?"

"I can't imagine."

"Your garden. I'm through for the day. What are the chances you can get away?"

Later she might tell him that it would mean breaking an appointment. "Excellent. In another hour, that is." The 6:00 p.m. date she would cancel was with a rather obnoxious bride and her even more obnoxious mother. She would gladly refund their deposit if they'd just get angry enough to go elsewhere. "Now, tell me, Dennis, if you were a key to the rear door, hiding somewhere nearby, where would you be?"

He looked around and spied a potted begonia near the back door. "Under the flowerpot?"

"Precisely. Help yourself, if you like."

She was there within the hour. When he heard her key in the door, his heart began to hammer inside his breast and he was a goner. He hadn't felt like this since he was a young man...a virile young man. He stood next to the dining table, a glass in his hand. When she was inside, he put the glass down and, without a second's hesitation, she was across the room and in his arms, his lips devouring hers and hers surrendering passionately. All talking aside, he swept her up into his arms and bore her across the little house to the bedroom before he put her again on her feet. Their lips never parted as they pulled and tore at each other's clothing. The scrubs were easily dispensed with and lay in a heap, but the wedding planner's pastel suit took a little more doing, what with all the silk and stockings and whatnot. For the first time in forever, Agatha didn't bother to gently fold away her things, and was happy to see her clothing lay in an urgent pile with his while they tumbled onto the bed.

For Dennis it was like a rebirth. He hadn't wanted a woman with this kind of fever since Sarah, and though there had been women in his life, he had been certain it would never be like that again. And for Agatha, it was like breathing clear air again after years of taking only painful breaths. Quickly sated, they lay naked against each other, holding tightly to what they both secretly feared could be fleeting. And for a very long time they were completely silent.

It was Agatha who finally spoke. "Does this mean...?"

He sighed deeply, a sound of disappointment. "I'm sorry—it doesn't mean I've been able to finally have that talk with Charlene." He lifted himself up on an elbow and looked down into her bright eyes. "I lied to her."

"Oh, Dennis..."

"I'll lie again, Agatha. Again and again. I can't help myself anymore. I wanted to be the perfect gentleman and dissolve my commitment to Charlene before taking another step into this relationship with you, but I failed. I went to her office specifically to talk to her, but she was in a bad place, her ex-husband was there and she'd spent the morning in court declaring her mother incompetent to make her own medical and financial decisions." He shrugged. "I flat out lost my nerve."

"Are you sure you weren't angry that she was there with her ex-husband?"

"I'm sure I *was* angry about that! But not because I was jealous. I've been trying to get a private word with her for two weeks. But he seems to have no trouble getting an appearance." He sighed. "I just wanted to get out of there."

"Well," she said, touching his cheek with tenderness. "What's done is done."

In truth, it didn't matter to Agatha. She wanted him

to end his engagement, but whether he did or not, she could no more resist him than he could her.

"It would be tidier if I'd done things the way I planned."

"That goes without saying, Dennis. But, well, here we are."

He kissed her gently. "Aggie, I never thought I could be this happy again. I think of nothing all day and all night but you. And how I want you. And how I can't live without you."

Her eyes welled with tears. "I haven't been called Aggie since I was a girl."

He pulled her close, held her tight and rolled onto his back, bringing her atop him. She was light as a feather; tiny and trim. Her skin was white and freckly, the hair on her head colored a tame brown while the hair down there was the fiery red that matched her hidden spirit, the spirit that seemed to come to life just for him.

Just thinking that way brought him to life again. At first the sensation caused her eyes to widen in surprised response, then they fluttered closed as her lips found his. Their kiss was long and deep and at its end she said, "I'm wanton, Dennis. I don't care about anything but being here, like this, with you. I'm wicked, cruel, because I don't care about poor Charlene and all her problems. I don't care if you lie. I don't even care if I'm stupid. All that matters to me is this. Right now." She kissed him again. "I didn't think I'd ever feel this again. I thought I was dead down there."

A devious smile curved his lips just as he moved his hips. "Far from dead, love. Far, far from dead."

As suited as they seemed to be for spending hours, if not days, abed, romping, laughing, talking and making love, even the most passionate of lovers needs nourishment. They showered, and while Dennis wore one of her oversize white terry robes, Aggie phoned the corner Italian bistro and ordered a meal of spaghetti and meatballs to go.

She waited just behind a small brunette who apparently had similar notions. "Yes," she heard the woman say, "I thought I'd take it to my fiancé at work. He's had to pull a double shift tonight."

"This is a lucky guy," the waiter said. "My girl, she expects me to bring home the pasta every night."

Agatha and Dennis enjoyed their takeout by candlelight with Chianti and bread, and it took them no time at all to find themselves back in bed. She wanted the night to never end. By his behavior, he was of a like mind.

Someplace in the dark, the trill of his cell phone rang out and he sat upright. He listened for quite a while, but let it go. Then he dialed up his voice mail and heard the message. Next, he called her and made his excuses. And then, of course, he pulled Agatha into his arms again.

"You've lied once more," she whispered to him.

"I have," he said. "I couldn't leave now. It would be too hard."

"You know, it's been said that if a man will lie to

his girlfriend to be unfaithful with you, he'll one day lie to you to be unfaithful with another.''

''Has it now? And is that what you fear?''

She turned her head. ''I'm a wretch. I don't even care.'' She turned back. ''How could I care? Answer me that. This is the first time I've felt alive in five years.''

''And for me,'' he said, ''it's been twenty.''

At a respectable time the next morning, Dennis called Charlene and said, ''I guess the timing was wrong last night. We're like ships passing in the night. Want to try again?''

She took the call on speakerphone at her desk, while, as usual, she did about three things at once. ''I have a hearing at eleven, so I can't guarantee lunch, and a client I've been putting off for some time now has asked to meet with me late in the business day. What if it were to be a late dinner? Eight or after?''

''I'll take what I can get. Would you like me to drive out to your place?''

''Since I don't know when I can get there, let me call you?''

''I'll wait to hear from you. Don't work too hard.''

She looked at her desk, at the calendar, at the stack of files. ''Okay, sure,'' she said, and clicked off the phone. ''Dammit!'' she cursed. Again she hadn't said goodbye. And Dennis was already feeling wounded. No wonder he wanted to postpone the wedding. He was probably feeling completely unloved.

But she honestly didn't think about it...or him... again.

The court hearing was a painful plea from her clients to turn off the respirator and disconnect the IVs from their nineteen-year-old son. Ordinarily, this wouldn't require a court hearing, but there was apparently some brain activity. He was morbidly injured, however. Even if he survived, it would only be with partial use of his mind, devastating injuries and terrible pain.

The court was convinced. Charlene was unable to feel a great deal of victory in that. She wished her clients well and promised to stop by the hospital later in the day to see how things were going.

The next appointment of the day was a stately woman of sixty to whom she had to deliver potentially tragic news. Mrs. Polk was convinced her husband was having an affair with a much younger woman. "I'm afraid our detective brought us much more damaging information than you suspected. It seems Mr. Polk has another family, including children, whom he keeps in a very nice home in San Jose. We were unable to ascertain whether he has committed bigamy, but the relationship appears to have been long term." She passed Mrs. Polk a file folder that included pictures of her husband with a woman in her late thirties and two teenage children. "I'm not certain whether these teenagers are your husband's. How would you like to proceed?"

Mrs. Polk pursed her lips and lifted her chin. Charlene could see her struggle against tears. The Polks were quite well-to-do. It would give Charlene considerable pleasure to settle Mrs. Polk with a handsome retirement and let the old fool live out his days with the other woman.

"With this information at hand, we could secure a no-fault divorce and—"

Mrs. Polk lifted her hand regally, to indicate Charlene should stop. "I'm going to have to think about this," she said. Her voice was faint. Weak. "I'll be in touch." She stood to leave, took three steps toward the door and fainted.

"Shit," Charlene swore, jumping from her desk. "Pam!" she yelled. She was always ready for tears, but she was never prepared for a faint. It didn't happen all that often, but it wasn't unheard of.

"Call 911. I'm not letting her drive home." By the time she'd said that much, Mrs. Polk was already coming around, but because of her age she was taken to the hospital for an examination.

Charlene had promised to meet Sherry Omagi, the owner of the goose, Frankie, and go with her to her ex-husband's house. Kim Omagi had taken the goose in a fit of anger, but had finally relented and agreed to return Frankie. "What I won't do for money," Charlene said to Pam as she left for the day.

Fifteen minutes later, exhausted by the typical events of a long day in family law, she pulled up in front of Kim Omagi's house and parked right behind Sherry's car. These people are nuts, she thought, and not for the first time. Even though she'd represented people in custody fights over dogs and cats and horses, even over a tankful of fish once, she couldn't get over feeling that this was beyond crazy.

Sherry got out of her car and waited on the sidewalk. She was wearing a big grin. "I have a surprise for Frankie. I got him a playmate. Johnny. I might be going into the goose business pretty soon."

"Well, now, that makes some sense," Charlene said. But she didn't ask any questions because she was pretty sure Sherry had no intention of breeding these geese for down comforters or Christmas dinner.

Sherry rang the doorbell. She was bouncing excitedly on the balls of her feet. "I knew he'd come around. He's been so angry with me for getting the divorce. He isn't even interested in Frankie...or in animals of any kind."

They heard someone yell for them to come in. Charlene opened the door to the very pleasant aromas of dinner, and was reminded that she hadn't eaten much all day.

"Oh my God!" Sherry gasped. She clutched at Charlene's arm. "Oh my God!" Then she ran into the house and began shrieking.

Charlene followed. There, in the dining room, on a candle-lit, beautifully appointed table, was a stuffed and roasted goose.

It was nine o'clock before Charlene was able to call Dennis as she drove toward her house. She described her day and apologized once again. She did not have another ounce of energy for anyone, not even him. "But tomorrow doesn't look as bad, Dennis. If I promise to call you about dinner, will you forgive me again?''

"Yes, Charlene,'' he said. "I'll wait for your call.''

On Thursday, just after lunch, Lois was in the house listening to music and paging through a catalog while Jasper cut the grass in the unseasonably warm weather. Then Lois got a notion. She closed her magazine, picked up her purse and walked to the house next door where her car was still parked in the garage.

Even though the necessary paperwork had been signed to allow Stephanie to make decisions without Lois's permission, it had not seemed necessary to take away her keys. She hadn't driven in a very long time, after all. Not since that embarrassing episode in the grocery-store parking lot. And, of course, she still had her checkbook and credit cards and saw no point in giving them up until such time as she missed payments, for example. But none of this came to mind now.

She had always loved books, so she drove to the book superstore and began to browse, soon deciding that this was definitely the place to be if you had an interest in birds. Before long she had loaded fifteen large picture books into the back seat of her car. She went back and got some more—standard hardcover editions, paperbacks, Audubon Society resource books, large print. In some cases two or three copies of the same title. The cashier said, "You must be setting up your own store.''

"I have a purpose, believe me,'' Lois replied.

She went to another bookstore, this one the competitor at the end of the very same strip mall. She didn't have nearly what she'd been wanting in the way of books about Africa, and not just the large picture books, but also the travel books, novelizations, guidebooks, animal books, children's books and political books. They also sold movies.

In the two bookstores in the mall, she decided to stock up on American Indian lore and literature. And women's suffrage. Fair Oaks alone had a couple dozen bookstores, Sacramento must have a hundred, Rancho Cordova had probably twenty, from small independent stores to megastores. Lois preferred the megastores because they had carts. But this was harder work than it might look. Books were *heavy*.

Lois had been, before her retirement, the acquisitions librarian at the city library. Every day she went through magazines and catalogs, read reviews, studied sales figures, examined her budget and bought the books that stocked the shelves. Even though she absolutely never went to a store to buy the books, it did not seem in the least bit unusual to her to fill up her car with books.

The moment Jasper noticed that Lois was gone, he called both Stephanie and Charlene. They chose to drive around the vicinity in search of her, while Jasper stayed at home. And though Charlene thought it was too soon to panic, she didn't think a little police intervention would hurt. She called Jake—an idea enthusiastically endorsed by Stephanie—and an all-points bulletin was issued to squad cars. Jasper thought the odds were pretty good that she'd eventually just drive herself home, because her periods of dementia were relatively short and widely spaced. And she did return.

She had only been gone for a little over three hours when he called Stephanie and Charlene back and said that Lois had come home. When they got to Jasper's house they found Lois seated in the family room, leisurely sipping a cup of tea while tall stacks of books, totaling one hundred and seventeen, teetered and rocked around her.

"Mom?" Charlene asked, dumbfounded.

"Peaches?" Stephanie echoed.

"Your Peaches has been to a few bookstores," Jasper informed them. "Thanks to the car and the credit cards."

Lois smiled, sipped her tea and looked perfectly serene, totally at peace with this decision to buy all of these books.

"She has all the receipts. It seems she favored the hardbound books, mostly nonfiction and quite a number of coffee-table books, at a cost of roughly three thousand five hundred and ten dollars."

Charlene gasped and Stephanie choked. Then they looked at each other and slowly, tremulously, their lips began to quiver. They started to tremble with barely concealed laughter and had to cover their mouths with their hands and flee the room. Thank God they had Jasper to stay with Peaches, though at the moment she was not the least disturbed by their behavior. She was in another place altogether, enjoying her tea and her purchases.

Jasper ignored the younger women and sat on the edge of his sturdy coffee table. "Looks as though you've had an exciting afternoon."

"All in a day's work," she informed him. She looked at him in a way that had become familiar to him—she couldn't place him at the moment.

"You must be very tired," he said.

"Why?"

"Carrying all those books to the car. Then into the house."

"Oh that. I had help. At the store, then here. You helped, so it was easy."

"Did it seem like something you just had to do?" he asked, genuinely curious.

"Not at all...just something that..." She frowned. In fact, she couldn't remember why she'd done anything at all. "Albert?" she asked. "Where in the world did all these books come from?"

"Well, as a matter of fact, you bought them. Took your car out of your garage, drove to a few bookstores and brought them home."

"Oh my," she said. "This is going to absolutely piss off what's-her-name. You know."

"Charlene?"

"Her, too."

At that moment, Charlene and Stephanie came back into the room and stood like naughty children before Jasper and Lois, still trying to control their laughter. "So, Mom, you feel like doing a little reading?"

And Stephanie crumbled into a heap of helpless laughter. It became contagious and Jasper found himself trying to stifle a chuckle. Then Lois joined in, laughing lightheartedly, though she wasn't sure what she was laughing at. Pretty soon the four of them sat on the couch, embracing each other fondly and giving in to the laughter until tears ran down their cheeks.

Later, Charlene and Stephanie began the difficult and time-consuming process of loading one hundred and seventeen books into Stephanie's car, gathering up the receipts and driving around town to return them. Jake met them at the first store and lent a hand, toting heavy books and helping to pick through the stacks to find which books went to which stores. "I've seen this sort of thing before," he said. "Manic-depressives do this kind of thing—go on sprees—but they almost always buy frivolous and unaffordable things like jewelry. Only Peaches would load up on books."

"It's not as though it makes no sense," Charlene said. "She was a librarian all her life, for heaven's sake."

"And she just about could be again," he pointed out. "She has a good start on it."

Not surprisingly, it took almost twice as long to return the books as it had taken Lois to buy them, even when they split up and went in three directions. But it was with great relief that they found the store managers understanding and willing to take them back.

By the time this project was complete, Charlene and Stephanie had laughed together enough to feel closer than they had in a while. They were leaning against the trunk of Stephanie's car, in the parking lot outside the last bookstore, commenting on their sore arms, sore enough to have been stacking wood, and wondering how little Lois had managed to heft all those books, when Jake pulled up.

"That it?" he wanted to know.

"That's it, Jake," Charlene said.

"Thanks, Dad. You're a sport."

"Yeah, yeah, I'm a sport. A *hungry* sport. It's after eight. How about a pizza?"

A stricken look came over Charlene's face. *"Damn!"* she whispered. And then thought, *I am in so much trouble!*

Dennis's shift ended at three-thirty; there were no messages from Charlene. He had time to kill while waiting to hear from her, and the late-April weather was so warm and sunny and inviting that he drove to his sister's house to see what the kids were up to after school.

He didn't bother to ring the bell at Gwen's house because he heard the squeals of the kids coming from the backyard, mingled with the other familiar but premature sounds of summer—splashing, the *boing* of the diving board and that telltale "No running!" coming from his sister. It was still a little nippy for swimming, but they were kids. They'd start begging on the first warm day and wouldn't let up until they won the fight to dive in. And if he knew Gwen, she'd probably heard enough and said, "Fine. Go in." She would sit lifeguard for the ten minutes it would take them to freeze and then she'd pull them, blue, from the icy water. She would ask, "Cold?" and they, with chattering teeth and purple lips, would shake their heads and say, "N-n-n-no."

He came around the corner. "Well," she said, smiling. "Just in time for dinner. What a surprise. You bring Charlene?"

"Ah...no," he said. He indicated the kids with a nod of his head. "You gave in, huh?"

"I give in earlier each year. My only firm rule is the pool doesn't open before taxes are due. We almost made it to May. But next year I'm just going to let them swim all winter. That oughta cure 'em, huh?"

"Got beer?"

"Sure. I hide it in the refrigerator."

He went into the kitchen, came out with a bottle and lowered himself into the patio chair next to Gwen. He took a long pull, followed by the requisite, "Ahh."

"Is Dick around?"

"Nope. Work. How about Charlene?"

"Good question."

She turned in her chair and stared him down. "What's going on?"

"What do you mean?"

"I mean, you bring your sulking self over here more often lately. Alone. You've never been more morose than since you announced to me that you're getting married. Your fiancée has invited me out to lunch tomorrow. And for the first time since you started seeing

Charlene, you have no idea where she is? Do I look stupid, or what?''

A childhood memory reached out and pinched him, made him smile. "Yeah, but you're probably not."

She whacked him across the arm and turned back to the kids. "Okay, that's enough. Get out now! You're blue! And Uncle Denny says you're going to be sick."

"I did not," he yelled out. "I told your mother she's sick. In the head." Then to Gwen he said, "Relax. It's a beautiful afternoon. Probably not warm enough for the pool, but they're kids...they have no brains."

"No kidding. So, don't keep coming over here looking all depressed if you're not willing to talk to me."

"Fair enough. But it's going to put you in a bad spot if you're going to lunch with Charlene tomorrow."

"Not to worry. I'm a consummate liar."

"You might be sorry you asked."

"I usually am, but I'm insatiably curious."

"Charlene came to this decision to get married very suddenly. First it was just a dash off to city hall, then it evolved into a wedding. I'm not sure how that happened. I think because I said if we were getting married, I wouldn't mind having guests. A wedding and reception. Stephanie and Lois egged her on, then there were all these upheavals. Lois's health problems, her house fire, et cetera.

"Charlene likes to pretend she's handling all of

this—especially this situation with Lois going through these upsetting bouts of dementia—with her usual cool and calm control. But she's not. Almost from the moment she agreed to have this wedding, she's moved away emotionally. Become distant. Aloof. She's been crying.''

''Well, Jesus, Dennis, what do you expect? Here she's made a major life change, a huge commitment for a woman who's been single and independent all her adult life, and at the same time her elderly mother is falling apart mentally. And practically killed herself!''

''I've made myself available to be her support through this, but I don't seem to be what she wants or needs right now. In fact, I seem to be the last thing she needs.''

Gwen shrugged. ''Maybe this is a family thing… something she and Stephanie and Lois have to manage together. I mean, they're actually not used to having men in the family, are they? She sounded perfectly normal when she called me the other night, inviting me to lunch.''

''She doesn't want to do this, Gwen. She won't even talk about it. But when I suggested that she not worry about any wedding right now and just take care of Lois and her practice, she insisted we go through with it. She said everything would be fine, she'll have things under control when—''

''Wait a minute,'' Gwen said, stopping him. ''Wait a minute,'' she said again, as though she had a thought that was starting to gel, then vanished. She grabbed the beer bottle out of his hand by the neck, took a swig and handed it back to him. Then she got up, pulled a thick fluffy towel from the pile on the nearby picnic table, shook it out and quickly filled it with a skinny, bluish, shivering little boy. Right behind him, quivering from head to toe, was her daughter. She enveloped them, rubbed them and sent them into the house with instructions to take warm showers and shampoo.

Then she sat down next to Dennis again. "Wait a minute."

"You said that already. I think you're the one who's getting dotty."

"Oh, that goes without saying. But Dennis, *you're* the one who doesn't want to get married."

"Where did you get that idea from?"

"I got that idea the first time we talked about it. It took making an official announcement for you to realize that, while you're very fond of Charlene, you're not in love with her in the way one must be to get married."

"I never said that!"

"No, you aren't saying it, but it's true."

"I'm the only one who's done anything about this damn wedding! I'm the one who has met with the wedding planner three times now—and all three times Charlene stood me up!"

"Not in love with her the way you were with Sarah," she persisted.

"But I'm not the one in denial. In avoidance."

"It's you," she said again. "And you're frustrated

because you can't get Charlene alone long enough to convince her to agree you shouldn't be planning a wedding right now. Then, when things settle down, you're going to tell her you shouldn't be planning one at all.''

"What is it you think you know?" he demanded angrily.

"You," she said, and she said it firmly and calmly. "When was it? Two, three weeks ago? Four? When did you realize that it wasn't right, that it wasn't going to work?''

He seemed to suddenly deflate. He let out his breath in a huff and looked down. "Almost immediately," he said.

"Oh God.''

"I knew right away. The day after we agreed to get married, I knew. We had no business planning to get married. Two people who see each other two or three days a week? Who are so independent they don't even want to live together? But I'm fifty, Gwen. And I don't want to be alone. I thought maybe the most anyone should ever ask for is to marry a good friend. You and Dick are good friends.''

"Denny, we didn't start out as good friends. We started out hot as pistols.''

His cheeks began to color. "I met someone.''

"Oh Denny. Oh God.''

"And that's when I knew that it wasn't okay to go along with the wedding idea. I have to end this, but I can't get Charlene alone long enough to even talk to her about the issue.'' He looked at his watch. "She's supposed to call me. We're supposed to get together for dinner tonight. But every time we try, she has to cancel."

"This is going to be so awful. This is going to kill Charlene."

"No, Gwen, that's what I'm saying," he tried desperately to explain. "She's doing the same thing I was doing. She's going along with the marriage thing for whatever reason—because she doesn't want to be alone or because she thinks she needs me to help her make decisions about her mother or whatever—but not because she's in love with me and wants to marry me. Don't you see, over the past few weeks I've gotten closer to the wedding planner than to my own fiancée! We're practically best friends!" He took a long pull on his beer. "Shit," he said.

Gwen took the bottle out of his hand and took her own deep swallow. "Hmm. Lunch tomorrow should be a real gas."

Fourteen

Dennis was good enough to call Gwen and warn her that he had not been able to talk to Charlene. Some incident with Lois had commanded her immediate attention. Gwen lunged at the phone every time it rang that morning, praying Charlene would call and cancel lunch, but no such call came.

On her way to the restaurant, the oldies station on her car radio played, "Oh, girl, I heard you're getting married, heard you're getting married..." Denny had refused to tell Gwen who the woman was, no matter how she'd begged. He promised she would be the first to know, once things were settled with Charlene. All Gwen could think was that this was going to be a mess.

When she got to the restaurant, she found her brother's fiancée waiting at a table set for six.

"I hope you don't mind," Charlene explained. "It's just that I've been so remiss in my share of the wedding chores, I thought lunch today might be a good way to break the ice and get some things done."

"Get some things done? What kind of things, Charlene?" Gwen asked. "Who are the others?"

"Well, its mostly the wedding party. There's my

mom and Stephanie. My assistant, Pam, is going to sneak away from the office for an hour. And if she can, Agatha Farnsworth, the wedding consultant, is going to stop by for dessert and coffee. She sounds like an absolutely delightful young woman. Dennis said he's enjoyed meeting with her and thinks she'll be very helpful.''

"Full speed ahead," Gwen said, then she gulped.

"I thought we'd just toast the engagement, throw out some ideas about what would make an interesting wedding, and by the time we've had some fun and some food, Agatha will be here. How does that sound?"

"Bring on the wine," Gwen said with a nervous shrug.

Gwen began to sense some of what Denny was trying to explain. Charlene was going through the motions. But why? She'd had the fortitude and courage to resist the conformity of marriage all these years. Why tumble into it all now, if it wasn't genuinely what you yearned for?

"I just have one question, Char?"

"Hmm?"

"Why marriage? Why now? You and Denny could certainly live together if you chose…and Lord knows, you have a great relationship now, with this sort of separateness and intimacy all at once…."

"Well, why did you get married?" Charlene countered.

"We wanted to have children, because we had no idea how messy and expensive they were."

Charlene laughed, and it had a hollow sound. Gwen frowned. One of Charlene's great gifts was a laugh that was deep and rich and contagious and from the heart. And Gwen, who had a wicked sense of humor, always found it so easy to make Charlene laugh, and so enjoyed the task.

"Wait till I tell you what my mom was up to yesterday," she said, not answering the question about marriage, but instead imparting this sad but sweetly funny story about Lois's purchase of thousands of dollars' worth of books, and Charlene and Stephanie's exhausting attempts to return them all. "How she managed to buy and transport all those books without dropping from fatigue is one miracle. How we were able to get them all back in the stores by closing time is another."

"Just you and Stephanie?" Gwen asked.

"Well, mostly. I had called Jake earlier, before we found my mom, because I thought we might be able to use the help of the police...so he was on hand to help out a bit. You've met Jake? Stephanie's father?"

"At her graduation, I think. A long time ago. Now, is Lois aware that she—?"

Before Gwen could complete the question, Stephanie and Lois migrated toward their table. Lois was animated, happy, lucid and excited to be talking about a wedding. The answer to Gwen's question was that between these periods of dementia, Lois was very nearly her old self. But it was apparent she was tired; perhaps it was the strain of illness and confusion showing on her.

And...speak of the devil, it was Jake escorting them. Stephanie kissed her mother's cheek and said, "Dad dropped us off. He's going to take my car to the garage to check the brakes...so they don't gouge me."

He pulled out Peaches's chair, told Stephanie to call him to be picked up and and joked a little with Gwen by asking, "Do you think it would be too much if I offered to give Charlene away?"

"You never gave me anything before," Charlene said in good humor.

Jake made the motion of a strike to the heart by pounding his fist against his chest.

No one else caught how their eyes twinkled. Gwen blinked to clear her vision, but even with the second look, it was there. The way they looked at each other. Jake and Charlene gazed at each other—though very briefly—with some kind of secret, and Gwen was left to study them, knowing something, but not knowing what.

Pam arrived, looking harried and pressured and less than her usual radiant self. She was wilting under the pressure of running Charlene's office with very little help, Gwen assumed. Wine came to the table and Pam waved off the glass, opting for water, while Gwen consciously instructed herself not to guzzle.

Then things adjusted. After a glass of wine and some good food they melted into the experience. They became five women—friends—talking about men and weddings and houses and dresses. Gwen found herself forgetting, for the moment, that this wasn't really going to happen. Instead, she got into the idea of a wedding party. Together, they came up with some fun ideas—a black-and-white wedding, a swing band for dancing, theme weddings from Mardi Gras to western. Before long they were a bunch of loud women, laughing at lewd jokes about the wedding night. Gwen completely dismissed any suspicion of Charlene and her ex-husband, and quit worrying about the fact that Dennis was probably going to break up with Charlene that night.

Then she walked in.

"Nothing could please a wedding consultant more than seeing the wedding party having a glorious time ironing out the details."

"You must be Agatha Farnsworth," Charlene said, half rising from her chair.

The waiter pulled out her chair for her, but before sitting she stretched her hand across the table and took Charlene's. She smiled pleasantly, somewhat shyly. "Ms. Dugan, the pleasure is entirely mine."

"So glad you were able to come. My mother, Lois Pomeroy, my daughter, Stephanie Dugan, my assistant, Pam London, and—"

Gwen's eyes fell on Agatha's face and things began to come together for her. *I've met with the wedding planner alone so often we're practically best friends!* She frowned. Do you continue to take meetings with a wedding planner if you knew you weren't going through with the wedding? Not unless you were taken with the wedding planner! She hadn't taken a breath, so stunned was she by this turn.

"Well, this is Gwen, my fiancé's sister. Gwen? Is something wrong?"

Oh God, they were all with the wrong people! If you put them in a room and played a little sexy music, they'd leave their partners and gravitate toward the people they were meant to be with. And the only thing in the world that could have her brother this screwed up would be if he'd already discovered the secret pleasures of the wedding consultant.

"Gwen? What is it? Gwen?"

"Jesus Christ, someone slap her!"

"Is she having a seizure or something?"

Gwen shook herself, took a sharp breath…and inhaled an olive. Her hands went to her throat. She couldn't breathe in or out. She first turned bright red, her eyes watered, her lips became blue around the edges.

"She's choking! She's choking!"

"Hit her in the back!"

"No, do that thing where you get her from behind!"

"Anybody know how? Get the waiter!"

"Help! Help! She's choking to death!"

Gwen stood on shaking legs and the room started to sway. Her eyes bulged and she felt as though she was looking at the women through a curved glass. Then their voices began to fade even though they were standing, shouting, waving hands, jumping up and down. The room began to darken as though she were entering a tunnel.

"Step aside, step aside," a deep growly voice instructed. The women parted and a huge man moved against Gwen's back, put his arms around her, his hamlike fist in her sternum, and gave a sharp, powerful squeeze. She felt the olive move in her throat. He did it again, harder, and the olive popped out of her mouth and shot across the table right at Agatha.

Agatha leaned right as the little green missile shot past her head. Gwen went limp in the big man's arms and he gently lowered her to the restaurant carpet.

"She'll be all right. She's breathing," he said. "But someone should call 911. A little oxygen wouldn't hurt. And sometimes I don't know my own strength. Maybe you'll want to X-ray those ribs."

Gwen's eyes fluttered open and she looked into the face of her savior, a fellow named Stan who was an off-duty fireman and paramedic. She began to sit up, and winced.

"You better stay down," he advised. "You actually lost consciousness."

"I'm fine," she said, trying again, wincing again. "Ugh."

"And I squeezed you pretty good."

In the end she was taken by ambulance to her brother's emergency room.

When Dennis looked down at his sister, her mascara running in rivulets down her cheeks from the choking and watering eyes, he said, "Gwen, what the hell happened?"

In a weakened and scratchy voice she whispered, "The wedding consultant came to Charlene's little luncheon."

"And?"

"What do you mean *and?*" She grabbed a fistful of his scrubs, and by the twisted look of pain on his face, perhaps a little chest hair as well, and pulled him closer. "Denny, I know what you've done."

"I don't know what you're talking about," he said while his cheeks began to slowly grow crimson.

"You'd better tidy this thing up, Denny, or a lot of people are going to get hurt. Or *killed!*"

Charlene waited in the E.R. She stood from her chair when Dennis came out.

"She *is* going to be all right, isn't she?"

"She'll be okay, but you can go. I'm going to tape up her ribs, which are only bruised, but still painful, then take her home. I'll be off in another hour, by which time she'll be wrapped and the X-rays, which we ran only as a rule-out precaution, will be back."

"I sure know how to throw a bridal luncheon."

"You didn't mention you were going to do that," he said, annoyed.

"You didn't expect to be invited, I hope. It was a girls' thing."

"Charlene, I want to see you tonight. No excuses, no last-minute cancellations."

"Dennis, I told you, I'm very sorry about yesterday. First Peaches was lost, then we had to deal with over three thousand dollars' worth of—"

"I know that, but we really must talk about this wedding business. We haven't even had a discussion about it in weeks. I'll be at your place at seven. I have a cell phone. If you're not going to make it—"

"You're still angry. I said I was sorry I was too preoccupied to call you— I was frantic. I don't want to get together if you're just going to yell at me."

"I never yell. At anyone."

"Well, I'll have to check and see if Peaches—"

"Seven!" He turned and walked away.

Charlene stood frozen, staring at his back as he disappeared. Then she gathered up her purse and keys and left. She'd never seen that side of Dennis. This was a new aspect to his personality. She'd seen him angry a couple of times, but it was so mild and so quickly gone it was almost fleeting. Dennis was too civilized to lose control. Nothing like Jake, who was like a white-hot flash of light.

Jake. He just kept turning up. Gwen had probably mentioned that Jake had been at the restaurant; that had probably turned the heat up under Dennis's impatience. It seemed that every time Charlene had to cancel or forgot to call, Jake was in the vicinity. It was pure coincidence, of course. Today he had offered to take Stephanie's car to the garage for her; something about brake pads being replaced. He often did that. Come to think of it, he'd done it for Charlene before Dennis. Men, just by virtue of being men, fared better at the auto repair. It had nothing to do with being together.

There also had been no sex between her and Dennis since the official engagement, which was a very strange turn.

Charlene had heard that planning weddings brought out the weirdest behavior in people, but she never would have been convinced of this bizarre turn of events. The first and probably strangest thing in her mind was the simple fact that she and Dennis had not grown closer in the past three weeks, but had clearly drifted apart. Stranger still, she had been with Jake. Where had her brain been that night? And to put the frosting on that cake, she dreaded tonight. *Dreaded.* But what was there to be afraid of? Dennis had always been kind, easy to talk to, understanding.

She would have to make amends, grovel a little, promise a lot and ultimately put out. She couldn't remember a time she'd ever danced to that particular tune and wondered if this is what marriage did to women.

Stephanie's car wasn't ready at three, nor was it ready at four, so she talked Jake into going to the coffee shop in the mall across the street while they waited. "There's something I've been trying to work up the courage to talk to you about," she said.

"I hate when you want to talk to me about something that requires courage." They sat in a coffee shop that gave the illusion of being a sidewalk café, with a little fence around the perimeters, but it was inside the mall. Shoppers hefting their purchases hurried past, going from store to store. Muzak played in the background and potted trees dotted the indoor landscape.

"I haven't talked to Mom about this, yet, but I'm going to—soon. I just don't want to screw up her wedding plans."

"I have my own opinion about that, but go ahead...drop your bomb."

"It's not a bomb, Daddy. I'm going to make a major lifestyle change. I'm going to do it whether anyone approves or not, but I want you to know the details, up front."

"Let's see," Jake said, rubbing his chin. "This would be the ninth major lifestyle change for you in the last two years, right?"

She just smiled indulgently. "Something like that, yes. I'm taking a leave from teaching."

"Really?" he said, his eyebrows shooting up. The one thing that had been constant with Stephanie since childhood was her love of literature and her desire to either teach or follow her grandmother's direction and become a librarian. "To do what?"

"To take care of Peaches."

"Aw...Stephie. First of all, Peaches doesn't really need you to—"

"Here's what I want you to do, Dad. I want you to listen to my whole plan. Then you can say whatever you want."

"Okay. You give it to me. Then we'll talk."

"Peaches *does* need someone around, which is why she's staying at Mr. Conklin's house right now. She's having these spells...and has been having them for a long time. Much longer than she told Mom. It started out as just not being able to remember where things were, but not like your car keys—like your *car*. Sometimes she couldn't even remember where she was. She'd look around the grocery store and get all confused about where, exactly, she was. But you know what? Clever Peaches *faked* it. She just didn't want anyone to impose any...I don't know...*limits* on her. She shouldn't have done that, you know. She should've started medication to slow down the progression."

"She told you this? That these little periods of confusion go back a ways."

"Uh-huh. Of course, she wants to live in her house again. And of course she shouldn't. Not without help. There's really no way she can afford full-time care in her house. What I'd like to do is take a leave from teaching and move in with Peaches. It's going to be a long, long time before she'll need any kind of nursing home. She just needs a companion. Someone to keep an eye on her, help her out with transportation. And I am her legal guardian, you know."

"Yeah, I know," he said, but he struggled with it. He rubbed the back of his neck. "This isn't what I want for you, Steph. To be twenty-five and baby-sitting your grandma. You're too young to give up your youth like that. It's not a great idea. Your mom will—"

"I grew up in that house, Daddy. I love Peaches's little house. The one who really can't do it is Mom. She's too bossy, too fussy. Peaches would kill her in her sleep."

"Well, I didn't want to say this, but...I don't know if you can. I mean, there are certain standards of... Stephanie, you would have to clean and cook. And we both know you're better at reading."

Surprisingly, she only laughed. "I know. I've been pretty selfish, haven't I? Daddy, we're not going to have Peaches too much longer. Who knows how much lucid time she has left. I don't want to miss it. I don't want to regret how I spent this time."

At that moment, Jake was incredibly proud. "Have you told Peaches?"

"I did. She thanked me for the thought, but I don't think she thinks I'll follow through. Isn't that too bad, Dad? That there were so many times I didn't follow through?"

"Don't be hard on yourself," he scoffed. "You're just a girl. You got your degree, after all. You're a good teacher."

"I am," she said, sitting taller in her chair. "I don't think I'll be away from teaching that long. I have lots of years to teach, but Peaches probably only has a few years at home."

"What does Grant say about this idea?"

She instantly glanced into her coffee cup. Tears threatened and she fought to hold them back. "I haven't talked to Grant about this yet."

Jake lifted her chin with a finger. "Stephie, is there something else you want to tell me?"

"No," she said. "Except that I will talk to Grant about it. He's studying for finals right now, but pretty soon, when he's done with that... School will be out for me, Peaches's house will be finished, Grant will be on break, Mom and Dennis will be— Hey, you said something about having an opinion about that."

"I have opinions about everything," he said.

"On that subject?"

He shrugged. "Better left unsaid."

"You don't much like Dennis, do you?"

"Aw, he's an okay guy, I guess. For a *nurse*."

"You're jealous!"

"Jealous? Me? Ha! I offered to give her away, didn't I?" But Stephanie was no longer listening. She was distracted by the sight of a young man at the serving counter who was both flirting with a young waitress and paying for his coffee. Jake followed her stare and identified Fast Freddy Rainey. "You know that guy, Stephie?" Jake asked.

"I've met him," she said, watching him carefully. In fact, he hadn't bothered her lately—no phone calls, notes or flowers—and she was momentarily afraid he'd resumed his pestering and had followed her.

Freddy turned from the counter with his steaming cup and wandered into the café in search of a table. He was laughing to himself, no doubt over some wildly clever line he'd just laid on the waitress. He spied Stephanie and stopped short, sloshing hot coffee over his fingers. His eyes took on an instant panicked gleam as he saw Jake. Jake made the tiniest smile, an almost imperceptible nod, and Freddy began to back away. His heel caught on the leg of one of the café's wrought-iron chairs and he stumbled backward, spilling hot coffee on himself and a seated patron. He fell into a rack of cups and they went crashing to the floor in a pile of ceramic pieces, but Freddy didn't stop. He scrambled to his feet and, while looking over his shoulder to be sure he wasn't being chased, fled the café.

Jake picked up his cup and took a leisurely sip. "Mmm," he said. "Your friend is…what? A little shy?"

Stephanie looked at her dad through narrowed eyes. "Something's going on here," she said. "Freddy took one look at us and ran for his life."

"Really? Maybe he mistook me for someone else?"

She crossed her arms over her chest. "I *highly* doubt it."

The Bridal Boutique was crowded with the female members of a wedding party trying on their gowns for alterations. The seamstress was ready to pin up the hems and let in or let out the bodices, as the case may be. In a not at all uncommon response to stress, or perhaps some other biological event, the bride had put on nearly twenty pounds since choosing her gown. And her face was peppered with new acne. And she was mean as a badger.

"Moth-her! Look at this goddamn neckline! This goddamn thing was *not* like this when I picked it out!"

The seamstress, Mrs. Rodriquez, a woman in her sixties who had been doing this work for many, many years, slowly pulled herself up from her place on the floor where she worked on the hem of the gown, and tried to examine the neckline in question. "This is the same gown, miss, but if you like, we can fix in some lace or tulle—"

"Except I didn't buy a gown with any goddamn lace or tulle, now, did I?"

"Birdie, Birdie," the young woman's mother admonished. "Let's stay calm and fix these things as best we—"

"I can't even *breathe* in this goddamn dress!"

Agatha stood back and listened, unimpressed. There were five bridesmaids in various stages of undress, all picking at each other's dresses, pulling them into better fits by pinching inches of satin at the sides, the waist, complaining about the style, the color, the fabric. But at least they did so more eloquently than the beast known as Birdie.

"I knew this blue would look nasty with my complexion," said one.

"The color is okay for me, but could you possibly find an *uglier* dress?" asked another.

"At a thrift shop, maybe."

"Check out Birdie's," whispered the fourth. "She looks like a beached whale."

"I *heard* that!"

"Drug of choice? Chocolate?"

"Are you going to do anything about this?" the bride demanded of the seamstress, towering over the little woman like a bear cowering a pussycat.

"It's not a problem, miss. The seams have to be let out right here, and right here," she said, pointing to the sides of the gown. "Then, if you like, a little of the same lace on your train can be applied to the décolletage to make it slightly more modest. Here, you slip your arms out, lower the dress, we'll open the seam and see what we have.''

"We'd better have a perfect wedding gown in one week or I'm going to sue you!''

"Birdie, Birdie,'' begged the beast's mother.

There was the tinkling of the bell to the shop and Agatha went, gratefully. She was a little less grateful when she saw it was Dennis, and he wasn't smiling. "Hello, Dennis. I guess I should have expected you.''

"Why did you go to the restaurant, Aggie?''

She shrugged lamely but met his gaze bravely. "She called just before lunch, begged me to stop by if only to say hello, and my curiosity got the better of me.''

He lifted an eyebrow. "And what did you think?''

"Of Charlene? That she's very beautiful. Very sophisticated. And very much planning a wedding.''

"I had absolutely no idea she was doing that.''

"Well, the women appeared to be having a wonderful time. Until—'' She stopped and winced as a shriek came from the back of the store.

"*Ouch!* Be careful with those goddamn pins!''

Agatha shook her head in disgust, then turned her attention back to Dennis. "Ahem. They were having a wonderful time until your sister's mishap. Is she all right?''

"She'll live. As you get to know my sister better, you'll find she is very unpredictable.''

"And is that likely to happen?'' she asked. It was impossible for her to hide the sarcasm in her voice.

Dennis chose not to answer. "I'm on my way to Charlene's right now. I have no idea what to expect.

It might be a very unpleasant evening, but when I leave there tonight, there will no longer be wedding plans in the works.''

She clutched her hands together at her waist and looked down at the floor. She couldn't help feeling very sorry for Charlene Dugan. But, she reminded herself, calling off the wedding and ending the relationship were two separate issues. Dennis had already said he would stand by Charlene, support her through difficult times with her mother's illness. And, really, wasn't that the kind of man Agatha wanted in her life?

This could drag out for a painfully long time.

"Would you like me to call you later? When I leave her house?" he asked.

She lifted her gaze. "Dennis, that's entirely up to you."

"If it's not too late, I'll call," he said, turning to go.

"Try not to—" she started. He turned back to her and she was about to tell him to be gentle or to try not to hurt Charlene, but there was another sharp cry from the back. Agatha lifted her hand in farewell and returned to the wedding party in the fitting room.

The bride was standing before the mirror, her wedding gown opened in the back and lowered to her waist so that her arms were free. She wore a miserable-looking corset and girdle. Mrs. Rodriquez gently held the gown by the shoulders so that the bride could slip her arms into the gown and pull it up to her shoulders again.

Agatha had a vision of Charlene, so smart and stylish and fun-loving, crumbling to the floor when Dennis told her there would be no wedding. And Dennis, chivalrous as he was, lifting her up, consoling her, kissing her, holding her, giving in.

"If you could lift your arm high over your head, miss?"

"Like this?" she asked, holding up her arm.

"Perfect. Still now, while I measure and pin." Mrs. Rodriquez measured the girl's bust, scribbled the number, and with a mouthful of pins, began fitting the open side seams and underarms together, giving the robust bride a bit more room. "Ouch!" the girl cried out. And to Agatha's horror, she shoved little Mrs. Rodriquez backward. The seamstress might've fallen if she hadn't been pushed right into a rack of billowing gowns that cushioned her. "I *told* you to be careful!"

"That will do!" Agatha said sharply. She went to Mrs. Rodriquez, the sweetest little lady in the world, and inquired, "Are you all right, Mrs.?"

"Yes. Sure. But I try to be careful."

"Of course. You can go home now. And don't worry, of course you will be paid."

"Home? You're sending her *home*?"

"Go now," Agatha told the seamstress. "Yes, she's going home. Miss, I have been doing this work for quite some time. Tensions surrounding even the simplest wedding tend to be enormous, and people naturally have their anxious moments, but I'm afraid you've toppled the cart. You will have to finish your event without our help. I'll be glad to give you the names and phone numbers of other alteration shops, but Mrs. Rodriquez will no longer be able to help you. You've treated her quite horribly.''

"How *dare* you," the bride sputtered. "The old cow stabbed me! What the hell do you expect?"

"I expect you to leave immediately or I shall call the bobbies and report an assault. Once they've made your acquaintance, they certainly won't doubt the probability."

"Now, now," the mother of the bride simpered. "I'm sure if we all calm down we can work this out, smooth over ruffled feathers, make this event as beautiful as all concerned."

"It's doubtful, madam," Agatha said, standing her ground. "I'm not in a particularly forgiving mood at the moment. And I don't think I'll be feeling better anytime soon."

Fifteen

Without really thinking too much about it, Charlene threw herself into preparations for a spectacularly erotic evening. It was the least she could do, and odd though it may be, something she hadn't done before. Not that she and Dennis weren't romantic. They were very romantic. Also very civilized. *Decorum* was a word that came to mind. Or tame.

She went first to her favorite lingerie shop where she purchased something small, silky, lacy and red. Something meant to be worn briefly, then tossed. Before she could sign the charge slip, she added a long red silk robe to the purchase; she didn't want to catch a chill.

Then she went to her famous gourmet grocer where she procured, from the deli chef, Dennis's favorite—chicken and pasta Alfredo, Caesar salad, Boston cream pie and a really nice bottle of Chardonnay.

Then home to set the table in china and crystal, silver and candles. This was going to be very special, and no one appreciated classy table appointments like Dennis. She found herself looking forward to this dinner, to time with him. He was, above all, a good date, a good friend. They had had many a pleasurable evening together in the last five years, two to three times every week.

There was comfort for Charlene in routine. There always had been. Since childhood it had always produced grave anxiety in her when she didn't know what was going to happen next. A by-product, no doubt, of having an unreliable though desirable father.

But their comfortable routine would change, she thought as she placed the linen napkins beside the plates. They would be together, as Stephanie would put it, twenty-four-seven. Hmm.

She went to the master bedroom, laid out the red silk on the bed and drew a bath. As she soaked, relaxing into the bubbles and scents, she decided that they would live there. It was the only possible solution because Charlene couldn't give up this master bedroom and bath, and preferred her soft bed to Dennis's hard one. And the neighborhood was a good one; the property values were rising. Dennis would come around. He'd always been one to compromise if it made her happy...unlike Jake, who would argue with a million dollars.

Scat, Jake! Out out out! Not tonight, she admonished.

As the sun slowly sank, she warmed the Alfredo, put on some nice music, moved the Chardonnay and bucket to stand beside the place that Dennis would occupy at the table and placed the corkscrew there for him. Next she lit candles. The only electric light she was going to allow tonight was the small one over the stove. Otherwise, it would all be candlelight.

She went to the bedroom, threw off the terry robe and donned the red concoction. She looked in the mirror. Well, Dennis would probably not consider it ridiculous, but to her it seemed absurd. Those dimples in her thighs would not turn *her* on.

Once, twenty-five years ago, she had put on a candy striper's uniform for Jake and he had chased her around their little apartment all night long. It was possible Stephanie was conceived that night. It was the last night she'd done or donned anything so risqué.

The robe was an excellent idea, she decided, pulling it over the itsy-bitsy nightie with a single purpose.

At six-forty-five she made sure all the lights were off but that one, all the candles flickering from bedroom to dining room. She sat at the table, waiting. It was beautiful. Romantic. Meaningful.

Artificial.

Then she knew. In a split second she knew. *It was all wrong.*

It was like falling from a forty-story building and having your life flash before your eyes, but for the first time she understood that it wasn't like a movie in fast-forward from birth to death, but rather a total life, seen all at once. Charlene at ten, waiting at the corner for her dad to come back and finally going home in the dark, disappointed; Charlene at seventeen, graduating from high school, Peaches alone in the commencement hall; Charlene at twenty, pregnant, standing over her father's casket; Charlene at thirty, getting her law degree, Peaches, Jake and Stephanie cheering; Charlene at forty, lonely, her child raised and gone, drawing up a list of qualities she would like in the perfect man and seeing them produced before her very eyes in Dennis. Finally, Charlene at forty-five, sitting in red silk and candlelight in a desperate attempt to be saved by marriage, to break the family curse of single women hooked on fallible men.

Suddenly remembering something she had known all along, she realized what she had done. She had re-created, with stunning accuracy, the life she'd had with her father! The minute she saw the resemblance of Jake to her father, she divorced him. But kept him in her life, on her terms, at arm's length. How often had she slept with him over the twenty-five years? As often as her father had come home during her youth? The life she thought she was freeing herself from, she had embraced. Had she really wanted to change the legacy, she'd have allowed Jake to be the husband and father he wanted to be—present, devoted and faithful. The things he'd ended up being anyway.

And Dennis? The perfect man? Certainly, but not perfect for her. Not who she wanted, really, but who she thought she should want.

Oh God, what have I almost done? she asked herself.

She stood up abruptly, almost panicked enough to run. First she would get out of the red, then she'd turn on some lights, then—

But the doorbell rang and, before she could even consider not answering it until she'd changed her clothes and her mind, she heard his key in the lock. Busted.

Dennis came into the foyer and just stood there as if letting his eyes adjust to the dimness, looking stately and handsome in his cream cashmere sweater and tan pans.

He didn't say anything. Charlene couldn't tell if he saw her standing by the dining table. She took two steps and turned on the chandelier light. Now it was certain he saw her, in all her glory. And she could clearly see his face. All that was there was disappointment. He was sorry for her that she'd made this dreadful presentation. This wasn't what he was looking for at all. When he said he wanted to talk to her, "talk" was exactly what he meant.

"Oh, Dennis, I'm sorry," she said, sinking into her chair. "This isn't what I want," she said, waving a hand over the table. "It isn't what you want, either. I can tell."

He walked slowly into the room. "Have you any idea what I want?" he asked. He stood behind the chair that was to have been his.

She gave a little embarrassed laugh and shook her head. "You want to live in your house," she said. "And I want to live in mine. And I was going to make it my mission tonight to convince you we should live here."

He pulled out the chair and sat down, but somehow they both knew he wasn't going to be staying for dinner. "Well, I admit, this is an interesting way of going about it. Do you think it would have worked?" he asked.

"That question should be to you, but never mind. Dennis, I don't want to get married. I'm sorry."

He actually slid back in his chair, shocked. He hoped his face didn't show relief. "When did you come to this conclusion?" he asked.

"You won't believe this—moments ago. As you were ringing the bell, I was having a sudden epiphany. Like lightning. Like a blow torch. All at once, I realized... I'm totally crazy, but at least I understand."

He thought for a second, then said, "It's probably not a good idea to think about things like weddings when you have other serious change in the family. Like illness. Or a fire. Or both."

"You're right, of course. But that's not really what I mean. My realization went a lot deeper than that. I'm not talking about having some common sense for a change, though wouldn't that be nice? I'm talking about one of those moments people pay therapists thousands of dollars to experience.

"Do you remember that night?" she went on. "That miserable, rainy night that you waited here for me with hot chocolate and dinner? And I burst into the house, a drowned rat, and asked you if you still wanted to get married?"

He reached for the wine and began to wrestle with the cork. "It's seared in my memory for all time."

"You'd understand perfectly if you knew what had gone on earlier in the day. Stephanie called to complain about Grant and she was threatening to leave him, after a little less than a year. In the course of all her bellyaching, she let fly that she didn't want to end up like me! Less than two hours later my mother got lost in the grocery-store parking lot and I realized I didn't want to end up like *her!* And that if Stephanie did leave Grant, she was *exactly* like me! I left Jake in less than a year. But here's a little something I never shared with you—I let Jake come back just about as often as my mother let my father.''

His hands stopped manipulating the cork as his eyes snapped to her face.

''You didn't tell me every detail of your life before me, either,'' she said. She knew the value of a well-placed lie.

''That explains Jake's constant resistance to me. He probably still loves you.''

''Only if he's completely stupid,'' she said. ''But, who do you suppose chased me down on my way home that fateful night that I proposed? Oh yes, himself. At which point he threw at me that I was probably the smart one, refusing to have a committed relationship…right after he asked me if I'd gained a little weight.'' She shrugged lamely. ''Didn't I just walk in the door and with one simple question change everyone's destiny?''

The cork popped like an exclamation point.

He poured himself a glass, then poured her one. ''I wonder how many proposals actually come out of panic,'' he said.

''You don't want to get married either, do you,'' she said. It was not a question.

''Charlene, I've only seen you in passing the last four weeks. We haven't even had a conversation about—'' He took a breath. Without this wedding fiasco, there would be no Agatha. And Agatha was what made his heart beat. Gentleman to the end, he said, ''That wasn't fair. No. In thinking about it, in looking at where we are in our lives, no. I don't.'' He took a small sip of wine.

''When I think about you, I think of you as nearly perfect. You're handsome, have good taste, you're very smart, gentle but strong. You have the greatest hair in California.'' He laughed. ''But I need a break. Thinking space.''

''Is that so?'' he asked, suspiciously calm.

''I have some things to figure out and I'm this close,'' she said, demonstrating roughly an inch with thumb and index finger. ''I'm sorry I hurt you.''

''We're breaking up, aren't we?'' he asked.

''Maybe. Do you hate me for all this?''

He took another drink. It was good wine. He smiled his appreciation and said, ''I may be at a similar place in my life. But I swear, no one's ever broken up with me in a red negligee.''

She leaned her chin on her hands and studied his handsome face. ''Is this the craziest night of your life? We've gone from having a perfectly lovely relationship to having a terrible betrothal to breaking up altogether in the space of three or four weeks. Tell me something, Dennis. And tell me from your heart. If we could turn back the clock, go back to April first, would you want to?''

He pondered this for a moment, out of kindness. He wouldn't hurt her with all the truth, all the facts. There was a big difference between needing "thinking space" and having been unfaithful with the wedding planner. "Truthfully? That perfectly lovely relationship must have been lacking a few things for us to end up here."

"You must be right. Again."

"I'm relieved you discovered this now, before the children came."

She burst into laughter. He stood to leave.

"This is the most civilized breakup in the history of the world. I should have videotaped it for my clients. But then, that's you, Dennis. To the last cell, a perfect gentleman." Jake had put his fist through the door and spent four days roaring drunk. "Would it be tacky to kiss you goodbye?"

He reached out a hand to pull her to her feet. "I'd be disappointed if you didn't."

But the kiss, like the ending, was bereft of passion. A peck, nothing more.

"Fabulous wine, Charlene. You have a real gift."

"Would you like to take it?"

"No, thank you. Put a cork in it. Enjoy it later."

"You know, Dennis, once I got used to the idea, I started to really look forward to trying on wedding dresses. How silly is that?"

"Charlene, you may need me. There will be medical questions with Peaches. Don't hesitate. No matter what your thinking space produces, we'll always be good friends. I'm more than happy to help in any way I can."

"Thank you."

He let himself out and she sat back at the table. She blew out the candles and stared at the door. My mother and I, she thought, were so hooked on my father that we missed him when he was gone and ached for his return, even though he would hurt us again and again by leaving. And when I took stock of what I had with Jake, I left him at once. I wasn't going to put my daughter through that life. I wasn't going to repeat my mother's mistakes.

But I did. I never left Jake. I was close to him for twenty-five years...sometimes closer than I should have been. I was the one who made our relationship *exactly* like the one my parents had had, when Jake would have gladly had better. When Jake wanted more.

It was me.

It was me.

It was me.

Charlene went to the kitchen and retrieved the Boston cream pie and brought it to the beautifully appointed table. She put it on her plate, picked up a fork and began to eat. She didn't cut it into neat little wedges or take servings one at a time. She started in the middle and fully intended to have her fill.

Pam could have simply looked for Ray. It was possible he had a listed phone number. She could call him, tell him she was embarrassed by her behavior and ask if they could get together for a drink sometime. But she was afraid his mother would answer and ask who was calling.

He's twenty-five, Pam, not fifteen. He probably gets the occasional call from a woman.

Instead, she went to the Plum Tree after work every evening for sushi and saki. Then she headed home for a long walk with Beau.

One evening a young Asian man came to her table and presumptuously sat across from her. She recognized him as someone who worked in the restaurant, perhaps one of the owners. "Hello," he said. "I couldn't help but notice you over here by yourself."

"Oh? Is there a problem with that in this establishment?" she asked in good humor.

"You either have an insatiable hunger for sushi or you're waiting for someone."

"I don't think I'll ever get enough sushi," she said, when in truth she didn't want to ever see another fish. "Yours is wonderful. This restaurant was recommended by a friend. Ray Vogel?"

"Yes, Ray has been coming in here for years. How do you know him?"

"We worked together, before Ray left the law firm where I work. I've been wondering where he went."

"It happens I know. A job came through for him, one that he's been waiting for. He's clerking for a judge in the Bay Area. He had almost given up—"

"Clerking for a judge?" she asked, shocked.

"He's a law graduate. Very recent. A week or two back? Takes the bar in August, I think."

"Gone to the Bay Area," she said.

The young man smiled handsomely. "I'm sure he won't forget his friends."

"We weren't very good friends, obviously. I didn't know he was a law student. And here I am, a paralegal working for a lawyer."

"Oh, of course. At the firm just down the street. Yes," he said. "He worked as a security guard there. He not only had time and quiet for study when he worked nights, he also used their law libraries."

Well, she thought, at least I don't have to eat any more fish and rice.

"If you ever happen to run into him, tell him Pam says hello." And sorry. Tell him sorry.

The work on Lois's house progressed nicely. The new appliances were something she should have had anyway, but being a penny-pincher, she would have waited till the last possible moment to replace the old ones. Some of the furniture cleaned up nicely, some had to be replaced because the acrid smell of smoke crept into the fibers and would remain till eternity. All her clothing had to be washed or dry-cleaned, and some had to be thrown away and replaced. The home-owner's insurance took care of almost everything; Charlene took care of the rest.

Charlene and Lois stood in the family room and looked into the kitchen. There was still plastic draping work areas and construction debris everywhere.

"And no more avocado-green kitchen," Charlene said with reverence.

"I've always liked that green," Lois said. "I'm not sure I like this black granite countertop...or these black appliances. You're sure they're 'in'?"

"You're going to love them," she promised. It was a lucid day, Charlene thought with a smile. So she asked, "Mom? I have a question about Daddy. Do you mind?"

"I didn't think you'd ever talk about him again," she answered. "I don't mind, but I don't know what I'll remember."

"Just tell me, why didn't you divorce him?"

"Why should I have?"

"Well, maybe because he was unreliable, and unfaithful, and never helped support us."

"And would divorcing him have made him faithful, reliable and supportive?"

"No, but you wouldn't have had to put up with him showing up once or twice a year."

"But Charlene, that was the only part I actually liked!"

"You liked that?" she asked, confused.

"Listen, you're a bright girl. It was the fifties. I was raising a daughter alone. I couldn't have boyfriends— I would have lost my job at the library. And even though you've thought of me as a dried-up old lady since you were on roller skates, I happened to like the by-products of having a male visitor who spent the night once in a while. He did more than fix the back step and paint the fence, you know."

"Mother!"

"Besides, if I'd divorced him, he'd never have visited *you*."

"But he was no good!"

"I know it."

"Didn't you ever want him out of the picture so you could start over? Maybe meet a man who would prove to be a little more...I don't know...substantial?"

"Good Lord. With all the trouble that man was, you think I'd want *another* one?"

"Oh, Mother." She laughed. "What would I do without you?"

"Charlene, tell me something. You've been happy, haven't you?"

She put her arm around her mother. She had spent so much energy on perfection, with the ultimate goal being happiness, that it took breaking off her relationship with Dennis and giving her life a long, hard honest look to find the answer to that question. "Almost every single day, Mom. Almost every single day."

Charlene hadn't seen Dennis in a week. She found herself thinking about him with gratitude and tenderness. She had not yet told Jake that the wedding was off, but she was certain Stephanie had. He was probably turning purple with the desire to gloat. He was a terrible winner. There was one thing she felt compelled to do, and that was apologize to Miss Farnsworth.

It was a warm and sunny day, the first of May, four weeks since the announcement of the engagement. The spring rains were dried up for good and the green on the hillsides were growing lush and rich. Charlene went to the Bridal Boutique only to learn that the wedding consultant was having a day off. "She works almost every weekend, as you might imagine,'' the store manager said. "And with June brides gearing up—"

"Sure. Weddings," Charlene said. And wasn't she almost an accidental June bride.

"She'll be working out of the shop this weekend, then she'll be back on Monday."

Charlene thanked the woman, but once in the car she realized this could be turned to her advantage. She looked in the phone book under Farnsworth and found an address. She consulted her city street map and, sure enough, the wedding planner didn't live far from the shop.

Charlene purchased a large potted plant from the first nursery she passed and decided to take it to Miss Farnsworth, with her thanks and apologies. Since the consultant had graciously chosen not to charge them for her wasted time, this was the very least she could do.

Miss Farnsworth lived in an adorable little cottage-like house in a section of Sacramento that had become popular among young professionals. As she pulled up, Charlene noticed that the windows to the little house were open, and as the spring breeze wafted in, the classical music drifted out. She stepped up on the porch and rang the bell.

"Get that, will you, darling?"

Darling? Oh, she hoped she wasn't disturbing—

The door opened and there, shirtless, shoeless and holding a newspaper at his side was none other than her former fiancé—darling Dennis.

She was speechless.

"Sweetheart, who is at the—"

Behind him, donned in a white terry robe with wet tendrils of curling red hair dropping to her shoulders, was the wedding consultant.

I may be at a similar place in my life?

Charlene shoved the huge potted plant into Dennis's midsection, causing him to grunt in either surprise or, she hoped, pain. "Sorry for the *inconvenience!*" She turned on her heel and stomped back to her car. Only then did she notice that Dennis's car was parked along the curb, under the huge elm at the house across the street. She hadn't even noticed it on her way up the walk.

"Charlene!" he called, starting after her. "Let me explain!"

She looked over her shoulder to see him limping along barefoot behind her, carrying the plant. "Leave me alone! Do you think I'm stupid? You didn't just meet this woman! You were meeting with Miss Farnsworth without me! This has been going on for—" She had absolutely no idea. Since the idea of a wedding was born? "Just leave me alone!"

She got into her car, started the engine and peeled away from the curb. Dennis looked perfectly ridiculous standing there, looking after her, holding the potted plant.

She made a right turn, then a left, then another right. She wasn't exactly sure where she was, and the tree-lined residential street was deserted. She pulled over and began to cry, loud, wailing, angry sobs punctuated with words like *bastard* and *asshole*. She pounded the steering wheel. And then, pulling her hands away from her face, noticed that they were dry. At the same moment she realized that, while she'd been in bed with her ex-husband, her fiancé had been boinking the wedding planner. She fell sideways onto the front seat of her car and was reduced to almost hysterical laughter. Which, indeed, brought on the tears.

Stephanie sat at the bar where Grant worked. If he was surprised to see her there, he didn't show it. He put down a napkin, flashed her his sexy bartender smile and asked, "Diet Coke with a cherry?"

"Thanks," she said. "And when you have a second…?"

"It's not very busy. Why don't I take a little break?"

"That would be nice. Meet you in the booth?"

She tried to keep her heart from pounding, but found it difficult. She wanted to grab him, hug him, hold him close. It had been weeks. She missed him so.

He placed the drink in front of her. "How've you been?"

"Okay. School will be out in a few days. Are you done with finals?"

"I am. I think I did okay."

"Okay…or dean's list?"

He smiled. "I think I made the list. How's Peaches?"

"You know how she is," she said coyly. "I know you talk to my dad all the time."

"What makes you think that?" he asked, the mask of a frown on his face.

"And I know you and my dad did something to Freddy. Did my dad tell you? About the coffee shop?" Grant tried to cover his emotions with a look of confused consternation, but it didn't work. His sly grin popped through. "You're going to have to work on your facial expressions before you start interrogations for the police department. I think you've been in the apartment, too. A small piece of tape on the inside of the bedroom door indicates it's been opened in my absence."

"What makes you think it was me?"

"Actually, I was a little afraid it was Freddy, except that I couldn't figure out how he'd have a key to the place."

"Okay, you got me. The apartment looked great, Stephanie. Like you changed your habits entirely."

"Sort of," she said. "Actually, I only changed my priorities. I hope my dad didn't tell you everything I came here to say.... I hope he left some things for me."

"I only called him a few times to make sure you were all right," Grant said. "And I only went in the apartment to get a couple of CDs I like to study with. I was pretty shocked, to tell the truth."

"I didn't do that to get you back."

"I figured not...or I would have heard from you."

"Well, the lease will be up on that apartment pretty soon—"

"Damn! That's *right!* I forgot. Well, don't worry, I'll still help you with—"

"No, Grant, that's not what I came to talk to you about. The lease is almost up and you can renew if you want to, but I'm going to move in with Peaches. She needs a companion. She's not so bad right now, just has these episodes of forgetfulness and confusion that come and go pretty quickly. The rest of the time she's fine, her old self but older. And Mr. Conklin, next door, he's a wonderful caretaker, and he'll spell me whenever I need it.

"As for Peaches and me? She needs a little more than a companion—she also needs activity and stimulation. It will keep her younger longer. Can you think of anyone more perfect with whom to read, play board games, go for long walks? Plus, I think I've found a good senior center for daytime activities—if she'll go."

"Moving in with her? Seriously?"

"You didn't know, did you? Dad didn't tell you!"

He shook his head. "Not a word. It's pretty drastic. I'm...well..." He scratched his head. "Shocked. I'm shocked. When are you doing this?"

"As soon as school is out. I'm just going to substitute next year, with Mr. Conklin as my day-care assistant. We're attending a support group for families of patients with Alzheimer's, even though her diagnosis still isn't official."

"You know what you're getting yourself into?" he asked.

"Oh yeah," she replied a little nervously. "Right now it'll be kind of fun, but I know that in time it could be a serious challenge. One day at a time, huh?"

"Wow."

"You really are stunned. You thought I was too selfish for this. Too immature."

"Well…"

"Never mind, so did everyone. Including me. But I feel really good about this. For the first time in a long time, I feel really good about *me*."

"And Stephanie? What about us?" he wanted to know.

"What about us, Grant? You were the one who left. You said you didn't have anyone on your team, and there was no one with a team you could get on."

"What you're doing for Peaches… I could get on that team."

"Oh?"

"You think Mr. Conklin would spell you so we could go out sometime?"

Going out was something that had rarely happened before, given his schedule. Maybe, Stephanie thought, she wasn't the only one who had things to learn about being a team player…or half a couple. Maybe, just maybe, she hadn't been one hundred percent selfish in asking him to give her a little more time, a little more attention.

"I'm certain he would," she said.

"Could you use some help moving?"

"Dad will help me, but I'm sure it would go faster if you lent a hand. You going to keep the apartment?"

"I'm fine at my folks' for right now. It lets me save a little for the future, whatever that might be."

She reached for him and squeezed his hand. "It might be a little brighter, starting from here."

Sixteen

At the beginning and end of every workday, Charlene and Pam met for strategy and wrap-up. In the morning they planned—short-term, midterm, long-term. In the early evening, they had a debriefing conference. Starting today, Stephanie had moved in with Peaches and Charlene was officially back in the office full-time. She found their wrap-up meeting especially gratifying, knowing this.

"Well," Pam asked. "How does it feel?"

"Like coming home."

"Like coming home to more work than you can get done in a month of Sundays?" she wanted to know, humor in her voice.

Charlene cast her assistant a sincere smile. "But this is what I do," she said. "I'm comfortable here. Much more comfortable than sitting at home. Besides, you did an amazing job of keeping up. If you hadn't been here, I'd have been defeated before I began."

Pam sat down in the leather chair facing Charlene's desk. "Are you ever going to tell me about it?"

"About...?"

"The wedding? Dennis?"

"Oh that. Well, what can I say. Everything's off."

"Charlene, I know that," Pam said. "But what happened?"

"Absolutely nothing. And that was the problem. In a fit of panic, I asked Dennis if he still wanted to get married. I'd had a really bad day, I was worried about spending my old age alone and I leaped. It was stupid and impetuous. I didn't want to marry Dennis."

"I thought you loved him."

"Of course I loved him. I still love him. He's a very, very special man. Kind, generous, strong. He has a million attributes to recommend him. But our relationship was entirely superficial. We had everything in common—we liked most of the same things and we enjoyed doing those things together—but we weren't at all in love."

"You're saying it was all a mistake?" Pam wondered.

"Yes and no. Had we actually married, we might have had many compatible years together. That's not all bad." Charlene shrugged. "You live with a man with whom you're very compatible, Pam."

"My father!"

"Yes, I know. And the situation has a lot to recommend it. Yes? And given a choice between living alone and living with your father, you've chosen your father."

"He has a big house. He travels a lot. It's practical. But it's not marriage."

Charlene smiled. "Exactly."

"Well, I guess I see your point. So, what made you realize that?"

"Maybe the way we stopped talking or seeing each other the minute we decided to get married. Aside from phone calls—mostly about doctors and tests for Peaches—we were completely estranged. I forgot about him for hours. I missed several attempts at dates, and not just because Peaches needed me. My mind was elsewhere. I missed a couple while I was working with Jake, and that didn't go over so well. And in the middle of all that, Dennis found someone else."

"No way! Dennis?"

"The wedding consultant."

"No! I bet you could sue her!"

"I'm told by his sister that the new couple are very happily in love and planning a trip to Europe to meet her family. I wish them the best."

"Very nice, but really, Charlene—the wedding planner? That's too tacky."

"Or too funny," she said. Even though Pam was her best friend and she trusted her implicitly, she was still not going to mention her tryst with Jake. "I kept missing those appointments, Dennis managed to keep them. I'll bet he fell for her immediately. He started working double shifts, or so he said, and I started having little family emergencies, and the next thing you know, we're over."

"No tears?"

"Pam, Dennis is a wonderful man, but he almost never made me laugh. I could enjoy myself with him, but I rarely had fun. I should have guessed we just weren't right for each other. We kept our own houses. We kept that compulsive independence."

"Now we're getting to my real question. Explain women like us. There's nothing wrong with us. We're not bad-looking, not dumb, not messy, not bitchy. Why? Are we destined to be alone? Because I don't want to be—but there doesn't seem to be anything I can do about it."

"Well, everyone has their own stuff to sort out, but sometimes we don't make room for the right person. I can't speak for you, but I found out something about myself that was a little embarrassing. I thought I was afraid of having the wrong person, the wrong relationship—like I remember my parents having, like I remember having with Jake. And then I found out that I was really afraid of myself."

"What? I think of you as fearless."

"Well, good." She laughed. "Then it worked. I make a point of acting fearless. But I have a deep fear of letting go, of losing control, of making a fool of myself. Seeing my mother begin to lose it really brought these fears into sharp focus. And I had to face them. Facing your fears changes you." She put some papers in her briefcase, snapped it shut and looked again at Pam. "I'll tell you who's fearless. Peaches."

Charlene didn't have Pam's full attention because Pam was thinking about fears of her own. Fear of being embarrassed by falling for a much younger man, or being made a fool of by a mere kid. And yes, fear of letting go of the controls.

"Pam?"

"Oh, sorry. Contemplating."

"You've been working too hard. As soon as we get

some of the accumulation taken care of, why don't you take some time off. Get a temp in here to keep up with the filing and typing, and go somewhere warm and sandy and get a good tan.''

"I just might.''

"You going to lock up soon?'' Charlene asked.

"Another half hour, no more.''

"I'm going to my mother's for dinner, then home.''

"And you have the Samuelsons in the morning.''

"Ugh.''

"They've been very patient. Not necessarily polite, but patient.''

"I'll get up early, put on my armor.'' Charlene headed out the door. "Have a nice evening.''

"And you,'' Pam called back.

Pam took a few moments to freshen up in Charlene's private rest room, and in those same moments did a little thinking. She had not been in the least morose about her singleness until Ray came along and opened her mind to some emotions that had previously lain dormant. This, she decided, was not a bad thing. The bad thing was not acknowledging him or his feelings when he had tried so hard.

She made up her mind. She was going to find him and at the very least, explain. She'd been afraid. Her father was right—none of us knows how much time we get. It's foolhardy to ignore any chance at genuine happiness.

She turned off the lights in Charlene's office, locked the door and went to her desk, upon which was a rose.

"Ray?" she called, but there was no answer. And no note.

She quickly got her things together, turned off her computer, left her calendar open on her desk, switched the phone to voice mail and hurried from her office, her heart hammering the whole time. She passed several young clerks and associates as they labored on, saying good-night to each one.

He stood in the elevator foyer, leaning against the wall between two large decorative urns. Of course she stopped dead in her tracks; she couldn't take another step. She hadn't been this nervous since the junior-high dance when she saw Roy Robards walking toward her across the gymnasium floor.

Ray looked different in his starched white shirt and patterned tie, but no less handsome. He smiled when he saw her and stood straighter, taking his hands out of his pockets. "I heard you were asking about me," he said.

"I heard you're a lawyer."

"A law graduate. I haven't passed the bar yet."

They met in the middle of the foyer; he took her tote and led her to the elevators. "I've been wanting to…how do I say this? I want to apologize for the way I acted the last time. You know, when you brought the Chinese? And I yelled…?"

"I was coming on too strong," he said. "I do that sometimes."

"No, you were fine. I was… Well, you must have noticed. I was afraid it was a terrible idea to get involved with someone so much younger."

"Because…?"

She sighed. "I don't know why, Ray. Because it's not usual. Because I was worried about what people would think. Because I couldn't believe you were serious."

"Did I ever seem insincere?"

"Never," she admitted. "I was surprised by how much I missed your flirting. And by how disappointed I was to learn you'd left. I was sure I'd driven you away."

"I would have explained, but I thought you were angry."

"I was, but not with you. And I had just decided, this afternoon, that I was going to find you, to make amends and ask for another chance."

He smiled at that. They were saved from further conversation by the arrival of the elevator. Inside was a cleaning lady with her cart; they each stood on one side of her. Neither of them had noticed the elevator was going up rather than down. When they got to the fifth floor, the cleaning lady pushed her cart out and the doors closed. Neither of them had pushed a button so they sat, idle, alone in the elevator, doors closed, unmoving. Then Ray pulled his keys out of his pocket, put one in the key slot on the control panel and made the elevator begin to move down, slowly. Then it stopped—between floors.

He let her tote gently fall to the floor so his hands were free, but soon they were on her waist, pulling her toward him. His lips were above hers, nearly touching. "San Francisco?" she asked.

"It's not so far," he said. "It's a nice place to spend a weekend."

"We should start with dinner," she suggested.

He kissed her softly at first, then harder. Her arms went around his neck, holding him closer, while his hands ran smoothly over her hips and thighs, around behind her, pulling her hard against him.

His lips rose from hers and he said, "I'll be glad to start anywhere you want, Ms. London."

"You can start by calling me Pam."

"Pam," he said, kissing her neck. "You're no longer unsure of this?"

She tightened her embrace. "Unsure? I'm not sure I'm ever going to let you out of this elevator!"

"Unfortunately, Pete's going to want his key back. But there are other elevators, Pam. And I think we should try them all."

It was nearly midnight when the doorbell rang at Charlene's house. Knowing it was Jake—who else would be rude enough to do that, without even calling ahead—she answered the door in her pajamas. "Oh no," she said to Jake. "Is everything all right?"

"Everything is great. I got a couple of updates, a couple of questions."

"I know you have my phone number."

"This had to be done in person. You gonna let me in?"

"Oh, Jake, it's midnight. You aren't going to get me all upset, are you?"

"Not unless you want me to," he said, stepping inside. "Can a guy get a drink around here?"

"If a guy drinks herbal tea," she said.

"Ugh. After all I've been through for you?"

"Sit down, I might be able to find you something. But really, Jake, you should have called me," she said, going into the kitchen.

He followed her. "This is going to make your day. Merrie and her two daughters got together with the Jersynski kid. The three little girls are instant best friends, and the eleven-year-old wants to help her sister with the bone marrow."

"Are they a match?"

"I don't even know the answer to that. What I do know is old Rick wants to help Merrie out a little bit...and I think the whole struggle is over. She says she owes it all to you."

She put a few ice cubes in a glass and poured him a bourbon. "But we both know better than that, don't we? You probably laid that giving-as-opposed-to-getting philosophy on her and she decided to do the right thing. I was all for getting money out of him."

"Well, there will be some of that, too," he said, taking the drink. "So, question. Stephanie told me the wedding was off, which I took as good news. Then she told me you and Denny were kaput. What's that about?"

"We weren't right for each other, Jake. You knew that before I did."

"I suspected that, but I didn't expect you to figure it out," he said, and took a sip, bracing himself.

"Button," she said.

"Button," he agreed, and smiled.

"You keep me confused about a lot of things, Jake, but I know you don't really think I avoided relationships for twenty-five years."

"No button pushing, Charlie. I never could figure out you and Denny."

"Why? He's a wonderful guy."

"He's so...stiff."

"Stiff?"

"No jazz. No sparks. Stephanie says he's nice and steady."

He sat down at her kitchen table and she joined him there, elbow on the table, chin on her hand.

"Jake, nice and steady can be worth a king's ransom. I get enough excitement at work."

"Then why'd you break it off?"

"What makes you think it was me?"

"Wasn't it?" he asked.

"It was, but that was an accident. He was on his way over here to break it off when I came to my senses and beat him to it. And the old dog, he never let on. I found out a couple of weeks later, he'd been fooling around with the wedding consultant."

Jake was at first stunned into rare silence, then he nearly fell off his chair in laughter. "Denny?" He laughed, slapping his thigh. "The wedding consultant? I have a whole new respect for this guy!"

Men, Charlene thought. Disgusting down to the last one.

"You came all the way out here at midnight to ask me why I broke up with Denny...I mean Dennis?"

He was still laughing. "That had to really piss you off, Charlie."

"Jake! What are you doing here?"

"Gimme a minute, will you. That's hysterical."

"I'm going to kill you. I mean it!"

"Okay, okay," he said, wiping tears from his eyes. "But I mean, Jesus, that's so rich." She made a movement. "Okay, *okay!* No, that is not why I came all the way out here. I came for a much more ridiculous reason. I wanted to ask you, where'd we go wrong? You and me?"

She frowned, and stared at him, mute.

"Was it just the screwed-up thing you had about your dad? Was it me? Was it you? What was it?"

"What makes you think we went wrong?"

"Charlie," he said somewhat impatiently, "we were so much in love we didn't know if the sun was up or down. We could hardly get out of bed long enough to get married. We were going to save the world. Then all of a sudden you couldn't stand me because I spit and watched ball games. Now, I'm not saying you didn't always have a case. I've never been good enough for you. But where'd we go wrong? Why couldn't we, different as we were, ever find a common ground? A compromise? What happened?"

"I'm serious, Jake. I'm not sure we went wrong. I used to think so. I used to feel like a failure, if not because I married you, then because I divorced you.

But now, looking back at the last twenty-five years, I think we did exactly what we were supposed to do.''

"Huh?"

"I think we managed pretty well. We were so intense when we were young, we were almost combustible. The two of us, both doing law enforcement work, under the same roof, raising a little girl—it might've been disastrous. Maybe we were just too much for each other. Maybe not living together was the best way to go. Not for everyone, but for us.''

"Hmm." He considered this. "Think so?"

"It's possible," she said.

"You hated me so much," he said.

"No I didn't," she said, smiling. "I couldn't have relied on you so heavily if I'd hated you. And there were those times…you know…''

"Those times…I know…."

"And you were a wonderful father, all things considered. I mean, she doesn't spit anymore.''

He laughed. "Not when you're around, anyway.''

"I never found anyone else. That has to say something.''

"You think we were just too much for each other? We just couldn't manage a full-time relationship? Is that what you're saying?''

"I guess that sums it up," she said. "There's a lot of powerful energy between the two of us.''

He finished his drink in a gulp, then stood. "Well, I just had to ask. I was…I guess you'd say I was *compelled* to ask. Tonight.'' He started for the front door.

''I don't think that's *still* the case. However.''

He slowly turned. ''You don't?''

''Naw. I think I can handle you. Now.''

Epilogue

There was a night in June—the third Saturday night to be exact—that would have emerged as the selected wedding date for Charlene and Dennis. But it fell apart in the worst possible way with the best possible results. So, on that particular night, at about the approximate time the bride would have been walking toward the groom, this is what the participants were actually doing:

At a table in Peaches's brand-new kitchen there was a game of gin rummy going on, and she was doing pretty well. Playing were Grant and Stephanie, Jasper and Peaches. Grant had decided that, since he was economizing by staying with his parents, he could afford to give up one night of the weekend and spend it socially. Peaches was on medication that was having very positive effects, and her periods of forgetfulness and confusion were few. Stephanie and Jasper kept her active and busy with mind-exercising games and physical activities.

There was some talk about Grant moving into Peaches's house in about a year if things were still compatible between the young couple. But for Stephanie, life had taken on a new meaning. She spent valuable time with Peaches, went to support-group meetings with her, took over her grandmother's job of volunteer reading and began to see a counselor to help her sort out her own personal issues. Also, she'd become tidy, but not dangerously so.

Jasper was going through the process of being licensed to manage an assisted-living facility for the elderly. He hoped to have three, perhaps a couple and a single like himself.

In San Francisco, in a very nice hotel, a striking couple dined in a restaurant on the wharf. Pam London and Ray Vogel found out that, in addition to bodybuilding, they had dozens of common interests, not the least of which was the practice of law, and not a weekend passed that they weren't together. Before summer's end they would announce their engagement and plan a wedding date with absolutely no hesitation due to ages. In fact, Ray's older sister, forty-two and pregnant with her first child, was a beacon of hope for the couple.

Back in Sacramento, in Gwen and Dick's backyard, there was a barbecue going on. The kids and Agatha were in the pool playing Marco Polo, a game she had barely mastered, while Dennis and Dick turned burgers on the grill. Gwen observed her brother's newfound happiness with deep personal joy. That the children were about the ages Agatha's would have been made it even more special.

Across town, against all odds, Mr. and Mrs. Samuelson reconciled. But that didn't necessarily mean they had stopped fighting.

And in a little suburban nook east of the city, at Charlene's house, Charlene and Jake were dressing up for a black-tie dinner.

"I feel ridiculous," he said, tugging at his tie.

"You don't look ridiculous. You look very handsome."

"Is this absolutely necessary? Can't I just wear a sport coat?"

"It's for a politician. It's for a cause. Grow up."

"But I'm not comfortable."

"You're also going to dance."

"Aww…"

"With all the stuffy old matrons…"

"Charrrrrlieeeee…"

"And charm them, and then they will give you money for your foundation."

"I should never have let you talk me into all this…."

She fixed an earring. "I'm the best thing that's ever happened to you."

He looked over at her—in her strapless black evening gown, at her narrow waist, her silky shoulders, her long neck, her sparkling, happy eyes—and knew this was so, so true.

"I will wear this for you, and do you know why?"

"Yes I do," she said. "Because I'm making you. And because I'm right."

"That is correct," he said. He couldn't keep his hands off her. He grabbed her around the waist. "And because you're the best thing that's ever happened to me.''

She gave him a kiss. ''And so are you. Now, don't mess up my makeup.'' She smiled. ''Yet.''

A little attitude goes a long way...

CHARLOTTE HUGHES

MIRA®

Marilee Abernathy's life is a mess. *Everyone* in Chickpea, South Carolina, knows about her husband's affair with the town floozy, her son's moved into *the other woman's* mobile home, and she's left alone to pick up the pieces. What she needs now is a new attitude—at least, that's what her neighbor Sam Brewer thinks. But Marilee's learning on her own just how far a little attitude can go, taking charge and taking chances in ways she'd never imagined. As for Sam, watching Marilee blossom reminds him of some long-forgotten dreams of his own. Now he's just got to convince her to turn some of that new attitude his way....

A NEW ATTITUDE

"A hilarious book...full of Southern charm
and unforgettable characters."
—Janet Evanovich

Available October 2001 wherever paperbacks are sold!

Visit us at www.mirabooks.com

MCH863

USA Today Bestselling Author

SUSAN WIGGS

Abigail Cabot has discovered the man of her dreams. Only, he's not interested…yet. So the lady astronomer, whose passion for measuring stars has left her woefully lacking in social graces, seeks someone to educate her…someone who is a master at the art of seduction.

Jamie Calhoun's handsome looks and easy charm have made him as popular on the Senate floor as he is with the capital's most attractive women. But secretly he loathes the cynical, manipulative man he's become. Initially, he befriends Abigail as a means to a political end. But somewhere along the way the plan goes awry.

For a man convinced he's incapable of love and a woman who believes she can reach the stars, could this be a match made in heaven?

HALFWAY TO HEAVEN

"Susan Wiggs delves deeply into her characters' hearts and motivations to touch our own."
— *Romantic Times* on *The Mistress*

On sale October 2001 wherever paperbacks are sold!

Visit us at www.mirabooks.com
MSW837

MIRA®

He gave her his name...but
would he give her his heart?

LINDA HOWARD

A tragic accident took everything that mattered to Rome Matthews—
his wife and their two little boys. And it robbed Sarah Harper of her
best friend. In the years that followed, Sarah wanted nothing more
than to reach out to Rome, but a tightly guarded secret kept her
away: she had been in love with her best friend's husband for years.

But now Rome needs her, desperate to lose himself in the passion he
feels for Sarah. Knowing that his heart belongs to another woman,
Sarah agrees to be his wife. Then an unexpected fate rekindles her
hidden hope that a marriage of convenience could become a
marriage of love....

SARAH'S CHILD

"You can't read just one Linda Howard!" —Catherine Coulter

Available October 2001 wherever paperbacks are sold!

Visit us at www.mirabooks.com

MLH861

MIRABooks.com

We've got the lowdown on your favorite author!

☆ Read an excerpt of your favorite author's newest book

☆ Check out her bio and read our famous "20 questions" interview

☆ Talk to her in our Discussion Forums

☆ Get the latest information on her touring schedule

☆ Find her current besteller, and even her backlist titles

All this and more available at

www.MiraBooks.com
on Women.com Networks

MEAUT1

If you enjoyed what you just read,
then we've got an offer you can't resist!

Take 2
bestselling novels FREE!
Plus get a FREE surprise gift!

Clip this page and mail it to The Best of the Best™

IN U.S.A.
3010 Walden Ave.
P.O. Box 1867
Buffalo, N.Y. 14240-1867

IN CANADA
P.O. Box 609
Fort Erie, Ontario
L2A 5X3

YES! Please send me 2 free Best of the Best™ novels and my free surprise gift. After receiving them, if I don't wish to receive anymore, I can return the shipping statement marked cancel. If I don't cancel, I will receive 4 brand-new novels every month, before they're available in stores! In the U.S.A., bill me at the bargain price of $4.24 plus 25¢ shipping and handling per book and applicable sales tax, if any*. In Canada, bill me at the bargain price of $4.74 plus 25¢ shipping and handling per book and applicable taxes**. That's the complete price and a savings of over 15% off the cover prices—what a great deal! I understand that accepting the 2 free books and gift places me under no obligation ever to buy any books. I can always return a shipment and cancel at any time. Even if I never buy another book from The Best of the Best™, the 2 free books and gift are mine to keep forever.

185 MEN DFNG
385 MEN DFNH

Name	(PLEASE PRINT)	
Address	Apt.#	
City	State/Prov.	Zip/Postal Code

* Terms and prices subject to change without notice. Sales tax applicable in N.Y.
** Canadian residents will be charged applicable provincial taxes and GST.
All orders subject to approval. Offer limited to one per household and not valid to current Best of the Best™ subscribers.
® are registered trademarks of Harlequin Enterprises Limited.

BOB01   ©1998 Harlequin Enterprises Limited

USA Today Bestselling Author

Stella Cameron

SNOW *Angels*

Since the tragic murder of her husband, Libby Duclaux has lived a reclusive life in the snow-covered mountains of Italy. Then Aaron Conrad arrives from across the Atlantic with a plea for help, and reawakens the fragile memories of a world waiting for her.... But back home in Washington State, Libby discovers the temptation of remembering what life was like before she stopped living. Could she allow her heart to leave its cold, wintry depths and warm with the promise of new beginnings?

Stella Cameron's novels "keep readers thoroughly entertained."
—*Publishers Weekly*

Available October 2001 wherever paperbacks are sold!

Visit us at www.mirabooks.com

MSC840

ROBYN CARR

66545 THE HOUSE ON OLIVE STREET

                  ___ $5.99 U.S. ___ $6.99 CAN.

66609 DEEP IN THE VALLEY

                  ___ $5.99 U.S. ___ $6.99 CAN.

(limited quantities available)

TOTAL AMOUNT $_____

POSTAGE & HANDLING $_____

($1.00 for 1 book, 50¢ for each additional)

APPLICABLE TAXES* $_____

<u>TOTAL PAYABLE</u> $_____

(check or money order—please do not send cash)

To order, complete this form and send it, along with a check or money order for the total above, payable to MIRA Books®, to: **In the U.S.**: 3010 Walden Avenue, P.O. Box 9077, Buffalo, NY 14269-9077; **In Canada**: P.O. Box 636, Fort Erie, Ontario, L2A 5X3.

Name:_____

Address:_____ City:_____

State/Prov.:_____ Zip/Postal Code:_____

Account Number (if applicable):_____

075 CSAS

*New York residents remit applicable sales taxes.
  Canadian residents remit applicable GST and provincial taxes.

MIRA®

Visit us at www.mirabooks.com   MRC1001BL